HEARTLAND

On the Side of Angels

HEARTLAND

On the Side of Angels

TERRI SEDMAK

THE
LIBERTY & PROPERTY
LEGENDS

This novel is a work of fiction.

Visit www.terrisedmak.com
Official website of THE LIBERTY & PROPERTY LEGENDS

My heartfelt thanks to my family, for all their wonderful input, support and
encouragement. To my focus groups, thank you for your illuminating
contribution. To Michael at Blow–Up Design Pty Ltd, who really does know how
to save my art. I gratefully acknowledge the assistance of the
Wyoming State Archives.

Credits: *We Will Not Be Slaves*, Sons of Liberty Traditional; *The Psalm of Life,
The Children's Hour, Snowflakes, The Courtship of Miles Standish, The Cross
of Snow, Song of Hiawatha, The Old Clock on the Stairs*
by Henry Wadsworth Longfellow.

Published by Vivid Publishing
P.O. Box 948, Fremantle
Western Australia 6959
www.vividpublishing.com.au

National Library of Australia
Cataloguing-in-Publication Data:
Sedmak, Terri.
Heartland : on the side of angels / Terri Sedmak
ISBN: 9781921787393 (pbk.)
A823.4

For Francis
Who is never short of a story,
and who generously encouraged
this one out of my laptop and onto these pages.
Thank you, from my heart.

'In story we're told, how our fathers of old
Braved the rage of the wind and the waves,
And crossed the deep o'er, for this far away shore
All because they would never be slaves, brave boys,
All because they would never be slaves.

The birthright we hold, shall never be sold,
But sacred maintained to our graves,
And before we'll comply, we'll gallantly die,
For we must not, we will not be slaves, brave boys,
For we must not, we will not be slaves.'

The Sons of Liberty

Luke...

"Call your next witness, Mr Faraday."

"Your Honor, the prosecution recalls Miss Keaton."

A hush deeper than silence envelops the courtroom as their key witness determines her way to the stand. As this is not the first time she has given testimony there is no swearing in. But it will be the most significant... the most damning... of all.

Aged-summer heat stews the pungency of shellac applied to lately milled wood, compresses all breathable air into brow-mopping droplets, and is disturbed only by the rhythmic swiping of white lace fans in the public gallery. For a moment the room is so quiet Luke thinks he hears the fans humming. Then someone coughs; then another. Still, in these seconds before it begins, a shiver wriggles down his spine. This is the spectacle they have packed themselves in to see.

Cam, with an air of casual benevolence, permits the jury time to admire his angelic-looking witness, and their eyes are fixed on her, while the witness herself certainly shows no objections to such scrutiny.

Luke shifts his attention to old Ed sitting beside McKinnon, the harried defense counsel.

Yesterday was a torrid day and not once did Ed show any emotion. One fanless woman swooned and needed to be carried from the courtroom, she... Concentrate, he tells himself, and rounds up his thoughts. The heat and the relentless intensity take their toll in every quarter.

Cam's previous witness for the prosecution had been an expert from the university in St Louis who testified to the age and condition of the evidence in question.

About moisture damage to the paper and the time it would take for this damage to occur in the ground approximately eighteen inches below the surface, while wrapped separately in two pieces of leather since January, surviving the thaw of winter.

The expert confirmed it; yes, there *was* moisture damage to the paper, consistent with the amount of time the journal was exposed to the conditions. The journal was definitely below ground for at least six months and had been exposed to the winter thaw. There was no way that such damage could have been created artificially in a short space of time, and no attempt to repair the journal in any manner had been made. Cam thanked his witness and gave McKinnon the floor.

When McKinnon stood, however, to draw breath and speak, Ed reached out and clutched his arm. McKinnon looked down at him in surprise. Ed gave a brisk shake of his head. McKinnon cleared his throat and told Judge Callaghan that he had no questions for the witness. The Judge asked the professor to stand down and then directed Cam to call his next witness.

And so she sits there, wide-eyed, her blue gaze fixed on Cam, waiting to begin. He holds the journal and is about to give it to her. Her eyes follow it as he puts it into her hands. It happens slowly, as though time has changed its course, like a small stream that skedaddles round a bend and meets the wide, gainly river.

Judge Callaghan reminds her that she is still under oath. Her expression sharpens in response.

From across the courtroom her glance collides with Luke's and sticks; he swallows hard, managing a tight smile as that bright blue scrutiny reaches deep into his memory.

This Cheyenne courtroom is ready to hear the truth at last.

"Miss Keaton, you hold in your hands your brother's journal. Correct?"

Truth, whole and nothing but.

"Yes."

That reaches into memory…

"Would you open the cover please?"

…and holds fast.

ONE

The heart has its own memory,
Like the mind,
And in it are enshrined
The precious keepsakes...

Henry Wadsworth Longfellow

❧◦❧

Luke

Diamond-T ranch, Wyoming Territory
Summer, 1869

Luke ambles along on Taabe liking the look of that bright blue sky, a summer sky, not a speck of cloud. Taabe's coat is chestnut but so glossy that sometimes sunshine bounces right off of her; that's why they named her Taabe, Comanche for sun; she used to be called Tamu (rabbit) on account of she was kinda small; then one day they saw her standing in the sun; her size no longer mattered; she was Taabe.

He heads for the River. Just yesterday he found some of Nathaniel's strays; he'd seen the brand on them. They were helping themselves to his grass and water. Those city cousins of Nathaniel, who went and took over the unlucky man's spread, obviously don't know what they're doing to be letting their beeves stray so far. Been a month since the new folks moved in; he ain't seen hide or hair of 'em. Ma might have, since she gets to meeting folks in town. But so what? He ain't interested in city types.

As soon as he makes it to the River he sees the strays, about a dozen in all, with the NC brand on their flanks. Pa and Nathaniel had been good friends and Pa always asked Luke to round up Nathaniel's strays and drive them back. This he fully has a mind to do now.

He's dug out at least four or five from the rough around the riverbank and stops to rest and wipe his brow when he hears voices and the tread of a pony over the pine needles in the forest. He dismounts and leads Taabe to cover behind a compact stand of young pines.

The voices become more distinct. They sound like children. He peers carefully through the trees and spots them. Never seen them before, but they've seen the strays and are dismounting, whatever

5

for he can't fathom, a small girl with long curly yellow hair sliding off the back of the pony with considerable daring, and a boy about his own age getting off the conventional way. The boy's expression is serious compared to the girl's lively features. She is talking to him without hardly drawing breath and he ain't liking it.

Luke don't blame him.

Why would anyone want a half-pint like that along when you're trying to work?

"I'll help you, Mart."

"Why didn't you just stay home like I said?"

Brother and sister…

"You don't think I can do it, but I tell you I can," she insists.

This feller needs help. Not only does he have a girl in the way, but he looks like he ain't got a clue. For sure, these are Nathaniel's relatives from Philadelphia. City kids.

The boy is telling the kid about the River, making some pretty fair judgments about it too. This is a deep and dangerous stretch of the River, with undercurrents and submerged traps. Even Luke is forbidden to play in the River anywhere along this section. But this boy knows rivers. Respects them. He is warning his sister in no uncertain terms that if she goes anywhere near it he won't never take her with him nowhere ever again. Good for him. They start walking around, exploring, he silent and the girl yammerin' about all kinds of things she finds. Very soon Luke's hiding place will be discovered – it's time to reveal himself.

Wait… wait…

He leaps. And throws in a loud and throaty *grhh* for good measure. The result is very satisfying. The boy's jaw drops and the little yellow-haired thing squeals. While the boy stands his ground, his sister jumps like a rabbit and takes cover behind her brother.

Luke chuckles.

"Now what did you go and do that for?" the boy exclaims. "Don't you know you can kill people scaring them that way?"

The boy's cool head is a surprise. Luke expected them to clear off like frightened fawn, instead this kid barely blinked.

"Are you dead?" Luke mocks him.

"Well, that's a stupid question." This bit of cheek comes from behind the boy – the voice of the yellow-haired rabbit.

"No, we ain't dead," the boy answers him, "but we could be. Didn't your Pa teach you better than that?"

Luke clenches his teeth. "My father's dead."

The boy frowns. "That's too bad."

"Mart, stop your talking to that nasty boy. I want to go home."

"Hush up, Kel, he's all right. And come out from behind me." The boy reaches around and yanks his sister out from behind his back. She finds her feet and looks up at her brother with a very pitchy look on her face.

Luke bursts out laughing.

"I want to go home," she yells. "He's horrible and I don't like him."

"How can you not like someone you just met?"

The girl looks Luke squarely in the eye and makes him uneasy. She looks like she don't like him, and like she don't even want to try. "He's mean and scary."

"It was a joke, Kel," her brother says and then takes a couple of steps towards him. "I'm Mart Keaton."

Luke eyes him, suspicious. "Well, Mart Keaton, your strays are on my land."

"Don't worry. I'll get them off – somehow."

"You don't know how, do you?" Luke don't want them to like him anyhow. Who needs them? "And how are you gonna do it with that scrawny kid sister gettin' in the way?"

"You see, Mart, he's not nice," the girl says. "He's just insulted me." She turns on him with her hands on her hips. "And I'm not scrawny!"

Mart Keaton grabs her arm and pulls her back. "Behave yourself, Kelley," he mumbles.

The girl looks up at her brother like she's going to cry.

"Fine," she squawks and walks off in a hurry.

Luke watches her go, wondering if she knows where she's going to.

Mart Keaton gets his attention again by saying, "Will you help me round up our strays? I sure could use your help. I ain't so good at it yet."

Luke stares at him. What's his game anyhow?

"What's your name?" Mart Keaton asks.

"What's it to you?"

"If we're gonna be neighbors…"

Luke ain't sure whether to play this Keaton boy's game or just let him have it.

"MART!"

It's the kid. She's screamed so loud he thinks she must have found a grizzly.

Keaton reacts at once and clears off towards the scream.

Luke follows.

They find the annoying pip-squeak on the edge of the river-bank. There actually *is* a she-bear, but over on the opposite bank.

As grizzlies go it ain't so big, but it's growling since her cub is close by.

"Keep still and stop caterwauling," Luke says.

"What'll we do?" she asks.

Luke looks at her white face and big eyes. "I just told you."

"I'm speaking to my brother, you…"

"Kelley, don't you dare!" Keaton cuts in at once.

Luke shakes his head. A scrawny kid with a mouth – just grand. "I feel sorry for you, Keaton."

"She grows on you," Keaton says, his eyes tight on the bear. "Do you think we can leave now?"

"Hec, I don't plan to stay here till the old girl thinks about crossing over, even if your kid sister does look like her supper."

As they back away Keaton's sister says, "I told you he's a horrid boy." A moment later she falls backwards over a rock and lands with a thump.

Luke reaches down and pulls her to her feet. "You okay?"

"What are you doing…" Keaton groans at her.

"I fell over a rock," she says, "and I'm fine in case you were wondering."

As she brushes herself down, Luke starts laughing at them. They're funny and he begins to like them even if the scrawny kid is determined not to like him.

"We'd better keep going," he suggests.

They pick up speed and make it back to the horses.

"I think we should get these strays back to your place before that bear decides to take a closer look," Luke offers.

Keaton smiles at him. "Thanks. We'd be obliged."

Luke leaps onto Taabe's back. "My name's Luke Taylor."

"So what," says Keaton's sister.

"Get on the horse," Keaton orders her, "and keep your mouth shut."

If Luke didn't know better he thinks he sees tears in her eyes, and for a moment he feels sorry.

"What are you staring at?" she scowls.

The remorse leaves him. "Not you, half-pint."

He hears Keaton chuckling as the city boy settles himself in the saddle. "When we get these steers back you should come up to the house and have some of my mother's pie. She's a good cook." He turns to his sister quickly. "And don't say a word."

"If you want this wild horrid boy for a friend, Mart, that's your business."

"How can your sister be so little and talk so big?"

"Pa says she was born talking. And Mama says she was born with an opinion about everything."

"Well, I ain't horrid."

Keaton grins at him. "You don't look so bad to me neither. You got a mother?"

"She bakes good chocolate cake. She'll make some if I say we're having company. You can come over tomorrow if you want."

"Chocolate!" the kid pipes up. "I like chocolate."

Luke has decided he don't want her around. He's gonna have to like her from a long way off.

"People who think I'm horrid ain't invited."

She bites her bottom lip and glares at him, madder than a wet hen. "I'm never going to like you. You can give me fifty chocolate cakes..."

He don't hear the rest. He and Keaton turn their horses and set about the job at hand.

That night, before he falls asleep, he thinks about things like he usually does. For the first time since Pa died he don't feel so empty inside. He likes Mart Keaton and he reckons they could be friends.

Mart

Keaton ranch, Bright River, Wyoming
August 1883

Impatient that the words won't come, Mart dabs the nib roughly into his ink. He sits bent over the page, cradling his head in his hand, his fingers anchored to a thick clutch of hair. The lamplight wavers; a distraction, another irritation. He drops the pen, the impact splattering black ink over the journal. From beside it he snatches up the letter he has been desperate to avoid. He must read it again and work out what to do. He reads aloud, desperate, mumbling like a maniac...

"In the Fall, dear brother, I will be coming home. What do you say to that? I can hardly believe it myself, but it is true. I have terminated my exile. Five years in that exile has taught me three things about myself. One, that I am a survivor. Two, with enough determination I can achieve whatever I set my mind to do. And three, other people's expectations of me are only there to make them feel comfortable, and not necessarily for me to meet. I am not bitter, however, merely desperate to answer the call in my heart.

"In case you have forgot, I have reached an age when most young women profess a degree of maturity – I am twenty, and I have achieved the refinement and education our parents have required of me. After all, they sent me East to become someone, and I have carried out their wishes. But now it's my turn. My dreams, my reality, my way.

"There is no ingratitude intended. The notion I intend to prove is that my heart belongs in the Wyoming of my childhood and not in the Manhattan of my youth. I think you of all people will understand when I say that I need to reclaim my freedom; my heart yearns for its pure essence with desperate longing.

"In my understanding, freedom does not come into being as a result of privilege or wealth, as so many people would have you believe; freedom belongs in the realm of love and truth, recognized by, and as part of, the human spirit in every age and circumstance.

"I have always believed freedom is exulted in earth and sky, in forest and river, in mountain and valley, existing in my surroundings, giving free rein to the body and so, the spirit. And I still do. Truth, however, that higher philosophy, decrees in her righteousness, that there is a superior way of exulting freedom – in the hearts and the souls of people. For then can the spirit truly soar, and freedom ring. I am unsure if I have the courage to test this insight, but the call in my heart insists that I find out. I must begin the quest in the place where the joy of freedom began for me – home. I am counting the days till I see you once again after so long. Your loving sister..."

Dear God… He tosses the letter aside and wants to swear and cuss until God sends a lightning bolt to strike him down.

Anything…

But there's nothing. In the end he is so shaken by the letter's passionate and honest expression he gives in to it. At the heart of it is the wild heart of his crazy sister sounding suddenly grown up and yet just the same as always. How can one scrawny individual be so intent on proving she is free in a world where freedom is so deceptive?

He retrieves his pen and resolves to keep faith with his main objective. The truth. Hard. Concrete. Providing temporarily relief from the despair of not knowing what to do about Kelley and how to protect her. He at last writes more than the date:

20TH AUGUST 1883: Ed did not win his challenge to the Bill. He constantly harasses Luke and me. He has two dudes with him at present who like to stop us in town and push us around. Luke and I made a firm agreement that we will not push back. We agree that Ed will step up his harassment in other quarters if we do. Surely Ed will soon see in light of our reasonable treatment of him that he is wrong.

Kelley

Two weeks later
September 1883

The stagecoach thunders along a mountain stretch.

Having glimpsed the perpendicular drop to the valley floor on her right once, at this pace Kelley would prefer not to again and keeps her eyes averted.

Opposite her are the only other passengers, a young woman who introduced herself as Mrs Edwina Adams, and her small cosseted son, Colin.

In a raised voice, Edwina says, "You know what they say…"

The stage takes an acute bend and throws them all right and left. Colin, free of his mother, thrusts half his small body out of the window and lets out a lusty whoop of delight. His little hat flies off his head and disappears.

"No," Kelley says, gripping what she can, "what do they say?"

Edwina grabs her son.

"That they keep the cattle trail to Laramie better than they keep the road."

"A little more upholstery."

"A little *less* speed."

The boy escapes once more and starts tearing around, throwing himself this way and that.

"Colin, sit down at once!"

Kelley remembers being Colin's age, which she estimates about six years old. Observing Colin and his frenetic behavior it is hard to believe he has any other interest than being wild, but in the heart of that tiny body beats a promise…

Kelley ceases watching Colin and stares out the window instead. A common mistake, in her view, is to doubt that a six year old can be passionate about something.

Moving from Philadelphia with her family in 1869 to live surrounded by hundreds of acres of prime beef country in frontier Wyoming began it for her. From the very second she breathed Wyoming air she realized what this daily activity she'd been doing, living, was all about. She understood the promise.

This was her life.

A different life.

But the kind of life her father had always wanted to live, in fact experienced as an adventurous youth and longed to return to. He infected his children with the same dream, something Kelley hadn't realized until it all materialized around her.

Working a comfortable job on the Philadelphia railways occupied the first twelve years of her parents' married life and was deemed by her father as a necessity. His patience and sacrifice for the welfare of his wife and children was eventually rewarded when it so happened that an ill-fated cousin bequeathed his large cattle ranch to her parents. The man was tragically killed on the property; however, their excitement overtook any grief for someone they hardly knew and who had their *un*dying admiration.

Her Pa was cock-a-hoop. She and Mart followed ecstatically. It was difficult to know who was more excited – a twelve year old boy with a yearning for adventure, his wild-hearted baby sister, or a man who was about to have his dream come true.

The jubilation was chastened somewhat by the thought-provoking utterances of the woman who would have to bear the brunt of frontier life – their Mama. Of course, she bore it far beyond her own and everyone else's expectations, and after the mandatory initiation period expired, the Keatons were a frontier success story.

Her father was back in the saddle where he knew he was always meant to be, and simply, they thrived. As for the passion, it never died, neither did it wear thin, nor disappoint. Her only disappointment came when she was forced to leave and the promise was broken. She hopes that doesn't happen to Colin.

Half an hour later, as they emerge from a valley forest, the road begins to climb once more. It doesn't seem to matter what section of road or type of surface, their driver maintains the same catapulting speed.

And then come the ruts.

Kelley's head bounces back and forth on her neck.

"Urrrrr," the boy ululates. "Listen, Ma, to my voice. Urrr..." His voice wails up and down as they strike rut after rut. It is not at all appropriate in company but nonetheless comical.

"Stop that," his mother snaps.

"Aw, Maa maa maa..."

Then, amid the thundering, the rumbling and Colin's vocal capers comes a loud crack followed by a heart-stopping shudder and a grinding moan.

They all grip tight, even Colin. The stage begins to slow and eventually stops. The driver, mumbling under his breath, walks past the door. Kelley and her companion swap glances. Colin sticks his head out the other window this time.

"What's up, mister?"

The driver's face appears at the window. He's a middle-aged man and despite his penchant for speed, he has proven an easy-going manner, with a friendly countenance on top of a strong physique, all preferred attributes for driving stagecoaches.

"Sorry, folks. Snapped a couple of spokes on the back wheel. Me and Jericho are gonna have to change it." He shrugs.

Jericho, their older co-driver, also appears at the window. "Can't figure how it happened."

"Well, we had kind of a mix up in Laramie, Jericho..."

"Sure, Harry, but..."

"How long will it take?" Kelley asks.

"Not long I hope. Why don't you ladies step out, stretch your legs, and get a eyeful of the view."

Jericho opens the door and Colin hurtles out. "That's the ticket!"

Edwina disembarks and Kelley follows. For several moments it seems like the whole world is spinning.

Leaving exasperated mother and child with the drivers, Kelley walks around the back of stage and negotiates the road.

A cool wind envelops her and a thousand smells blend into one undeniable scent. She takes a deep breath, clamps her hat on her head and looks up.

A thousand visions blend into one glorious sight.

A thousand memories come home...

My Home
by Kelley Keaton, aged 15.
Oh, heart's desire, come, for I have waited long,
My majestic mountain land.
My winter wonderland of snow and ice.
My summer land, rich in pasture,
sustaining peoples past and present.
My eternal place, where end of land and edge
of sky meet to dance together in timeless ritual to the
song of constant wind.
My river land, where a diamond-studded snake hugs
the road from the gorge below, or sweeps away at its
own bidding, absorbing color from the sky
and brilliance from the sun.
Come, be in my heart and in my soul for ever more.

That's very nice, Kelley, and your penmanship is definitely improving, but it's all been arranged, and you're going.

Mama, didn't you understand what I just read to you. I wrote it. It's
how I feel.

Very descriptive. And all the letters are slanting the same way. Aunt
Edith will be pleased. And so will you, at your new school...

I won't go.

You will go.

You are kicking me out of my own home?

No. You will have two homes. Your Aunt and Uncle are expecting
you.

I'm to live with strangers?

Edith is your father's closest relative. His sister, for heaven's sake.
Hardly a stranger. Besides, I know you must remember them a little...

I don't fit your mould so you want me gone.

That's nonsense and you know it. This is an opportunity...

If I go it's the last time you will ever see me. I won't come back. I'll
never speak to you again.

Gratitude would be nice for a change.

You want me to give in without a fight? Why can't you understand, Mama, I love it here. I don't want your opportunity. I want to stay here.

In New York you'll have plenty of adventures, believe me. It's clear that you don't know what's good for you.

What's clear is that I can't stay where I'm not wanted. What's clear is that Auntie wants me and you don't!

We want what's best for you. And that's your Aunt and Uncle and New York. End of discussion.

"Certainly is a magnificent view." Edwina Adams steps up beside her. "Goes on forever like this, don't it? Just beautiful…"

"Yes."

"That's a smart dress you're wearing. You're not from around here, are you?"

"Actually, I am, but I've been East. New York."

"That explains the dress."

Kelley glances at her and they smile. "What about you?"

"I took Colin to Cheyenne for treatment. He was very sick. There's a doctor there who is very good at treating children. She…"

"She? A woman doctor?"

Edwina smiles. "My husband was very unhappy at first until I began to write that Colin was improving. I heard about Dr Sullivan from a friend. You know how word spreads."

"And her treatment worked, I mean, your son seems perfectly well."

"Yes, it worked. She's young and has a way with children. We had to stay in Cheyenne for a month. It was worth it though. Colin is our only child. But, I've been missing my husband and our home."

"A month!" Kelley exclaims. "Try five years."

"Oh, my. I should have guessed from the way you've been devouring the scenery. Memories?"

"Thousands. When I got to New York I couldn't work out what was missing – it was the wind."

Edwina grins. "My husband and I love it here too. It hasn't all been easy, but no one could ever make us leave. We live near Dickson, so just a few miles to go for Colin and me. You?"

"Bright River."

She nods. "The next stop after."

"Yes. Not long."

They hear Jericho warning Colin to stand back.

Edwina excuses herself, saying, "I hope Colin's father is prepared for the new Colin."

No one could ever make us leave. Five years ago Kelley threatened to disown her parents after they made *her* leave. In New York, she refused to communicate with them for six months; her mother called it the biggest temper tantrum of all time, but Aunt Edith recognized profound hurt and grief when she saw it, and only Aunt Edith's persistent encouragement finally induced Kelley to relent her position. Goodwill and communication was re-established.

Let go of all that stuff and nonsense and see each of life's episodes as part of your life's journey. Aunt Edith the philosopher.

"Yes, Auntie..." It is time to deal with the past by facing the present, no matter how daunting. She has plenty of strength on which to draw, not the least being Aunt Edith's unconditional love and devotion, of which her parents will soon see she is definitely a product.

She smoothes her outfit, straightens her hat and returns to the stagecoach to inspect the driver's progress with the broken wheel for herself.

Luke

Bright River

Amy: "Where could it be?"

John: "Just been held up. You know it happens."

Amy: "But two hours?"

John: "You're gonna wear the sidewalk clean through if you don't quit pacing like that…"

If Luke could be anywhere else he would.

Waiting for the half-pint to hit town again after five years of peace and quiet is a dreary pastime.

And John and Amy are making him stir-crazy.

He shoots a glance of frustration at Mart.

"Patience is a virtue," Mart tells him.

"This much patience is reserved for relatives. Don't know why I let you talk me into this."

"It's neighborly."

Luke peels himself off the stage depot wall. "I'm taking a walk."

"How many does that make?"

"I haven't been counting."

Luke turns away. He surveys the town, and even though the open Fall sunshine gives it scope, with one sweep of his eyes he has seen practically all of it: general store, saloon, barber shop, livery, guest house, bank, sheriff's, school, telegraph office, a few houses…

The half-pint might notice a couple of differences since she's been gone – they refurbished the schoolhouse, painted the stage depot yellow and added a couple of extra tables to the lunch room, and there are a few more people about – otherwise it looks like nothing's changed.

"Try the church," Mart suggests, "you haven't been there yet."

White building, steeple and bell, doubles as a community hall. Cemetery out back.

Luke turns around to counter Mart's wisecrack, but something interesting at last catches his eye – two riders approaching from the same direction as they are expecting the stage.

"How many people did Amy and John tell?"

"That Kelley was coming home? You know them; everyone." Mart now follows Luke's line of vision.

"Harris and Richards," Luke murmurs, moving to the edge of the sidewalk.

"I see them."

"Maybe they know what happened to the stage."

"Ed Parsons ain't responsible for everything that happens around here."

"Not the good things, no."

"Will you relax? – look at you…"

"Better to watch these two."

Harris and Richards ride up to the slip rail alongside the stage depot, a few yards from where Luke and the Keatons are waiting. They dismount and tie up their horses, with Richards sporting his trademark eagle beak taps. Luke notices John stiffen as the two men pass by to take up the bench that Amy had given up an hour ago.

"Seems like someone knew the stage would be late…"

"Luke, leave it…"

But Luke takes a casual wander over in their direction. "You two wouldn't happen to know why the stage is late?"

Richards, the taller of the two, looks up. He gives Luke the once over, then looks away, saying, "How should we know, Taylor."

"It's a fair question," Luke counters lightly. "I mean, the Keatons have been waiting nearly two hours and here you are…"

Harris says, "We're expecting a package."

"Shut up, Harris," Richards says out of the side of his mouth.

Luke smirks. "Like I always say, when anything goes wrong in this town just ask Ed and his boys, they'll know why."

Harris charges to his feet, eyes hard, nostrils flared.

Luke's pulse quickens a fraction. "That stage better arrive soon with everyone on board in perfect health…"

Richards gets to his feet. He's the same height as Luke but heavier and barrel-chested. "Or what? What are you gonna do, Taylor?"

Luke stares hard at Richards, right down deep into the mean and sorry state of his pathetic being.

"Luke."

"What?" Luke says through gritted teeth.

"Let them pick up their package."

A familiar sound shudders on the air.

"It's coming," Amy announces and breathes, "at last."

Luke shifts his eyes from Richards' face to spy the stage horses strutting with unusual politeness around the corner, followed by the coach, as they enter Bright River at the top of the street.

Amy adds, "Luke, leave them alone and behave yourself."

Luke slides his gaze back to Richards. "What happened to it?" he asks quietly.

"You tell me," Richards mutters.

"I'm asking you," Luke counters.

They stare. Mart steps up beside him. The stage creaks to a halt close by, its shadow falling across them. Dust hovers in the air with the smell of sweating horses.

Driver Harry Hobbs's boots resound on the sidewalk. Followed by Jericho's prattle…

"No cause for alarm folks, we just broke a couple of wheel spokes as we were coming through the ruts. Had to change the wheel. No other damage and everybody's right as rain."

A slow, insolent smile spreads across Richards' face.

Luke is vaguely aware a reunion is taking place; curiosity gets the better of him and although he should know better he turns his head to look. A pretty blond girl in a smart dress is standing in front of John, biting her bottom lip.

He looks back; Richards glances at the stage. Harris steps forward. Mart counters Harris' movements. Richards sees this and looks back. They all stand face to face. Richards snarls; Luke senses what's coming but with Mart standing right there he hesitates. Richards slams his fist into Luke's mouth.

Luke feels the stinging pain right to the back of his head even before he hits the sidewalk. It ain't no picnic.

"Why don't you just kill me…" he gasps at Richards from the ground, "and get it over with."

"Don't give me any ideas."

"God forbid… you should ever have… one of your own."

Richards appears to want to have another go, but Luke can just make out Harris holding him back before Mart steps in front of them.

"That's enough," Mart says.

Richards shouts instead, "When are you ever gonna learn?"

Luke sits up best he can, and with the taste of blood staining his tongue, splutters, "When hell freezes over."

"So, I guess I'll see you there then."

Luke is spent; he has no more retorts. He cuffs at his bloody mouth while he watches Harris and Richards swing away like a couple of schoolyard bullies; who knows, they could've been, although it's unlikely they ever went to school.

"The package… see if they get their package…"

A moment later Mart says emphatically, "No. No package."

"What did I tell you?"

"And how many times do I have to tell *you*?"

"Tell me what?" Luke fingers his mouth.

"I give up."

"Luke Taylor, you get up at once." More chastising from Amy.

"Yes, M'am," he calls politely.

"It's not what we agreed," Mart continues.

"I didn't lay into him – that's what we've agreed. If I can't hit them then at the very least they gotta know that we know."

"Know what?"

"Mart," he growls, frustrated with him. He looks up; Mart's frowning but offering Luke his hand.

"You antagonized them."

Luke takes his hand and Mart pulls him to his feet. And it happens that, as he does so, Luke catches sight again of the pretty blond girl. He double takes and then stares. A light and airy sensation starts bobbing about inside him. She's not biting her bottom lip anymore; she's watching him, and Mart, her eyes flitting between them. He sleeves his mouth again and says, "Don't look now, Mart, but I think your sister's back in town."

Mart turns sharply. The half-pint raises her gloved hand and gives her brother a tentative smile.

"No one can change that much," Luke mutters.

"Does that really matter," Mart counters, regarding her with a stupid grin on his face.

"Maybe not to you," Luke says, and gives him a shove in the half-pint's direction.

He bends down and retrieves his hat. Nothing's ever gonna change around here, not while they stand back, pretend, and do nothing.

Kelley

Mart grabs her hands and squeezes them hard; she becomes the object of intense study. "Kelley... look at you..."

Her Pa chuckles. "Yep, she sure is a sight for sore eyes."

"She's beautiful, and no one could say otherwise," her Mama says.

"You look incredible."

"I'm still the same," she tells him dryly. Except that now she stands eye to eye with her Mama.

"You're grown up," he says unnecessarily. Or maybe he needs to say it. Either way, his approval warms her.

Mart's height seems to have averaged now that Kelley herself is taller, but he has acquired her Pa's well-muscled and broad-chested build. The gray eyes and long eyelashes, though, have always been like their Mama's, and the thick dark-blond hair exactly like dear departed Grandpa Olufsen's in the days before old age robbed him of it. If anyone is anticipating a family resemblance between brother and sister, it is there, but you need to look for it. They take their looks from opposite sides of the family.

Mart was just twenty-one when she left Bright River and she remembers him as a boy, but this person before her... Her parents seem barely changed, a few wrinkles, a little gray hair, but when did her brother become a man? Of course, all the correspondence they exchanged over five years should have prepared them for the changes they are now intent on seeing in each other, but even the honesty she poured into every letter could not possibly reveal the outward transition. Indeed, when the promise was broken so was the hour glass; time stopped all those years ago and for her to survive the adjournment everything and everyone in Bright River needed to stay the same, particularly Mart.

"What was all the commotion about?" she asks.

"Ah, Luke thinks he can take on Ed Parsons and his cronies..."

"Why would he want to do that?"

"It's not important now."

From the look on Taylor's face, it is important to him. He never used to be one to back away when challenged, which depending on how you looked at it was possibly his only redeeming quality. Her Mama is pushing a clean handkerchief into his hand for his bloody mouth but he's refusing it. Well, that's gratitude for you. And that's Taylor for you.

He walks up to her; she'd forgotten how intensely blue his eyes are, that he is some inches taller than Mart, although six months younger, that his strength is leaner and shoulders squarer, that his hair is light brown when he thinks about removing his hat, or in this case when it's removed for him. And she'd forgotten because she damn well chose to.

Clearly, he has forgotten nothing if that serious, narrow-eyed gaze is anything to go by.

"Hello, Taylor," she says, determined her memory should be longer than his.

"Kelley." A deeper, firmer voice than she expects. He looks like he wants to ask her something but thinks the better of it. He settles his hat squarely back on his head and turns to Mart, studying him from under the brim. Something silently yet eloquently passes between them.

After a sharp glance in her direction, Taylor acknowledges her parents and strides away.

Mart turns back to her. "Come on; let's get you home. You're probably tired."

"What was that all about, son?" her Pa asks quietly.

"Just Luke getting hot under the collar. It's nothing, Pa."

Her Pa's brow knits tightly and he says, "If you say so."

One hour later, she stands in her bedroom in danger of feeling as though she never left.

The rush of memories thrusts Aunt Edith in her wonderful brownstone, the whole of Manhattan and everyone she knew there into another world altogether. Here is girlhood, where time stopped and truth waited: her many treasures, her soft quilted bed, her precious books, her best doll... all laid out exactly as she left it. They hadn't cleared it away and converted it for storage; or rented it out to itinerant workers; or used it for visitors. This is *her* room. She presses her pillow to her face; it still smells of lavender. Never in her wildest dreams did she imagine *they* would treasure her childhood.

Just on sundown, Kelley persuades Mart to climb to the rocky outcrop that they named The Lookout a lifetime ago; here they witness the sun set over the green spread of their father's finest grazing pastures.

"So, Mart, what was the commotion in town today?"

"I thought I told you already."

She smiles. "I know a hedge when I hear one, Mart Keaton."

"Yeah?"

"And another. Are you and Taylor all right?"

"What do you think?"

She gives a nod; she knew the answer anyway. "But the situation today, when you stood there and Taylor, of all people, let that big man punch him, what's that all about?"

"It's a new approach," he hedges again.

"Come on, Mart, you know I am not about to let this go."

"We never wrote you about the Alliance?"

"No, you didn't. Are we at war or something?"

"No, but we needed a strategy. The Alliance means that the Taylors, the Benchleys and the Keatons have formed a pact to keep Parsons off our backs."

"By letting his man punch Taylor to the ground?"

"No. Look, it's complicated."

"It sounds serious," she murmurs. "I mean, The Alliance – that's so militaristic. Who thought of it?"

"Can't remember exactly. We were all talking a while back and it sort of happened."

"Is it working?" she asks, while temporarily overlooking his vagueness.

He gives her such a look that she feels it in her toes. "I think so."

She swallows hard and returns to the view. "They call it appeasement, what you and Taylor are doing."

A minute passes in silence.

Finally, he says, "You've been reading too many books. It ain't like that."

"What's it like then?"

Again, he declines an answer; he merely sighs.

"Have things changed that much?"

She feels his strong arm around her shoulders. "You're changed that much, why can't we?

"Because you were supposed to wait for me."

"I guess we waited a couple of years and then…"

"What?"

"Suddenly things were different."

A moment of mutual contemplation falls between them. The dusk grows heavy and evening begins. The suffuse pink of the sun's blush dissolves; the hills move into shadow, the pastures begin to fade.

"Still, this is the same," he murmurs. "If it should ever change…"

She glances at him in surprise; he catches her eye and clears his throat.

"Supper must be about ready." He faces them in the right direction and they start walking. "Did you learn anything useful back East?"

"Well, that depends on your context…"

"A yes or no answer to a simple question would be useful…" He continues to tease her all the way into supper.

Despite the light-hearted banter and the delicious homecoming meal their Mama has prepared, Kelley's conversation with Mart hangs in the air between them.

He hands her the potatoes. "Let it go, Kel."

"I can't. I don't understand and I need to."

"What are you two talking about?" her Pa asks.

"Mart told me about this Alliance with the Taylors."

"Good heavens, it's your first night home." And her Mama shoots Mart a rare look of disapproval.

"Amy," says her Pa, "our daughter may not be a signatory, but she is a member by right of blood."

"What does that mean?"

"Kelley, it's the men's business."

"Are we at war with Ed Parsons, Pa?"

"Certainly not!" her Mama answers. Her Pa opens his mouth then shuts it again. Mart chews his food.

"And why are we allied with Taylor?"

Her Pa opens and shuts once more as her Mama grunts at him.

Kelley looks from one to the other. "Oh…"

Mart swallows his mouthful and forks another. "These vegetables are great. Good crop this summer. You probably don't know, Kel, that your Mama's gone into selling a quota of each harvest."

"To the neighbors," says her Pa. "Even Daily's in town buys them from her to sell in the store."

"This season's crop is nearly done," murmurs her Mama.

"And folks have caught on to her herb remedies too. Had to build another greenhouse."

"Congratulations, Mama," Kelley says.

"It's really nothing…"

In another age, her Mama might have been burned at the stake…

They fall into silence, chewing diligently.

Aunt Edith would say *name the moment, don't suffer it*. But Kelley isn't with Aunt Edith.

Whatever this alliance is, her Pa's explanation will have to wait.

Sleep beckons.

The thought of being related to Taylor in any way, even by pact, is not her idea of a good idea, although the others in Taylor's family group, namely his mother and the Benchleys, are definitely worthy.

Wearily, she makes a mental list of her concerns: exactly how much allegiance is expected of her in regard to Taylor; and, why is such a coalition necessary?

Then she turns her cheek into her lavender-scented pillow for that long awaited first sleep in her own bed.

Kelley

During the week subsequent to her return, Kelley becomes reacquainted with the ranch. She inspects her Mama's greenhouses, markedly changed in five years. There are two potbelly stoves in each house in which she slow burns fat logs during winter. In one house Kelley imagines what being in a jungle probably feels like, luxuriantly verdant and enclosing, while the other is crammed with countless herbs and medicinal plants, all arranged methodically on shelves, each plant precisely labeled and emitting various fragrances that strike your senses as you walk by them. Her Mama takes her from plant to plant saying, "You remember this one…" or "Now this one is new, you won't know this one…" When it comes to names and application, her memory is vague and her interest obligatory.

Her Pa revels in showing her the improvements made to all the ranch buildings, and of course his great love, his horses, now reside in the best horse barn and finest corrals in the district.

And then there's Dancer. From the moment this creature came into this world as the sweetest, dearest foal ever born Kelley loved her; she'd be nearly twelve years old.

"She remembers me," Kelley says.

"Ain't likely to forget you. Not after the adventures you had together. You never went anywhere that I can recall without Dancer."

She hugs her warm neck, scratches her ears, kisses the white star on her nose and palms half a carrot into her mouth.

"Remember in the old days how you used to get into trouble and Dancer would take off and bring Luke back." He starts chortling. "Of all things. Not Mart. Or me. Luke! Your Mama and me used to chuckle about that…"

Her Pa is far too enthusiastic.

"Well, I never laughed," she tells him, but he only chortles harder.

"You used to get so mad with Luke for comin' to your rescue. And he wouldn't be too happy neither but he always did the right thing."

"May we change the subject?"

"Let's go for a ride after lunch. The old gal will love it."

Her parents have indeed prospered and despite the difficulties, which her Pa defines as winters (nothing new) and Ed Parsons (still nothing new), they are content.

And somewhere in all this re-establishment her concerns about the peculiar partnership between her family and Taylor fade. There are no signs of war, and no sign of their allies either.

In fact, her greatest problem is that she can never find Mart. After that first day his attention to her has dwindled. They pass at breakfast each morning and supper every evening when he barely says a thing no matter how cleverly she tries to contrive some conversation.

"Is something wrong, Mart?" she asks, eventually trying the direct approach.

He looks up from his plate; he sports dark, smudgy half-moons beneath his eyes. "No."

"You look tired."

He sighs and says, "Let it go, Kel."

Let it go seems to be his favorite saying.

The following morning she helps her Mama load the break-fast table with every delectable breakfast food imaginable. Juicy steak. Salty bacon. Creamy oatmeal. Pancakes. And small bowls of fruit preserves. Any of New York's finest eating establishments would be happy with this lot.

"The outfit will be busy today. Want to feed up your Pa..."

Her Pa comes in, rubs his hands together, gives the cook a hug around her middle as she pours his coffee, sits down hurriedly and digs in.

Kelley slides her spoon into her oatmeal. "Can either of you tell me what's bothering Mart?"

"No," says her Pa before he forks steak into his mouth.

Her Mama salts her eggs. "Just going through a spell."

"What kind of a spell? It's odd, don't you think? I mean, he's the consistent one, usually."

Her Pa swallows his steak. "Not for you to worry about."

"He's not eating breakfast?"

"Should be."

Kelley continues her oatmeal in silence.

Mart tracks in after a while and she smiles a sheepish good morning. His in return appears even wearier and more remote than the last.

"The fence is down along the south flat," he says to her Pa.

"That where you been?"

"We're fighting a losing battle."

"With the fence?"

"It's costing us."

Her Pa considers him, chewing thoughtfully.

"Eat your breakfast, son."

Kelley slowly sips her coffee, glancing from one to the other over the rim of her cup, as, she notices, is her Mama.

Several days later, Kelley has fallen into a typical routine – her Mama's. They clean up after breakfast, working quietly, getting the job done. Kelley knows her Mama's thoughts are on the next. She used to say, *give some thinking time to your next chore while you're busy with the one in your hands.* Kelley often thought about other things while doing chores, and rarely was the next chore among them.

"Mama?"

"Mm…"

"How well do you know Aunt Edith?"

"Well enough, and I'm very fond of her."

"She taught me a great deal."

"I know," her Mama says. Her hands on the pot she's scrubbing slow a little.

"She said that you should know why I came back."

"I figured you thought it was time."

"Aunt Edith taught me that my life, the way I think, is complicated. She taught me to think through things and apply philosophy and strategy."

"Go on," her Mama says with a lilt in her voice.

"I must have clear objectives and keep them prioritized. I must stick to them. And I must seize my opportunities."

Her Mama drops the pot and looks up. The pot bobs around in the dishwater. "What are you getting at?"

"There is something I need to do, Mama. One of these objectives, you see. The first of course was to see you and Pa and Mart, and I've done that and I'm very happy…"

"Go on."

"You know how much I loved living here, how free I felt…"

"From the way you begged me not to leave, it was quite clear."

"I need to rediscover that feeling again, to know if this is where I am supposed to be."

Her Mama picks up the pot and resumes her scrubbing. "I thought you had."

"I came home to reconnect."

"Kelley, I wished you'd get to the point…"

"I need to take a trip into the hills, maybe camp out for a night…"

Her Mama drops the pot. "Absolutely not."

"If you had been away from your plants and greenhouses and herbs for a long time, the first thing you would do after kissing Pa would be to go straight out there and tend to them, see how they were, get them back to rights if they looked peaked and droopy. You would, wouldn't you?"

"It's hardly the same…"

"You would reconnect with them."

"Kelley…"

"You love your plants, don't you?"

Her Mama's shoulders sag.

"Mama, I have no one to talk to about this. What if I'm wrong? What if my objective is only a child's whim, because I can feel that child in me, Mama, protecting herself, wanting everything to be just perfect, the way it used to be. What if…"

"I won't let you go out there by yourself. Mart could go…"

"If I could find him to ask; he's never around. And he doesn't talk to me. Look, Mama, I know it's hard for you to understand…"

"But obviously Aunt Edith would, is that it?"

Kelley swallows. "I'm not practical like you, Mama, my heart tells me what to do. And I have to do this."

"Finish the wiping up and we'll talk about it later."

"But the day is perfect…"

"I said later."

"It's now or never, Mama. Don't say I can't go. Just say you advise me against it, if that will make you feel better. I'll face Pa when I get back, and Mart. Anyone. I just hoped to make you understand."

Her Mama stares at her.

Kelley grins. "I could have just left a note."

Kelley moves through drifts of grazing cattle until she comes to the boundary of her Pa's land. Beneath Dancer's footfall the ground is hard and the grass a little dry as summer leaves its mark, but as she and Dancer ford the river shallows and lope across the plains, the grass grows thicker and greener in the shadow of the hills.

To the north lies Ed Parsons' ranch, to the south the Stewarts'; some of this open space belongs to the Taylors, but there is a green corridor which leads up into the hills which everyone can use, and it was definitely well-used when she was a girl.

She pushes her hat hard to her head and gives Dancer the opportunity to stretch her twelve-year-old legs; they gallop onto the open plain and defy the inevitable swirling wind. When she eventually pulls up at the top of the trail leading into the hills she's laughing breathlessly.

"When was the last time you did that, Mart Keaton," she breathes.

She and Dancer rest here for a time and look back at the way they have come. The cattle appear like tiny brown dots; in fact everything seems far away. The sky bows like a massive blue vault, cloudless and intense, containing everything beneath it.

Is that why she came here so often as a girl? To see things from afar? To make sense of it through the perspective of distance?

She mounts Dancer and they start on the trail, soon winding their way up a forested hillside. She is careful to mark a precise trail so that she will find her way back. Mart taught her how to do this when she was seven, although she always insisted that her sense of direction was perfect and she didn't need trail markers. Without the five-year interval she still wouldn't need them, but there is no sense in getting lost from lack of practice and proving her mother right. Anyway, there are far worse fates than being lost out here.

This is where heaven touches the earth with its big toe.

Your imagination gets worse by the day, Kel.

Come on, Mart, you know you agree.

Mart tended to agree quietly; a boyish agreement.

After the open plain, the forest feels like her Mama's greenhouse, warm and encompassing. The earthen trail, covered in leaves and pine needles and veined with tree roots, is still well defined; branches overhang it in some sections; higher up fragrant conifers line it like an avenue. It is full of sounds; bird song, wind moving in the treetops; chattering, darting animals.

Memories flood back. Any recollections of the times she was by herself or with Mart or her friends are sacred; any that remotely have Taylor in them, but particularly those her Pa gleefully recalled earlier, are banned.

They reach the stream a couple of hours before sundown. She scoops handfuls of sweet mountain water into her mouth; Dancer slurps in the shallows beside her.

"Well, Dancer, I think we should get back on the trail and find a place to set up camp." Wearily, she swings her leg over Dancer's back. "I don't know about you, but this trail riding is considerably more exhausting than I remember."

Luke

Darkness encroaches, steadily, like an enormous shadow. Luke must hold the lantern closer in order to examine the broken branch properly.

Twisted. Crushed. Deliberate.

"Over here, Mart."

Mart rushes across and inspects carefully.

"It's her?" Luke asks.

Mart nods and looks ahead this time. "This was her favorite trail."

"Yeah, well, I remember that too, Mart, but what I'm saying is that she did this, not the bear."

"I know!" he snaps.

Gees, he's jumpy, bear or no bear.

"Well, good for her."

Mart reproaches him with a look. "Okay. Let's just keep going."

They push on. One eye on the trail she's clearly marked. One eye on the darkening forest. Painful girl. A wounded bear on the loose won't enhance her camp out. Well, that's Kelley. It has to be her way, her time and to hell with everyone else.

As for the bear, no one knew how it got wounded, only that it had been seen several times in the past two days and had eluded its hunters.

From out of the eerie silence between them, Mart says, "I know you're annoyed, but…"

"Ain't you?"

"I'm gonna wring her neck."

"So?"

"So let me do it."

Luke sighs and spots another broken branch. "Well, you'll be pleased to know we're on track."

It seems like an hour later that they hear a horse whinny.

"Dancer?" Luke whispers.

Mart nods. "Take it easy. We don't want to spook her."

They dismount and continue on foot, walking into a clearing a few minutes later. Dancer whinnies again. She's calm because she knows them; knows their scent and their approach.

They look about with their lanterns high, the golden light casting long shadows.

Luke grounds his lantern in the center of the clearing, then crosses to Dancer and grabs her bridle. "Easy, girl, easy now... She hasn't lit a fire."

"There she is," Mart says suddenly. Luke watches him stride quickly to an old hollow tree stump. His lantern illuminates a figure curled up in a blanket. Sure enough, it's her. And she's asleep.

Luke gives a snort. "Is she in one piece?"

Mart is waking her gently. Pity. Once her eyes are open it's like releasing the brake on a wagon facing downhill. And the forest is so peaceful.

"Mart..." A sleepy voice. "You came. I was remembering all the adventures we..."

"Kelley, we're taking you home." She has to know that when Mart is that direct he...

"What for? What's the matter?"

"Well, what do you think? Come on, get up."

"What's the matter with you?" She emerges from her hideaway; for a fleeting moment Luke expects to see that annoying adolescent.

"I'll get a fire started," he says.

"What's *he* doing here?" she exclaims.

Yep. That's more like it. He enjoys the brother and sister exchange as he gathers firewood.

"Of all the chuckleheaded stunts. You can't come up here on your own."

"Well, if you had been around, Mart, I would have asked you along. Not that I expected you to come. You barely give me the time of day."

"When you didn't come home before dark Mama started to panic. Don't you ever think?"

"What did you expect me to do, Mart? Keep house all day with Mama. I thought you knew me better. That's not why I came back."

"Why you came home is not the point…"

"You don't think so? If you had been away for five years, would you sit in the house and look out the window day after day? I think not! So don't lecture me."

She can talk her way out of anything.

Almost.

"It's not always about you!" Mart grinds out.

As Luke gets back to the clearing, they stop.

The half-pint glares at him.

"What are you doing here?" she shouts, obviously expecting an answer this time.

"Nice to see you, too," Luke says and goes about setting the fire. He glances up to see her retreating to her tree stump.

"Shouldn't we just go," Mart suggests.

"I'm beat and I want some coffee," Luke tells him. "The fire should keep any unwelcome visitors away."

Mart joins him; he sits down and lets out a long sigh.

They never did mind an argument these two, not since he'd known them; they loved each other, but they occupied different planes of existence.

Amused, Luke prepares the coffee.

There are few flavors in the world like coffee made on a campfire. Even Mart seems to enjoying his.

"Want some coffee?" he calls to his sister.

"No, I do not! I can't believe you did this. I am not a child."

"That old tree stump talks," Luke chuckles.

"And tell him to mind his own business."

Luke gets to his feet and ambles over to her; she is sitting up, hugging her knees.

"Didn't you learn to be nice when you were away?"

"Luke…" comes Mart's hushed call. "Gonna scout around."

"Why?" Luke asks. "Everything's quiet. I don't think we should split up."

"I won't be long. Mind the half-pint."

He'd rather face the bear. "You mind her. I'll scout."

Without warning, Kelley stands up and brushes him aside. She strides to the fire as Mart saunters off armed with his rifle and the lantern turned down low. Luke watches her while she warms her hands. She's pretty, he decides. Well, he decided that when he'd seen her in town, only by firelight she is prettier. He returns to the fire himself and picks up a clean cup.

"Coffee?" he asks carefully.

"Thank you."

He pours out a small amount of the strong, bitter brew and passes her the cup. He watches her blow the steam and take a sip.

"For crying out loud, Taylor," she splutters. "Are you trying to poison me?"

"Hadn't thought of that," he says.

She dispatches a scathing look. That's pretty too and he grins at her through the spindly column of smoke. Well, he's only human.

Kelley

Philosophies and strategies are easier to learn than they are to apply. The thick skin, for example. One can simply become oblivious to everything, or learn to apply old-fashioned self-control. Either one stretches her ability to the limit, but to sit around a campfire with Taylor after what's just happened requires every-thing she's got.

Breathe, my darling, just breathe; it is the key to control.

She wishes she had asked Aunt Edith for a Taylor strategy, but she breathes anyway.

The flames bob and sway.

She watches the reflection of their spirited dance move across his face. He doesn't say anything; offers no criticism, makes no judgment. After she spat out his six-shooter coffee he had smiled at her, which was interesting. Then he lost interest, silently staring at the flames.

"How long will Mart be?" she asks him.

He shrugs. "There's no telling; he's taken a liking to his own company these days."

"Why?"

"Your questions are annoying, didn't anyone ever tell you that?"

"Only you."

His piercing dark-eyed glance silences her at last, but the fire crackles cheerfully, filling the surly void. Short flames penetrate the darkness, flicking wriggles of light onto the bushes and up to the tops of the trees.

Presently, Mart returns and sits down on her right.

"I was just thinking before," he says. "Old Ozark – this reminds me of him."

Taylor smiles. "Well, I guess he must be here in spirit then."

Kelley gapes at her brother; now this is what a thick skin is all about. One minute you tear strips off your sister and the next you can sit and recall legends like it never happened.

"You wanna tell it, Kel? You liked Ozark a lot I recall."

"No, I do not want to tell it. And if this is your way of smoothing over what just happened, Mart Keaton, you can think again."

Mart frowns at her. They sit in smoky, crackly silence.

Ozark.

An old Indian fighter, employed as a scout by the Army at Fort Laramie, who had more stories about his Indian fighting days up on the Ozark Plateau in Missouri than you could poke a stick at. According to the legend, the Army re-christened him 'Ozark'. His real name they never found out; it didn't seem important. He would visit from time to time on his expeditions; *never had kids of m'own*, he used to say, and he would take them into the hills when Kelley was still small and make a fire and tell his stories. He could speak a number of Indian languages. She used to think he had special powers and would never die until the Sioux killed him along with General Custer up on the Big Horn seven years ago. She remembers Taylor saying he died the way he lived – on America's frontier fighting Indians; and that with his death the Sioux had avenged many.

The fire crackles on… to speak the stories, and dance the legends… and they don't take to being ignored.

"You realize this is the first time the three of us have been together for a long time," Mart murmurs.

Now he's really pushing his luck.

Make the best of the situation.

She breathes. And breathes some more.

Taylor adds more wood to the fire. It crackles furiously for some moments before it settles down to become the perfect campfire. More coffee is consumed in a silence that is growing increasingly awkward.

"May we please just go home?" she says.

Mart sighs. "I was thinking we could do with a yarn."

You would, Mr I'm-over-it-why-ain't-you.

"No," she and Taylor say simultaneously.

"Liberty and Property," Mart says. "That's your cue, Luke."

Taylor stares at him for some time, poker-faced. "What's got into you?"

"I just thought this was a good opportunity to…"

"To what, Mart?" she scowls.

Mart doesn't answer. Typical.

"Never mind," says Taylor. "I guess if we got your company, Mart, we oughta make the most of it."

"What do you mean by that?" she asks.

They are staring oddly at one another and ignore her.

Furious, she says, "You realize that this was *my* adventure and you two just come barging in here, ruin it completely and take over…"

Mart regards her gently. "Kel, you love campfire legends. You know you do. And no one tells them better than Luke. So in honor of your return, let him tell one."

She looks at Taylor. He shrugs lightly.

"I'll risk it," he murmurs.

Such graciousness.

She sighs. "You two… Oh, go ahead."

He gives a broad grin – something unexpected – and begins.

"Matthew Taylor, originally from England, seeking freedom and better prospects for himself and his wife, Elizabeth, set sail for America.

"He settled in Duchess County, New York. He was an outspoken advocate against the British Stamp Act and became an active member of the Sons of Liberty. He was injured in the Battle of Golden Hill in New York in 1770. Later he fought in other battles of the Revolution.

"His son, Daniel, my great grandfather, was only a lad at the time, but he also fought under the banner of 'Liberty and Property'. In 1779, Matthew, Elizabeth and Daniel left Duchess County like many of those Sons and took routes westward to a frontier that was free and where land was begging to be got.

"On the shores of the Ohio River they settled down and raised livestock. Many others from Duchess did the same and they kept together to strengthen their endeavor and for protection against the Indians. Others from Duchess settled along the Mississippi.

"Anyway, Matthew and Daniel raised their beeves and when it came time to market them they loaded their stock onto flat boats – rafts – to float them down river to the markets in New Orleans. For the journey home they broke up their boats, sold the lumber and returned on horseback, north along the Natchez Trace, the old Indian trail. They and their partners stuck together for protection against hostiles. They were river men and horsemen – half alligator, half horse.

"Tragically, Matthew and Elizabeth were killed by Indians. Daniel though, he survived and became quite a frontiersman. Later he married a much younger woman named Roberta Howard. Said to be so pretty he called her 'Angel' and made her sleep with a shotgun under her pillow."

"Must have been damn uncomfortable," Mart remarks.

"Mm... I always thought it was romantic in a frontier kinda way. Anyhow, Daniel and Roberta had one son: James. He loved raising livestock just like the Taylors before him. At twenty-one he married Lara Proulx; her family were originally refugees from the French and the English fighting over Quebec. James and Lara had two sons: Richard and Morgan.

"Now Morgan set off as a young man of twenty; he went to Texas in '46 and rounded up longhorns for the ranchers that were thriving there. Before he left, James, who was close to Morgan, gave him Matthew Taylor's Sons of Liberty ring, which got passed down from father to son. He said Morgan seemed to have inherited his grandfather's love of the frontier. But Morgan never saw his father and mother again; they died in a winter epidemic in '47. Even though he wrote to *them* often, his useless brother never wrote and told him that they were ill. Just as well Morgan had Texas. According to him, Texas was the grandest place in the whole country."

"Liberty and Texas!" Kelley cries.

"Keep quiet or I won't go on."

"So it's all right for Mart to make comments but not me?"

"It's not supposed to be part of the story," he says, turning towards her.

"Well, far be it for me to add something to your sacred text, Taylor."

He rolls his eyes, then looks back into the fire. "Morgan set up his own ranch at a place called Diamond Bend along the Red River, said to have originally belonged to some Spanish lord. He and Ethan Benchley spent eleven years making it the success that it was. In the meantime, Morgan met Sara and she changed his life. My mother was the daughter of one cattleman who decided he'd get out of Texas. His descendants came from Denmark, who originally settled in a small enclave in New York. Sara's father grew tired of ranching, but not before Morgan met Sara. She was ten years younger than he and real pretty. Ethan likes to tell that Morgan fell head over heels in love with her. Her family spoke Danish and kept Danish customs, and Morgan liked that. They were married in '54. Her folks moved back East. The clan died out, leaving only Sara. A sad thing, after all that moving, settling and striving.

"My sister, Katrine, was born in '55, three years later I was born. When I was five, Pa and Ethan joined the Confederate army and went off to the War. My mother begged Pa not to go but go he did."

"Could've been a Liberty and Texas thing," Mart remarks.

"Probably. Ethan, a pure-born Texan, sure, but Pa… I guess the thought of Texas changing didn't sit right. Anyway, they were both captured at Vicksburg in '63; eventually got paroled; they lived to fight another day, to finally return home, sick and sore and weary, only home weren't nearly the way they left it."

It occurs to Kelley that the strain of surviving the War for Taylor, his sister and especially his mother would have been almost unbearable. In fact, a woman's perspective is sadly absent in Taylor's man-orientated telling of Liberty and Property. They either die unceremoniously or have to put up with an awful lot.

"It must have been dreadful without your father and Ethan all that time," she says, staring into the flames. He is silent and she glances up to find him looking at her with an unreadable expression.

"We survived," he says gruffly. "I told you not to interrupt."

She glares at him, but he ignores her and continues. "When Morgan and Ethan returned from the War, the ranch was in disarray. My mother had enough to do just keeping us alive, so most of our stock went missing, was scattered or got confiscated. We weren't the only ones. Ranches all over got devastated. So…

"Like other Confederate soldiers returning to their ranches in Texas, Morgan and Ethan found that thousands of longhorns had strayed and multiplied; here was their chance. They rounded up as many as they could muster, branded them all with the diamond-T and started again. With the War over, they found out that they stood to make some good money if they could get their cattle to northern markets. So in '66 they drove a couple thousand head up the Sedalia Trail to Sedalia in Missouri. The railroad was pushing through and beef was in high demand.

"Trying to run cattle out of Texas in those days was a treacherous occupation. But Morgan and Ethan did it. They had some brave men that rode with them. Through all kinds of weather and terrain. Stampedes, river crossings, rustlers. You had to be tough. How they never got killed by red-legs, nesters or Indians, or by riled Kansans worried about cattle ticks, is something. They collected $35 a head for their trouble. So they gave it another try the following year and took the Chisholm Trail to Abilene, a cow town specially set up by a man named McCoy to get Texas herds to northern markets in St Louis and Chicago. They made a great deal of money.

"Before going back to Diamond Bend, they undertook a little exploration, hearing from traders that lands west of Fort Laramie held great promise if you could survive the Arapaho and the Cheyenne. They started to explore the pastoral prospects of this part of the country. The state Texas was in after the War was such that they laid eyes on this country and decided that they could settle down right here in the high grazing pastures and green valleys of these mountains. Get out of the South and get closer to the markets and potential markets promised by the railroads. Made sense, they reckoned.

"They bought a large spread from a feller named Connors who was fed up with the Indians and wanted to push on westward to California.

"Connors had had the land surveyed and documented by the Army to keep the railroad from getting their hands on it; my father and Ethan paid a handsome price for it and called it the Connors Bill of Sale. Connors' herd was in good condition but kinda small, so they purchased shorthorns for breeding from cattlemen who were crossing the district over the Oregon Trail. Then they went home, sold Diamond Bend, gathered up their families, their horses and a handful of their best breeding stock and headed north."

Taylor pauses here for a long moment. His eyes have got the fire in them, like porcelain glazed midnight sky.

"On the way our party was attacked by Kiowa-Apache. They kidnapped Katrine and later she was found, murdered. How they could do what they did to a girl just fourteen, I can't understand. I mean, I can understand they would be touchy about white men taking over their land, but to do what they did to a just a kid... and why her? Why not me? I had a gun; I was shooting at them. She wasn't. She was just being Katrine, telling me what to do..."

He kicks at hot ash, causing dirt to fly up and into the fire. He never used to tell this part of the story with so much feeling. He used to say that the Kiowa-Apache attacked their party and killed his sister, and hastily move on to the next part. Now, it seems that he knows the answers, has always known them, but has been reluctant to speak them, or give voice to his emotions for that matter.

She dares the question: "You were only a boy, how did you find out what they did to her?"

"I overheard two men from our party talking. They found her. You don't want to know what they said."

"I... oh," she says.

"Anyhow," Taylor continues, his voice low, "Pa and Ethan set up the ranch and called it the Diamond-T. They survived Indians, blizzard, storm, flood, wind and Wyoming winters to create the beginnings of a prosperous ranch." He clears his throat. "Then, early in the summer of '69, Morgan was driving the herd to the rail yards. The cattle stampeded at night in a thunderstorm. He was crushed by the herd."

Yet another occupational hazard of catastrophic proportions.

The Keatons arrived late that summer when the Taylors were deeply mourning the loss of husband and father.

Her Mama used to say that they came along just when Taylor needed a family. What her Mama failed to understand in her desire to do good was that Kelley didn't need an obnoxious eleven-year-old upstart in theirs.

"Meanwhile, Richard Taylor, who years before had parted Morgan's company on bad terms, ignored Sara's letters. He had ignored her pleas for help during the War, so what was new? Did he care about his brother? Give a dime about us?"

Taylor stops and looks fit to swear. She and Mart exchange glances. It is no secret that Taylor despised his uncle for what the man did, or rather didn't do.

"Maybe it was the fact that your father was a Confederate," she ventures. "There is still division between North and South to this day."

"But the Bible says you're supposed to take care of widows and orphans," Mart says.

"That's beside the point, Mart," she argues. "Maybe Richard Taylor doesn't believe in the Bible. Taylor's father didn't."

"You seem mighty sure of yourself. How do you know what Morgan Taylor believed in?"

"It's obvious. His son doesn't believe in the Bible. Those things get passed down."

"Not always. Faith gets lost as much as it gets found..."

"Hey! Remember me? The son?"

Sheepishly, they look at their storyteller.

"I think the closing chapter is long overdue," he growls.

"Oh. Please, continue," she says.

"Thank you. With Ethan's continued partnership, we carried on. Despite difficult times, the Diamond-T eventually prospered. In the spring of '75 we upgraded the Diamond-T stock with five hundred head of short-horn cattle. The end."

"1875?" she exclaims. "Are you joking?"

"Do I look like I'm joking?"

"Liberty and Property could certainly do with an update. Pa's got some nice, fluffy, plump Hereford roaming about, and I can't imagine you missing out on that."

"Very funny. That's all for today, children."

"But I would like to know why women always get the short end of the stick in your story? I mean, whatever happened to Elizabeth's story, and Roberta Howard's – she must have been more than a pretty face; or Lara's? Her family was from Quebec, she must have been French, you have French blood..."

"*Now* we are leaving." Taylor shakes coffee dregs from his cup and stands.

"With a story like that runnin' around in your blood, is it any wonder you can't make up your mind to go or stay," Mart remarks curiously.

The two of them eye one another, Taylor with good-natured forbearance and hands on hips.

"That so?" Taylor says, his tilted chin looking square by the light of the fire.

"What do you mean, Mart?" Kelley asks.

Mart throws a smiling glance in her direction. "Luke's got the blood of a frontiersman, Kel. And right now it's making its own war of independence with a head full of rancher's common sense that's saying stay right here and make a life."

And what is she supposed to make of that? Besides, who cares if Taylor stays or goes, particularly goes?

Taylor's feet shift impatiently and she swings her gaze back to him.

"I ain't going anywhere," Taylor grinds out, still with a smile curling his lip a fraction.

Curiously, he is twisting his Sons of Liberty ring around his finger – Matthew Taylor's ring, which he never takes off. She vaguely recalls overhearing him telling Mart once that he put it on when his father died and swore he would never take it off.

"Give it time," Mart says.

Taylor lets out a huge sigh and rolls his dark eyes.

"What was that song, the one from the Revolution…?" Mart continues. "The Sons of Liberty song… something about *our fathers of old… far away shore... ah, I remember… The birthright we hold, shall never be sold, but sacred maintained to our graves, and before we'll comply, we'll gallantly die, for we must not, we will not be slaves, brave boys, for we must not, we will not be slaves.*"

"Not bad."

"A feller can't hang out with you all these years and not know it. There are better ideas to believe in, in my opinion."

Taylor gives a lopsided grin. "I know what you think about the Sons of Liberty… I know, I know."

Now what are they talking about?

It's always the same when Taylor's around. They leave her floundering. It vexes her. Deeply. And her patience with it wore out long, long ago.

"Keep the fire until we're fully ready to leave," Taylor says. "I'll see to the horses."

Who'd dare to disobey?

Mart stands up then, clutching his rifle, chuckling softly. "Kelley, get your gear packed up. Be back in a minute."

She crosses to the hollow stump and rolls up her blanket. She looks up and notices Taylor watching her. "Well?"

"This little escapade of yours – if it makes you feel any better I would have done the same thing."

"Would you just?"

"Maybe it's a liberty and property thing."

"I doubt it. Liberty and property is not for me." She strides across to Dancer and ties the blanket to her saddle. Heaven forbid she should ever want *his* understanding.

"It seemed to me that you enjoyed the story."

"I *want* to go home."

Unexpectedly, Dancer whinnies; her ears stand erect, she stomps her feet. Kelley soothes her but then hears movement in the bushes beyond their clearing. Taylor has heard it too, probably before her because he has already engaged his rifle.

"Mart," he calls in a hushed tone.

"Where *is* Mart?"

"I'll let you figure that out. Get back to the fire."

"I don't have to do what you tell me."

"You'll wish you did," he says and strides over to her; he grabs her arm and drags her to the fire.

"Just what do you think you are doing!"

"Mart, get your ass back here!"

It isn't Mart who appears. It's a bear – a huge grizzly who bellows with jaws dripping with saliva from a posture on all fours about ten feet away on the other side of the fire. The horses screech and bolt. Taylor raises his rifle and simultaneously pushes her behind him. She steps aside to see what is happening. The grizzly lumbers towards them, its ferocious jaws emitting a howling scream. Taylor fires his rifle.

The explosion is shattering and the bear takes the full impact and roars in agony. But the bullet hasn't stopped it. The enraged creature lunges at them. She feels Taylor yank her to the side. Then she's on the ground and Taylor is no longer with her. Frantically, she looks up to see the grizzly's finger-length claws lashing out at him, catching his arm, slashing through his coat, knocking him to the ground.

Rifle fire blasts out of the dark and the bear roars in confusion and agony. It turns away from Taylor and stumbles back onto four paws again, one huge claw shakily lashing out at the air.

She scrambles to her feet to see Mart taking aim at the creature. He fires three more times and the grizzly crashes to the ground. The air it displaces causes the fire to roar and flare. Orange sparks and smoke career into the sky.

Then there is silence.

Shaking, she stares at the animal's motionless form. An erratic thumping in her ears breaks the silence. She clutches at her chest as her heart pushes against her ribs.

"Kelley, are you all right?"

"Yes… yes…"

"Luke's hurt," he says, but she loses sight of him in a dark cloud of shock.

"He… he pushed me aside…"

Luke

Luke is unsure what wakes him, but it jerks him into consciousness and causes the pain in his shoulder and arm to freshen.

"Dang…"

"Easy, Luke."

The scent of juniper and pine fill his nostrils as he draws a recuperative breath and becomes aware of the sharp coolness all around him. Slowly, he opens his eyes. Daylight.

"Mart…"

"Can you sit up?"

"I think so. What happened after I passed out?"

"We finished cleaning you up. Mind your bandage."

"Thanks. Am I still bleeding?"

"It's likely. Doc Lewis is gonna have to stitch your arm."

"Biggest, meanest sonofabitch I ever saw."

"The grizzly?"

"No, Doc Lewis…"

Mart chuckles. "Want some coffee?"

He nods gingerly. With his eyes actually beginning to focus, he manages to get himself in a position to survey their camp. The grizzly makes an interesting centerpiece. Close to the fire and wrapped in blankets is Kelley's sleeping form.

"How's the half-pint?"

Mart pours steaming coffee into a tin cup; its stout aroma lends comfort as Luke battles with the pain in his arm and the tiny person with the huge hammer running around in his head.

"She'll be all right." Mart hands him the cup. "She said you pushed her out of the way."

Luke blows on his coffee. "I did?"

"Thanks."

"Don't mention it."

"Guess I'd better wake her."

"Pity."

Mart's eyes flash at him. "She ain't that bad."

"You're right. She's worse. Go on. I'll see to the horses."

"You stay put till I tell you."

Luke gets to his feet, accompanied by his tiny pal with the huge hammer and a bout of dizziness, while Mart gives his sister a gentle nudge. Luke watches her sit up while his head clears. She refuses Mart's offer of coffee and drinks water instead. Then she turns her bright blue gaze on him. Should be used to that adventure-crazed face... tousled hair and smeared cheeks... seen it a thousand times. As he returns her gaze, he remembers something long forgotten; he used to call her 'K'. Hating him the way she did, she never called him by his first name... Taylor this and Taylor that... but he could never bring himself to be quite as harsh towards her. So he shortened Keaton to...

"I thought I told you to stay put," Mart says to him.

Luke turns away towards the forest. "I heard." He whistles; all three horses come sheepishly into the clearing. It puts a smile on his face, and he hears Mart and Kelley laughing softly. He lets Mart pack their gear; his arm hurts so that all he can do is stand there, hold it to his side and concentrate on not passing out again.

"Some water before we start?" Kelley holds out the canteen to him.

"Thanks," he says and takes it.

"I think you should let Mama apply a poultice to your arm," she suggests. "Who knows where that bear's been..."

He raises an eyebrow at her.

"It was just a suggestion," she murmurs and turns away. He watches her mount Dancer with consummate ease.

"Need a hand?" Mart asks him.

"No."

"Okay. Let's get out of here."

As he lies in bed, stitched up, bandaged and helpless, Sara stands over him with her arms folded and her eyes narrowed. There's a bony line to her mouth too.

"So tell me what happened."

"I told you what happened. Mart came over and asked me to help find the half-pint. I went. We found her. That wounded bear attacked me. Mart brought me home."

"I believe that a grown girl of twenty is entitled to a full measure."

"A full measure of what?"

"Respect."

From the other side of the room Ethan whistles softly.

"That'll be enough of that, Ethan," Sara says, but there's a wobble in her voice. "You should have come straight home. None of this campfire legends and coffee. It was a rescue not a social occasion. Thankfully, Doc Lewis could assure us there'd be no lasting damage. Again."

Luke is too sore and too fed up with the whole thing to argue. As it is he's gonna have to stay in bed all day. Sara straightens his coverlet and walks out.

"Well, Ethan, got nothing to say?"

"You're alive, ain't you?"

"Yes, I'm alive."

"Then I got nothing to say. But when you do finally get yourself fitted out for a pine box, then I'll have plenty."

Kelley

"I know we all got some adjusting to do. All of us living in this house are adults now and we trust each other."

"Yes, Pa."

"But that don't mean if we believe one of us might be in trouble we stand by and ignore it."

"Yes, Pa."

"Living here has never been just free and easy. There are things to consider. Always has been. And we've always known we got to work together. Said it a hundred times, I know, but it never hurts to say it again."

"Yes, Pa."

"And, daughter?"

"Yes, Pa?"

"Be sure you pay your respects to Luke and Sara tomorrow."

"Very well, Pa."

When he has finally gone, she slumps into a chair.

Mart regards her with laughing eyes. "Could've been worse. Supper dishes for a week."

"Probably escaped your notice that I do those already."

"I'll take you to Morgen tomorrow."

"Suddenly I'm the focus of your attention again?"

"Don't be like that. I'm trying to make it up to you."

"Well, I'm not sure I want you along."

"Oh, that's rich, that is. When I think of all the times I had to drag you along everywhere I wanted to go alone."

"That was different."

"Come on, Kel. It'll be like old times."

"That remains to be seen. What is Mrs Taylor like these days? She was a very good woman as I recall; Taylor has driven her to drink by now, has he?"

"If Pa and Mama didn't take up the bottle on your account, then Sara had no cause to resort to drink because of Luke."

"I only asked what she was like these days."

"You're on your lonesome there. It wasn't my fault Luke was out looking for you instead of being home all tucked up safe in bed."

Kelley blinks. "You asked him to help you. And when was Taylor ever tucked up safe in bed?"

"Now that right there – Sara ain't gonna like it. That's what the old folks call a bad attitude."

When they finish laughing, she says, "Been a long time since I visited the Diamond-T. I guess I could use your company, as long as that's what you'll be – company."

the following day

"Mart!"

His attention is fixed on something way off in the distance.

"Mart!"

"Mm?"

"Look at me."

Reluctantly, he takes his eyes off the scenery. "What?"

"You know, I've always loved the road to Morgen which is just as well because I might as well be on it alone."

"What are you talking about?"

From the bewildered expression in his dark gray eyes, he clearly doesn't know.

"I've asked you at least a dozen questions and you haven't heard one."

"Sorry."

"What were you looking at?" Kelley cranes her neck. "Something interesting…"

"No, it was nothing."

"No, *it* was something…"

"No, nothing."

She sighs. "Well, if I remember rightly we're nearly there. The road dips just up ahead, there's the gully, then the rise…"

His attention begins to wander again. "You're gonna love the view from there…"

Asking why would be a complete waste of time, so she follows his lead and watches the countryside.

Much of the trail to Morgen is river country: her diamond-studded snake never more obvious, with its flowing and intensely blue deeps, babbling silvery washes and smooth pebbled shallows. It meanders through shady roadside forests and across undulating grassland. And then there is the exhilarating panorama of the distant mountains and the wild beauty of the plateau, which cradles the Diamond-T on its northern boundary. She feels no disloyalty admitting that the Diamond-T is more beautiful than her father's ranch, and she feels no shame in declaring that Taylor is unworthy to live there.

She and Mart head down into the wide, deep gully. They discovered many years ago that anyone riding through the gully disappears from the sight of anyone outside it. There's a shallow creek running its length connecting several small waterholes, with a picturesque bridge of split logs for crossing. This is the kind of homeland scene she hungered for in New York, but as they clatter over it, a covey of grass fowl takes flight and shoots upwards, whirring madly. As the birds scatter every which way, Mart whips out his colt. The afternoon sun winks sharp against the metal, blinding her for a second.

"Mart," she cries as she pulls tightly on Dancer's reins.

Mart pulls up also, his eyes following the birds as they career through the gully.

"What happened?" she breathes, her pulse racing.

His eyes come back to hers, his face white. "I'm sorry."

Trembling, still holding tight to Dancer, she stares at him. "What is it, Mart?"

He looks down to replace his colt. "The birds startled me. Come on or we'll never get there." He digs in his spurs and takes off.

Not until they make the rise has her trembling eased and heartbeat returned to normal.

Pulling up at the top, Mr I'm-over-it-why-ain't-you says, "Now, this is what I wanted to show you."

Mart

Through her stunned eyes, Mart appreciates the Diamond-T home ranch all over again for himself.

"These days the Diamond-T is a pretty stylish place."

The small log dwellings once looked like a couple of blots on the grassy plain, dwarfed by mountain range and plateau, but now they are large houses, properly landscaped with extensive and well-planned outer buildings.

"When did this all happen?"

"The past two years."

"Just how prosperous is the Diamond-T now?"

"These past three to four years they really started to turn a substantial profit. Luke came up with a whole bunch of ideas. Ethan liked them, so did Sara, and they haven't looked back. They've overtaken everyone else in the sale yard."

"Where did Taylor come up with these ideas?"

"Why don't you ask him?"

She throws him a glib smile.

They pass through the gate which bears the name Diamond-T and the cattle brand – a half-shaded diamond shape, followed by a tall T. The corrals are lively with cowhands and horses.

"There are two houses," she says. "*That's* Ethan's house?"

"He and Tip renovated too. Built up around the old cabin, same as Luke…"

"Who would have thought Taylor could have done such a good job," is her backhanded compliment.

"You're the only one he needs to convince."

"Why would he even want to try?"

"Maybe he does and maybe he doesn't," he says, because he can't resist.

Luke

Her hair is richly yellow, one even shade right to her scalp. As Tip whirls her about, the sun tracks it and spins it gold, and her hat flies about down her back. She's wearing riding clothes, expensive-looking ones.

From his chair on the front porch, Luke watches them give each other arm holds and secret handshakes, all the while laughing and joking. Makes him wonder what it would actually feel like to be pleased to see her again

"I can't get over how tall you are," she's saying.

Tip takes her hand and spins her genteel-like, dance style. "I should stay a boy just for you?" he replies, grinning from ear to ear. "Don't worry. I remember how good you were at getting into trouble."

"And I remember how you were always trying to talk me out of it."

Glad someone tried.

"So," Sara says from behind him, "this is the new Kelley."

Luke gets to his feet, favoring his shoulder. The doctor insisted he wear a sling for as long as he could stand it. By the end of the day he will have had enough.

"I'd forgotten how well she and Tip used to get along," Sara continues. "Pity Ethan's not here to see this."

"Pity's not the half of it. But for this shoulder I'd be where Ethan is and Ethan would be here."

Sara turns to look at him. "It wasn't worth it?"

"For the Keatons' sake," he mumbles.

"I think she is very pretty and I think Tip thinks so too. And Mart looks very proud."

Often it wasn't worth debating stuff like this with his mother.

One of the ranch hands, Dan, calls out, "Tip, come on..."

Tip shrugs at her. "Sorry."

The half-pint goes quiet; gives a nod and a wave. She and Mart turn their attention. As they move towards the porch, she straightens her clothes. Luke meets them at the archway.

"Well, to what to do we owe this honor," he says.

K thrusts a small package towards him. "Mama sent this."

He takes it. "What is it?"

"Some weird and wonderful concoction to apply twice a day to your wound."

Just the thought of touching his wound makes his stomach weak. "Doc Lewis says I can't get the stitches wet."

"Well, why don't you drink it then."

Mart chuckles. Sara clears her throat.

Luke glares into her bright blue eyes and says, "Tell your mother I said thanks."

"Kelley," his mother says, suddenly eager, "what a lovely surprise!"

"Hello, Mrs Taylor. It's good to see you again."

"And Mart... Good of you to bring Kelley over to see me."

"It's the least I can do."

Luke studies him for a moment. Despite all the talking, laughing and his gallant reply, he looks pale and uneasy. It could be the prospect of sitting in a parlor with a couple of females, drinking tea and talking about the good old days, or maybe – probably – not.

"Please come in," Sara invites. "I'll make tea..."

Luke says quickly, "Mart and I have some things to do in the barn."

Mart's expression renders relief almost at once, but Luke's comment incurs some intense female scrutiny. He looks about, particularly in the direction of the corral. "Tip and Dan could probably use some help."

"It's not very polite for the sick person to wander off and not allow themselves to be visited upon," K says.

Luke resists his routine cynical response because there's an inflection in her voice that interests him. And he notices her observation is now of Mart.

"Maybe not in this case," Luke suggests.

"I think it perfectly fine," she says.

Did they just agree on something?

"Certainly," Sara says. "We got a great deal of catching up to do, and you know how men are about that kind of thing."

Luke steps down off the porch, clamps his good hand on Mart's shoulder and steers him away.

Mart murmurs, "You're my hero."

Luke shakes his head. "No offence, Mart, but the last thing I need to hear about right now is your sister's stay in New York. The doc said I shouldn't strain myself."

Kelley

Kelley wonders what Sara Taylor remembers about her. A nuisance. The bane of her son's existence. A trouble-maker. The warmth of the woman's greeting is promising, however; maybe time has dimmed her memory.

"I'm so glad you came," she says.

Braided hair a-winding her head, a soft shade of brown not unlike her son's. A splash of rose in each cheek...

Sara Taylor is a woman who just by standing there says a great deal about who she is.

In her youth she would have been considered captivating. As Kelley recalls Luke's recent telling of Liberty and Property, she places his mother amid the pioneering days of hardship and struggle and war; she sacrificed her youth to them, and her husband and daughter.

With the blush of youth since faded, clearly wisdom and endurance have given her mature beauty a quality all its own. Agelessness. In her sparkling blue eyes, in that small upright stature, the shrewdness of a survivor lingers with deceptive delicacy. Gowned in her jade-green satin skirt and blouse of pale lavender, a cameo pinned at her throat and a cream lace handkerchief at her wrist, she reminds anyone who cares to look that a more civilized age has arrived.

"Let's go inside, my dear."

And something Kelley had forgotten: she speaks with a charming hint of her Scandinavian heritage.

Through the spacious entrance Mrs Taylor escorts her, highly curious, to a large yet cozy parlor. A generous stone hearth, framed by an intriguingly-carved redwood mantelpiece, draws the eye immediately upon entering. Silver candlesticks guard each end; framed photographs in between. Above hangs a long horizontal mirror of slender proportions, reflecting light and enabling the guest to admire certain details of the room twice over. Large colonial windows with fine lace curtains offer an admirable view of the front yard and allow the light to inundate the whole room. A wide, brightly cushioned window seat offers extra seating to two plump chintz armchairs and a brown leather Chesterfield arranged around the hearth. There are bookcases with all manner of books, cabinets with glass doors displaying knick-knacks and collectibles, on the walls paintings and sketches of various size and composition, a small writing table and chair in a corner near the windows, an unfinished tapestry on its frame, and matching occasional tables with fancy feet beside each armchair.

"Such an interesting room," Kelley remarks, as she pulls off her riding gloves and places them inside her hat. "Mart was telling me as we rode over about all the changes that the Diamond-T has undergone. What a remarkable transformation. It's beautiful."

"Thank you, Kelley. I am very happy with the way everything has turned out. It has taken some time to get it just right, but it has been an enjoyable exercise. Now tell me, how does it feel to be home after such a long time?

"Strange," she answers truthfully.

"Mm. You have come from a large, sophisticated city back to your father's ranch. I can understand that it must feel strange. But look at you, so grown up…"

"I guess it had to happen sometime."

Kelley is invited to the kitchen where Sara Taylor prepares their refreshments.

"Goodness… this kitchen must have everything you could want."

"It has an excellent stove, for sure."

"Good natural light, and this handsome table and comfortable chairs for amiable fellowship."

"It's mostly amiable," Mrs Taylor smiles. "Take a seat."

"Thank you."

"So, how do you like living in New York?"

"I liked living with my aunt and uncle very much. And I found New York very interesting. Challenging. What I learnt has been invaluable though and I'm glad I have had the experience."

"If I remember correctly, you weren't so happy to go."

"No," Kelley says, grinning at Mrs Taylor's arched tone. "I wasn't."

"You talk as though you don't plan to go back. New York must have everything you could desire."

"Everyone thinks that. When my uncle passed away he left Aunt Edith a great deal of money and bequeathed me a generous annual allowance from his estate, so in that sense I want for nothing, but there are things that money can't buy. I believe those things are here. When I'm here I feel this sense of… well, I believe it is freedom."

"Mm. Cities tend to make people more concerned with material needs and clever ways of getting them, rather than acquiring those things of lasting value. The simple life is a gift. It is easier to distinguish between what is good and bad for you when you are living the simple life…"

"Yes, well, I'm afraid my desire to recover my sense of freedom didn't do your son a great deal of good the night before last, and for that I am very sorry. He was protecting me. You must have been very upset when Mart brought him home yesterday."

"At first," she acknowledges. "But Luke and danger do have an attraction for one another. On the other hand, for you the whole thing must have been a terrifying experience. How brave you are."

"No, I think you are overstating my part." Her son was the courageous one, but admitting that out loud was never going to happen, along with the grudging admission that his scratched face and bandaged shoulder were on her account.

"Will you have one of these?" Sara Taylor positions a plate of small cakes in the center of the table. "My Danish grandmother's recipe. And if you like, I can show you the rest of the house when we've finished."

"I should like that very much."

Sara Taylor takes great delight in showing her home and it is everything Kelley's first impressions had anticipated. The richness of Mrs Taylor's European tradition is evident throughout the house.

"You know, Kelley, all my things, my treasures and heirlooms, some over one hundred years old, had no place in a frontier house made of logs; they have been in crates in the cellar for years. Luke's father never even saw some of them." Sara Taylor's face is aglow with the joy of giving her whole life its freedom. "Memories don't belong in boxes."

They continue their bright chatter and exchange many ideas; Kelley shares the many similarities she finds between Sara's taste and Aunt Edith's.

"And yet we live worlds apart. Fancy that. Oh, down the end of the hall is the original house. Luke occupies that. He's fixed it up the way he likes, which means he has kept the original logs. He has a study as well, with a wonderful view of the plateau."

"Mrs Taylor…"

"You must call me Sara, my dear. We're on equal terms now, wouldn't you say? We're both adults."

"Yes. Thank you. I… I was going to ask you about the Alliance. I know nothing about it, but… Are we on the brink of war with Ed Parsons?"

"I hardly think so," she says. "The men take the Alliance very seriously though."

"Are you a member of it, Sara?"

She fiddles with her handkerchief. "I believe I agreed to something…"

"Pa said I was a member by right of blood. I don't under-stand. And I certainly don't believe in war. I've studied history; men make wars and women suffer them. Loss of fathers, husbands, sons… Politicians in cabinet rooms and generals in war rooms… The war between North and South, for example, was fought to free the slaves, but it couldn't change the color of their skin…"

"That's very commendable, Kelley, and I understand exactly what you're saying, having lived through that particular war, but I don't think our Alliance quite fits into the same category."

Don't preach to people. Express your ideas; don't ram them down people's throats.

Yes, Auntie.

Sara smiles and suggests they make some fresh coffee.

When you are too busy preaching, you are not listening.

Sara never does get around to explaining the Alliance, and Kelley can't bring herself to mention it again.

"Come and see the view from Luke's study."

Taylor's study retains the log walls of the original house and features leather furniture. Beyond a desk, which sits with grand efficiency in the middle of the room, is a large window similar to the one in the parlor but without drapes, and beyond that the reason why there are no drapes: Nature in all her splendor; the green broadloom of pastureland, the graceful jade curves of rolling hills, the rocky walls of the mountains, and a cloudless blue sky. Kelley's spirits lift in one glance of it and she heads straight to the window. Why there are no paintings either... who needs them... what else could anyone possibly need...

"We kinda need to be leaving, Kel..."

Mart. She turns around to see him standing with Sara and Taylor at the door. "Oh. Of course."

She passes by Taylor on her way out.

"I get the impression you like the house," he says.

"Yes, well, a house don't maketh the man," she retorts. "Besides, you only *framed* the view."

"Never claimed otherwise."

"Oh, really?"

"Thanks for coming."

"Don't mention it."

On their return, they find their father and ranch foreman Jim Aldridge deep in discussion in the kitchen.

Mart steps forward, anxious. "What's happened?"

"Rustlers," her Pa says tersely, grim-faced, his eyes glinting.

Jim appears similarly affected. "Could be fifty, sixty head from North Ridge."

Mart swears under his breath. "I'll get on to it."

"No, I'm going," says her Pa. "I want my steers back and I'm gonna get them back. Jim, tell Will and Dave to get their gear together. They're coming with me. Mart, you and Jim and the others keep a close eye on things here. I want the herd watched day and night, understood? And you better get word out there's rustlers in the district. Kelley, go tell your mother."

TWO

Let us, then, be up and doing,
With a heart for any fate;
Still achieving, still pursuing,
Learn to labour and to wait.

Henry Wadsworth Longfellow
The Psalm of Life

Ed

...lights his cigar.

Through drifts of fragrant smoke, he watches a horse and rider tear into the yard at breakneck speed. When the dust settles he approaches the edge of the porch.

"Well?" he barks.

The rider, the blond-headed kid with a snout for snooping and a talent for running horses into the ground, removes his hat and thrashes it against his thigh. His horse, slick with sweat, finds the water trough.

"Did Keaton go after the cattle?" Ed urges, impatient with the kid.

"Not Mart. *John*. Took a couple of hands and hit the trail. Mart stayed behind to mind the herd."

"Dang!"

"He's hardly ever at the house but. The women are lonesome all day."

"Mm. What about Taylor? Anyone from the Diamond-T accompany John?"

The kid shakes his head. "Business as usual at the Diamond-T, Mr Parsons. I watched 'em good for half the morning. Ethan, Luke and Tip were in the feed barns checking their winter feed. Luke still favors his arm."

"From the bear incident. How unfortunate. Keaton women are alone, you say?"

"Yes, sir."

All is not lost. For Mart to stay home John must have put his foot down.

"Anything else, boss?"

"Tell McCurdy I want to see him, pronto."

The kid mounts up and takes off again.

Ed puffs thoughtfully on his cigar. Might not be so bad after all. If Taylor can manage to keep his nose out of other people's business, that is. He resumes his seat on the porch, stretching out, contemplating, enjoying what's left of his cigar. He imagines his life when this is all over and he has what he wants; he sees pictures of it in the last wisps of smoke like other people make out shapes in clouds. But the pictures dissolve as another horse and rider materialize in their place. He sits forward and can't believe his eyes. He gets to his feet and crushes the cigar butt under his boot heel. How did *he* get in here? He steps to the edge of his porch just as Taylor reins to a halt. Taylor ain't alone, naturally. The half-breed watches his back. Standard Alliance crap. But Ethan taught both boys to shoot fast and straight; they can fight these two, and the half-breed is a freak of nature when it comes to sniffing out trouble before it comes to that.

"What do you want? And how did you get in here?" Ed greets his visitor.

Taylor relaxes on his saddle horn. "You forgotten I've lived here since I was ten years old, Ed? I know every back way there is, including the ones you don't."

Tip Benchley calls out, "There's four, Luke. Hayloft. Barn. Two at the bunkhouse."

The half-breed's got eagle eyes. Taylor straightens and looks around. Ed knows what he's thinking; they might have to fight. Can't say he ain't tempted.

"You answered *one* of my questions," Ed taunts him and slides his hands in his trouser pockets.

"Hayloft just engaged," the half-breed reports.

Taylor tips his hat back. "King among your faults, Ed, is your predictability." Son-of-a-bitch ain't even rattled. "We saw Blondie snooping around this morning. I know you're not concerned about our ability to feed our herd this winter, so we kinda assumed you had something else in mind. Care to share?"

"You're crazy."

Taylor smirks. "We just came to tell you we don't like being spied on. Blondie looks like the kinda kid who would crack handily under a little interrogation. If we see him or anyone else snooping again, Ed…"

Ed laughs. "You'll what, Taylor?"

"Ask him a few hard questions. Maybe take him to Laramie. The Albany County Sheriff might..."

"Might what? Charge him with trespassing?"

"Sure, Ed. Hey, I'd be happy to have anyone who works for you charged with swatting a fly when it comes right down to it."

Ed glares at him. Taylor returns it brazenly. He straightens his hat, turns his horse, collects Tip Benchley and they canter away.

So what? Blondie's done his job. And Taylor's threats are full of Alliance code horseshit. Pacifists.

There will come a time, Taylor, when you and Mart Keaton will rue the day you thought of it.

Kelley

Her Mama knots her stitching, holds up a pair of her Pa's drawers to the light, scans her fastidious mending with a critical eye and says, "And this week you had planned to catch up with all your old friends, the ones that still live in the district anyway."

Looking at her, no one would suspect she is nervous and fretful and has been that way since the search party left several days ago, except that she has skillfully patched the underwear in double quick time. She wants Pa to find the cattle but not the rustlers. She doesn't sleep well; she eats very little. And when Kelley coaxes her she is accused of being bossy. There is no lack of organization, however. Kelley's immediate chore is ironing linen, something she has seldom engaged in. In fact, ironing is not a strong point as Aunt Edith well knows and soon, Kelley hopes, so will her mother.

"Mama, may I stop now? The iron is heavy, I've scolded myself three times, I feel flushed, my arms ache, and I've got a headache from trying not to scorch anything."

"Yes, dear. Make sure the edges are nice and crisp."

Clearly, her mind is elsewhere.

Later that morning, when they have progressed from ironing and mending to preparing food, a buggy pulls up outside the house. A glance through the curtains reveals a slender, dark-haired young woman stepping down with considerable aplomb. She smoothes her stylish dress and straightens her smart hat, then looks up at the house.

On opening the door Kelley is set upon by a pair of navy-blue eyes alight with friendly if somewhat jittery anticipation. The young woman's dark hair swirls around her head and under her hat like waves of shadow. Her complexion is fair and smooth, the perfect canvas for her long black lashes, smiling mouth and even white teeth. She seems familiar somehow.

"Good morning."

"Good morning. I… I'm very sorry to bother you, but I am looking for the…er… the Diamond-T ranch. I was given some directions in town, but I… I think I'm lost. I…"

"I'm sure we could help," Kelley says and opens the door wide.

"Oh, I couldn't intrude."

"You're not. It's no bother."

The young woman enters hesitantly.

Her Mama offers a greeting.

Their visitor launches into another nervous speech. "My name is Tressa Taylor. I've come from Omaha, that's in Nebraska…well, I'm sure you… well, I'm looking for the Diamond-T ranch. I… I am Luke Taylor's cousin. I don't know him… have never met him… at least I don't think so… Oh… er, you do know him, don't you? I am in the right county?"

"Yes," they drone, stupefied.

"Oh, good. From the looks on your faces, I thought you'd never heard of him."

"Known him since he was a boy," her Mama offers.

"I'm so glad… I mean… because I really need directions."

A poised silence follows.

"You must think us so rude," her Mama says suddenly. "We haven't introduced ourselves. I'm Amy Keaton, and this is my daughter, Kelley."

Kelley offers her hand in her usual forthright fashion, but Tressa Taylor is slow to take it. Her eyelids flicker several times.

"Pleased, I'm sure…"

"Would you like something to drink, tea, coffee… a cold drink, Miss Taylor?"

"Water, thank you."

She offers them one of her charming smiles.

As the water is procured, and sipped, they discuss the idea of Kelley escorting Tressa to Morgen as a neighborly gesture.

"Morgen?" asks Tressa.

"Yes, that's the name of the Taylors' house."

"After my cousin's father?"

"Well, there is a story about it. You could ask your cousin when you finally meet him."

"So, you're from Nebraska?" her Mama continues as Tressa sips her water.

"My father, Richard Taylor, owns Taylor Mining. The head office is in Omaha. We moved there ten years ago after Papa quit our ranch in Montana. My father prefers mining to cattle. There is an ancient dispute between my father and Luke's family that has never been resolved. I... I'm hoping... Mm, well, I have an older brother. Ben. Oh," she blinks, "I'm rambling."

"No, not at all," her Mama fibs. It's informative ramble at least.

Tressa smiles. Mm, this girl has innocent, unaffected charm, but will it be enough?

"What's my cousin like?" she asks.

He looks like you! Yes... about the eyes.

"I would hate to prejudice your first impressions in any way," Kelley replies. "You'll be pleasantly surprised I'm sure, won't she, Mama?"

"Pleasantly," grins her Mama.

As the green miles roll in every direction like a huge welcome mat for an honored guest, one can only hope the welcome stretches to Morgen's front door.

With Kelley at the reins, Tressa seems more relaxed. They chat easily about their families and their homes. Tressa tells of how at the age of sixteen she was sent to a ladies college in Boston and majored in Art, that she loves to draw and paint. Her mother's family live there.

At nineteen she returned to Nebraska accomplished in water-colors, in particular botany and landscapes. She is now twenty-two years of age. She doesn't much like living in Omaha, and she would prefer to live in Boston, or do something useful such as assisting her father in the business, but he won't allow it. The desire to paint and exhibit professionally was forbidden by her father upon her return to Omaha, although she is permitted to paint occasionally for friends and she has an extensive portfolio of work.

In turn, Kelley shares some of her New York adventures and Tressa listens attentively.

As they enter river country, Tressa begins to take more notice of her surroundings. "This is truly beautiful."

"This is the Diamond-T."

"My cousin's property. Oh, I love this river. It's wonderful. So picturesque..." Tressa cranes her neck in all directions. "Does the river cross your ranch too?"

"Further to the north."

"And your properties, they're not fenced?"

"No. As far as I know. That is, they never have been."

"Amazing," she mutters and lifts up her face into the wind.

The road narrows, winding its way through wooded country for a time. Shafts of sunlight illuminate the spaces between the trees. The fragrance of pine and cooled earth fills the head, and the freshness of the forest offers relief from the warmth of the day.

The edge of the forest comes into view and glimpsed beyond are the rolling pastures of the Diamond-T. They leave the woods, where an outcrop of boulders guards the exit, and are drenched in pleasant sunshine. Kelley explains some points of interest in the land that sweeps so boldly before them, and Tressa keenly remarks how inspirational the scenery is for an artist.

However, by the time they pull up outside Morgen she has turned pale again and is wringing the handles of her purse.

"Kelley, I... how do I... will you come in with me?"

Kelley hesitates, but daunted by those pleading eyes, relents. "Just to the door then."

Thankfully, Sara is there with a warm greeting. "Kelley, how relieved I am to know you are..." Her eyes fall upon Tressa. "Who are you?"

"I... I'm... My name is Tressa Taylor."

There. That wasn't so hard, was it?

She adds, "Richard Taylor's daughter."

Now, that's one heck of an admission.

"I'm your niece."

Sara's eyes pop. "Oh my. How... Who... How did you get here?"

"I... I took the stagecoach from Laramie to Bright River. I became lost on my way out here and ended up at the Keatons. Kelley brought me from there."

Sara mutters something to herself, then says, "From Laramie. Do you live there?"

"No, M'am. Omaha."

"I'm sorry, but I can't believe it."

"You won't turn me away, will you?"

"Turn you away… Gracious, child. That's not something we do in these parts. You stay right where you are. Kelley…"

"I really can't stay, Sara. With Pa away I promised Mama I would go straight home."

"But I want to hear how you're coping. Luke was only saying this morning that…"

"We're fine, Sara, truly. You're not to worry." She presses her cheek against Tressa's. "You know where we live and you are always welcome."

Luke

Several days later

A simple cup of coffee is pretty darn civilized this way, sitting around the kitchen table with a pressed white cloth on it, the good china and cake on matching plates. But it depends on who is serving it up that really makes the difference. Can't be just any individual – got to be your long lost cousin, of the kind you didn't expect. A female who tears at your heartstrings as soon as look at you.

What were you thinking – she'd have horns, poison under her fingernails and a barb on the end of her tail? Ethan. Think he read more than he let on.

Luke sighs at his napkin, uses it and stands up.

"Where are you going?" Ethan asks.

"The Keatons."

Ethan and Sara gape at him.

"Wouldn't you like another piece of cake?" Tressa asks him. Upside down caramel coconut somethin' cake…

He already had two pieces. Best he ever ate, next to Sara's chocolate cake.

"Later," he tells her with a smile.

"Why?" Ethan demands to know.

Luke walks to the door to unpeg his hat and coat. They are still gawking at him as he threads one arm in a sleeve. "Because the last time I spoke to Mart was three days ago. Worries me when he thinks he's too busy to come over and talk. And I don't think John's back – we'd have heard."

"You're worried about the women," Ethan concludes.

Luke gives a nod.

"Oh," Sara murmurs.

Tressa sits round-eyed, grave and silent as she stares at him.

Ethan, ever quick on the uptake, says, "You think Kelley's got trouble."

Luke adjusts his coat collar. "If there's trouble to be had, she'll be right there having her share of it."

Sara becomes busy biting a grin off her face.

"Aw, you think too much," Ethan dismisses him and punctures his third piece of cake with his fork. "Besides you don't seem to mind getting into trouble right alongside of her." He picks up his cup next.

"Getting her out of it, Ethan; and more times than I care to remember."

"I remember," he chuckles and then has a slurp.

"Anyway, you're coming with me."

Ethan chokes on his coffee.

Grinning, Luke fixes his hat just the way he likes it. "Come on, Ethan. We haven't got all day." To Tressa he says, "Thanks for the coffee and the upside down cake."

"You're welcome," she says and lowers her eyes. While he's come to realize she's shy by nature, her father has also poisoned her thinking and she's still not sure if Luke's gonna turn into an ogre and demand she be thrown out.

He's gonna have to talk to her about that. Yep, clear the air once and for all.

"Best I ever ate," he says to reassure her.

"Thank you."

And Sara chuckles.

Luke wrenches open the back door and tells Ethan he'll be saddling the horses.

As they mount some minutes later, Ethan says, "You really got a hunch."

"Wish I didn't." They set off at a canter out of the yard.

"Well, I ain't even seen her yet, since she came back. Had to do your trip for you and missed her the other day. I'm looking forward to it."

"Well, good, Ethan," he replies, but his tone incurs a reproachful glare. He puts his head down and says, "Go in by the forest trail?"

"I reckon."

Sure enough, as they emerge from the Keatons' forest and trot into the yard, there's more than enough trouble. There's a bearded stranger on horseback and K on the porch with her chin in the air. The stranger has a Smith & Wesson on his hip, which he seems itching to get his hand to when he sees them dismount. Calmly, they extract their rifles from their saddle holsters; Ethan has a Sharps rifle, a prized souvenir from his war days. It's a single-shot breech-loader, but Ethan only ever needs one shot. Luke's prefers the security of fifteen rounds that his Winchester provides. They approach the scene.

"Can we do something for you, stranger?" Luke calls out as they move to position themselves between K on the porch and the stranger. Ethan looks over his shoulder and winks at her.

"Where's your mama, honey?"

"Hello, Ethan. I'm very glad to see you. Mama went into town."

Luke exchanges glances with him.

"I'm looking for Keaton," the bearded stranger says. "Not you, whoever you are."

"What do you want with him?"

"None of your business."

"He's a friend of ours, maybe we can help…"

But K jumps in, "I told you three times that Mart is not here." As weary as she sounds she expands, as she tends to do, by saying, "I have also warned you that you are on private property. Please leave."

Luke says, "Well, that's pretty plain and simple for a man like you. Have you got a problem with it?"

"Yeah. Where's Keaton?"

"Your problem seems to be your hearing, mister…"

He's aware of movement behind him; he looks over his shoulder. K has gone into the house but quickly reappears on the edge of the porch with a Winchester of her own – well, it's John's. He always leaves a loaded rifle by the front door – every day since they got here fourteen years ago.

"You been holdin' out," the stranger complains. Then, in a smoother voice, he says, "Now, folks, there's no call for all this fuss."

"When you're outnumbered three to one," Luke says.

"Now leave this ranch and don't come back," K shouts.

The stranger looks at the three of them in turn, his horse fidgeting.

Ethan says, "You heard the lady."

Snarling and cussing, the stranger turns his horse recklessly and rides away at a brisk pace. Luke relaxes but K keeps her rifle trained till the stranger disappears from view. Luke watches her, amused.

"What are you staring at?" Ethan rebukes him.

"Okay, okay..." He steps up onto the porch and starts pulling the gun from K's tough little hands. Then he sees that those hands are white and smooth and all her determination and courage has made them strong. He looks down into her face and the bright quivering blue of her frightened eyes.

"With that beard'n all, he reminded me of the grizzly," he says lightly.

She is speechless, however, one of only a few times he can recall.

"You take care of things here; I'm gonna follow him," says Ethan.

"Watch yourself."

"Yeah, yeah..." Ethan steps up to K, grins and pats her cheek. "Good to see you, honey. You went and growed up just fine. Mind what Luke tells you now."

They watch Ethan mount up; he proceeds out of the yard slowly, with his head up.

At last she speaks. "I don't think he should go."

"Ethan knows what he's doing," Luke assures her. Besides, in the War for Southern Independence, Ethan was a not-so-honored guest of Billy Yank, and you don't come home from that with a Sharps rifle because you're short on knowing a thing or two; and the story of how that came about is a perennial favorite on the Diamond-T. Even K knows it. Or she should.

"That stranger looked evil," she says.

There was no disagreeing with that.

Ethan

Ethan pulls up and removes his hat, training his fingers through his hair which is damp with perspiration.

In frustration he surrenders a hard and fast "Dang," and the pinto whinnies and throws her head.

"Easy, girl, easy now," he soothes.

With his hat back on his head he sighs, resigned to the fact that there ain't nothing more he can do for now.

By his reckoning he is two miles west of North Ridge. The long way round by anyone's reckoning. The forest only gets thicker from here on till the top of the Ridge; on the other side is John's highest grazing land. Those rustlers must have used the narrow pass on the east, he thinks, and then realizes he is making a connection between the two separate happenings: the nabbing of John's cattle and the appearance – and disappearance – of that oily-looking, rifle-toting stranger.

He turns east himself, of a mind to link up with the main cattle trail from the Ridge. It's the quickest way back; besides the stranger's had him wandering all over the place and he's sick of it.

Sometime later, he breaks out of the scrub and encounters the worn trail. He encourages the pinto into a steady lope. A few miles down the trail he spots Luke moving along at an easy pace. Ethan gallops up, then drops into pace beside him.

"Well?" Luke asks, pushing his hat back a little.

"Absquatulated."

"Figures."

"Where have you been?"

"Spoke to Mart. He's gone home."

Ethan studies the boy. "What are you thinking?"

"I'm thinking if we can't get any sense out of Mart then we're gonna have to go around him."

"None of this adds up. We got rustlers and a stranger who vanishes."

"Where did you lose him?"

"Two miles west of the Ridge."

Luke turns his eyes on him. "Reckon he knew where Mart was all along."

"Could be."

"So why did he come to the house looking for him?"

Ethan shrugs. "Kelley did all right. How is she?"

"She'll recover. She thanked us. Praised the devotion of Alliance members…"

Ethan chuckles. "That girl…"

"Mm. Wanted to know who the stranger was. Told me Mart was up on North Ridge when I asked her, then couldn't wait to see the back of me."

"That girl…"

"Yeah, she's a peach. Ethan…"

"I'm listening."

"If that stranger knew where Mart was all along and went to the house deliberately, then K was in danger."

"She would have shot him," Ethan says.

He glimpses a small grin on Luke's face. "Probably would have."

"This is a strange kinda Alliance."

Luke points a glance in his direction. "You think this is connected to Ed in some way."

"I'm just saying that alliances are supposed to work together against the common enemy whoever it is, and sometimes young Mart seems to be choosing to be out there on his own and lonesome."

"Yeah," the boy mumbles, "doing God knows what."

"But you're thinking about Ed and all this, ain't you?"

"I can't see how it fits, but you just know with Ed that nothing's too dirty. I still think we should go to Laramie and tell the sheriff."

"And tell him what? That our neighbor is a bully? Ed's too clever to make even that stick."

"Ethan, I've got proof, you know I've got proof."

"You wanna stick your neck out with that crazy file of yours?"

"Ethan…"

"All our necks?"

"Why is it so hard for you and Sara to accept that my file is proof?"

"It's dangerous."

"Why? Because it means taking a risk?"

"A risk we all agreed we wouldn't take."

The boy goes quiet.

Ethan clears his throat. "Knew a sheriff once; had a problem in his town. Said: sometimes, Ethan, sometimes you gotta let things play out, only that way will you know the right time to act. Never forgot that. Never will. And I want you to remember it too."

Kelley

That evening Kelley adds another chapter to her latest letter to Aunt Edith.

"Without Ethan and Taylor I'm not sure what would have happened to me. Ethan did seem pleased to see me, and I was worried and disappointed when he decided to follow the stranger. But no harm came to him and all is well again. When was the last time I told you the legends surrounding Ethan?

"Firstly, you may remember that his wife passed away four years ago from complications after a bout of pneumonia. She was Eka Tomoobi, Comanche meaning Red Sky, so named because she was born at sunset.

"Ethan Benchley met Morgan Taylor working on the same ranch in Texas back in the '40s. Ethan was very young. They became friends and realized they shared the same goal. Their own ranch. They worked hard and made the dream a reality and that of course is how Diamond Bend was born.

"Well, it so happened in those early days that Ethan found himself a young wife, his first; however, barely one year after they had married she tired of ranch life and ran off with a high roller. Ethan tried to find her, but according to the story, she and her gambling man were killed in a shoot-out with a vicious debt collector.

"Morgan married Sara Mortensen in '54 (interesting similarity with their names, don't you think?).

"For Ethan there was no one until he found Red Sky.

"In the period after Ethan and Morgan returned from the War and before they migrated north to Wyoming, Red Sky was a young woman and

82

the daughter of a chief of a Comanche band whom the Texas Rangers confused with another raiding band. The Rangers' attack on her people, therefore, caught them by surprise. They were wiped out. Red Sky was not in the camp at the time of the attack and escaped the slaughter. She spent many days wandering alone, hiding from the rangers, cold, dazed and unwell, her family slaughtered, unable to locate any survivors of her band. Ethan found her while he was checking on stock in a remote corner of the ranch and gave her much needed assistance and protection. He concealed her when rangers came looking for survivors. Red Sky saw that he was a good and brave man, and gave him her trust. By the time it was safe enough to go looking for survivors, Ethan and Red Sky had fallen in love. They found no survivors. They were married. She said Ethan had strayed onto her path just when she thought it had ended, but it was a change of direction, she realized, not an ending. In spite of what happened to her, she was a woman of peace. And it was well known that, although she did not seek revenge, she prayed that honor would one day be restored to her people, the band of Tuhu Piaisa, Chief Black Wolf, of the Nakoni, people who return.

"I remember Red Sky as being both strong and gentle, and she treated me with kindness and humor, even though I probably tried her patience. Their only child, Tip, is just a little younger than I and we always got on well together. His Comanche name is Waha sia Sumu tosa, which means Two-feathers-One-white. That's what the 'T' in Tip stands for. The 'i' stands for Isaiah. The 'p' for peace, not a word or name exactly, but a sign, of peace between two bitter enemies, the Texans and the Comanche. I always thought Tip had a lot to live up to, but he never behaved that way; he is one of the nicest boys you will ever meet, courageous, with a cheeky wit and full of fun. His parents were understandably very protective of him. At times he bore the brunt of terrible discrimination, as did Red Sky and Ethan. Red Sky said it made them strong. Comanche was, and still is I imagine, a major language at the Diamond-T. They all speak it with varying degrees of ability. Taylor speaks it as fluently as Tip. They speak it when they are together, or they used to. I suppose they still do. Tip was immensely fun to be with and together we *excelled at adventures. I'm looking forward to seeing more of Ethan and Tip. This is your chapter for today, Auntie. Meanwhile, I pray constantly that Pa will be home soon."*

Her prayers are answered late in the afternoon the following day; her Pa returns, unhurt and with the missing cattle.

They get word that he's back and wait at the slip rails.

When he finally rides in, weariness on every part of him, he reaches for her Mama and stays quietly in her arms for a very long time.

"It's done," is all he says.

It isn't his nature to be this way. He is a vibrant, boisterous sort of man of Irish descent. He is tall and well built, with a handsome face. His finest feature, his bright sky-blue eyes, are like flames that never dim. But absent from their midst is their normally gregarious hero, not to be seen those storyteller arms waving like bells tolling his triumph, nor the blaze of success in his eyes.

What has happened?

The next day Kelley must seek out Dave for details. He and Will have the day off, and the promise of extra pay in their wages apparently.

"We picked up the trail almost straight away but lost it a couple of times. Those rustlers sure gave us the run around. At last we was a day's ride from Casper and we rode into a canyon. Will spots half a dozen prodigals. And then more – well, they was all there. We trailed them right through that canyon and cross t'other side. We took a day to round 'em all up, scattered all over the place. Lucky they didn't drove 'em across the Platte. We'd have lost 'em for sure. Strangest thing, there was no sign of the rustlers. It don't make one bit of sense to run cattle all that way and leave 'em for somebody else to nab. Anyhow, we drove the poor critters back safe and sound. Mighty strange exercise."

The cattle rustling episode was a mystery.

Despite her Pa's somber mood and his reservations, her Mama convinces him that a family celebration is in order – *humble gratitude* – and she invites the Taylors and the Benchleys to supper for Saturday evening. She says she hasn't seen Sara for some time and that she'd like to see Tressa again. At that point her Pa interrupts to ask who Tressa is and she informs him with much pleasure.

"Luke's cousin!" he exclaims. A spark re-ignites in his Keaton-blue eyes. He hitches up his britches and they giggle helplessly. "By all means, let's see Luke's cousin. I'm down right intrigued."

"She's very refined," her Mama warns him, "so you'll have to be on your best behavior."

"Goes without saying," he says.

"And she's very fetching," Kelley adds.

"I can handle that," he continues, "I'm used to being surrounded by good-looking womenfolk."

After Mart retires for bed that evening, Kelley takes her Pa aside and tells him about the stranger and what Ethan and Taylor did.

"Pa, something else… I didn't tell Mama. She was so worried about you I didn't have the heart."

"Don't say a word to your Mama just yet. You're right. She's had enough worry."

"Are you all right, Pa? Truly all right?"

Very gently, he pats her cheek. He says, "You did well with the stranger. Now go to bed."

Ethan

Saturday evening

As Ethan eases himself into the parlor, two pairs of eyes pin him to the rug. Feeling a little naked, he folds his arms.

"Where have you been?" Luke frowns. "We're gonna be late, and that ain't like you when Amy's cooking…"

"Yes, Ethan, where have you been?" asks Sara.

"I went to see Ed," Ethan declares, unfolding his arms.

Luke gawks at him. "On your own? What happened to our agreement – one of us talks, the other watches his back?"

"Didn't seem necessary. Besides, John's busy celebrating, and you…"

"What about me?"

"You get steamed up and…"

"What does that mean?"

"…and you know you rub Ed the wrong way. Now don't take it personal."

"How do you want me to take it, Ethan?"

Sara, raising her hand, interrupts them. "What did Ed say?"

Ethan clears his throat. "Well, he said he don't know nothing about a stranger in the district, or that John's cattle had even been pinched – that's a lie, everyone in the district knows. Well, a new feller was there. City type. Much too high and mighty for a minder. And Ed don't need a new lawyer that I'm aware of. We wasn't introduced so naturally I was suspicious."

"I guess I'll see what I can find out about this character," Luke says.

Ethan feels the hairs on the back of his neck prickle. The boy is like a bloodhound. "You're gonna have to be careful. You be sure you pull your head out of the dirt before someone goes rubbing your nose in it."

"I'll be careful, Ethan. Although you might like to think about that yourself next time you decide to go barging in on Ed on a Saturday evening."

"Aw, Saturday evenin's fine; he's had a few drinks. His dogs have had a few drinks... Makes it a good night for taking a snoop around."

"Ethan, that is reckless thinking," Sara says. She's wearing her blue dress.

"Now, Sara, there's no call for alarm. I'd rather go Saturday evening than Monday morning. Well, now, don't you look nice."

She rolls her eyes. "You had better clean up..."

But Luke asks, "Did you get a close look at this city dude?"

Sara jumps in before Ethan can answer. "Not now, Luke. We're already late."

The boy heads for the writing table, saying, "You just go see what's keeping Tressa. Ethan and I'll be ten minutes, that's all."

She looks to him for help.

He tries a grin. "It weren't me that taught him to draw, Sara." She did a fine job, too.

"This file will get us all into trouble someday," she mumbles while she leaves.

With Luke sitting at the desk, Ethan wanders across to join him. "What happened to Tressa?"

"She came in late. Very cagey about where she's been."

"Mm... A body could be excused for thinking that girl's afflicted with shyness and a tender heart. But she's a Taylor, it's natural she's cagey about where she's been. Still..."

"Ethan?"

"What?"

The boy has his pencil poised in his left hand ready to sketch.

"Oh. Sure... where was I?"

Funny to see that strong rancher's hand sketching exactly what Ethan tells him; ten minutes later the city dude's face is staring back at him. But who is he?

Kelley

The delectable aroma wafting from her Mama's kitchen and through the rest of the house has her Pa checking the mantle clock every few minutes as if keeping track of the Taylors' lateness will make a difference to it.

Her Mama's succulent pot roast, prepared from a well-hung side of beef, is her Pa's favorite. Being a cook who has a fondness – and a prodigious talent – for using garden-fresh herbs, her Mama creates a flavor that is comparable to none. Perfectly prepared vegetables from the prolific variety of her kitchen garden accompany the meat, with fresh-baked bread for sopping up her mouth-watering gravy.

Ethan likes her chive biscuits, so she baked those as well.

Her green thumb and intuitive knowledge of the use of all things that grow in soil is never more evident than when she produces a meal such as this.

Eventually, their guests arrive to greetings warmed by anticipation and welcome. Kelley looks for Tip to discover he is not among them.

"Gone to Laramie for a spell, honey," Ethan explains. "Back on Monday."

She overlooks this disappointment to focus on Tressa.

Predictably, her Pa likes her from the moment they meet. And Tressa herself appears a little more at ease since that significant day when she arrived. She greets Kelley and her Mama as *her oldest friends in Bright River*.

As they speak together, her Mama returns to her cooking and Taylor steps up in her place. His scratches have faded, restoring his dark blue eyes to their rightful status.

"So, Taylor," she says boldly. "How do you like your brand new cousin?"

He bestows upon Tressa the gentlest of grins, which Tressa answers with a shy but comfortable smile of her own. If they intend to elaborate, it's all too bad.

Her Pa distracts them by putting a drink in everyone's hand; he's bellowing, "Bought this wine for a special occasion. I think now's as good a time as any."

Keaton code for: who knows what tomorrow may bring? So let's eat, drink and be merry, etc, etc.

He makes a toast: *to friends mostly old and some delightfully new.*

They drink her Pa's wine. It's rich and sweet and in those seconds when it swirls around her palate and tingles her tongue Kelley can almost believe that Aunt Edith will appear. Her eyes meet Taylor's as they lower their glasses. The encounter feels odd, different, but before she can analyze it, her Mama is calling for her help.

"Put this on the table." Her Mama transfers two serving bowls of vegetables into her hands.

"I miss Aunt Edith," she blurts out.

Her Mama raises her flushed, excited face. "You're in a house full of people who love you."

"I guess."

"It will pass if you concentrate on the others."

"I just need to talk about her..."

"Supper conversation? Excellent idea. Anything but those dreadful rustlers. Right, let's go..."

Her Pa gathers everyone to the table and says the blessing.

"Lord, it seems like we're celebrating Thanksgiving kinda early, but we just want to say how grateful we are for your blessings upon this family, for our friends gathered here with us, for this food, and for bringing me and the men and the cattle safe home. And I personally thank you, Lord, for the safekeeping of my family while I was gone."

Everyone responds with a hearty 'Amen'.

Kelley's eyes fall upon a respectful if not prayerful Taylor, sitting at the end on other side of the table with Ethan beside him.

They have been the safekeeping of this family. A strange occurrence: her being thankful for Taylor. As the various bowls of vegetables are passed around, the serene face he had shown in prayer gives way to that disarming smile of his. God has made him very pleasing to look at. That odd feeling returns and she is determined to understand it. She is spooning beans onto her plate when it occurs to her that she no longer sees Taylor through a child's eyes but a young woman's. Exactly what that means she's not sure, but it gives her quite a jolt and keeps her quiet for some time.

Her Mama's pot roast surpasses all their expectations, and she is most gratified. Her Pa is very happy. Despite all that her Mama suffers on his account, she likes to please him, which is a contradiction and a mystery, although their attentiveness to each other since her Pa's return she completely understands. Her Mama's nervous pining has disappeared and her Pa's spirits are lifting little by little as she cares for him.

Other impressions are being made, but one in particular. Mart seems happier than she has seen him since her return home. Smiling and talking the way he is tonight, it seems as though nothing has ever been wrong. If it's within his power to be this way, why does he choose to be miserable and uneasy? He and Tressa appear to find one another's company quite agreeable, and together with Taylor, the three at that end of the table appear to be enjoying themselves.

Meanwhile, Ethan helps himself to more pot roast. "You know, Amy, I haven't had pot roast this good since the last time you made it."

"That would be Mart's birthday, June the twenty-second," her Mama says, passing the gravy along.

"Yep, we were due," Ethan declares, hastily cutting his meat.

Sara engages Kelley in an interesting exchange about New York. And Kelley gets her opportunity to talk about Aunt Edith. Her Pa finds the stories about his sister particularly entertaining, while Sara asks questions that invite details about Kelley's life in New York which, not surprisingly, her parents hadn't thought to ask.

After this, her Pa, obviously feeling restored by the warmth of family and friends gathered in celebration, tells Sara that he has the sheriff looking into the whole rustling mystery and hopefully they will soon find some answers.

"Don't count on it," Taylor responds and their heads turn in his direction. "McCurdy couldn't find his way out of a gunny sack at the Fourth of July picnic races."

"Well, I ain't about to sit back and do nothing," her Pa retorts. "Now, I'll get indigestion if we have this talk now. We'll talk about it later."

"You brought it up, John."

"I wasn't talking to you, I was talking to your mama. Your ears are always perked to hear things they weren't meant to."

There's an awkward pause and then Taylor apologizes.

"But, Pa..." Kelley begins. Regrettably, her question regarding the dubious sheriff must be swallowed under the shadow of her Mama's stern eyebrow, which she raises as she sees Kelley draw breath. "Never mind."

Her Mama brings chocolate cake to the table for dessert.

They infrequently had chocolate cake as children; special occasions... when you got your hands on cocoa you tended to make it last. Sara used to bake it from time to time and if she did she would bring some over to share. Kelley recalls the day she and Mart first met Taylor by the River. He asked Mart over for chocolate cake but she wasn't invited. Meeting Mart was clearly special; she loathed Taylor on sight.

As each slice gets passed along, once more she catches Taylor's eye. There's mischief there. He is remembering that first day by the River, she's sure of it.

"This is not my recipe, Amy," Sara says.

"Well, I could never do justice to yours, Sara. It's tradition. No, this I found in that new journal I subscribe to."

"It's very light and soft. The whipped cream in the center is nice..."

"I like the frosting. Chocolate, mm..." says her Pa and he winks at her. Sometimes she thinks he needs grandchildren.

"Did you learn to cook in New York, Kelley?" Sara asks.

"A little." Her abilities, or rather her inadequacies, are not open for discussion in supper conversation. Not after the meal they've just consumed.

"I have read that there are schools that teach only cooking – such as the French mode of cookery schools."

"For the career-minded," Kelley tells her. "And a French chef would be accepted anywhere in the world. The rest can only emulate. To go to a Paris school is the ideal, but to be an apprentice to a French chef is highly sought also."

"Yep, all those fancy restaurants need fancy cooks," Ethan remarks. "As luck would have it, we got ourselves a couple of fancy cooks right here – who needs Frenchmen."

"Here, here," says her Pa.

Her mama giggles, which is kind of sweet.

"How gallant of you, Ethan," Sara says dryly.

Ethan can be quite charming when he chooses.

"There's a school for everything now days," her Mama says.

"What course did you most enjoy at school, Kelley?" Sara asks.

"I think History."

"Mm, and what did you learn from studying history?"

"That as human beings we tend to repeat our mistakes."

In the ensuing silence, Kelley forks cake into her mouth. She is determined to refrain from saying anything her Mama will prevent her from finishing.

"Think you're right about the frosting, Pa."

"Well," her Mama admits, "*that* I did pinch from Sara. Hers can't be bettered. More coffee, anyone?"

Sometime after the conclusion of their meal, when the men go out onto the front porch to talk, and the women begin to clean up, Mart disappears from their company.

Kelley

As Kelley rummages through the linen chest in the parlor for extra dish towels, with her emotions over Mart pendulous between frustration and confusion, she overhears her Pa, Ethan and Taylor talking on the porch, discussing the possibility that the bearded stranger looking for Mart and the cattle rustling are connected. Her Pa calls the recovery of his steers a wild goose chase.

"With me gone and Mart on watch, my Amy and Kelley were all alone... Is that a coincidence?"

"We think maybe he knew where Mart was all along," Ethan says.

"Putting all of us in a precarious position," Taylor concludes.

Indeed.

She returns to the kitchen and begins to wipe dishes. That bearded man might be waiting for her anywhere. He threatened her once without any qualms, what if he tries it again? She'd thwarted him this time, with a rifle no less – and Ethan and Taylor. But what if she meets up with him somewhere and she has no way of protecting herself? What if...

"Kelley, for the last time, wake up! You're going to rub the pattern right off that plate. Whatever's the matter with you?"

Stammering an apology, Kelley stacks the plate she had been wiping and then reaches for another. Her Mama checks her feeble attempts by snatching her towel and declaring that a better use of her time would be to take the leftover chocolate cake to the bunkhouse.

Kelley begins to protest. Her Pa, Ethan and Taylor come in from the porch just as her Mama is securing a cloth-covered dish in her hands. While their serious faces deepen her anxiety, her Mama, who rightly or wrongly still knows nothing of the stranger, will not listen to any excuses.

"John, I wish I knew what's got into this child. She seems to be uneasy about walking across the yard in the dark. Since when? Only a few days ago she was determined to stay out all night in the wilderness all by herself. What do you make of that?"

Her Pa is on the verge of speaking when Taylor steps forward and offers to accompany her. He heads towards the back porch, smiling slightly as he passes. Considering her predicament, she follows him. He holds the backdoor and she steps out into a windy night lit by a star-washed sky and a three-quarter moon. They stroll across the yard, passing the corrals and the barn to the bunkhouse without speaking a word. At the bunkhouse there is only the yellow glow of a lantern to greet them.

"Where did everyone get to?" She places the cake on the large table in the center of the room. Lying on the table, folded to highlight one particular article, is a copy of the local newspaper. The article runs:

PARSONS LOSES CHALLENGE.
DIAMOND-T DENIES ITS WATER.
DESPERATE ED TO FIGHT ON.

"What are you doing?" Taylor asks impatiently from the door.

"There's an article in the paper here about Ed Parsons."

"There's always an article about Ed Parsons. He owns the newspaper."

"Since when?"

"Two years."

"Why would he buy a newspaper?"

"I could be obvious and say he wants to see his name constantly in print, or…"

"Or what?"

He moves inside from the door, draws up a chair, swings it back to front and straddles it. "A man like Ed is interested in only one thing – power."

She returns to the newspaper and runs her eyes over the article; she then unfolds the paper and turns it over to peruse the back. "It's full of local news, information and advertisements, just as I remember it."

"Mm. Makes people think everything's usual."

She looks up. "But it's not?"

"Nothing in there about your father's cattle being nabbed. Would've thought that was local news. And that mean, ugly stranger in these parts, everyone should read about that. Did a reporter come and interview you?"

"No."

He shrugs and looks down at his hands. "Once you start controlling what people read about, well..."

"Well what? Shouldn't people know that the Alliance has denied Ed water?"

His eyes dart up. "Where did that come from?"

"What *is* the Alliance, Taylor?"

"I thought your father would have told you by now."

"Are you stockpiling weapons or something?"

He regards her steadily. "No."

"So you and Pa are not about to wage war?"

"The war is already being fought."

"I don't understand."

"Well, I don't expect you to. You are a person who looks at life in extremes. Go, stop. Fast, slow. Love, hate. There's no middle ground with you."

Rankled that he should know her so well, she replies, "And that's how you contribute to a perfectly reasonable and objective discussion – personal criticism? I want to know about this Alliance and I want to know about Ed. Now unless there is some rule excluding Alliance women from knowing, I expect you to tell me."

His dark-eyed stare is extremely unnerving. "Very well. The Alliance was formed between your family and mine to protect us from Ed Parsons. His questionable tactics to obtain land in this district and to maintain some kind of power base we consider justifiable reasons for a formal association in order to take whatever action necessary, which excludes violence, and blood-shed – except as a last resort, in self-defense."

"That was a mouthful. Sounds like you wrote the book on it."

"The cattle barons have their Association and we have ours."

"So, you're saying whatever measures you take they have to be legal."

"That's about it. We are playing by different rules."

"You're not convinced?"

"United we stand…"

So divided they fall? Is he serious?

"What about the sheriff?"

"The law and order around here is as interested in justice as the local newspaper is in freedom of the press."

"The sheriff is on Ed's side?"

"Like I said, different rules."

"What can you possibly hope to achieve?"

"It's simple, K. We keep our land. Some have already lost theirs."

"Will it come to bloodshed?"

"Hard to say. Ed might start shooting."

"You believe that land is more important than people?"

"When did I say that?"

"What would be the point of the land without people?"

"The Shoshone, the Arapaho and the Cheyenne might take offence to that, K."

"We're not talking about a belief system."

"Sorry to disagree," he says, standing up. "It's all about believing. I believe in liberty and property."

"Well, I believe in peace and fairness."

"Very noble, but are you prepared to fight for them, because if people never fought for what they believed in, you and I would not even be here. You studied history, you ought to know that."

"Why you…" she says through clenched teeth.

"Now, I think we have a bigger problem than Ed at the moment. We need to get Mart to open up. Think maybe you can do it?"

Arrogant, condescending, upstart know-it-all…

"I don't know," she mutters.

"Maybe you could give it a try."

"Don't tell me what to do!"

"Wouldn't dream of it."

He'd been useful up to a point.

"I think I've lost my fear of the dark," she says and strides hastily to the door.

Flippantly, he's saying, "Glad I could help, but you really could show more gratitude."

She stops in the doorway and glares at him. "I don't think so."

An intriguing sparkle surfaces in his eyes.

She studies its warmth and humor for a moment, then, realizing what she is doing, she turns abruptly and continues on her way back to the house.

Luke

Luke sits down again for a spell, wondering if there's a way through that prickly hide of hers. Well, she hates him and it won't be easy...

Suddenly, she reappears in the doorway, a pale imitation of her former self.

"What's the matter?"

She can't speak, so he gets up and pulls her away from the door.

"Well?"

"I was walking... the horses were unsettled... I stopped and I felt... I felt..."

"What?"

"Like someone was out there. I had the feeling they were watching me... Could it be him?"

"I don't know. I'll take a look around. Stay here."

"No. Let's just go back to the house."

He considers the fear in her eyes. "Very well." They step out into the wind and darkness. "Could be the wind spooking the horses." She is walking at his side, just a little behind him. He feels a strong urge to protect her and an even stronger perception that she wants it. "What do you think?"

"He's still out there," she says.

"Great."

"Can't we walk a little faster?"

"And let him know we're scared?"

"You're not scared."

No, but she sure is making him twitchy...

Suddenly, an owl swoops across their path from the trees and into the barn. K lets out a squeal, and he flinches as she grabs his arm. They stand there in shock for a moment until he manages a deep breath and then lets it out. Slowly, her hands release his arm.

"All right?"

"Yes," she replies breathlessly. "It was just an owl."

"Seems that way." He looks down at her trembling by his side.

"...your injured arm. Did I hurt you?"

"No. It's almost healed." Then her large troubled eyes are all he sees, staring up at him in the windy moonlight. She steps back abruptly.

"I'm sorry to be such a baby," she says and walks off quickly to the house.

He's not sure what just happened, but it leaves him with a curiously warm feeling.

THREE

I have you fast in my fortress,
And will not let you depart,
But put you down into the dungeon
In the round-tower of my heart.

Henry Wadsworth Longfellow
The Children's Hour

Kelley

Days slip by and weeks unfold...

Kelley writes to Aunt Edith constantly, letters with small chapters of consecutive days. Her love of writing has been encouraged by Auntie's enthusiastic appreciation of it; she says Kelley should write about everything and by and by she will have accumulated great wisdom. Kelley is not sure about wisdom, but she certainly finds comfort in her ability to readily express her opinions and emotions, which brings her order and clarity of mind. So, in her letters she is able to put words to her disquiet about Mart and the uncertainty she is now experiencing about being home – and how keenly she feels both.

Meanwhile, she and Tressa visit one another frequently; they walk, ride, read together, play chess, bake, help out and discuss life. This authentic and affectionate rapport with Taylor's cousin perplexes her in quieter moments, and in others she is aware that it rescues her from prodigal introspection, particularly when they are at Morgen with Sara.

And in her own home it would be easy to envy Tressa's innate ability to be naturally pleasing, but Kelley can only feel relief that there is someone who is able to make her Mama happy other than her Pa, since she and Mart are failing spectacularly.

And then there are the challenging times she rides with Mart, mostly early in the morning, along their boundary with Parsons.

No truly sane person would relish rising so early, especially as the morning cold is really beginning to bite, but attempting to discover what bothers Mart has become a pressing concern. He protests at first, ordering her back to the house, only resigning to his fate when she persistently meets him at the stables every morning with no intention of letting him ride alone.

"Why do you always ride fences, Mart? We never used to."

"Things have changed," he says.

"Has it got something to do with that stranger who came looking for you?"

He doesn't answer.

She doubted the direct approach would produce the desired effect; he is a master at ducking and weaving and basically clamming up. So she pretends to want to do her part when it comes to boundary riding, adding that it gives her an excuse to spend time with him. But if gaining his acceptance was difficult, enticing him to converse about anything is impossible; he is so quiet, so determined to be alone with his thoughts.

As for the dark and slippery stranger, he has vanished, although her anxiety still lingers. Her Pa, though, has changed his routine and is frequently about. And while Kelley can't be sure if her Mama has since acquired knowledge of the bearded gunman, she doesn't seem to question her Pa's increased presence about the ranch house. Similarly, when Kelley visits the Diamond-T, Ethan or Taylor seems to be there. If they go into town, Tip accompanies them; these trips are immensely enjoyable in his lively company and they get on as well as they ever did. Nevertheless, the womenfolk are under the watchful eye of the Alliance. She writes Aunt Edith that:

...apart from some happy consolations I do not care to live this way, and I am very annoyed about needing the men's protection...

Auntie writes in reply:

You must be patient, for you are so used to your independent life here with me in New York that you must become re-accustomed to living back home with its frontier ways and peculiar dangers. Surely it is worth it, indeed a necessary part, in order to fulfill your quest. However, I am deeply concerned for Mart, and you must keep me informed. Goodness such as Mart's is not often corrupted but it can be manipulated. As for that stranger, I am not too worried on your account. If anyone thrives on danger, darling, it is you.

This is news to Kelley and she is not sure how to take it.

One morning, she asks Mart if he still keeps the letter she wrote him before she came home. He takes it out of his bureau, hesitates before he gives it to her and orders her to put it back when she has finished with it.

With her confidence waning by the minute, she feels the need to revisit her feelings: what had been her motivation for returning? She reads of her longing for freedom, to breathe it into her soul and exult in it. And then there is something about truth and hearts and righteousness…

Someone else must have written this; the voice in her dreams that called her home is silent. Could she have been so naïve as to believe that home would remain the same as the day she left it, that she would *feel* the same as the child who left? She folds Mart's letter and places it back in his drawer.

She saddles Dancer and heads west, away from the River and her father's pastures, towards the Shoshone forest (which is the name the locals christened it and not its official name), a magnificent old forest of giants: ponderosa pine, lodgepoles, box elder, cottonwood, spruce and quaking aspens. In mid-fall, as it is now, its golden spectrum is breathtaking, and it is alive with game and wild creatures. A tentacle of the River irrigates it with cool, clear water. The Shoshone once hunted that game and fished the stream; the forest is sacred to them. Now the Shoshone are far away on their reservation, away from their treasured forest. She imagines they have never forgotten it, she imagines that memory is the magic of this place, that when the Shoshone tell their stories far away, the memories come to life here.

The forest is located on the border between her parents' ranch and the Stewarts', who, in stark contrast to Ed Parsons, are good neighbors and pleasant people who tend to keep to themselves. The stream marks the boundary and both parties keep this without any fuss. They both fish and hunt, although hunting is kept strictly to their respective sides.

On the Keaton side, the forest has a well-worn trail that winds gracefully through the huge trees. Even on the hottest summer day the temperature is always cool, the heat and light repelled by the forest's dense ceiling of branches and foliage.

They stop to drink and rest at the stream; while Dancer slurps to her heart's content, Kelley gazes into the water wishing an answer to Mart were forthcoming. She wonders if the urgency she had felt to return home was born of some instinct for knowing Mart was in trouble, and had nothing to do with all that other sanctimonious stuff. And as for the courage she is supposed to be testing, she needs Taylor to protect her from an owl!

Back in the saddle.

Dancer ambles along the forest trail while Kelley's thoughts take less simple trails in her head. *What would you say, Auntie, if I told you I am not sure any longer about my quest? What would you think of me? What would the others think of me? Will I ever truly know what I want? – and where I am meant to be?* The trail through the Shoshone forest winds smoothly on, while the gentle pulse of Dancer's hooves on the firmly packed earth beats a counterpoint for the occasional call and answer of birds. The trees in all their grandeur weave Shoshone memory magic. On the morning breeze they whisper to each other of times long ago…

Gunfire suddenly explodes. Two sharp cracks that lock the breath in her lungs and drill shock through her body. Dancer pitches steeply. Kelley loses her balance. She can't hold on. With a cry she crashes to the ground. Fierce stabbing pain follows. She hears Dancer bolt away into the forest.

"Dancer… Dancer, come back…"

But the forest has closed in. The pain intensifies and she dissolves into the trees.

Kelley

"Kelley, you're safe; for God's sake, open your eyes..."

She can't focus.

Lavender... she smells lavender.

Where is she?

Her head aches.

Soreness pulses down one side of her body.

Confusion, in her head, all over her... why she is thinking about the Shoshone forest?

"Kelley?"

A face slowly comes into focus and upon it a measureless frown.

Mart. With a look in his eyes that she finds quite alarming.

"Mart, what's wrong?" she says.

"What's wrong?" he gasps. "Luke brought you home with concussion and you ask me what's wrong."

Taylor brought her home?

"The doctor says you're not allowed out of bed until he says so and you ask me what's wrong?"

"I'm home? Where was I before?"

"Luke found you in the Shoshone forest."

"Oh. I... Dancer..." A memory stirs... "I... I can't... I..."

"You came off Dancer."

"I got dusted?"

He sighs and pushes his hand through his thick blond hair. "Yes, little sister, you did. I'll go tell Mama you're awake."

Mart disappears from her line of vision and a long confusing silence settles in her room.

For a week she's as sick as a horse.

Her Mama administers a variety of restorative concoctions.

Willow bark for the pain.

Peppermint oil and comfrey poultices for her bruises.

Lavender compresses and thyme to relieve her headaches.

Sage for her memory.

Elderflower tea to calm her... The doctor also has some say in her treatment. Gradually, however, her recollection of the main events and her strength returns. And after eight days of endless treatment she threatens to mutiny if she is not allowed to lie on the sofa in the parlor tomorrow for at least some part of the day.

Her Mama capitulates.

That night she tells her Pa everything she can remember about the incident.

"Are you sure it was gunfire?"

"I believe so. On our side of the creek."

"And you saw no one?"

"No one before it happened," she assures him. "I don't remember anything after the noise of the shot. What are you thinking, Pa?"

"Don't know what to make of it yet. What I insist on, and I mean it, so you pay attention..."

"Yes, Pa."

"You have to take more care. I'm serious. Real serious."

"Yes, Pa."

The next day she is allowed to rest on the sofa in the parlor and have one visitor for a short time. This is Tressa, who has been waiting for word about visiting hours, and she showers Kelley with a lively narration of the latest happenings at Morgen, with get well messages and flowers from Ethan and Tip, and a package of Sara's special shortbread.

The following day Kelley decides to exert some of her so-called independence and take herself down to lunch. Apart from anything else, the aroma is terribly inviting. She manages the stairs by supporting herself with the banister. On the bottom landing she looks up from her efforts to see Taylor sitting at the table, his interest firmly anchored in a newspaper. The landing tends to creak and Taylor glances up.

"Need any help?"

"No. I can manage." She begins her assault on the final three steps. "Why are you here?"

"Amy invited us. She said you needed company."

"Us?"

"Tressa and my mother are outside inspecting some unusual herb Amy's got growing in her greenhouse. She claims it has rare medicinal properties."

"Mm. I'm probably living proof that it works."

He relinquishes the newspaper, stands up and pulls out a chair as she approaches.

"Is that Ed's newspaper?"

He resumes his seat. "No. It's the Bugle; from Cheyenne…"

"Yes, I remember." A little weary, she sits down on the chair he pulled. "What's news?"

"The latest gold shipment heist; the railroad detective could be in on it so they called in Pinkerton's. The coal miners are pushing for better pay and conditions. And Statehood's back on the agenda. So, how are you?"

"I'm recovering. Mart told me you found me and brought me home. How?"

"How do you think? – you know that horse of yours is part bloodhound. She came and got me."

She stares at him and waits for what is surely coming.

"It's not the first time," he continues with a smirk.

Brash upstart. "I suppose I should thank you."

"Only if it don't cause you any more pain, K. Wouldn't want you to suffer a relapse."

"Why do you have to be so sarcastic? Weren't you just being a diligent Alliance member anyway? Duty calls and all that."

"If that's how you see it, K, then I guess that's how it is."

"Don't take that tone with me – you always do it."

"Can't you say thank you and mean it?"

"Why is my sincerity important to you?"

"It ain't."

"Then just…"

His eyes flash. "Just what?"

She draws breath. "Stop it."

Silence. His very blue eyes glare at her.

She tenses for what surely will be a sharp retort.

"You're right. I don't need your gratitude." Then he jerks his newspaper up to his face and disappears behind it. She stares blankly at the newsprint, her hands trembling. Abruptly, the newspaper comes down and those clever eyes catch her out.

"I don't want to fight with you," he says.

She struggles for words. "I... I..." Precisely in the middle of this stingingly witty retort the others return and she must greet them. Lunch proceeds, typically exceeding the expectations of its aromas.

After half an hour Taylor excuses himself and says he has to get back to work.

"I hope you remembered to thank him, Kelley," her Mama says when he has gone.

"Yes." But her gratitude had lacked sincerity. Then, feeling decidedly headachy, she also excuses herself and returns to her room.

Another long week passes. The doctor declares his approval of her improvement and she is allowed to go about her business as usual except for riding.

"Another fall wouldn't be helpful," Doc Lewis says, frowning at her from over his big droopy moustache.

"Couldn't agree more," her Pa booms. "Don't worry, Doc, she'll be taking the buggy wherever she goes from now on."

Great news indeed, she remarks, and Doc Lewis barks a laugh from *beneath* his big droopy moustache.

As he is leaving she overhears the Doc tell her Mama, "See if you can't arrange for something to pick up her spirits. Head injuries do strange things to even the most cheerful mind."

Tressa visits during the week. She looks a little down herself.

"I have received a telegram from my mother. My uncle is not well. My mother's brother. He lives in Boston. My mother is talking about going to see him. If his condition becomes worse I'm afraid she'll go to Boston and I'll have to go home."

A bleak prospect. Surely Doc Lewis didn't have this in mind.

Two days later, word comes from Morgen that Tressa's uncle in Boston has passed away, and a telegram from her mother insists she is to return home at once. It is agreed that Kelley should visit Tressa first thing in the morning.

Kelley

The following morning her Mama takes great pains to ensure that Kelley has everything she needs before she sets foot out the door: coat, scarf, gloves, and rug for her knees. Apparently, the buggy is ready and waiting by the slip rail. Her Pa has insisted that he take her to Morgen himself – just more of the same; constant vigilance for protection of womenfolk. Independence for Alliance members equates to manhood; at least in New York a woman of independent means can exist within the social and moral code and take care of herself – it is frowned upon but achievable. But here at home, short of packing a gun, she needs a man.

Meanwhile, why they besiege themselves this way and not apply to the county sheriff is a mystery... so entrenched are they in their little war.

Outside the cold stings her cheeks. She walks to the top of the porch steps and looks up from the business of pulling on her gloves. On the other side of the buggy a very heated debate is in progress between her Pa, Taylor and a man she has never seen before. They don't notice her approach, so she stands quietly beside the buggy and listens.

"Are you telling me, McCurdy, that you are just going to stand by and let Ed's boys shoot at John's outriders and do nothing?" Taylor rasps.

McCurdy?

So this is the dubious sheriff. Fairly tall, thickset, dark-eyed, hair slicked back off a low forehead, immaculate charcoal-colored suit, knee-length coat to match, hat of similar quality resting in leather-gloved hands. He is obviously a man of means; surely not a town sheriff's means, and a small town at that? Bright River is hardly the place to impress. Maybe he thinks he's got folks believing he is on the up and up...

"I'm telling you, Taylor," McCurdy retorts, "that if you retaliate before I have investigated why the incident happened in the first place, I'll put you in the lock up."

"Investigate? You get over to Ed's, McCurdy, and you tell the bastard that if he tries it again you'll put *him* in the lock up. And while you're at it, you tell him for me that if he does try it again, I won't be playing the stoic."

"Just what kind of fool threat is that? You want to start a range war, Taylor. Is that it?"

"This ain't the range, McCurdy, this is John's land and my land. Bought and paid for. This ain't about who owns what and who's entitled. We got the papers to prove these lands have been ours for a very long time. You remind Ed of that while you're investigating."

She's never seen Taylor quite this impassioned before. Didn't know he was capable of it. His body is rigid with indignation.

"This Alliance horseshit has gone on long enough," McCurdy mutters.

"You make me sick. I think you oughta leave."

Her Pa removes his hat and busily sets about reshaping it. "I called you out here, McCurdy, for some reasonable response. I can see you ain't about to give it."

"I said I'd investigate. What more do you want, Keaton?"

"We have families to consider, Sheriff. We want an assurance that it won't happen again."

"How do I know you didn't start it?" McCurdy asks. "All I get from you people is complaints. You got rustlers, Keaton, and strangers with guns looking for your son… so maybe you should be talking to Mart…"

Kelley catches her breath. What follows is a terrible silence. No one speaks; instead hot breath pours out into the cold morning as furious white clouds.

"Like I said," Taylor finally grinds out, "you'd better leave. *Sheriff.*"

McCurdy slides his quality hat over his carefully oiled hair. She observes him stride to his horse, a finely groomed and saddled black stallion which must account for the entire year's wages of a Bright River sheriff.

He mounts it easily and rides away without a backward glance.

A rather colorful cuss draws her attention back to the slip rail.

"Calm down," says her Pa, jamming his hat back on his head.

Taylor looks like he won't even get close to calm. He begins to pace.

"Let's face reality. Where would we get enough hired guns?" her Pa asks him.

"We only need one. The right one. I'll find him. Let's face it, the territory's crawling with them. How hard can it be?"

"No. We agreed to do this right."

"Fine. Let's go get Sheriff Ransford in Laramie."

"You want to keep the Diamond-T, don't you? And you want to live there, not in the penitentiary or six feet underground in a pine box? Well?"

"Yes, but…"

"Let the sheriff be till we know for sure that such a course of action won't make things worse."

"Things are getting out of hand, John."

"So I want you to calm down and we'll see what happens when McCurdy's talked to Ed."

"John, I keep telling you that Ed's lining McCurdy's pocket."

"But you've got no proof of that."

"He lives like a king, for God's sake!"

"That ain't proof."

"Looks suspiciously like proof to me. But fine – you want more proof, I'll get you more proof."

"I want you to go home and calm down, start thinking with that smart brain of yours. You got that?" Her Pa grabs Taylor around the side of his neck with one hand and gets his attention. They stare at one another. "Now you do as I say," says her Pa in a choked voice, "while I go find Mart."

Kelley clears her throat, loudly. They don't hear her.

She shifts her feet…"Pa?"

Her Pa turns her way, nonplussed.

"Would you rather I not go see Tressa?"

She has claimed Taylor's attention also; the heat still burns in his eyes.

They straighten, glance at one another awkwardly and generally try to compose themselves.

"Luke's going home; he'll take you," her Pa mutters. "I'll come for you later." With that he walks off towards the corrals, the crunch of his boots echoing across the yard.

Taylor lets out a sigh and adjusts his hat. "Get in, K."

"You don't have to do this," she says.

"No. You were going to see Tressa and she needs a friend right now."

He could do that: put aside his own problems to concern himself with someone else's? Somewhat mystified, she watches as he tethers his horse to the buggy.

"Get in the buggy, K," he repeats patiently, as though he understands her hesitation. They end up doing it at the same time. He picks up the reins and urges the patient mare forward. They travel for miles in absolute silence and his eyes stay fixed on the road.

Luke

When they emerge from the dense mist of the forest, and he breathes once again the clear air of the Diamond-T, Luke finally feels calm enough to talk to his passenger. She hasn't said one word; he didn't know she could actually hold her tongue for that long.

"About Tressa…"

"Yes," she says quickly.

"She seems to be taking her uncle's death pretty hard, but she's reluctant to go home. And it's not like she can't come back…"

"Perhaps the situation at home is not what it seems. I mean, has she ever told you why she came in the first place?"

"She said she never understood what kept our families apart. Now that is she of age she decided to take a stand and told her father that any quarrel he had with his brother ages ago shouldn't influence the relations between cousins. It's been a personal decision; her brother hasn't come to the same conclusion."

"Yes, she told me about Ben, and exactly what you just said. Perhaps her father resents her for what she has done and she is scared to go back."

"I'm sure that's what it is," he says. "That he allowed her to come in the first place says a lot about her determination."

"Allowed her?"

"Don't imagine for a minute that he helped her to the station with her luggage, kissed her on the cheek and said go enjoy yourself. Who knows under what ultimatum she left. Campfire stories aside, my uncle hates us. Returning will probably involve a great deal of humiliation on her part."

Silence.

"Well, anyway, all that I get, but I think there's something else going on; she's not saying what and it's driving me and Sara crazy." He glances at her profile. "Maybe you can get it out of her."

Again, she doesn't reply. She is looking at something with a deep frown on her face. He follows her line of vision to a stationary rider about a half a mile away on a high knoll that overlooks the road. He pulls up at once and tosses the reins in her lap.

"What are you doing?" she asks.

"I'm gonna see who that is." He jumps down from the buggy.

"You're leaving me... Luke, don't leave me..."

As quick as he decided to investigate the rider on the high knoll he decides not to, and instead heed the swift return of that curious warm feeling, to focus on something else that he can't believe just happened. He turns and studies her tense face as she keeps her eyes on the rider. Not only is she pretty, but she has eyes the color of a summer sky... and the cold has made her cheeks rosy red and her lips pale... It ain't a good idea to get romantic about her is what he keeps on telling himself; she's trouble and heartbreak all rolled into one. Still, thinking about it is kinda interesting.

"You called me Luke."

"Don't be ridiculous."

Suddenly, her large, scared eyes come to his face and he has to swallow. Maybe they are deep river eyes. Maybe those pale, cold lips need warming up. Maybe she needs some reassurance that the rider on the high knoll's never gonna get her while he's around to protect her. Maybe she thinks he is good for something after all.

She looks away; picks up the reins. "Are you getting in?"

He looks at his feet to hide the grin he can't keep off his face.

"Well?" she demands.

He climbs back into the buggy and lets her drive it. He knows she won't talk to him, so until the road changes direction he keeps his gaze fixed on the spot the rider on the high knoll has since vacated. "Looks like our dark stranger has returned."

"How do you know it's him?"

"I know it as well as you."

Her silence confirms it.

Kelley

"My mother has gone to Boston and I'm supposed to return home and run the house in her place. For how long, I don't know, but it will be for some time. My father and Ben are expecting me." Tressa dabs at her wet cheek with the back of her hand.

"I admit I don't want you to go."

"Thank you, Kelley. At last someone who isn't trying to give me advice. My mother hasn't been back to Boston for years, and her family situation is complicated. I might not return here for a very long time."

"Then tell them you can't leave, that you have a very good reason for staying, that you will be home when you can and they can hire someone to housekeep, that's what it sounds like they need anyway."

Tressa gives a tearful laugh. "I wish I could take you back with me. You are precisely what they need."

"No. I don't keep house very well at all. Ask my mother."

"Don't joke," she says.

"You could try keeping a sense of humor. It might work."

Tressa shakes her head.

"Tress, how do you feel about your family, truly?"

"Mama is loving and sweet, and Ben is strong and sure; I love them both, very much; but a person doesn't love my father; you fear him, respect him, and don't dare cross him."

"You crossed him once to come here, didn't you?"

"I… Yes."

"Then do it again."

"No, they are my family after all. Families rally in a time of need. And my mother asks this of me. How can I let her down?"

"Then what is the problem with going back, Tress? – since you know what is the right thing to do."

She shakes her head. "I really can't say. Kelley, I need your confidence. And I wish I had your strength – you stand up to people when you believe in something – and you see your mistakes in a positive way. I've been taught differently. So much is at stake whatever I do. I'm not prepared to make these decisions."

"You're an intelligent, level-headed woman; you are perfectly capable."

"No. I'm not." She turns back to the stove.

Kelley understands what Taylor had tried to explain earlier. There is something else.

"The kettle's boiled," she says. "I'll make the tea."

A rustle of skirts and Sara walks in. "No, let me do that."

The tea is made in silence.

Sara picks up the tray. "Let's take this in the parlor by the fire."

Taylor is stoking it as they enter, a frown on his face and a shadow of preoccupation in his eyes.

He says, "I'll take you home myself, Tress."

At this extraordinary piece of gallantry Kelley catches her breath.

Tressa's eyes shoot up. "No! You can't leave here." She detects their surprise at her outburst and repeats softly, "You can't leave. I won't let you leave. I'll go myself. Tomorrow..."

"I didn't say that to push you," Taylor says. "It's the only thing I can think of to help you."

"I know. And considering the implications it is indeed the most generous offer of support I have ever known in my whole life. But you are right. I should go. This indecision is ridiculous. After all, the only difference between wisdom and folly is the outcome and whatever happens, happens."

"Tress, what are you saying? It is wise to stay and folly to leave... what...?"

"What price loyalty?" she murmurs.

"A high price, clearly," Kelley replies.

"Yes," Tressa says with a sad, resigned smile. "One can only hope that it is worth the price. Thank you for coming by, Kelley. I should pack now. Will you excuse me?"

"Of course. When will you leave?"

"Tomorrow."

"I'll come see you off."

She nods and raises yet another melancholy smile.

"I'll help you pack," Sara says.

When they're gone, when Kelley can hear them on the stairs, she exclaims, "This is terrible! I don't know how to help her, short of going with her. She jokingly suggested it."

"Did she?" Taylor queries softly.

"Perhaps she really meant it. I have no idea what good I would be."

"She's gentle, and unsure, and she's looking for strength. To stand up to her father and come here must have taken a great deal of courage. And now, to go back, she needs more."

"Well, I agree, but I still don't know what that has to do with me," she says, warming her hands before the fire.

"She's sees you as brave and strong."

"Huh! We both know that's not true."

After a moment's silence, he says, "I went looking for the rider."

"Thought you might."

"He's vanished." He comes and stands beside her at the hearth. "There's no shame in wanting protection when it's genuinely needed."

"I never needed protection in New York," is what comes pouring out of her.

"No bears, or strangers with rifles, or rocks to fall on and bump your head, or mysterious riders watching you as you innocently go about your business."

"No. There are none of those."

"So," he says in a brighter tone, "you'll be going back to New York then."

"I don't know."

Then, "Why did you come back, K?"

She walks away from the hearth. "Well, I had... I had this dream. The same one over and over. It was like someone calling to me, come home, this is where you belong. Night after night, the same dream. I could smell the grass and the forest, and the river country, feel the sun on my face, and sense the incredible freedom you get when you're alone on the range with blue sky all around you. The quiet and the serenity, the majesty... All the things I loved when I was a child. I missed them and I came back for them. But nothing's the same as it used to be…"

With this off her chest, she realizes with whom she shares her confidence. She can't decide what is worse: divulging her secrets to Taylor, or realizing that she wants to. His willingness to protect her has bestowed a sense of confidence in him that she finds at once startling and satisfying. She sits down on the sofa, not caring if they don't speak another word. She needs to be here in this house, with the sense of security that he gives her.

"Well, it happens," he says. "Even happened to me."

"How?"

"I went to San Francisco."

"I didn't know that. Oh, that's what Mart was referring to before… er, before the bear…"

He gives a brief smile. "Went not long after you went East. Stayed away for about a year and a half. Ethan managed here; gave Tip a chance to come on. Though Sara wasn't impressed. But there comes a time when you gotta find out what's going on in the world apart from raising cattle and selling them at the best price. I needed to find out if living here was really for me, or if there was something else. I got the 'your father would be unimpressed because he intended for you carry on' lecture. Ethan convinced her to let me go, and I pointed out that my father made his own choices, why couldn't I? She couldn't argue with that. I pestered Mart for weeks to come with me, but you know Mart, he's always been happy where he is, so we shook hands and off I went."

"What did you do?"

"A lot of things. I worked my way west across the country. Wrangling, chopping wood, even a stint tending bar, anything that came my way. Eventually I got to San Francisco and saw a whole new world. I put myself through a college course. I worked some and studied some and came back with a bunch of new ideas. I kinda fell in love with San Francisco. Discovered the ocean. Never saw it before in my whole life and I'll never forget what it felt like to see it for the first time. I guess I felt like I was going to die just looking at it. It goes on forever. The color. The way it moves. It makes you want to jump right in. And it's constant. I guess it storms and gets wild, but it never dries up or floods; the tide comes and goes…"

She is astonished; touched that he can speak from his heart this way.

"King tides," she murmurs.

"Sorry?"

"They move in and flood coastal areas."

"Oh, I see. And then there was *all streams flow into the sea yet the sea is never full...*"

"Poetry?"

"Not exactly. You'll find it somewhere in the Bible, according to Sara. She liked to quote it every day after I got back. She said it was her way of reminding me that I couldn't escape my destiny. Annoying really..."

"It would be. Why did you come back?"

"Red Sky wrote and asked me to come home."

"You adored her, didn't you?"

"Pretty much," he says with a passing smile. "Her health was failing. I think she knew she was dying and she was worried about Ethan and Tip. She said if I searched my heart I'd know that I wasn't on the right path. That wandering wasn't good for me. The path of one's destiny, she said, begins in the home country, in the heartland. But I think you understand that. You answered the voice in your dreams and came back."

In the ensuing silence, she begins to feel awkward about this creeping intimacy between them.

"When I got home Red Sky fessed up that she had a dream about me. I was a Comanche 'crazy' warrior in battle, rolling out my sash and fixing it to the ground with my lance, making a stand, with bow and rattle, singing songs until victory or death."

"Only a member friend of your shield group allowed to free you," she murmurs, trying to imagine him as a crazy warrior, particularly the singing part, and not having any success.

"You remember."

"Yes."

"u que ka nada thuu moi tui tan."

Meaning, *let us sit down and tell stories.*

She can't help smiling just a little. "Yes. I remember lots of stories. Red Sky's stories..."

"This is our land. Our precious land."

"Mm. What were you fighting for in Red Sky's vision?"

"She didn't say. It hasn't happened yet," he says in a self-mocking fashion, "so I guess the day is still to come."

"Is that how you see yourself – the crazy warrior?"

"No," he says, his gaze fixed. "But when Red Sky asked me to do something I listened. So I came home."

"She certainly had a way about her." She stands up and smoothes her dress. "I should be going home. I don't know what's happened to Pa, but since he was going to look for Mart, he might have forgotten about me."

"I'll take you."

Three words she simultaneously dreaded yet wanted to come from his mouth. "You should stay here with Tress..."

They stare at one another for a somewhat long, intriguing time. Until he says, "You're right. I'll get Tip."

"Yes..."

He grins with such gentle humor that her heart leaps. And then he steps up to her, puts his hand under her chin and looks into her eyes.

"What are you doing, Taylor?"

"I've got no idea."

"Well, stop then."

"Not in a million years."

"That's..."

His lips touch hers with feather softness.

"...ridiculous."

And again.

"We don't even like each other."

"I think we do." The softness goes from his lips and he kisses her firmly, properly. Unexpected feelings stir her to the unthinkable... kiss him back. Then suddenly it is over and he is stepping back in a hurry; she can only stare at him in complete astonishment.

"Sorry," he murmurs.

"You certainly should be."

"That was strange. I mean..."

"I know what you mean."

"I'll find Tip."

"Thank you."

The following morning her Pa pulls the buggy to a halt one block down from where the stage, six horses, Harry Hobbs and Jericho are ready and waiting to depart for Laramie. Kelley spots Tressa standing with Taylor; his hands lightly rest on her shoulders while he speaks to her, their faces earnestly engaged.

"Are you coming, Kelley?" her Mama calls as she and her Pa wait on the sidewalk. "Are you feeling all right? You seem preoccupied."

"I'm just concerned about Tress."

She receives a sympathetic smile. Her Mama has not an inkling of a whole new problem Kelley has concerning Taylor, which is the opposite of the one she used to have. Even her fourteen-year-long predilection for calling him Taylor is wearing thin.

"Tressa will be fine. Now let's just say goodbye."

Tressa's departure was never going to be as simple as 'goodbye'.

Just because a person tortured by dilemma finally decides what action to take doesn't mean that person will be fine.

Wisdom or folly?

Consequences are a fact of life; doesn't her Mama know that?

Kelley

As Tressa's stage rumbles out of town, the last shred of Kelley's belief in her decision to leave Aunt Edith and return home disintegrates into something very like the cold dust spun out from beneath the wheels of the stagecoach.

"Why didn't Mart come?"

Her Mama gives her a guarded look. "Because he wasn't to be found."

The frustration and disillusionment, which have been building for weeks, seize the upper hand.

"He's never to be found. He's lost, Mama, when are you and Pa going to do something about it?"

"You're making a big fuss over nothing. Your brother is a grown man…"

"What happened to if we believe one of us might be in trouble we don't just stand by and ignore it?"

Her Pa strolls up, having just checked for mail. "Daughter, your voice is raised and people are staring."

"Aunt Edith would never let this go on."

Her Mama bristles. "What has this got to do with Tressa leaving?"

"I don't know," she says and swallows a painful lump in her throat. "But it must be something. Something around here has got to make sense eventually."

"Will you calm yourself…"

"I don't want to be calm."

She takes off down the street, striding briskly, her goal the cemetery behind the church, with its fresh and sweeping vista to the valley beyond (voted by a panel of churchmen as the best view from a cemetery in the county). People hastily sidestep as she advances; she marches the length of two blocks before a figure in black remains fixed and she must stop. When she tries to sidestep him herself, a black arm shoots out and prevents her.

"Something troubling you, M'am?"

She lifts her eyes to the face with the deep voice. McCurdy the sheriff stands there.

"Step out of my way," she says.

"You're causing a disturbance along the sidewalk, so until you calm down and..."

"And what?"

"I'm the sheriff and it's my job to keep things peaceful."

"It's your job to enforce the law, sheriff." She reaches up and starts prodding his chest with her finger. "There are things going on that you don't seem to give a damn about."

"Don't do that, M'am. You can't do that to a sheriff."

"Not in the rule book?"

The man's nostrils flare. A red stain appears in his cheeks.

"My best friend in Bright River just left town; she probably won't ever come back. My brother is in trouble and what are you going to do about it? You're the big man around here..." She prods even harder. "Do something!"

"M'am, I'm gonna have to ask you to step inside the office here until I can fetch your father to take you home."

"We've never met. How do you know who my father is?"

Strong fingers close around her arm and grip.

McCurdy begins to hustle her into the sheriff's building.

"You can't do this. I have certain unalienable rights. Unhand me..." Her protestations go unheeded. She's bundled inside and released. McCurdy closes the door.

The sounds of the street are cut off.

As she rubs her arm and looks around, reality begins to sink in.

McCurdy circles her.

"What are you doing?" she asks.

He stops a few paces in front of her. "Tell me about your brother's troubles. Maybe I can help."

"I don't have to tell you a thing."

Again, he circles her; the cloying scent of hair oil mingles with that of expensive fabric. She doesn't recall ever being in here before. It is dark and boxy; there is a gun rack on the wall replete with half a dozen Winchesters; and in the far corner a door leading to the jail cell, its metal bars just visible. McCurdy's boots sound deeply on the boards as he walks.

"Don't do that," she breathes.

"But you just asked me to help you."

"I... I was upset and I didn't know what I was saying."

At the same moment McCurdy moves to take a step closer, Taylor bursts in. She flinches and gasps. The room explodes with light and sound.

"You don't want to take that step, McCurdy."

She looks from one to other.

McCurdy's face is a blaze of color; Luke's, on the other hand, is as cold and stony as a rock carving.

"She was causing a disturbance, Taylor."

"I was walking down the street."

"I've got plenty of witnesses. I could charge her."

"I will not go to jail..."

"K?"

"Yes?"

"Be quiet."

She folds her arms.

"Now, come here to me."

She walks up to him. He glances at her briefly, but his eye generally remains fixed on McCurdy.

"I will only agree to release her to her father," McCurdy says.

"I didn't do anything wrong. Okay, I prodded your suit a little but it wasn't personal...and I've recently had a head injury. You scared me and hurt my arm..."

Luke looks at her. Puts his finger to his mouth to quiet her. She watches him, fascinated. He takes her by the hand and her breath gets caught in her windpipe. Gently, he leads her out of McCurdy's office onto the sidewalk and back up the street.

"Keep walking, don't look back," he tells her.

"He's mean and scary."

"He's a lying coward. Did you say he hurt you?"

"He grabbed my arm. Luke, I didn't mean to cause trouble."

"I know."

"You do?"

"Yes."

"I was upset."

"About Tressa?"

"Yes. And Mart. Always about Mart. I don't know what to do."

"You might have noticed we've started a club for people who don't know what to do about Mart. Ethan and me are founding members. You're welcome to join."

She removes her hand and slows. "You asked me to get through to him and I have failed."

He adjusts his pace to hers. "Club membership rule number one. You must have failed to get through to Mart."

Her parents stand waiting on the sidewalk ahead.

"I don't want to be a member of the club. I want to know what to do."

"That's membership rule number two."

"No, honestly, Taylor, in Mart's life I've never made a difference; I'm his kid sister and he tolerates me."

Luke stops and she must also. They face one another. He frowns, and then smiles, and frowns again; a wriggling frown-smile.

"To help him is my vanity, not his desire. He has to want to be helped."

"He loves you, K."

"He has our parents and he has you."

"What are you saying?"

She can't tell him. Not here. Not when her thoughts are still so disconnected.

"Nothing. I... I..." she looks along the sidewalk to where her Mama and her Pa wait; they're holding hands. "Look at them."

He watches, bemused. Then, "Go home, K. Get some rest."

She sighs. "I guess."

"And stay out of McCurdy's way. Alliance members are his favorite meat."

The following day dawns with a hardy chill.

They eat breakfast. Mart leaves early.

Kelley follows her Pa to the stables.

"You should be helping your mother," he says.

"I know. I will." She struggles to keep pace with him. "Pa, there's something I have to tell you."

"It can wait."

"But…"

"I've got work to do. So have you." His stride quickens; she completely loses ground and gives up. She returns to the house, assists her Mama, endures her curious glances and then returns to the stables. Her Pa is nowhere to be seen.

Luke

Ethan's comment when Luke told him about K's run-in with McCurdy was, "This ain't the time or place for a high-spirited girl."

Yep; he had that right.

The trouble with K is she takes everything too hard.

He ambles into the yard like he always does when he calls in on the Keatons. Call? Call as in…

He thinks twice about dismounting. No one has to know he is calling on her; it's more of an inquiry anyhow. Besides, it would be impossible to count the number of times he wanders by the Keatons for no reason. Could very well be one of those occasions. Anyone would think so.

When he can't rouse anyone in the house, although Amy's baking is spread out across the table, he tries the stables.

K is giving Dancer a rubdown, a vigorous grace in her strokes; but when she repeatedly wipes her face, he suspects she's been crying.

She catches sight of him. "Where'd you come from?"

An improvement on *what are you doing here?* Gotta be.

He doesn't answer her; he props himself up against the stall and gives her a hard look.

"You've been crying."

"So?"

"Why?"

"I'm…"

"You're what?"

"…thinking of leaving."

She studies Dancer's brush.

He swallows. "When?"

"Soon." And then she resumes grooming. "I haven't worked out how to tell them yet."

"I know this is hard for you, but..."

"You know nothing," she cuts in, turning her teary eyes on him. "You have no idea. I don't want your sympathy or your under-standing." She shelves the brush and makes a move to leave. He loops his arm around her waist and maneuvers them both back into the stall. She gasps and stares at him in surprise. Even he doesn't understand it; his feelings are confused and he is acting purely on the emotion she is stirring inside of him.

"I can protect you," he says.

"I know," she murmurs.

"Then let me."

"No..." Tears drip from her eyes. "I don't want to be protected. Not the way you mean. This is not the way I want to live my life."

He slides his arms around her waist, drawing her against him. To hold her this way makes his head light. He feels the tension in her body ease even though he expects her to push him away. He smiles into her eyes.

"K, I don't think you hate me anymore."

"Are you happy now?" she retorts, making him laugh.

"I never hated you, you know."

"That's not how I remember it."

"Well, you were the one who called me horrid as soon as you laid eyes on me. You never gave me a chance. You expected me to take it and not give it back?"

She is silent, biting her bottom lip. Finally, she says, "There is too much in our past..."

"I'm not thinking about the past," he tells her; he's thinking that this is how they start putting it behind them.

"But I have to. I know you, Luke."

"You only think you do," he says.

"No, I do. I always have."

He kisses her forehead, then her cheek, then her lips. She is soft and lovely, and the idea of kiss and make up with her fascinates him. For one all too brief moment he feels her kissing him with the same fervor. Then she pushes him back.

"No. This is not what I want," she breathes. "*You* are not what I want."

She shoulders out of his grasp.

He swallows hard, realizing that for all the progress they had made, she is still the same wild-hearted girl she always was. And since he never had cause to doubt her word in the past, there is none now. Reluctantly, he steps out of her way and she brushes passed him.

Ed

…watches the stage fumble its way out of town, tapping cigar ash on the sidewalk and releasing a thoughtful sigh. He ain't the only one; John and Amy Keaton stand arm in arm on the sidewalk at the depot.

McCurdy steps up to the doorway of the sheriff's building with his hand on his Colt. Loves his guns, McCurdy does; strokes them like a lover. Don't actually need to use your Colt so much when folks see you treating guns the way McCurdy does. Messes up their heads just fine.

"What are you looking at?" McCurdy asks.

"Keaton's sister just got on the stage," Ed replies.

"Yep. A good thing too."

Ed glances at him. "Maybe it is and maybe it ain't. They got less to worry about now."

"Well, we can give them more, Ed."

Ed turns to him and gives him a hard look. "I'll decide what and when, understand?"

"Of course, Ed. You're the boss." McCurdy says this and then he tenses.

"What's the matter?"

"Taylor. Across the street."

"Don't tell me he's staring dewy-eyed at the stage as well."

McCurdy shakes his head. "He's heading this way."

"Damn son-of-a-bitch." Ed turns and walks to the edge of the sidewalk. Sticks out his chest.

Taylor can stay in the dirt.

"Pleasant day," Ed greets him.

Taylor, however, has other ideas; he sidesteps Ed onto the sidewalk and they come face to face. Ed doesn't despise the upstart for nothing.

133

The trouble with Taylor obviously began with the kid's father; he never beat him; never showed him who was boss, so he never learnt. A father who don't teach his son these lessons can't expect much, but then Taylor reveres his father's memory; Ed has hated his pa to this very day while he is grateful for teaching him how a man can get what he wants.

"So, Ed," Taylor says, "what are you and McCurdy gonna do for fun now that you scared the girl away?"

Ed holds the insolent gleam in Taylor's eyes for a moment. "Sheriff?"

"Yes, Ed?"

"I wish to make a complaint against Mr Taylor."

Taylor lets out a laugh. Shakes his head.

"What would that be, Ed?"

"False accusation."

"I'll make a note in the file."

"You do that, Sheriff," says Taylor. "Cause I've already made one in mine."

"What does that mean?" Ed asks him, narrowing his eyes on the punk.

"For me to know, Ed… for me to know." Then he grins and walks off in the direction of the Keatons.

"There ain't enough opium in China for the pain he gives me," Ed grinds out.

"I know what you mean," says McCurdy. He's massaging his fist into the palm of his other hand.

"Get word to Bodecker and Donnelly I need to see them."

"Sure, Ed. That all for now?"

"For now."

FOUR

Out of the bosom of the Air,
Out of the cloud-folds of her garments shaken,
Over the woodlands brown and bare,
Over the harvest-fields forsaken,
Silent, and soft, and slow
Descends the snow.

Henry Wadsworth Longfellow
Snowflakes

Kelley

New York

The station veritably steams with the crush of people, back to back and in the chaotic process of arriving and departing. It is precisely the self-occupied type of crowd that severely tests a woman's ability to pin her hat securely – a different test to the physically bone-wrenching stage ride from Laramie to Bright River, but in the relative scheme of things one no less critical. Life seems to be a constant series of meeting expectations, her own as well as other people's. But Manhattan measure-ups are no longer her concern; she couldn't care less. If she fails the test, so be it. As her cab driver ferries her across town, she is absorbed into New York's winter fortress.

Soon, in the cold silence of the afternoon, Aunt Edith's brownstone stands before her with complete dignity and utter common sense, almost as if Aunt Edith and the house are one. Symbols are powerful things, where a person lives and the work of their hands perhaps the most powerful of all: her Pa and his ranch; Luke and the Diamond-T; and Aunt Edith and this house. The cab driver handles her luggage, places it on the stoop and accepts his fare with a worn smile.

A chilled breeze stirs leaves from the sidewalk; some float while others tumble. Coming back to Manhattan for peace of mind makes a complete mockery of all the soul searching and sleepless nights that demanded she return to Wyoming. And yet, while suffering the irony to the marrow of her bones, she cannot deny that here she will find the safety and peace she craves.

Inside, the house delivers its potent remedy; all will be well now.

As dear as a home away from a girl's parents can be, it has its own comforting peculiarities, and she deposits her bags at the foot of the stairs soothed by the serenity of sophistication at ease with itself.

Nothing self-conscious here.

She unpins her hat and removes her gloves, all the while wondering at Aunt Edith's whereabouts.

After placing her things on the hall table, she crosses through the doorway on the right into Uncle Keith's library.

Wall to wall shelves of countless books. Leather furniture and rich woolen rugs. Mahogany desk, buffed to perfection. Ornate fireplace. And overlooking the street, the expansive bay window where Uncle's drawing table remains positioned at an angle that best catches the light. This room has remained unaltered despite her uncle's passing three years ago.

Keith Austin Edwards achieved significant standing as a naval architect and marine engineer; he was, as Aunt Edith put it, an exceptional man, and she vowed that as long as she lived the legacy ensconced in this room would remain as he left it; the rest sails the high seas. On his death from a heart attack, Aunt Edith was left a comfortable living to compensate for a lonely existence. That year was bleak, and Kelley set out to cherish her widowed aunt with a fresh vigor.

In Uncle's desk, inside the left-hand drawer and fixed to the back, is a secret compartment. Kelley removes the false back and reaches in. She extracts a black velvet pouch. She fingers this for a time knowing that the round, heavy object within belongs to her. After drawing the pouch strings apart, she slides Uncle's gold watch into the palm of her hand and smoothes her fingers over its shiny casing. A beloved keepsake. And yet a practical bequest, for: *In life, Kelley my dear, timing is everything; remember that...*

"What time is it?" comes a rather sharp demand.

"Time to regroup," Kelley murmurs, quoting one of Uncle's favorite sayings.

"Is that so..."

"Yes," she says and swallows hard. She looks up and across into Aunt Edith's face and some of that hard emotion lifts. "He would have said as much."

"Mm. You look pleased to see me," Aunt Edith says dryly, her Keaton-blue eyes twinkling madly.

Kelley grins at her. "I am. Very." She replaces the watch in its pouch and sets it back in the drawer.

"You know, my darling, every time you take out your uncle's watch, look at it and put it back again, it tells me that you are scared to commit. You wouldn't take it home with you and now I find you here again. What on earth are you doing?"

"I needed to come back, Auntie." She crosses the room to where Aunt Edith stands by the door in her bronze-brown satin, with her silver-brown hair all coiled and coiffured, her extra-ordinary barely-wrinkled complexion, which Kelley hopes she's inherited, and hugs her. She absorbs the comfort of her arms, the reassurance of her larger than life presence. "I've missed you."

"Well, that's very nice, darling, but you don't have to ruin your life."

"Ruin my life? What are you talking about?"

Aunt Edith sets her back and looks with perspicacity into her eyes. "You look like you need a rousing cup of tea and a sandwich. It never fails. Roast beef?"

"Maybe not beef."

"There may be a little lamb left from dinner. We roasted a small joint."

"Perfect."

Aunt Edith sighs. "This had better be good."

In her large solid kitchen, complete with winking copper pots and pans and all manner of kitchen gadgets, Aunt Edith makes their refreshments herself.

"Laurette is marketing. If I had known you were coming, and refusing beef, I would have asked her to order more lamb."

Kelley picks up the eggbeaters from the table and gives them a spin. "Laurette keeps this house just as beautifully as she ever did."

"As housekeeper-companions go, she is a treasure." Auntie glances up from the lamb. "In fact, she is still a young woman. Like when you were here. She has barely aged a day all the time you were away."

"Well, it feels as though I have been away for years."

"You were away for the Fall, darling, and only the Fall. Drink your tea while it's hot. Are you going to tell me now why you are back? I know things were not as you had hoped, but nothing you wrote me seemed bad enough to warrant this."

"It will take some explaining."

"I can hardly wait. Tell me – your father and mother, are they well?"

"Yes."

"And Martin?"

Kelley shrugs.

Aunt Edith frowns and drives a knife through the bread. "Such a good, solid boy Mart."

"Yes, but I am resigned to the fact that where my brother is concerned I am useless."

"Just tell me, darling. What of this Alliance?"

"I have a limited understanding of it…"

She explains it as best she can.

"Mama and Sara Taylor don't ever want to speak about it; the men run it."

Kelley proceeds to give her a complete account of all the things that have happened to her and other events as well.

"I can't live that way, Auntie, needing an escort, feeling secure only when men are around."

Auntie dollops mustard on the bread and spreads it neatly. "So with all that, what you are telling me, darling, is that the freedom you returned home for no longer exists…"

"In five years they obliterated it."

"…and that your independence was smothered by an organization dominated by men – as if that could possibly be anything novel."

"Those men, Auntie, include Pa, so it's not that they don't care. They just ruined everything."

Auntie arranges slices of cold lamb on the bread. "*They* being your dear father, Martin, Ethan, and the young man, Mart's friend… Taylor?"

"Yes."

Auntie tops the lamb with another slice of bread and pads it down. "You know, I'm wondering what he thinks about your brother's odd behavior. Surely, as his best friend, he must be able to do something."

Kelley needs both hands to place her teacup on its saucer. "The situation is very confusing. I think he's doing what he can."

"Well, if you say so."

Auntie cuts the sandwich in quarters and wipes her hands on a towel. "You never did get along with Taylor, did you? I think you must have told me a number of times you hated him with a lifelong commitment."

Kelley picks up a lamb sandwich and sinks her teeth into the bread. "This is delicious. Laurette did a good job with the lamb."

Aunt Edith nods with one eyebrow arched.

"She's amazing…"

"Yes, we established that. You didn't kill him, did you? – and now you're on the run from the law?"

"That is ridiculous."

Kelley stuffs the rest of the sandwich into her mouth, all the while under severe scrutiny from Aunt Edith.

"What's he like these days, this Taylor? And is that his Christian name?"

Kelley points to her full mouth.

"You want me to guess? I love the idea. Let me see. Aloysius. No? Adrian. Not an Adrian? Andrew – a name I like. No? Ah, what about Augustine…"

God forbid, she's only in the 'A's. Kelley swallows quickly. "Luke. His name is Luke."

"Mm. A nice name. Strong and to the point. I like it."

Kelley picks up another triangle. "There are better names."

"I didn't seem able to think of one," Auntie counters. "So, I believe I asked you, darling, what is Luke like these days?"

"Auntie, I've told you all I know about the Alliance."

"Who said anything about the Alliance? I was speaking of Luke."

"Luke… the Alliance… it is all the same thing."

"Well, if you say so, darling."

"I do. I do say so."

Auntie tops up their tea. "He must be quite something."

"Why would you say that?"

"Just a hunch," she says. "Well, my darling, men get zealous about all sorts of things that women can only sit back and wonder about. I need to know – is this Alliance necessary?"

"*They* seem to think so."

"But you are not so sure."

"I know there is some kind of trouble – the sheriff is quite unbelievable; but my quest, Auntie, I went back to rediscover freedom and now I'm not sure what that means any more. I was a child to think everything back home would be just as I left it."

Aunt Edith smiles sympathetically. "Don't be so hard on yourself. A young woman like you needs to search for the meaning of her life. Some don't. They are quite happy to follow the pattern of womanly existence handed down from generation to generation, and I don't mean to be critical of them. But not you. There is a destiny for you, my darling. Surely finding out what that destiny is will be the most exciting adventure you can imagine."

Surely.

Edith

The Wells' Yuletide party is held on the Saturday before Christmas each year without fail. Everyone they know is invited. We belong to their set by the very fact that my Keith and Julia's Arthur had known one another since school. And now, with both our husbands passed on, Julia and I look forward to the party more than ever. To explain: the organization of it provides welcome distraction, affording Julia some relief from bereavement of her absent beloved which is heightened by the holiday season; while the anticipation of it, excited further by her frequent blow by blow descriptions of how the plans are progressing, offers me similar consolation.

Kelley has attended since she turned sixteen; this is to be her fifth. The nervous excitement of her first had gradually given way to gracious anticipation over the years as she became accustomed to being in society. It should come as no surprise that the way my niece moves in society is not average. Her high spirits keep the girls of her age on their toes and the young men in confusion. She is naturally flirtatious, although her behavior is certainly never unacceptable. She is unaffected by her natural beauty. Her manners are always driven by her intelligence and not by hours of practice and regurgitation, although in her first year with Keith and I there were indeed many, many hours. But for several years now, young men do adore being with her and young women would rather that she stay at home. However, as I observe her speaking with Julia's youngest son, William, and a number of his friends, they in their fine black tail coats and she in her pink silk, something is definitely different. She is smiling, politely, and they are obviously doing their best to rouse her spirits, but her spirit is conspicuous by its absence.

"Kelley's sojourn over the Fall seems to have done her the world of good, Edith," Julia remarks.

"How so, Julia?" I ask, intrigued to know what she sees.

"Look at her; she's just as lovely, probably more so. I just think she seems more mature. Her posture is a credit to you."

I glance at Julia, highly amused. "Thank you, Julia. Always my fervent priority, her posture. Now go attend to your guests."

Julia does so with a smile. The music starts up and Julia's son dances with my niece. I continue my observation.

Gone is the sparkle from her eyes; the lighted-hearted way she makes eyes at her partner while she dances. Whatever has happened at home during the Fall, it has certainly made an impact. She has returned to me after barely three months, declaring she cannot bear the confinement of an organization dominated by men, her father (my brother!) the worst of all. But why run? Her normal tendency is to fight. Then there is Martin, who is troubled; unable to help him she has become frustrated. And lastly, the recondite Luke.

The music dies; William bows and returns my niece to me.

"Thank you, young man," I say. He is well-mannered and amiable, and when he has gone, I remark, "Charming boy."

"Boy? Auntie, he is twenty-five years old."

"Ah, they never really stop being boys. They disguise it with careers and professions and all kinds of distractions."

She is quiet; and for a time she stares at me as though she doesn't see me. Then, "Do they? With war?"

"Definitely with that. Kelley, whatever is the matter?"

"Nothing, Auntie. Although I think I would like to go home soon. Whenever you are ready."

Whenever *I* am ready? Since when?

Christmas and New Year's come and go uneventfully. My joy at having my darling girl back with me is perhaps a little selfish, but she fills my life as the child I was never able to have. And whatever challenges her problems present, I want to postpone addressing them if it means I may have her with me, at least until the end of the long, dreary winter.

Mart

Bright River

2ND JANUARY 1884: I am ready to go. I write this the evening before I intend leaving. I have what Luke calls a gut feeling and that I might not be coming back and that this is my final entry. If I am wrong then no harm is done. But I don't want this journal to fall into Ed's hands so I will hide it in a place I have prepared and leave a message that Kelley will understand. I know she will take good care of it.

I don't know what the future holds. Maybe more of the same. Maybe not. I want my family to know that I love them and I respect them and I am grateful to them for a full and privileged life and grateful for the Faith that they handed down to me and that I have fought for them the best way I knew how. I want Luke to know that...

The call to supper floats through the lonely recesses of the upstairs story. He answers promptly that he will be down in a minute. Sadly, he stares at the incomplete last line while he waits for the ink to dry. Will they ever understand?

Outside, a bitter wind howls and whips sleet against the window. Perhaps supper will provide some comfort. He locks the journal away for the time being.

Of one thing he is certain; he will not return without some resolution of this foul, damnable business.

Kelley

It was while on the train to New York that she had conceived her plan. Unsure if it would be needed, she waited. But now the time had come...

She walks the streets of Manhattan, from Harlem's fashionable residences to Little Italy and perilous Chinatown.

She crosses Roebling's recently completed bridge spanning the East River; investigates the bustling population and industry of Brooklyn and Kings County; wanders around popular Coney Island; revisits the shipyard where Uncle Keith had undertaken his apprenticeship; and once again pays silent homage to Henry Ward Beecher and the Abolitionists at Plymouth Church.

She ventures through the agrarian settlement of Queens County: Flushing, Jamaica and Long Island City. She braves the ferry to Richmond Borough, a growing seaside resort deserted for the winter.

She makes forays into areas where well-bred young ladies never go unescorted: the slums of the poor, the unemployed and racially discriminated; the immigrant communities of Jews, Greeks, Poles and Italians in Bronx County.

In some quarters she finds good-hearted curiosity and ready acceptance, and in many others she is numbingly and totally ignored. She suffers suspicion, proposition and alienation. Whether fearful or stimulated, and she experiences both, she relishes each prospect and dreads failure.

For when Aunt Edith takes her afternoon nap or sees her own friends or pursues her own business, Kelley pursues hers.

Nearly every day she goes out into a world that is as diverse as it is singular in its pursuit of a common identity.

That the rights of people are being consumed by a *laissez-faire* style democracy appalls her; they must all get ahead as they may. And yet there are wonders, not the least of which is the day-to-day pursuits of the many, powering the city like a huge engine beneath the consciousness of the gilded elite. Ultimately, it is not wealth that she wants from this city. Her independence is *her* Holy Grail. In so vast an array who would deny one small woman what is fundamental to their Constitution? When so many are denied decent living conditions and fair wages, her desire seems self-centered and shallow. And yet the city is bombarded weekly with the cries of the suffragettes. Isn't their cause hers also? How do women define and declare this urge to be free from unfair constraints, to have rights that should be theirs? Do they band together? Or do they step out alone and make their mark? To this end, her upbringing has not prepared her for group defiance, or to do anything in a group for that matter; her parents tried but she has always done things her own way. Aunt Edith understood this and taught her that her strength lay in her individualism. So she takes her protest to the streets of New York on her own.

And standing in the middle of an icy, bleak-looking Central Park on a late-January afternoon, after weeks of testing herself, she believes she has succeeded.

"Where have you been?" Aunt Edith exclaims when she arrives home later than planned. "You look frozen."

"In the park watching the skaters. I saw Mariah Milford – her skating hasn't improved one bit."

"It's just so cold today... What possesses you?"

"Don't fret, Auntie, I'm fine."

"I think it's time for that talk we've been putting off."

"Yes, I think it could be."

"Come and warm yourself by the fire. If I didn't know better, I'd say you have been roaming the streets as well. Look at you; wind-blown, red face, and how do you account for those dark circles under your eyes..."

The fire is comforting. "All right, I confess that I have been roaming the streets... for some time."

"For what purpose, may I ask?" Aunt Edith sits down and grips the arms of her chair.

"I was... I was looking for my courage. Or more accurately, testing it."

An intense look surfaces in Auntie's eyes. She speaks softly, however. "Your courage? Whatever do you mean, darling?"

"When I arrived here, all those long months I was homesick, and I would weep at the pain I felt in leaving the ranch, you used to tell me that I was your brave soldier – remember? And then when I got scarlet fever. I was so ill and yet I can remember you whispering to me: *my brave little soldier...* It made me feel strong. And I began to think I was brave. That I always had been brave. Auntie, when I went home again I still believed I was. Then one frightening thing after another happened, until I needed... and wanted protection from someone. I am not brave, Auntie. I am not who I thought I was..."

"The someone wouldn't happen to be a man, would it?"

"Yes, but you're not listening to me."

"Indeed I am. I know the pain you felt, and the need you had to be understood. I would not make light of these for anything. And you were brave indeed, my darling. But that was then."

"Auntie..."

"Nothing saps a woman's will to be brave more than a man who is willing to take up the task for her. Of course, she would have to be attracted to that young man..."

"Attracted?"

"Mm."

"That's absurd. I'm not attracted to..." Kelley stops herself. And keeps her lips firmly together.

"Say his name, darling. You will feel a whole lot better."

She fights a silent battle; Auntie watches with obvious amusement. Surely all her profound insights gleaned from so many dramatic expeditions can't come to this?

One eyebrow arches; Aunt Edith demands an answer.

"Start with a description," she suggests.

"No. I want to discuss my problem, not... that."

Auntie chuckles. "Darling, 'that' is your problem. When did you feel the symptoms appear? After the bear, the stranger or the owl?"

Kelley gapes at her, forgetting to breathe.

Eventually, she mumbles, "I wrote you about the owl?"

"You did."

"Oh," she says. "It… it was the owl."

Aunt Edith gives her a smile of approval. "Now, that wasn't so hard, was it?"

She wants to scream *it's devastating, it cannot be happening.*

Instead, she gropes about for a chair and sits down. "He makes me feel safe. And my confidence in him grew the more he protected me. Only it's not supposed to be this way. We're supposed to detest each other. It worked exceedingly well for fourteen years…"

"I warned you, didn't I? I warned you that one day there would come a man and that headstrong streak in you would not be able to control your heart because hearts are more than capable of going their own sweet way. Oh, I'm dying to know all about him…"

"You're speaking as if this… *this* has some meaning in my life."

Aunt Edith looks surprised. "It doesn't?"

"I've walked the streets of this city and all its environs to prove I don't need him. If I don't need him here, then I certainly don't need him anywhere else. I have proved my independence."

"And what I am saying is that his protecting you and you wanting him to is a sign of something deeper. That's just how it's begun, and very sweetly I must say…"

"*Sweetly?*"

"Has nothing to do with your courage, although, as I said, romantic attachments can sorely dent your independence. However, darling, I must say that, personally, I am very impressed with your achievement – no wonder you look exhausted."

Kelley springs to her feet. "I'm going to have my bath… and, Auntie, there'll be no more talk about it."

Neither speaks again on the subject for some days, not until Kelley begins to experience weird dreams. The disturbance to her sleep is evident on her face and Aunt Edith pounces on it.

"This is the third morning you have come down to breakfast looking as though you need to go back to bed."

"I keep dreaming about Mart. Sometimes I see him clearly; he is calling to me, holding out his hand. We are always by the River on the Diamond-T... And sometimes I can't see him but I feel he is there as I toss and turn in my sleep." She sips her coffee and then reaches for the sugar bowl.

Aunt Edith contemplates for a few moments as she watches Kelley stir sugar into her coffee. "All this *brave little soldier* business... You have obviously completely overdone it and now you are ruining your sleep. We better plan some outings to get your mind off Mart – not that I am surprised that your concern for him is surfacing in your dreams."

"Yes, Auntie. But why are we on the Diamond-T?"

"Darling, you cannot keep Luke out of mind any more than you can keep out Mart, especially since you have finally stopped all this gadding about. You know how dreams are – they do your thinking for you when you won't do it for yourself. When did you last write to your father and mother?"

"Just after Christmas. I thanked them for their gift."

"February starts tomorrow. That's over a month!"

"I'm sorry." Her Mama's prompt reply had been general in content, with no news of Mart or escalating problems with Ed Parsons, so she had assumed that nothing had changed.

"I am not the one to whom you should be apologizing. Ignoring a problem, denying its existence, does not make it go away. Apart from all that, a letter might ease your concern for brother, reassure you – heaven forbid, Kelley, they might even write back!"

She writes her letter that evening, but the very next day, before she can send it, a letter arrives from home.

"An ominous coincidence," Aunt Edith murmurs.

"It might be nothing. Just a simple letter..."

Auntie's expression is grim. "All my feeling tells me otherwise."

Kelley stares at the envelope and her Mama's handwriting, feeling less and less like a brave little soldier.

"Read it aloud, darling. Please."

"Yes, Auntie… *Dearest Kelley, I wouldn't dream of interfering with what I imagine to be a busy life in New York but I need you here at home. I wouldn't ask you if I thought I could do without you. Mart departed from home on the second of January saying he needed to take one of his trips but he did not return in the usual time. Your father and Luke went to search for him. It has been a week since they left. His trail had gone cold and so far they have found nothing. They won't stop until they find him. When last I heard from them by telegram they had reported Mart missing to the county sheriff in Laramie as well as Luke's sheriff friend in Cheyenne, who both said they would keep an eye out for him. Your father and Luke decided to leave the territory and head east. They did not say why. Please let me know soon if you will come. My love to Edith as always. Love, Mama.*"

She stares at the words feeling as though everything in her body has shuddered to a halt. And despite all that the letter contains, it is her Mama's thinking that her own daughter would possibly ignore her plea that is the most upsetting.

Shaking, she cries, *"If I will come…?"*

Aunt Edith looks at her hands, a sure sign she wants to hide her dismay. "What will you do, darling?"

Luke

Missouri
March 4, 1884

Luke puts muscle to the door to shut out the howling wind while John relocates snow from his shoulders to the floor. They take a moment, then move to the bar; even this modest place, with a good fire in its hearth and the odd stove placed about, is a relief from the raging snowstorm. A tall middle-aged man, wearing a white apron around his tubby middle, approaches them.

"Welcome to Shorty's, pilgrims," he says. His face is lined and saggy, with flourishing salt and pepper eyebrows sweeping low over his eyes.

Luke removes his hat. "You're Shorty?"

"No. Sam Pike. Bought this place from Max Short." His eyes get a cagey expression to them. "So what can I get you?"

Luke places five dollars' worth of coins on the counter and looks up at the saloonkeeper. "Two hot dinners, a bottle of whiskey and some information."

Pike lifts those bushy brows and looks from Luke to John and back again. "A feller could think you were a might desperate."

"That accounts for a lot of folk on a day like today," Luke says.

"Just cold, mister," John adds.

Pike reaches under the counter and produces a bottle of his finest cheap whiskey. Luke shakes his head. "Not that. The bottle on the shelf behind you."

"That'll cost you extra."

"What's the grub?"

"Beef stew."

"Large plates. And pile on the bread. We'll be at that table," he says, thumbing over his shoulder at the table furthest from the door. He and John have had enough of snow and wind.

"What about your information?" asks Pike.

Luke gives him a grin. "Bring yourself a glass with that good bottle, Pike."

"Sure. But I ain't sure what kinda information you want."

"We're looking for someone. Now, we're kinda tired..."

The saloonkeeper nods. "Go on. Sit. Only be few minutes. Stew's good and hot."

Luke takes the bottle and two glasses from the counter. At their table they remove their heavy coats, and when they both sit down Luke reckons he hears their bones creak. John lets out a huge sigh, takes off his hat and gives Luke a hard look.

"What?" Luke asks as he pours liquid into their glasses.

"Think he knows something?"

"This is the only decent place to stop. We know Mart didn't go into Kansas City; his trail's led us too far south, although this town's got a rail spur all its own."

"It's a timber town, son," John tells him.

The whiskey disappears down the back of their throats. Luke refills their glasses. The second shot actually makes a dent in his frozen insides and he feels better. He watches the door open and snow sweep in with a big, heavily dressed man. "Woodcutter?"

John looks. "Mm."

Pike brings the food, bread piled high. He has an extra glass with him. John glances at Luke with a hopeful glint in his eye.

"You boys should eat something first. You look all in."

"What about your customer?"

"My daughter will take care of him."

Sure enough, a young woman appears.

Luke is too hungry to take any further notice; he consumes half his plate before he feels the need to stop. John is taking it a little slower and has indicated to Pike to pour himself a glass.

"Well," the saloonkeeper begins after he's bent his elbow once or twice and smacked his lips, "that's not half bad that is; so, what do you want to know?"

"We're looking for someone," John tells him. "My height and build but he's got blond hair, gray eyes. Same age as my friend here. Would have come through in the last day or two."

Pike stares at them. "Where are you boys from?"

Luke is about to ask why he needs to know when John cuts across him. "Wyoming territory."

Pike downs his whiskey. "A young feller came through here that fits your description."

"Can you recall what was he wearing?" Luke asks.

"Heavy dark blue coat and a green and blue plaid scarf... I noticed the scarf 'cause it looked like a fine article."

Luke recalls K sending Mart such a scarf from New York a couple of birthdays ago; Mart liked it but only wore it on special occasions. John remembers as well because his eyes have got a definite glint in them now.

"Who is this feller to you?" Pike asks.

"He's my son," John replies.

Pike nods some level of understanding.

"How did he seem?" John continues.

"Looked like you two. Cold, hungry..."

"Did he talk about anything?"

Pike smiles crookedly. "He could have..."

Luke reaches into his pocket and produces ten dollars. John sighs; the barkeep's eyes light up.

"Your son asked if a black-haired man with a beard and a scar on his left cheek going by the name of Cutter had come through. He were looking for him because they had business to attend to out Sedalia way. Didn't recognize the name, I told him, but an unsavory character answering his description had been by here. This character were even bragging he were going to Sedalia. It were weird, like they kinda knew each other, going the same direction, same place, but not together. This Cutter character gave my daughter a hard time and it weren't easy gettin' rid of him. Can't abide trouble-makers like that one. Anyway, your son ate and went on his way."

Luke feels frustration swell inside him. He brings his fist down hard on the table. John reprimands him.

Pike's expression hardens. "You got your information, your food and your whiskey. This is a peaceable watering hole for a lotta people. Keep it that way till you leave."

"Just one more question," John says, and the saloonkeeper eyes him suspiciously. "How long ago?"

"Yesterday afternoon."

Wilson Cutter

March 5, 1884
Thirty minutes out of Sedalia

Wilson at last manages to reef the coupling of the baggage car free. The Kansas City Express tears away, leaving the US mail and the baggage car attendant behind.

The car slows. After checking the condition of the attendant, who is unconscious and bleeding from a cracking blow to the head courtesy of Wilson's rifle butt, he wonders if he should put a bullet in him to keep him that way. He decides against it; alive he might come in handy when dealing with Keaton.

He wrenches open the loading door of the carriage. A bitter wind breaks in, hurling mail and other papers into the air and scattering them all over the carriage. He breathes deep and having secured his hat, leaps from the carriage and lands in a mound of soft snow. Spitting the stuff from his mouth, he sets off, trudging alongside the tracks until he spies the forest up ahead. Once there, he fires his rifle into the air; it resounds through the lonesome woods, then there is silence.

He enters the forest. "Keaton! Keaton, I know you're here!"

Light snow starts to fall. The forest is dim, stinging with cold, and eerie. What will happen here... no witnesses; the trees can't talk; nature don't even care. Murder goes against nature, they say. Cutter laughs to himself. Whose nature? Nature has two sides. Take this forest; it's pretty enough, but stay a night without shelter and you freeze to death. Same nature, two sides. He and Keaton are like two sides of the same penny. Just two men come into this world, stuck together by the same predicament, destined to be on opposite sides of Ed Parsons.

Poor Keaton. He gave it a shot, but he ain't cut out for spending a night in the forest and that's all there is to it...

"Wilson Cutter, you have one more chance to do the clean and just thing."

Keaton… Just his voice, but on the other side of a clearing. Wilson fires two impulsive shots in Keaton's direction, curses himself for being so stupid, then takes a steadying breath.

"Let it all go, Cutter; I know the sheriff will take it kindly," Keaton shouts, this time from another direction; ten yards west.

"I ain't surrenderin' to no one," Cutter screams back, and honing in on the direction of Keaton's voice, he fires just one shot. This time Keaton fires back. Wilson catches the orange flash and the gun smoke before it floats away in the frosty air. "Gotcha, Keaton. I'm too good for you, boy, and you know it. You're soft. Your life has made you soft. You can't win."

"I don't want you dead, Cutter, you know that. I just want the truth. It's why I got you here. I want you to help me be the bearer of it and we can turn this whole thing around. Your life, everything. We can do what's right. For once, just once, listen to me…"

"You talk shit, Keaton. Now hold still so I can kill you."

"Cutter, lay down your weapon and we can do this…"

Before Keaton's even finished speaking, Wilson fires his rifle. He hears Keaton cry out and feels a rush of excitement followed by a warm sense of satisfaction curling through his blood. But Keaton emerges from the trees with his rifle blazing. Wilson takes a hit in his thigh. Pain rips through him but he must retaliate.

"Now we are even. Now will you see sense?" Keaton says and grounds his weapon. "We can do this together. Set things right. Come back with me and let's end this before…"

"Shut up, Keaton, and pick up your gun," Wilson shrieks but Keaton keeps on walking and stretches out his hand.

"Keaton…" he screeches.

He aims at Keaton's oncoming figure and squeezes out a shot.

Keaton staggers to a stop, gripping his belly; he groans, "You shouldn't have done that, Wilson."

Then he drops into the snow and don't move.

"Keaton…" Wilson cries, shaking. This should have been a fight to the death for both of them. He limps forward, clumsy with pain. Closer, he sees a red stain spreading out onto the snow.

"You're soft, Keaton," he croaks. "Not me… not me…"

Sean (John)

Sean retrieves his son's lifeless body from the snow. He looks down at the white face and the blue mouth. The gray eyes, so like Amy's, are closed on the world, his mop of yellow hair darkened and matted. He pushes some of it back from the boy's forehead, gently removes snow and ice from his face and kisses him.

My son. My very own son. My beautiful boy. Too late. Too late. Oh God, no, *no, no…*

Luke forces Sean back. "Mart…Mart, can you hear me?" He attempts to bring Mart back to consciousness.

"It's no use," Sean whispers.

"But I feel a weak pulse." Working quick, his hands shaking, Luke takes a shirt from his saddlebag and covers Mart's wound, stemming the blood.

"It's too late, he's lost too much…"

"John, we need to know who did this. Mart… Listen to me. Wake up…"

Persistence brings results. Sean's heart leaps as his son's eye-lids move.

"Mart…"

The boy gives a pain-filled gasp.

"Who did this, Mart?" Luke insists. "Who did it?"

Not: don't worry, everything will be all right. But: who did this? *Yes… yes, who did this?* "Mart, can you tell us?"

With his son so close to death, Sean can't believe he would find the strength to speak.

But in the faintest of whispers… "Pa."

"This should be me…"

"Mart." Luke squeezes one of his hands and bends close to his face.

Mart's eyelids flutter; a muscle in his cheek twitches. "Luke."

"Tell us. I promise, I swear, I will bring whoever it was to justice. You have my word…"

Mart gasps, "Wilson Cutter. You have met him. You, Ethan, Kelley…"

"The stranger with the black beard?" Luke asks.

"Yes. Justice. Do it. Pa… pray for me…" His face freezes; his breathing is still.

"Sweet Jesus in heaven, no!" Luke cries, before he gets to his feet and storms off a ways, Mart's blood dripping from his hands.

"Please, God," Sean implores. "Please…" He gathers Mart to him and rocks him in his arms endlessly, praying aimlessly until the Lord's Prayer comes to him, aware of Luke standing by and trying to wipe tears off his face with bloodied hands…

At last defeated, exhausted, Sean stills himself.

"My dearest boy. I am proud to have been your Pa. Rest now in the arms of the angels."

He caresses his son's eyelids shut. The cry of anguish he hears echoing through the trees is his, he realizes; it comes crashing back to his ears.

How is he to tell Amy he was too late?

Luke

Two female figures, clad in mourning clothes, step down gracefully from the train and into the stinging cold. Clouds of steam obscure them momentarily.

"There," Luke says.

"I see them," John says in a crusty voice. As he hurries up to them, Luke hangs back. For all the fine talk and close affection over the years, these women are rightfully John's kin, not his.

They embrace and cling and make the grief a whole lot worse – if it could be any worse. And when he eventually reaches Amy, she hugs him tightly, strokes his cold cheeks and peers into his soul with her swollen gray eyes.

"It's all right, Luke," she whispers.

No, it's not, he screams on the inside.

"You did everything you could."

He says, "I'll get the bags."

As he moves away, he steps into K's path. They stare at each other. He thinks of nothing to say to her. And grief has caught her mute. She takes her father's arm and walks off with her parents.

"Where are we going?" Amy asks.

"Cheyenne Hotel," John tells her.

"I'd rather see Mart straight away," she replies.

"I don't think that's such a good idea, Amy…"

"But, John, I must…"

There is a dangerous wobble in her voice and John relents. He turns to inform Luke of the change in plans. The undertaker's is not far from the depot anyhow.

Luke says, "I'll take the bags to the hotel. You go."

John nods and escorts the women away.

They pass by the 'Welcome to Cheyenne' sign without a second glance.

Just as Luke is about to collect their bags, K breaks away and walks towards him. She hands him a white envelope.

"A letter from Sara and Ethan. Mama's been holding it since we left Bright River. She says sorry and that she doesn't know how she could have forgotten to give it to you."

"Thanks…" He swallows awkwardly.

"You… Are you all right?"

He avoids her eyes and pockets the letter. "Of course."

"I'll help you with the luggage."

Before he can protest, she has waved at her folks; they acknowledge and walk on without her.

"I'll only be in their way," she says, her eyes following them. Then the bags become the focus of her attention. "Here they are…"

This is only an overnight stay, so they have one small bag each.

"Do you mind if we walk to the hotel?" she asks.

"It's cold," he says.

"I know."

The walk from the passenger depot down 15th Street, up Ferguson for two blocks and left onto 17th is an uncomfortable slog through bitter cold and slush. The whole time her posture is perfect, as though she can sense where the rough patches are before they get to them. And there is purpose in her stride as she keeps pace with him. He is fully aware of her; it is impossible not to be. After her rejection of him in the Fall, however, and after some thorough deliberations on his part, which filled the many days he and John were searching for Mart, he is over his infatuation of her. They'd got passed their childhood conflict and that is enough for him.

Lost in his thoughts, the Cheyenne Hotel has crept up on him. He stops abruptly, opens the door for his companion and they enter. The hotel is comfortable without being extravagant.

He glances at K's face. She's been crying. On second thought, maybe extravagant would have helped.

As they check her in at the hotel desk, she uses a handkerchief on her tears.

The hotel clerk hands her a telegram. "This came for you, Miss Keaton, this morning."

She opens it immediately and very soon tells him it is from her Aunt in New York. She looks like she is going to break down but holds it in. He draws her away from the desk, carrying the bags, and walks her up the staircase to her room. Before meeting her train he'd got a fire going in the stove; it burns sturdily and the room is warm. He deposits her bag on the bed and places Amy's on the floor beside it.

"Will you be all right?" he asks before he leaves.

She swings her eyes to his face, swollen red eyes now. "I... I don't know how to deal with this."

He sighs. "You and me both."

"Oh. Could you... could you tell me what he said to you before..."

"He wanted justice, K, so that's what I'll be doing. Getting it for him."

Her eyes flood with tears and she looks away out the window overlooking the street. "I'll help you."

He is startled momentarily. "He wouldn't want you to be risking your..."

"Don't tell me what he would or wouldn't want."

God, she can still rankle even in this state.

"This is about Mart," she continues, "my *brother*...not your precious Alliance..."

Her fists are tight balls at her side.

In the silence that follows he takes the hint.

"See you at lunch," he says and leaves, gently snapping the door shut behind him, then expelling a deep sigh.

Her brother! What a... what a piece of work.

Overcome with weariness, he heads for his own room and a warm fire.

Kelley

In the hotel dining room, which is warm and clean, they eat a hot and nutritious beef stew. Her Mama believes that they should be together, probably laboring under the misapprehension that their grief shared is grief halved.

Once again Kelley is out of her depth when it comes to groups. The stew, however, is a good choice because it requires very little effort either to eat or push around her plate. She mostly pushes. On one rare occasion when she manages to put a piece of meat into her mouth she catches Luke's pitiful glance. She wants to be furiously angry with him but can't. He affects her in ways she is beginning to find a little alarming, and his anguish over Mart goes straight to her heart.

"I think this is just what we needed," her Mama remarks. Brave attempt. No one responds.

And no one will talk about Mart.

Kelley pushes away her plate. "I have started a letter to Aunt Edith. Do you want to add anything, Pa?"

He shakes his head.

"I wrote her what has happened. And that we are all here in Cheyenne to bring him home."

"She knows that, Kelley," her Mama murmurs.

Yes, a few terse words in a telegram. Hardly the outpouring of family sorrow that dear Aunt Edith, who loves them all so much, needs to share. What happened to grief shared?

Perhaps her Mama notices the tears welling in her eyes because she says, "A long letter, though, the kind that you write, is a good idea. Very hard for Edith, living so far away…"

"Edith always had a soft spot for the boy," her Pa says.

"She liked the fact that a boy could be so plainly good," her Mama explains.

"I used to give her grief when we were young'uns. She used to say, Martin certainly doesn't take after you, Sean."

Her Pa falls abruptly silent.

"I think Mart would like that hymn with the sheep in it," Luke says. They all look up. "At his service…"

"I know at least a dozen hymns with sheep in them," her Mama says. "That you know any, frankly…"

"And I'd like to say something…"

Her Pa frowns. "A eulogy?"

"I guess."

Her Pa nods.

"I've written a notice for the newspapers," her Mama informs them.

"Bet they charge like a wounded bull," her Pa grumbles.

"Which hymn with the sheep in it?" Kelley asks.

The dining room is barely half-full by the time they stop speaking about Mart and how to say goodbye; when the dam finally burst, shutting the floodgates wasn't so easy. Clearly, they all feel better for it.

As Kelley sips her water, she notices their waitress and a middle-aged man, who from his apparel looks like the cook, standing at the door of the kitchen. In earnest conversation with them is a striking woman with a keen expression and a brown canvas satchel hanging from one shoulder. Along with a certain style and poise, she has the most beautiful chestnut-colored hair. And an easy sophistication, although next to the cook that wouldn't be hard to achieve. She listens attentively to the cook's animated speech as the man keeps showing her his wrist. Hard to imagine what would be so fascinating about a cook's wrist that it would hold this woman's interest.

Kelley's attention is abruptly diverted. A tall, athletically built young man attired a smart charcoal suit strides towards them. Luke sees him and stands, extending his hand. They greet each other like friends.

"Cliff, good to see you."

"And you, Luke."

"Let me introduce you to the Keatons…"

They are formally introduced to the sheriff of Cheyenne, whose name is Cliff Ryan and who, like the woman with the brown satchel, appears to be a square peg fitting quite neatly and enigmatically into a round hole. He borrows a chair from an adjacent table and seats himself at theirs, his manner easy and elegant. He expresses his sympathy for their recent loss, that he knew and respected Mart.

"The last thing this territory needs is to lose men like Mart," he concludes. Her Pa appreciates this remark and thanks him. "And since Luke informed me of what happened I have made some discreet inquiries regarding Wilson Cutter's most recent activities. Your decision to keep the circumstances surrounding Mart's death quiet may actually be the best way of apprehending him. The saloonkeeper in a town up the line from Sedalia said he spoke to Cutter a couple of days ago. Cutter was bragging. And, he was wounded in the right thigh. Now one of our doctors here in town has just today treated a man who was bushwhacked by a man answering Cutter's description – thigh and all."

"Where?" Luke asks sharply.

"About half way between here and Pine Bluffs. Shoots him in the leg, beats him senseless, takes his horse and all his money and supplies. A Good Samaritan finds the poor unfortunate, Byron Sawyer, on the side of the road and puts him in his wagon. However, our Good Samaritan didn't realize how sick Sawyer was and his health got steadily worse along the trail. By the time the doc got a look at him he was in bad shape."

Her Mama says, "This Cutter is coming back. And so fast. Trains were supposed to be a boon to this country and all they do is assist outlaws."

The sheriff looks stunned for a minute. Her Mama's lack of compassion for Mr Sawyer is a little surprising.

"This won't be easy," Mr Ryan says. "A full-scale manhunt will drive him away. At the same time, you'll need protection."

"You mean you want us to lure him back here by doing nothing?" Kelley asks incredulously.

Sheriff Ryan's eyes search her face. "I can understand your dismay, Miss Keaton, but if we scare him away we might not find him again or discover why this has happened to your brother. Now, Byron Sawyer won't be going anywhere any time soon. The doc's taking care of him. And we've informed the saloonkeeper, Pike, that his testimony may be needed at some point."

"But, Sheriff, a full-scale manhunt might actually succeed."

"First, Miss Keaton, I have it on good authority that Wilson Cutter loves the thrill of a chase and excels at it, and secondly, we still have no clue as to why Mart was involved with a wanted outlaw, and believe me Wilson Cutter is wanted. He's hired himself out to anyone paying the right price. So the chances are that someone hired him to murder your brother and he will come back to collect what is due to him. That would be highly in our favor. In any case, a federal marshal may pick him up regardless for other crimes – that is out of our hands. Now, Mr Keaton," he says, diverting his attention to her Pa, "if you and your family are agreeable, and Luke as well, I'd like to wait and see where Cutter surfaces in the near future and where he may lead us."

Her Pa, to his credit, looks to his wife for the approval he obviously desires. To her Mama's credit, she asks, "How long will we have to live like this?"

"I don't know," he says honestly.

"You're not even going to put up WANTED posters," Kelley continues.

Luke gives her an exasperated glare.

"Miss Keaton, the baggage car attendant was probably the only person who could have placed Cutter at the murder scene and he was found dead. So at the moment we have no witnesses to the actual crime. Now I'm sure even you would concede that."

Sheriff Ryan has got her. Still, she says, "If my brother, in his dying breath, said Wilson Cutter shot him, then Wilson Cutter shot him."

The sheriff favors her with a rather sparkly-eyed smile and then promptly swings his gaze expectantly upon her Pa again.

"We go along with the plan, Sheriff."

"Good." Mr Ryan stands up, extends his hand to her father and they shake.

Luke stands also and says, "I'd like to talk to this Byron Sawyer."

Sheriff Ryan considers the request. "I'll check with the doc. Shouldn't be a problem. Good day to you all."

Her parents are polite as he leaves them.

Luke resumes his seat and looks set to bite her head off.

"Things are certainly moving along," her Mama remarks. "And he seems like an honest, capable young man."

Kelley is determined to keep her mouth firmly shut as she follows Sheriff Ryan's movements across the dining room.

The young woman with the brown satchel meets him half way with a charming smile, and he begins speaking earnestly to her. Looking at them, they could be greeting one another in a restaurant in any city back East… They provide a focal point for her tension; before long her eyes are stinging with pent up emotion.

"What are you staring at?"

She blinks several times to discover Luke scowling at her.

"Nothing. Just… just that woman and Mr Ryan… Listen, you, it's my business who I stare at…"

Luke ignores her and turns to take a look for himself.

A casual glance at first, but his scowl fades. His observation lengthens; the angry line of his features softens, and that observation becomes a comfortable gaze.

She follows that gaze with supreme curiosity. The woman. Well, it certainly wouldn't be that sheriff… Her heart begins to pound rather strangely.

Soon after, Sheriff Ryan and the woman with the brown satchel move away. Luke's attention drifts. He doesn't look at anyone for a while, pushing at the remnants on his plate; she watches him out of the corner of her eye as they converse around him. Finally, his sapphire gaze meets hers. She doesn't understand the look in it and it makes her nervous.

"I think I'll go upstairs and finish my letter to Aunt Edith," she says.

She also writes another letter; if Tressa is as fond of the Taylors and Keatons as she seemed to be, she will want to know about Mart. Kelley finds her words are stilted and faltering. In disclosing her brother's death to Tressa, it feels as though she is admitting it to the whole world. It is painful, and swamped by guilt she keeps the letter short.

Ed

…pounds the table with his fist and swears furiously under his breath. "It's too soon for Cutter to come back. Keaton ain't even buried yet."

McCurdy quickly mutters, "I'll locate him, Ed, and tell him to stay on the dodge till we say otherwise."

Ed moves to the window and stares out at the distant plateau that marks the high pastures of the Diamond-T.

A tasty curl of covetousness tightens to a knot in his stomach. He feeds his avarice like a man satisfies his lust for a beautiful woman. He brings it to its conclusion with triumph. He will have the Diamond-T. He will have it. He will. And no one is going to interfere with his plans.

"Keep Cutter out till I call him back," he grinds out.

"Sure, boss. I'll take care of it," McCurdy says. "I'll be away for a while but."

Ed grunts. "Give him something to keep him happy. And don't give Ryan a sniff, not a sniff, y'hear…"

Luke

Luke shaves with the utmost care.

His hands are trembling and his eyes won't focus.

And in his gut lurks a churning, gnawing agitation that just won't quit.

When at last he's done, the clean-shaven face in the mirror taunts him: do you really think you can hide a night of sleeplessness and anguish by looking like you care what other people think?

Tears well in his eyes. He splashes cold water on his face. He clenches his hands together to stop them shaking. It doesn't work.

There hasn't been a day since he was eleven that didn't have Mart in it somehow.

Even in San Francisco he wrote him; sent back newspaper cuttings, and sketches he made of the city to amuse him, entice him to come; Mart wrote him back: it ain't for me but I'm glad you're doing it.

Don't matter anymore. None of it matters.

Cliff finds them at breakfast almost as if they never left the dining room since lunch yesterday. In fact, they spent some very separate and private hours the previous afternoon, came together for supper and then disappeared for the rest of the evening. This morning they will take Mart home. John and Amy's grief has been diverted by the need for practicality and as yet K hasn't said or done anything to irritate him.

Cliff draws him aside. "Byron Sawyer's condition worsened overnight. He's critical."

"Where is he?"

Even as Cliff is briefing him, Luke is on the move. Shaking all over, able to think of only one thing – reaching Sawyer before he leaves this earth for good and takes what he knows about Wilson Cutter with him – he rushes up 17th street, shouldering his way through clusters of ambling citizens, dodging wagons and horses, incurring the annoyance of all he passes. As Thomas St looms ahead, and he thinks he has missed his target, he sees the doctor's name – J.A. Sullivan, Physician & Surgeon – gold lettering on a wooden shingle fixed over a pair of half-paned doors. He bursts one of them open and flails a small bell, which drops with a thudding clunk onto the floor in front of him, bringing him to an abrupt halt.

Breathless, he looks up from the bell lying dead on the boards to what lies before him: a large room, vastly still and empty, veiled in the remnant of night that was breached the moment he cracked the door and admitted a fringe of pale sunshine. He closes the door and traps sunlight floating on particles of street dust inside. As his eyes adjust to the peculiar light, he sees a row of vacant chairs arrayed along one wall and in the middle a neatly arranged work desk. While he tries to steady his breathing, his senses are arrested by a nostril-sucking smell of utter cleanliness. His crazed, one-tracked thinking begins to shift, to slow, consider… It must, to enter into this orderly, strangely comforting, and curious world. Who created it? Even on the Diamond-T there is nowhere like this, to do this to him. Then to his heightened senses comes a sound, deep and penetrating, a perfect rhythm. It is his breathing. Nothing else stirs.

Suddenly, his eyes are drawn to a woman, wrapped in a full white apron, standing in a draped archway. Angelic, she is. Like the most beautiful painting he ever saw come to life. He muses: this world has its own extraordinary creature. Sweetness, both fierce and serene. Then comes recognition… The deep chestnut hair, pink-cheeked porcelain skin, the bright eyes. His Cheyenne Hotel woman. In the back of his brain niggles another fanciful thought that he's not surprised to see her here. He finds himself absorbing every curve and detail of her face. Her eyes are green and the longer he looks into them the saner he feels…

"You…" he mumbles.

One loose and curling lock dangles against her cheek. She is regarding him, calm but curious, as she folds the lock behind her ear. "Yes?"

"…created this place," he finishes in a whisper.

"I…" She frowns lightly. In a smooth, clear voice she says, "Who might you be?"

"…er…Taylor – Luke," he says and removes his hat. "And you are…?"

"Sullivan – Doctor."

"I broke your bell."

"So I see."

"I'm sorry. I'll pay to have it mended."

"That won't be necessary. How may I help you?"

"I need to see Byron Sawyer."

"Are you a relative?"

"No… you don't understand. I…"

"I'm afraid Byron Sawyer passed away a few minutes ago."

"Passed away?" he mutters. "He's dead?"

The world without Mart strikes back. His heart pushes hard against his ribs.

"Yes, he had suffered several blows to the head."

"He can't be. I don't believe it."

Not even this young… female… pretty… *whatever* can distract him now. He rushes past her through the archway and down a hall till he comes to an open door. From here he sees a man's body being covered by a white sheet. Another woman is doing it – a tall, middle-aged woman who looks right into his face.

"No," he breathes.

"A relative, young man?" she asks in an Irish accent.

"No…"

"Mr Taylor…" The female doctor has followed him.

His eyes begin to glaze and sting as he stares at the sheeted body. "I needed him…"

"I'm sorry," she says. "There was nothing anyone could have done. He drifted in and out of consciousness most of the time he was here. The sheriff and I managed to extract from him what had happened to him and not much else."

Luke looks into her face. "The man who did this to him murdered my friend."

"Oh," she murmurs. "I see."

"I needed him," he repeats.

"Duffy, I'm going to pour Mr Taylor a cup of coffee..."

The tall woman says, "A fine idea, Dr Sullivan. I'll finish here."

Luke doesn't understand why he allows himself to be led away by a woman doctor to her examination room; the episode at her front door was a unique and fanciful distraction – okay, kinda heavenly – but no medicine exists to cure what ails him.

"Please sit down, Mr Taylor," she says.

He doesn't right away. He stares at his surroundings, a little taken aback...

The room is unlike any room he's ever seen, full of bizarre gadgets and curious artifacts, and gruesome pictures of the human body and its parts. There are cabinets with glass doors packed with all kinds of oddities, including glass jars that contain unsettling objects pickled in liquid, and bookshelves crammed with important-looking volumes. It's neat, tidy and clean beyond any clean he's ever seen. But she has an old potbelly stove firing away and a steaming pot of coffee on top of it. Just like everything else he'd encountered so far, without her this wacky room wouldn't make sense. He eventually takes a seat.

She pours the coffee and he watches her graceful, efficient movements, fixing his mind on her, absorbing her. Picturing her in this curious world of hers day after day. Helping people, strangers... with that kind and beautiful face the first thing they see... Is she the treatment? – because it's working. It's a feeling beneath his skin, slipping through his blood, settling in his chest.

As far as he's concerned, she is 'puha'.

Powerful medicine.

"Sugar?"

He shakes his head.

"I don't think you would have got much more out of poor Mr Sawyer," she says, handing him coffee in a white china cup with saucer.

"Thanks." He swigs at his coffee; he can't believe it tastes strong like his campfire brew.

She pours her own and stirs in two spoons of sugar. He tells her it's good and she smiles.

"A dead witness is no witness," he continues.

"Did Mr Sawyer witness the murder of your friend?" She sips her coffee.

"No. It's like this..." It only takes a few minutes but Luke manages to tell her the story of Mart as he sits in her patient's chair and she sits thoughtfully behind her desk.

"I can see why you would be so desperate," she remarks at the end of it. "And I am very sorry for your loss. The Keaton family – is there something I can do for them?"

"I think they are coping better this morning. And we're leaving soon." He glances at the mantle clock behind her. In one hour...

There is a knock on the door. The woman Duffy is beside it and tells the doctor she has an urgent patient waiting.

Luke deposits his cup and saucer on her desk and gets to his feet. "I'm sorry to have taken up your time." He reaches into his pocket for suitable remuneration and places this on her desk. "For the bell."

The doctor's eyes flash in surprise. "Oh. It was no trouble. Good luck, Mr Taylor."

As he passes Duffy waiting by the door he murmurs politely, "M'am..."

The woman surprises him with a strident chuckle. "M'am he drawls. Blue eyes an' all. Be gone with you before I swoon."

Luke remembers the two women from time to time on the journey home. Calling the doctor to mind calms him in his worst moments. *Good luck, Mr Taylor...* There is precious little luck in the world to his way of thinking.

Sometimes, and this is one of those times, he wonders what life would have been like if his family never left Texas. His father would probably be alive. And Katrine too, a lovely full-grown woman who looked like her Mama and with a loving family of her own.

Katrine should've had that; she deserved it.

He wouldn't know the Keatons or Ed Parsons or anyone here.

He'd be a Texan, and he wouldn't be watching his life being whittled away by things he can't control.

From the train window he watches Wyoming being swept by the Chinook, which is melting the snow till the next blizzard. It's blowing faster than the train.

FIVE

...for it is the fate of a woman
Long to be patient and silent, to wait
like a ghost that is speechless,
Till some questioning voice dissolves
the spell of its silence.

Henry Wadsworth Longfellow
The Courtship of Miles Standish

❧

Tressa

Omaha, Nebraska

Her father's voice surges across the room as ear-splitting waves of rage: "You defied me, you lied to me. You married that useless boy against my express wishes and now you want me to welcome this...this child you are expecting."

Mama clings to his arm. "Richard, show some compassion..."

Gripping the back of the chair for fear of falling, Tressa says, "Papa, h...how can you speak that way?" She can't control her trembling; she can barely breathe... her words are slurring. "I can't deny the man I love any longer. He deserves better, we all deserve better..."

"Silence!"

"He's gone now, Papa."

"I told you to be quiet. It is clear to me that you will have to leave."

"No," Mama cries.

"Leave?" Tressa gasps.

"Think what you are saying, Richard. This child will be our grandchild, our first grand..."

Her father's expression becomes so dark that even Mama reels. "Caroline, you and I have not recognized nor blessed the marriage."

"Nevertheless, the marriage is legal. Richard..."

"I will not have a daughter of mine defying us in this way and taking no accountability for her actions."

"All right. All right. You don't want me or my baby. I... I will go."

"No," Mama gasps.

"I cannot stay here..."

"Where will you go?" Mama reaches out her hand but her father pulls it away again.

"Where I will be wanted. Do you understand at all, Papa? Where I know I am wanted." Before her father begins yet another spurious tirade against her Uncle Morgan's family, against Luke and Aunt Sara and Ethan, she says, "I only hope that Ben will come to his senses..."

"You would encourage your brother to defy his parents, dishonor us?" her father says and spittle flies from his mouth.

She shakes her head weakly. "Not defy. Only demonstrate some independence of thought, freedom of spirit..."

"You have the utter gall to call your defiance independence and your licentious behavior freedom?"

"Whatever my actions have been, stupid and naïve certainly, only you, Papa, see them as defiant and licentious. Others, those who love me, will not. They will know, they will understand..."

"You were not raised this way," he shouts.

"Are you sure about that, Papa?"

"Oh, I am very sure about that," he says, mocking her.

"Then I am very sorry."

"Tressa..."

"Do not worry about me, Mama."

"I will worry and fret and..."

"No, you will not," her father snaps. "Now say goodbye and be done."

She cannot bear the grief on Mama's face for long; they don't speak; they acknowledge the tears in each other's eyes. As Tressa turns and leaves, Mama's cry is drowned out by her father's harsh rebuke.

Ben stands in the hall, his eyes narrowed against her. In spite of this, she smiles at him. "If only you knew your heritage, knew Luke... You have his eyes, though you don't know it yet; we both do. Our great great grandfather Matthew's eyes. To see the world in another way. I won't give up on you, Ben. No matter how long it takes."

Kelley

The snow finally contracted to the high country, leaving ample room for wildflowers to bloom in gorgeous array. The liberated grasses, sun-rich, sweet and juicy, stretch ever skywards. Aspen and cotton-wood have budded into leaf, already quaking on the wind. The River and its creeks have swollen to flood. The men are busy with the spring roundup, a testing time with a man like Ed Parsons for a neighbor. Even so, on a ranch or on the range, this is a cowboy's favorite time of year, where his expertise with horse and cattle shines, and the tenderfoot learns the ropes.

A cloud hangs over the beautiful and the busy.

The cool and constant wind sweeps across the Bright River graveyard, which sits on the high ground behind the church commanding a view to horizon of the green-gold plains beyond.

Crouching beside Mart's grave, she places a fistful of wildflower blooms against the headstone. With her finger she traces the writing, not so very long engraved into the stone, and engraves them onto her heart:

In loving memory
MARTIN JOHN KEATON
Born June 22, 1857
Died March 5, 1884
At Peace

Mart made his choices, and they live with them.

She stands, the wind tugging on her clothes. She turns her face into it and looks out across the fields. Her Mama has tired of the wind and has retreated to the buggy just outside the cemetery gates, while her Pa, who today has lost interest in spring roundup, walked into town for no distinct purpose, leaving her alone with Mart.

Acceptance of God's will for Mart is a bitter pill to swallow; choking on it is a prospect never too far away, so these broken hearts decided to use life's rhythm and the monotony of days in order to keep on beating; these broken spirits decided to look to Spring as a symbol of hope, and they decided to refuse to go under. Decisions made over agony of hours, days, weeks... her parents so distraught she almost floundered in a sea of uselessness. At last, what would Mart have her say to them?

Some good will come from this, is what she told them.

So, they made their decisions and now they travel the journey of grief together, waiting when one or other falls behind, because alone there is only unspeakable dismay; no promise of new life.

She wipes tears from her cheeks with the back of her gloved hand. *What secrets do you keep, Mart? What do we need to know? Where do we find the answers?* The wind swoops down and across the plain like the immortal custodian of some ancient mystery.

Sundays seem to be the worst day of the week; it is good then that Sara often invites them to lunch or supper. She welcomes them warmly and has Ethan (who tries to be buoyant) and Tip on hand to help out. Luke is remote but not indifferent. Kelley longs to compensate for her inadequacy in Cheyenne, but he speaks very little to her and they rarely find themselves alone together.

This Sunday everyone manages to portray a lighter mood. There is just such a huge hole in their existence, such bewilderment over how it came to be this way, and more than a little anxiety waiting for Cutter to show up. Towards the end of the meal, Luke excuses himself with the intention of line riding Diamond Pass.

Disappointed, Kelley watches him stand.

"Excellent idea," says Sara. "Take Kelley with you."

They both gape at her.

"You both spend too much time alone. Go along now," she adds as though they are children and the grown-ups want to talk.

"I'm not dressed for it," Kelley points out.

"Well, that's never stopped you before," Ethan says.

"In the chest in my room there are some fine riding clothes that don't get used nearly as much as they should," Sara says. "Luke will wait for you at the stables."

She hears Luke's resigned sigh as he strides from the room.

With or without appropriate clothes, Luke has no intention of ambling. They ride apace for much of the way, with a spell at the River to water the horses, until they reach the mouth of Diamond Pass. They have not spoken a word.

Morgan Taylor named Diamond Pass many years ago, before Ed Parsons cut sway through their beautiful district. It is indeed a breathtaking place, a natural pass from one side of the range to the other. The pass itself belongs to the Diamond-T, although the base of the northern slope forms part of the boundary with Ed Parsons' property.

Tired of their silence, she slows her mount to a civilized walk. Luke appears to notice after a moment and turns back. He draws level with her, his face like a cranky question mark. She absorbs his attention with great satisfaction.

"There are other legends in Liberty and Property that are hardly ever told," she says, "and the one that features Ed Parsons they prefer not to tell. However, in terms of Luke's heritage it is highly significant."

"What are you doing?" he snaps.

"Ed Parsons is not the original owner of his large and ever-growing parcel of land. Many years ago some of it belonged to Nathaniel Collins and some of it to partners Morgan Taylor and Ethan Benchley. The owners had a serious dispute over water rights to the River. To solve their disagreement they redrew the internal boundaries of their respective properties so that both had equal access to water. Diamond Pass was to remain open. Let me know if I'm incorrect about anything, won't you?"

Luke grunts and keeps his eyes straight. He might not want to, but he's listening.

"Not long after this, Nathaniel wanted to raise funds to make improvements to his ranch, so he retained the best of his property and decided to sell off a substantial parcel in the north.

"Morgan and Ethan in turn decided to consolidate their best acres, so both parties sold the northern sections of their property to an eager buyer. That eager buyer was Ed Parsons and he proceeded to rankle about access to the River. The River does not flow through these northern parts; a tributary does, however, and the extensive high pastures are dotted with tarns, which are both picturesque and practical.

"All the relevant landowners, the Taylors and the Benchleys, Nathaniel Collins and John Keaton, have had written contracts with Ed Parsons regarding Ed's entitlement to their water. Ed paid the handsome price begrudgingly, but always wanting more for it.

"However, as my father informed me, when the contracts came up for renewal two years ago the landowners refused to renew. Apparently, Ed and all the fuss he generated were not worth the income produced by the contract.

"Morgan Taylor passed on in '69, not long after my mother's cousin, Nathaniel Collins, was killed by itinerant hostiles, and although it was rough and under-developed at the time of their deaths, the legacy they both left behind was rich and enduring."

She and Luke saunter through the opening of the pass, but such is the awesome beauty of the place, history and disputes are quickly forgot. Peaks shooting up like church spirals command the land-scape. The imposing majesty is softened by the generous, sloping grassland, and trees offering shade and shelter from the sun and weather.

As a young girl, Kelley ventured here only once or twice, and only to the opening. Even she was humbled by its splendor. She feared she would be lost forever if she entered.

Their old friend Ozark use to call Diamond Pass 'Luke's sacred site' because Luke revered it so. Ozark used to tell her stories about the 'real' owners of the canyon and how sacred it was to them too. Luke's cattle found it special also – the pasturing here said to be some of the best in the whole region.

And now, some years on, as she is permitted to tag along, she views this sacred place not with childish self-satisfaction but with an almost desperate desire to understand the one who holds it sacred.

There is no human to be seen as they ascend the lower reaches of the gorge, still dotted with patches of icy snow.

They move on; the sides rise vertically, perhaps thirty feet of rock worn by wind and water. The trees are old, their thick trunks and huge billowing branches adding to the magnificence of the pass. It is not so very wide here – a few hundred yards across at most – and the large trees and scattered boulders narrow it further. But as it cuts back it broadens and climbs, spanning out into a grassy crest that is perfect for grazing a small herd while offering the beasts some shelter. As they approach this section, they come across the herd – mothers and calves grazing peacefully. Spring has been busy here and the thaw complete, for there is sweet and juicy grass aplenty. The walls now are barely ten feet high. The air is cool and thin, the light sharp. This is the summit of the pass, this rich pasture, and visible on the other side is a spectacular view to the north, including Ed Parsons' property.

Her Pa liked to describe Diamond Pass as 'high, wide and handsome'. And indeed it is. Beyond even her expectations.

"Luke, it is truly splendid," she says and regains his attention with this remark.

"Well, I wish I could take the credit for it."

He continues to push on gently through the herd, which includes many calves, all with a fresh diamond-T on their young flanks. As the herd dramatically begins to thin out, Kelley realizes they are heading down the other side towards the boundary with Parsons. On the way down, following the slope, are a handful of mothers and calves, stubbornly grazing away from the main herd and seeking their own juicy patch. This side of the pass is not as bountiful as its southern sister, and it ends in rocky terrain and weathered boulders, which Ethan once told her stray cattle some-how still manage to negotiate if not coerced back up. *Ornery things'd rather climb over rocks than turn around and stroll back up. Well, cowboys are dang ornery too…*

They are nearing the bottom. Luke draws to a halt. Kelley does the same and they sit and survey the massive spread of Parsons' mustering cattle to the north.

"Are we looking at something in particular?" she asks.

Luke

"Ed Parsons' beef."

"Apart from Ed Parsons' beef."

She is being patient, quiet and unbearably demure. Without him saying much of anything she has already shared this special place with him for the first time. He is aware that her feelings towards him have changed yet again. She doesn't struggle with them; not like before.

"Luke, I really want to know."

He gives her a hard look. Deliberately. It is a test that she fails because she looks away and he senses that she is unsure.

"Sara is right," she says. "We do spend too much time alone. We bottle our grief and guard it jealously. Who grieves more deeply? Who hurts more, who has lost more... I would never presume to grieve for Mart more than you."

"I don't want to talk about Mart," he says.

Her eyes flash at him. "Then tell me what we are looking at apart from Ed Parsons' beef, or I will go mad."

He swallows, yet his throat remains tight. "I come here Sunday afternoons, except when I am away from the ranch..."

K brings around the young mare she's riding.

"Of that I am jealous," she says with a glint in her eye.

They are face to face. He must be businesslike, detached.

"What do you want from me, K?"

After a moment she says, "I think we need each other, Luke."

Six months ago if she had said this he'd be dancing, but six months ago the world was a different place. He has no intention of being gentle with her. "The only thing I need, K, is to find Mart's murderer and bring him to justice."

She steadies her mount. "I can help you."

"No."

"Don't tell me that it is not my place. My place is with you, to do this for Mart."

"Partners," he sneers. "You and me?"

Her expression freezes and she is staring at him. With mounting curiosity he returns her gaze.

"I will do whatever you want me to do. Just don't…"

"Don't what?" he prompts, admitting she is getting to him.

"Don't renege… or give up on me because I don't understand or I don't do things your way."

In spite of himself, he can't help grinning. "Well, maybe I should give you a little test. See if you're up to the task."

"Don't make me pledge allegiance to the Alliance," comes tumbling out of her mouth.

"Ah," he murmurs, nodding thoughtfully. "You seem to be putting forward a lot of conditions, K. I can't renege, I can't give up on you, I can't misunderstand you, I can't be in charge and I can't count on your loyalty."

She mutters hotly, "Damn you, Taylor."

This is more like her; the part of her he prefers.

"Thank you," he returns, his grin widening. She looks fed up. Now is the time to see if she is genuine. He clears his throat. "Let me know if I go too fast for you…"

"There is no need to be rude…"

"The bill of sale made between my father and Connors states that Diamond Pass must remain open. It can't be fenced, even though me and Ethan are in the process of fencing the Diamond-T. These rocks here, even they are kinda pushing the limits of the agreement, but we had to do something. Most of them were here in any case, we just rearranged them to stop Ed's raids on the pastures up on the summit. We'd go to graze a herd up there only to find Ed had moved in a herd of his own. They weren't happy occasions. As for the pass, I don't know why it has to stay open. Even Ethan says he doesn't know. It must have been some private deal, but it stands, all legal and binding, because it's a part of the original surveyor's charts that make up the bill of sale which constitute the official deed of ownership."

She interrupts with a question: "But why are you fencing? Pa has been doing the same and I don't get it."

"It's true, natural boundaries used to be good enough for every-one. Even Ed, although he always pushed them. Of late, however, he's been waging war on those boundaries and it seems the only explanation is that he's greedy and wants what he can't have. Our greenest grass and our strategic water supply. Not that he needs it – as you well know, he's got plenty of his own, I mean, just look at it. But, he'll try and convince you different. Lots of ranches are fenced these days, and homesteaders want to keep ranchers out, ranchers want to keep sheepherders out, and not everyone's got hills, gullies, rivers, creeks and mountains like we do. But *we* fence as a tactic to try to keep Ed at heel, frustrate him, stop him. He never did like playing second fiddle to men like your Pa and Ethan, or even me. He's got vested interests out on the range and elsewhere but he wants more. Wants a lot more. The River and our exceptional pastures are the most important possessions we got and I want them to stay that way – ours. Are you with me so far?"

She presses her lips together, which amuses him. "I believe I am."

"The current agreement for this northern boundary is that Parsons' foreman has to let me know when Parsons' herd will be down here and I have to keep the pass clean of his stock."

"Tricky."

"Mm. You can probably guess that Ed don't make much of an effort to keep his cattle out." Luke cranes his neck to view the near horizon. "One of his boys should be doing sentry duty… ah, there he is. Off in the distance. It's probably Carmichael. It's his day. At least there shouldn't be any trouble."

"This sentry duty is separate from the Alliance," she says, turning her horse to see for herself.

"Well, mainly it's to do with the bill of sale. But the Alliance between your family and mine was formed to protect both our interests from Ed. To help each other. Your father and I won't fence our properties from each other and, with round up being an exercise in mutual cooperation, natural boundaries seem to be good enough for what's left of our southern neighbors."

"Yes, I know. North, south, a kind of civil war," she remarks.

"Mm, and I suppose I'm to put up with your wisecracks in this partnership," he retorts.

To his surprise she looks contrite.

"You know, K," he chuckles, "I'm almost enjoying this." He ignores any reaction she might have and turns his attention on another figure, loping on horseback across the distant landscape. This figure catches up to the first and they stop to confab.

"Now what?" she asks.

"That's Ed down there jawing with Carmichael. Know that shape anywhere. Looks like we got more than we bargained for."

The two men are riding in their direction now.

"I haven't see Ed Parsons for years," she says.

"You've changed a lot more than he has." Luke secures his hat. "Come on." He heads off in the direction of the riders and she follows. They halt in the center of the border strip, which is barren and lifeless, a no man's land entirely devoid of grass, comprised of all sorts of rocks and gravel and boulders, and slightly treacherous underfoot. The cold wind blows hard here without shelter of any kind.

He notices that the second rider cuts away from Ed and rides back the way he had come.

K is busily splitting her vision between the two riders. "What can that be about?"

"We'll know soon enough."

Kelley

Soon enough, they come face to face with Ed Parsons. Indeed, his appearance has changed very little in six years. His stocky build, silver hair and round face make the perfect cover for a mean and relentless nature because, if he were not the bane of Bright River, he could be someone's grandfather; if only.

He and Luke glare at one another silently.

"Ed," Luke murmurs eventually.

"Taylor," Ed returns. There is an edge to the silky smooth patience in his voice; it raises the hairs on the back of her neck.

"K, you remember Ed," Luke says.

"Of course."

"Ed, you remember Mart's sister."

Ed's eyes switch to her face. "Miss Keaton, I wouldn't have recognized you."

"I'd know you anywhere, Mr Parsons. How are you?"

Ed's eyes sparkle; then he chuckles, a sly tone, again belying his appearance. "Well, I am just fine, thank you."

"So, Ed, to what do we owe the privilege?" Luke asks.

"No reason," he replies. "Thought I'd check out the pass myself today."

"Nothing's changed, Ed. This is still private property and I don't recall inviting you…"

"It's been checked," Kelley says quickly.

After a sharp glance her way, Luke steadies his horse.

Ed chuckles again. "How many strays would you count, Miss Keaton?"

"There are no strays to count. In fact, every flank wears the diamond-T."

"Now how do I know you are telling the truth?"

"What reason would I have to lie?"

"Is there nothing else, Ed?" Luke asks almost before she finishes.

Ed looks at them in turn. "No. I don't think so."

A wind gust, straight off the mountains, tears at them. She shudders, chilled to the bone.

"Good day, Miss Keaton," Ed says urbanely.

He turns his horse and moves off. Kelley takes note of the cold expression on Luke's face as he watches Ed negotiate his way back through the borderland. She also turns her horse, expecting Luke to do the same. Instead, he seems miles away.

"Luke. It's cold here."

His eyes come abruptly to her face. "What was that, K?"

"It was the truth."

"What do you really want from me?"

"Do you think so little of me, Luke? That I have no feeling or loyalty to my father, or to you?"

She rides away from him, heading for the shelter of the pass. In the upper reaches she slows her mare to a walk. There are cattle about. By a huge boulder she spots a young calf on the ground and its distressed mother nearby. Riding over, she sees that the calf lies limp and still. She dismounts and inspects the animal; it's not breathing. The mother moans as if to tell Kelley what she can see for herself; her calf has just died. Kelley kneels and takes the calf's head on her lap, stroking its soft face.

"Poor baby," she murmurs.

The mother punctures the air with a mournful call.

Luke rides up. Aware that he will want to inspect the animal for himself, she relinquishes the calf and stands up. In seconds he is beside her.

"Shame," she commiserates.

Without warning, she is hauled against him, tight up to his chest. "I want a straight answer this time. What do you want from me?"

It is not an unpleasant experience.

"The calf is…"

He kisses her none too gently; she understands his aim is to expose her motives or spleen his frustration, but she takes it gladly, trying to soften him towards her.

When he ends it as abruptly as he started it, they stare at one another. Perhaps now he has the answer to his question.

"What about what I want?" he asks.

"I thought you wanted this once."

"I seem to remember you saying…"

"I was wrong."

"And so was I, then. We're too much alike."

"No, it was my fault. I was confused. And being alike is considered a good thing."

"We stopped being children to one another last Fall."

"That's probably true."

"That's *all* that happened."

"I was *wrong* last Fall, self-obsessed, and I should have tried. We won't know if we don't try…"

"Last Fall was last Fall. Things are different now," he says and lets her go.

"I understand you now."

There's no mistaking the hurt in his eyes, even if she's not the cause of it. "I always understood *you*."

She is unsure if that is really true, but she refuses to beg any further. He crouches at her feet and attends to the calf while she stands in a shaky daze. Then he heaves the calf's limp body into his arms and drapes it over his horse, which patiently accepts the additional load. He takes a rope and lassos the distraught mother, giving her a long leash and securing the other end around his saddle horn.

"You coming?" he asks as he swings himself into the saddle.

Luke

One week later

The outfit is cutting calves from the main herd for branding, with a couple of the men maintaining the branding irons on a neat, very hot fire. They are about three miles south of home and it's been a long morning. Even though the sun is shining, it struggles to give effective warmth while the wind blows from the north; the men had drawn straws for firing the irons. Luke spots Ethan riding in as if he's got Apache on his tail. Ethan signals that he wants to talk and Luke removes himself from the melee of cattle and men to meet him.

"What's up?" he asks.

"Your mother wanted me to talk to you."

"Now?" Luke searches his face for some clue.

"Now's as good a time as any. Aw, don't look at me like that."

Luke unwinds the leather strap of his canteen from his saddle apple. He uncaps the canteen. "Like what?" he asks and takes a satisfying draft.

"You know how Sara is."

Luke gulps and laughs. "Yes, Ethan. I know how Sara is. She gets you to tell me what she thinks I won't listen to if she tells me."

Ethan's brow quivers. "Right."

"Well?" he asks and has another drink.

"We were talking, Sara mostly."

Luke looks around at the progress of the branding party.

"Go on…"

"Son, I'm supposed to give you the *it's time you settled down* speech."

He turns back again. "Like the one you gave me when I got back from San Francisco?"

"I hated doin' that," Ethan mutters. "Had to 'cause it was part of the deal for lettin' you go off in the first place."

"Appreciate that, Ethan. Go on..."

"Well, you're twenty-six years old. Ain't you old enough to know your own mind?"

"A body'd reckon. Come on, Ethan, just give it to me straight up. Let's get it over with, then you can report back to Sara that you've done it."

Ethan chuckles. "I like the sound of that." Then he clears his throat. "Luke..."

"Yes, Ethan?"

"It's time you found yourself a wife and settled down. This ranch needs stability, and a future. Sara and me, we ain't gonna be around forever..."

"You going somewhere, Ethan?" A particularly stubborn calf captures his attention.

"Be serious. This is important. Now Sara and me think that there's a woman who's perfect for you..."

"I think there is too, but there ain't a snowball's chance in hell of ever..."

"Aw, Kelley ain't like that really. She's just..."

Luke jerks his head to look at him. "K! You want me to marry K?"

Ethan seems surprised that he is surprised and swallows hard. "Well, who are... Sara thinks... Well, you love her, don't you?"

"K?"

Not even last Fall had he thought of marrying her. Even K's proposition the other day hadn't put marriage in his head. He's not even sure how much you have to love a woman to want marriage. To *survive* a lifelong commitment like marriage...

"Don't you?"

Love K? "Well, I...I guess I do, in a way," he says honestly. "But..." Marriage?

Ethan looks satisfied. "Well, there you see."

Luke stares at him, astounded, not knowing what else to say.

"Sometimes it just takes admitting to your feelings to get things going," Ethan continues. "Sara and me see how you two are together. She thinks Kelley's perfect for you."

"Ethan, I don't love K the way... *that* way. And she don't love me – *that* way. It's a game. She wants... something from me, but it ain't that, believe me." Doesn't anyone understand her the way he does?

Ethan gives him a sheepish look. "Sara thinks she does love you. Besides, there's the way you care for her. Look out for her. Almost know what's happening to her before she does. Sara says you have a connection."

Sara would. Luke secures his canteen and adjusts his hat. "I've got work to do. If I fall in love with K I'll let you know. So long, Ethan." Luke canters away and doesn't look back.

Marriage. Don't you have to be compatible for that?

Maybe he should be married, maybe he's at that age, but to K? He's distracted for the rest of the job and when he eventually returns to the ranch house, he avoids Sara till supper and then makes sure she knows he doesn't want to talk. They end the day with hardly a word spoken between them.

The following morning he eats breakfast before dawn, and then packs the wagon with provisions and the necessary tools and equipment for a job that everyone has been putting off for a long time. Fencing Bear Paw Marsh, a substantial wetland that drains Little Bear Creek in the northwest section of the Diamond-T.

About one third of it – up to and including the low mesa-like mound where the ducks roost – graces Ed's property, and the shyster has no qualms about borrowing the Diamond-T's two-thirds in summer when it's hot and he's looking to cool his cattle, which he allows to trample the peaceful place into a mud wallow. Mosquitoes repopulate the earth from the marsh in summer, so Ed's boys hate it. Luke is plain fed up. And in the mood for riling Ed.

He tells Ethan where he's going.

"Got your waders, son?" Ethan says, rubbing sleep out of his eyes.

"Got 'em."

"Got the putrid stuff to repel the mosquitoes?"

"Yep."

"The surveyor's map?"

"Got it."

"You'll need a hand," Ethan continues, reaching for his hat. He looks comical in his red woolen long johns, bare feet and his hat.

"No, I'll be fine."

"Well, watch out for low flying ducks."

"I will."

Ethan gives him a look of uncertainty. "You ain't mad at me about… you know…"

"Don't want to talk about it, Ethan."

Ethan nods. "Fine."

"Back for supper."

By mid-morning, he has five posts dotting a line from the highest point on the eastern side to about half way across the marsh, his posts leap-frogging the water. He has dug holes from twelve to eighteen inches deep in various points of high ground, jammed in the posts and back-filled with rock, dirt and river sand. He stops for coffee and sandwiches, appraises the scene, checks and rechecks his surveyor's map. He makes a mental note to clean up what he's disturbed when he's finished. The constant quacking is getting to him. And other birds tend to fly out of the reeds and long grass making his heart jump. Still, it's peaceful enough.

By the time the sun has passed overhead and it is early afternoon, he has completed the western half and now a long row of poles divides the sprawling marsh in two. His back is killing him and his body screams stop. But his mind needs this diversion. Needs it for too many reasons.

All that is left to do is thread the wire. Some men insist this is the worst part because it goes against the grain of the old time cowboy to fence anything other than a corral. Bane of the prairies, Ethan calls it.

As he commences unloading the coils of barbed wire from the wagon, he catches movement from the corner of his eye – a rider, approaching at a leisurely pace. He sorts through his coils until the horse and rider get close enough to identify.

Kelley

As Kelley rides towards her destination, she spies a long row of poles laced across Bear Paw Marsh, the mesa-mound behind. Almost at once they strike her as symbolic, while incorporating the complex and determined character of their architect into the landscape. Her Pa liked to say one of Luke's best qualities is that he's not afraid of hard work, to take on a challenge. This other side of Luke was hidden from her; no – she must be honest – she refused to see any other person but the one that it suited her to see. Of course, she is not about to idealize him – she may have overlooked his good points, but she has never been mistaken about the maddening ones; they definitely remain in the mix.

He is sorting barbed wire coils as she brings Dancer into his camp of wagon, tools, wire and everything else imaginable. He is as surprised to see her as she is sheepish about being there. Still, she is pleased when he leaves his wire and holds Dancer's bridle while she dismounts. He looks wet and tired, and ready for a long hot bath and a soothing rub with some of her Mama's famous lavender oil.

"You've been busy," she greets him.

He looks across the wetland at his poles with a grin on his face. He seems proud of them. Then he says, "You're not someone I was expecting…"

"Well, I went to visit Sara, to take her some of Mama's herbs. Is something wrong, because she gives me this…" she reaches into her pocket for the telegram she has been sent to deliver… "and tells me where I can find you and would I give it to you."

He takes the telegram. "You could've refused. This ain't exactly on your way…"

"She wasn't of a mind to have me refuse. She's sent food as well."

He is studying her and she finds it extremely unnerving.

She moves away and makes a show of admiring his poles.

"A good day's work," she remarks. "Don't know what Ed will say. A little provocative, don't you think?"

He comes to her side. "You know I don't care about Ed's opinion."

She glances up at his face. "Yes." Back at the poles. "Open your telegram."

She leaves him reading and unpacks the saddlebag of food from Sara. She can see for herself that Luke has packed himself plenty of provisions, so she's not at all sure why he needed more.

Luke joins her at the wagon, wearing a puzzled frown.

"Everything all right?" she asks casually.

"Not sure. I'll have to go to Cheyenne tomorrow."

She hides her disappointment by inspecting the packages of Sara's food. Fried chicken. Biscuits. Pie. A flask of lemonade. Picnic food. Well, if he is not expecting her, then it has to be somebody.

"I think you're supposed to stay and help me eat it," he says.

"Me...?"

He gives a polite chuckle. "K..."

She is determined to meet his eyes this time; she also clamps her hands on her waist. "Yes?"

"Anyone who can ride all this way to appreciate a row of poles deserves a helping of chicken and lemonade," he says. "If you decide where we should eat, I'll go wash up." He tosses his hat into the wagon with his gloves and heads off to the water.

She chooses a place away from the marsh, a sunny, sweet-smelling patch of grass and wildflowers. But she is too nervous to eat properly and there is an awkward silence between them. They had more to say to one another in the days when she harbored undying hatred.

"What's the matter, K?" It is a genuine inquiry; nothing flippant about it, and he swallows rather obviously to utter it.

"Nothing."

"I apologize for the other day, I'm sorry..."

She gets to her feet. "I'm not in the mood for chicken. If you have extra gear I'll help you with the fence."

"Sure, if you want. There's another pair of waders in the wagon. You'll need britches."

"I'll manage," she says and returns to the camp to find what she needs. Her split skirt, although good for riding, is not appropriate for wading through a marsh. Rummaging through the gearbox in the wagon she finds an old pair of trousers. She changes into them behind a thick clump of bushes, cinching the waist with her belt. Luke is waiting for her by the wagon. He is holding the long rubber waders and hands them to her. As she steps into them, he explains exactly what they are going to do. Then he puts a pair of thick canvas gloves in her hands and tells her to follow him.

The water is freezing cold, and the barbed wire is hideous stuff; she is extremely finicky about how she touches it. Meanwhile, the frustration of manipulating tools is mounting.

"I'm holding you up," she says after she drops the pliers in the water for the third time.

Luke, strangely patient and good-humored, dries them off and hands them back, saying, "No; honestly, I appreciate your help."

After this, she begins to relax. She drops nothing and actually appears to be lending some effective assistance. Conversation, mostly about what they are doing, begins to flow. They even make jokes. Duck jokes. Luke tells Mart's three best jokes. The presence of laughter between them is odd.

As the sun begins its afternoon descent, they have spun a line of wire across the bottom and half way across the top. When the light around them softens to violet, they have completed the fencing of Bear Paw Marsh.

They wade out of the water and admire their work.

"A thing of beauty," Luke murmurs.

Time to change.

When she returns from the bushes, the wagon is packed up and Luke is hobbling Dancer to the back of it.

"What are you doing?" she asks.

"Taking you home."

"That's not necessary," she tells him and unties Dancer's reins.

"You're tired, it's a long way and it's almost dark."

"Yes, I know that…"

"K…"

"It's not…"

"We can eat the rest of the food and watch the stars come out…"

His suggestion is not romantic, nor improper, as the words may imply. Watching the stars appear in the night sky like bright jewels and naming them, even making up names themselves, was something she and Mart and Luke and Tip did frequently as children. The wonder and beauty of the natural world absorbed them; breathing or their hearts beating could not have been more natural.

Nevertheless, she says, "My father will go insane."

He laughs. "Well, I reckon Sara will tell him you're safe with me…"

He takes her hand and immediately she flinches; it is sore from the wire. Abruptly, he lets go.

"Sara and your folks," he begins gently, "they want this…"

With her heart pounding against her ribs, she murmurs, "But it's not what you want. You made that clear."

"I was rough with you. I'm sorry…"

"You don't trust me, you think me capable of manipulating the situation."

"Is that how I've been treating you today?"

"No," she admits. "But you do think I want something from you…"

He doesn't answer right away. Then, "You want in when it comes to getting Mart justice."

"That's not what this is about…"

"K, it's been a long day; I don't want to end it with us at loggerheads."

He's not hearing her. Or doesn't want to. Old Luke.

She swallows and says, "Nor I with you. I've decided I like it better when we're not fighting."

"K…"

"For you this is an apology…"

"That's not entirely true. I…"

"…but for me it's another opportunity to understand you, to reach you."

"K, when it comes to Mart I can't be got."

At that she catches her breath. She is fully aware she is not the manipulative, worldly type who would know exactly *how* to get him (but neither does she think she ought to be, since she has always despised girls like that).

And at this moment they are a bundle of misunderstandings.

The irony is that he is also right; she does want in when it comes to getting justice for Mart.

How to get the two things she wants most is a challenge; after all, Luke has been her nemesis from the start. How does she break his thinking without breaking herself?

She unties Dancer from the wagon while he silently looks on. She mounts and, careful to keep even a trace of bitterness out of her tone, says, "I wasn't referring to Mart; I wish you would believe that. Thank you for an enjoyable afternoon. I always did harbor a notion to work on the Diamond-T. Goodnight, Luke."

She rides into the cool, fragrant dusk. If he is ever to reciprocate her feelings for him – if she is to rekindle that spark which began with his sweet offer of protection last Fall, the one she foolishly rebuffed – she must work to gain his trust, show him that her motives are pure.

Tressa

Cheyenne
the following day

On her way to the dining room of the Cheyenne Hotel, Tressa is handed a telegram by the desk clerk. She reads it at once.

"Thank God."

"Are you all right, M'am?" the desk clerk inquires.

She shivers a nod and goes on her way.

Breakfast is easier to eat; a little scrambled egg, small piece of toast, hot cup of tea...

She takes a walk after, away from the business district to an intersection with a church on every corner but one, then returns to her room and lies down, staring at the ceiling. A wave of nausea comes over her. She rushes down the hall to the bathroom and promptly loses her breakfast. She washes her face and hopes to revive herself with a short nap. But she cannot rest. She leaves her room and walks down the street to the opera house. It is an elegant stone building – Cheyenne has several elegant buildings, but apart from the curiosity they stimulate, the town doesn't interest her. Nothing can in this no man's land she haunts. Luke is her last hope.

The train is on time. She watches impatiently for him to step out. Then she espies his tall, strong frame with those shoulders set in that utterly reliable demeanor, savors his resolute expression, and feels hope rise from the ashes of her existence.

After greeting her with the love and concern of an older brother, he walks with her back to the Cheyenne Hotel. He doesn't seem to notice anything different about her since they last saw one another.

She asks him questions about Aunt Sara and Kelley, about the Keatons, Ethan and Tip, and the Diamond-T. He gives her typically male answers, short and not very newsy, although he mentions that they are coping best they can with Mart's death. She accompanies him as he checks in at the hotel and settles himself in his room.

"I'm hungry, how about you?" he says.

She has never known Luke not to be hungry, but the thought of food sends her reeling. Nevertheless, they eat in the dining room and eventually he looks her in the eye with the obvious question forming on his lips.

"I will tell you, Luke, but may we walk? I need some fresh air."

"Tress, you look tired and I think you should lie down."

"No. I need to walk," she insists. He eyes her curiously, then yields to her request.

She tells him her story as they walk. Very soon she realizes that this is a mistake because his step falters; he must stop. She watches him draw an agonized breath. People speculate and murmur as they pass by. Oblivious, he stares at her; shock has set in and she doesn't know what to do. His dismay becomes hers, freshened, doubled. Everything around her swirls and blurs.

"I'm sorry, Luke, I'm so sorry..."

But she can speak no longer. She collapses in a faint, into his arms.

Luke

"She's in good hands, my lad." A stern but good-hearted attempt at sympathy from that woman Duffy.

Where else should he bring a sick female but to a kind, smart female doctor?

"I know," he mutters. In actual fact, Luke knows little about the green-eyed Doctor Sullivan with the chestnut hair, but his instinct about her tells him plenty. Enough to entrust Tressa to her care. Besides, the way Cliff referred to her on his last visit to Cheyenne is a good enough recommendation; Cliff's judgment is eerily flawless.

He twirls his hat in his hands, staring at the floorboards. A woman and her daughter enter, distracting him. They speak to Duffy and sit down, eyeing him curiously.

The doctor finally appears under the arch and he studies her expression for clues about Tressa. She gives him a brief glance and then asks Duffy to show the woman and girl into her consultation room. She tells them she won't be long. Once they have left with Duffy, Dr Sullivan sits down in the chair next to his.

"Well?" he asks.

"You told me her name is Taylor. She tells me it is Keaton."

"Yes..." he murmurs and swallows awkwardly. "Keaton. It...it would be..."

"She has the marriage certificate in her purse. Mr Taylor, you look a little pale..."

Every time this woman sees him he looks pale – and acts like he hasn't got a rational bone in his body. "I'm fine. What's wrong with her?"

His question ignites a green spark in her eye. "This is a delicate matter..."

"Go on."

"Your cousin is expecting a baby."

"A baby?" he squawks.

"Yes, Mr Taylor."

"Holy sh… I mean… sorry, I don't know what I mean." He leans forward and rubs his eyes with a shaky hand. "I did notice she looked kinda tired, but…"

"Mm, shall I go on?"

"Should you? – I mean, am I supposed to know… details?"

"I always encourage people to be open and honest about such things. It is after all a natural part of life. And in this case, it would be far more helpful than propriety."

He'd rather help Tressa, he knows that much. Even if his insides feel as pale the outside looks. And since Mart ain't here… Shakily, he says, "Say what you need to say."

"Very well. I've examined her thoroughly and everything is progressing well. She is carrying relatively small and compact, which is not all that unusual for a first baby, concealing it well, I think. She is experiencing the normal symptoms. Nausea, light-headedness, fatigue, although these usually go away after three months. Mrs Keaton it seems is part of a select group of women who experience prolonged morning sickness, in some cases for as long as the entire length of their pregnancy. They need extra care so they receive the nutrition and rest both mother and baby require. Mrs Keaton is a little slimmer than I would like her to be, but of greater concern to me, however, is that she appears to be under great strain…"

He looks up, hoping she's done with the details, wondering what Tressa would think about him knowing them. "Can I see her?"

"Of course. Are you sure you are well?"

"It's just shock. I'm fine."

"Then I believe your cousin will be very pleased to see you. What… what I wanted to say though…"

He should've guessed the details were leading up to something. He looks at her expectantly.

"I know that what has happened is none of my business, but I can see that it is very painful for you both. However, in your cousin's condition, losing her husband, the terrible strain she is suffering, I believe that without your full support she will become melancholy, and melancholia is a grievous condition that is not good for her or her baby. She won't disclose the whereabouts of her family so I..."

He turns in his chair to level his eyes with hers. All leading up to this... "She will have the support and care she needs."

Dr Sullivan watches him as if her thoughts have run ahead of her speech. "No matter what?"

That instinct he feels about her alerts him to the depth of her compassion for Tressa's predicament. He clears his throat and looks down at his hands. *Widows and orphans...* He recalls the day his father died. Sara had said, *what is to become of us now?* – and for a long time he felt the nagging uncertainty.

He clears his throat again. "No matter what."

"Then, in the midst of so much pain, there might be room to be happy for her. This child is a great gift."

"Happy?" he exclaims and faces her again.

"How rare is it that when one precious life is taken, there is another almost immediately to ease the loss," she says, and smiles, at the sight of which he loses concentration. She appears to notice and the smile disappears.

He waits dumbly while she rallies.

"Take as much time as you need with her. And, I would like to have her stay here overnight so I can observe her condition more closely. Good day, Mr Taylor."

As he watches her stride across the waiting room and disappear into her wacky examination room with the potbelly stove, he wonders why talking with her feels like someone else is in control of his life.

Sara

Sara thinks of him at dusk every day without fail.

Morgan.

He loved to say that dusk was the best time of day. When the fading light signaled an end to the rigors of the day. A space for living between work and sleep.

And when Luke is away, and she is alone, her pangs of melancholy for Morgan intensify because she must think about both of them. Two very different men. Although in one respect they are very much alike. Luke is no more settled than Morgan was; outwardly it might seem the boy is entrenched in ranch life, that he is following his bloodline, but appearances can be deceiving. She knows how profoundly restless her son feels because they often differ so about his future; on the days that concern her most, his abilities seem to stretch way beyond the boundaries of the Diamond-T. Ethan keeps insisting that Luke's bloodline isn't ranching at all, that it's frontier, revolution and adventure...

"...and he's smarter than all of us put together - how do propose to keep all that cooped up on this ranch forever?"

But she is convinced, even if Ethan is not, that Luke will settle when he is married to the right woman, a bright, loving wife who understands this life, who will keep him true to Morgan's legacy with a stake in the future of this territory.

With the last of daylight gone, she returns inside and begins preparation of her lonesome meal. Waiting for Luke to return from one of his adventures has been a serious occupation since he was a very small and self-sufficient boy. She gave up chasing after him and let him explore the world to his heart's content – with a few definite rules that for the most part he obeyed; his education, the most important rule, which because he was smart and tended to be curious about everything, he kept up without much coercion.

Ethan said he should be sent East to college, but she couldn't bear to have him leave her for that long. He would never have come home again. He went to San Francisco anyhow, and got himself a higher education there, if only for a year. At least he came home. She half expected he would leave again, East this time, but he didn't.

Keeping herself busy in this period of waiting helps to numb her concerns, but it's never easy, particularly right at this moment with him gone to Cheyenne without explanation, and annoyed with her to boot. So, she focuses her thoughts on how the unlikely alliance between her son and John's daughter can be brought about.

They have always disliked each other. Well, in truth, Luke never really disliked Kelley; he reacted to her resentment of him. Sara had spent a good deal of time, when the Keatons first moved on to the Collins property, telling Luke that little girls who idolized their big brothers were bound to resent an interloper, and that he should be very patient with her and she would come around eventually. Well, the bold little creature didn't come around and it could only be assumed that the dislike for her son was personal. And he took it that way.

Yes, waiting for Luke is always a hard business. He takes the place of Morgan in that regard very admirably. She has lost too much and gained not nearly as much as she wants. But Luke will not often do things the way Sara wants or expects; if she pushes too hard he will resist and not yield at any cost.

A loud thumping on the front door startles her. She takes a lamp with her; before she can open the door, a deep voice thunders, "It's Sheriff McCurdy."

She opens the door immediately and he seems a little taken aback by it. His tall figure looms in her doorway.

"Sorry, Mrs Taylor, to disturb you."

"Whatever can be the matter, Mr McCurdy?" This man who calls himself sheriff is never sorry to disturb anyone. He makes a point of it.

"Is your son home?"

"No. He is not."

"Well, maybe you can help me. Ed Parsons was riding up around the marsh this afternoon. Reckons there's a barbed wire fence running straight through it."

"Well, I hope so. Luke spent a full day erecting it. He expects the men to begin fencing the dry boundary up there any day now…"

"Ed wants to dispute the accuracy of the boundary."

"Luke used the surveyor's map," she points out firmly.

"Well, Ed wants your son and Ethan to come into town and discuss the matter in my office. Tomorrow be all right?"

"I told you that Luke is not at home."

"When are you expecting him?"

"Of that I am uncertain. He didn't say how long he'd be."

"Well, I'll give him another day or two. Then I'll call back."

She narrows her eyes on him. "The fence had better stay upright and intact, Sheriff."

McCurdy has the audacity to smirk. "Of course, Mrs Taylor. But you know how cattle can be."

Detestable man. He bids her goodnight and leaves. She waits until he rides off into the darkness before she lights a lantern and hurries across the yard, passing the bunkhouse and the corrals to Ethan's house.

Luke

A spring morning in Cheyenne; a sharp breeze invigorates the slow-waking streets, even where the sun is busy. He arrives at the doctor's early. The repaired bell announces his entrance, but Duffy is not at her station.

After a moment, the doctor appears. Struggling with a line of buttons on the cuff of her white blouse, she hasn't even looked up to see who's walked in. She wears a fine wool skirt the color of corn-flowers. Loosely caught in a blue ribbon over one shoulder is her dark chestnut hair; it's thick and smooth, with shiny crinkles in it that catch the light. She looks up; the smiling recognition in her eyes makes him choke on what was gonna be his greeting.

He coughs politely, then finds his voice. "I'm too early." At least he's not pale.

She's making no headway with the buttons. "I thought I was running late."

"You don't have to be understanding," he tells her.

"Oh," she says and gives the buttons her attention, which gives him time to study her face. There is a pale sprinkle of freckles across her nose that fascinates him, a trail that draws his eye to the delicate frown upon her brow.

"I should wear this ridiculous blouse on a day when I am on time."

She seems younger every time he sees her. How can she possibly be a doctor? Doctors are old men with gray hair. She catches him staring and the thought falls out of his mouth, "Doctors are old men with gray hair."

She gapes at him; color has crept into her cheeks.

"Sorry," he says lamely. He clears his throat and pegs his hat; what is the matter with him?

"What did you mean by that?" she asks.

"Nothing... er, nothing." He doesn't think she'd like being told she's too pretty to be a doctor, so he points to her buttons and says, "May I help you with those?"

"Oh... no..."

"Least I can do. You've been helping me." He gives her no option. He steps up to her and takes her left wrist. There is no wedding ring on her finger. He makes his move on the buttons. They look like small pearls and flop about on their thread. The soft, smooth fabric of the blouse don't help either. "You're right. About the buttons."

"You're a little anxious this morning about Tressa," she says.

"Mm..."

"She spent a restful night. We talked at length before she went to sleep. She told me about your home and that she will be well taken care of. I apologize if I inferred in any way yesterday that you weren't up to the task of caring for her."

He lifts his eyes to her face. "You should never apologize for anything you say to me, Dr Sullivan. I'm likely to be needing to hear it."

A slow grin forms on her lips.

"What?" he queries. He's working blind on the last button; he can't take his eyes off the shape of her mouth, wondering how to sketch it to do justice to it. "What else did that cousin of mine tell you?"

"Nothing else," she says lightly. "You might get this last one if you actually look at what you're doing."

He does as she suggests. "Next you'll be telling me you roll up your sleeves about nine o'clock every morning."

"Well, I will wait till ten today."

For a moment after he's finished, her slender wrist rests in the palm of his hand. He has witnessed something of what doctors do; bloody stuff, things that make you heave, and he just can't imagine this woman doing them. "Seven buttons kinda seem like five too many."

He withdraws his hand and she places her wrist by her side.

"Does everyone call you Dr Sullivan?" he asks.

"My patients do." She moves away towards the archway. "I'll see if Tressa is ready for visitors..."

Then he hears Duffy bellow, "Miss Jennifer, what's keeping you?"

"Jennifer," he murmurs.

"Mm." She turns and walks backwards a few steps.

"That's a mighty pretty name," he says. "I'm Luke."

"I know, Mr Taylor," she replies.

"You don't have to call me Mr Taylor."

"No, I really think I should." She nearly cannons into Duffy coming from the other direction. Duffy reproaches her, then sees him.

"Ah, the blue-eyed boy himself, it is!" she exclaims. Miss Jennifer, meanwhile, has made good her escape.

Tressa has more color in her cheeks. She tells him that Dr Sullivan spent time with her last night teaching her how to take care of herself during the pregnancy, about the birth itself, and what to expect afterwards. Luke can see that it has eased her mind. Although he wants to talk about Mart, he is afraid that it will distress her, so he sets her mind on going home to Morgen, and to Sara, which appears to bolster her spirits. After half an hour, Dr Sullivan reappears. Her sleeves are still buttoned but her hair is up and neatly arranged. She examines Tressa briefly and tells them that everything is 'thoroughly normal'.

"And you are fit for travel," she announces.

"Is she fit for an old stagecoach, Harry Hobbs and miles and miles of bad road?" Luke asks.

"If there is no alternative, you should insist that the driver... Mr Hobbs?"

"That's the one."

"That he drive in a considerate manner, stop often and allow you to stretch your legs or rest quietly. This is a medical situation. Doctor's orders."

Luke would like to witness Dr Sullivan making that demand. He's thinking he might have to hire a horse and buggy in Laramie rather than risk Harry's penchant for speed, when a loud wailing travels down the hallway with Duffy's voice following it. A small child, a boy, appears at the door.

"What's all this?" Dr Sullivan says to the child.

The child throws itself against her skirt and clings. She calmly untangles the kid and picks him up. "I'll write the instructions for Mr Hobbs on my letterhead. Come on, little one… Excuse me, won't you?"

"You're excused, Miss Jennifer. I'll take care of these two."

"I like her," says Tressa after she's gone.

Duffy fusses about, tidying the room, although Luke can't see how it can get much tidier. "You're not the first and you won't be the last. Dr Sullivan has a way with people. The more troublesome they are, the more she likes it. She'll have that mischievous babe eating out of her hand in no time. Now, you will be needing assistance, Mrs Keaton. Out with you, lad. She'll be ready in a jiffy."

The agreeableness of the morning gradually dissolves as the miles creep by on the train.

"Say it, Luke."

"What?"

"I deceived you. All that time. You knew something was wrong and I didn't tell you. You should be angry."

He remembers the doctor's warning about melancholy.

"My only concern is for you and the baby. You're my kin, Tress, and Mart's wife. I would never abandon you. And I'm not angry."

Unlike your pathetic father who abandoned my family and me…and now you.

"I don't deserve it," she smiles shyly, "but… thank you for being the kind of man Dr Sullivan says would move a mountain if it got in your way."

"She said that?"

"I think she likes you."

Then her lovely eyes fill with tears as if to say she likes him too.

He takes her hand and squeezes it.

"What about the others?" she sniffs.

"Think they might surprise you."

Sean (John)

"Last December, Mart came to Omaha."

"Last December? I recall he wanted to take some time away from the ranch," Sean tells them, "it was getting cold and he looked kinda peaked, but I said okay…" Amy's hand comes down on his arm; her expression implores him to be silent.

Sean sighs away the hundreds of questions he has regarding his son so that in her small grave voice Tressa can tell her story without him interrupting; there are very few tears and he suspects something brutal has dried them all up.

"There didn't seem anything unusual about it; nothing odd about a young man looking at prospects in town. He came into my father's office one day when I happened to be there. I wanted to learn about the business and help my father, but my mother wouldn't allow it. She said that it was my brother Ben's place. I hoped to convince Ben to persuade my parents.

"Anyway, I was there at the front desk in Papa's offices… Mart walked in. I guess you could say we fell in love at once. I don't know if you think such things are possible. We just knew we belonged together. One week later we… we were married in Omaha. The preacher married us quietly with nobody knowing except for my best friend. You see, my parents had absolutely forbidden me to marry Mart."

She stops and draws a shaky breath. Sean reaches for Amy's hand; her fingers grip his like she daren't let go. Meanwhile, Sara sits perfectly still and straight with her hands on the table. Ethan leans against the doorframe staring out across the yard and hasn't said a word since they arrived. Silent tears drip down Kelley's cheeks. And every now and then Sean hears a restless sigh coming from the parlor where Tressa told Luke to remain; this was her duty, she insisted, and he was not to interfere.

"Did he give no clue about me?"

Sean answers. "He… he said he had a friend in Omaha, who he visited regular, but…" He shakes his head.

"He was never a deceitful person, I… don't…" Amy's voice trails away.

"Mart stayed in Omaha with me secretly for a while, then he went home. My father had said that if we married he would cut me off from the family. When I told Mart I didn't care what Papa said or did if it meant we could be together always, Mart insisted I never ever cut myself off from them. He went crazy, so I had to promise.

"Now I know why he insisted. For a long time I didn't know he was hunting that outlaw, but what he wanted to safeguard against happened – he was killed and I still had my family to look after me, as he wanted. It was so very bad, so painful, being separated from him. And then we had a fight one day when he came to Omaha to see me and it came out that he was hunting this Wilson Cutter. He refused to tell me why. I didn't know what to do; I had no one to turn to, and nowhere to go for help. I couldn't risk the upheaval in my family… it's difficult to explain how it is…"

"Leave that, Tressa, we understand," Sara says kindly. "Go on."

"Very well. I decided the only thing left would be to come here, and take my chances. You see, Mart told me so much about all of you that I felt that if I came here you wouldn't turn me away, and I could be close to Mart, understand him better, but mostly try and talk him out of this madness. You have no idea how many times I tried… I tried everything, over and over, but of course I didn't succeed; no matter what I did or said, I couldn't move him. I think he was driven by fear and he wouldn't listen to me. I… I thought he loved me but I began to think he didn't… and I feared for him. I pleaded on my knees for him to tell Luke or Ethan; I insisted that I would tell and he said if I go against his wishes then I could not love him. He said a wife is loyal to her husband. Then my uncle passed away. I didn't know what to do. Mart insisted that I go home, that if I truly loved him I would, but I should never have gone back. I should have told you what I knew, even if he refused to see me ever again. He needed me to do this and I failed him. I'm not used to… it's hard for me to…" She hangs her head. "How can there be any excuses…"

From the parlor comes Luke's exclamation, "I can think of one!"

"Luke, please..." Tressa gasps. "Let me go on."

"Please," Amy sobs, and it goes straight to Sean's heart. Until now, Sean has been too numb to feel anything and he wants to stay that way. He resists the temptation to put his arm around Amy and merely squeezes her hand.

"Before I left Morgen, Mart made me promise not to tell some-thing else – about our marriage. He said that if anything happened to him I should go on with my life the same way. What was one more secret? This would have worked out, but for one small thing..." Tressa finally breaks down. They all watch her, stupidly. Luke appears in the doorway.

And then Amy says, in a tone so quiet and dignified that Sean feels the hairs stand up on the back his neck, "You're expecting Mart's child."

Tressa nods. And tears seem to spill over her cheeks and waterfall onto her lap.

Sean feels Amy's fingers squeeze his hand, short and sharp.

"I know you would have noticed I look different."

Amy and Sara exchange glances.

"Why are you are telling us this, Tressa?" Amy asks.

Tressa, her cheeks now wet with heartbreak, stares at her. Sean looks from his wife to Tressa and back again. This seems a little harsh...

"My father still refuses to recognize my marriage to Mart, and he...he... I don't...I have..."

"That's all right, Tressa," Amy says calmly. "You don't have to say it. You have done the right thing. You're a brave girl, and I'm proud of you. One of the cruelest things in life is to live with hindsight tormenting you day and night. But no more. Mart should have listened to your wifely wisdom. You showed him true loyalty. Your reward shouldn't be pain and condemnation."

"You're not angry?" Tressa gasps.

"Are you more to blame than any of us? Definitely not. But dwelling on what might have been is unhealthy. You loved Mart and now you bring a living part of him back to us."

Sean, staggered by his wife, watches Tressa wipe her tears.

"So, when is the baby due?"

"August."

"Excellent." Amy turns to him with the return of that energetic smile of hers, warming his heart. "You're going to be a grandfather, Sean Keaton. What do have to say to that?"

It is truly the finest thing he's ever heard; now, if he can just get the words out.

Kelley

If Tressa presumed she would live with Sara and Luke, or even wanted to, and if Sara and Luke assumed Tressa would or wanted to live with them, such expectations are swiftly made redundant. John and Amy Keaton are very adamant about who will be responsible for mother and child. She is Mart's wife; she is carrying Mart's child. No more secrets. No more doubts or dilemmas, ifs, buts or maybes. Tressa will come to live with them in two days, which allows sufficient time for the energetic reorganization of the Keaton household.

"This is just what was needed," her Mama says. "For all of us."

For the Keatons anyway.

It could only be assumed the Taylors, and Tressa, agreed.

If they had objections, they were not voiced.

If they were disappointed, they didn't show it.

Tressa arrives as planned. As Luke deposits her things, her Mama invites him and Sara, Ethan and Tip to a special supper to welcome Tressa into the family.

He accepts, although he appears somewhat circumspect when her Pa announces, "Tressa is our source of hope and promise. That's the way she needs to see her life now. We all do."

As they mingle before supper, Luke remarks, "Well, K, who'd have thought you and me would ever be related?"

She can't mask shock at a comment like that, and he laughs in her face.

"This baby will be my first cousin once removed – according to Sara – and your niece or nephew, and that makes us some kind of relation…"

"Just what are you trying to insinuate?"

216

His smile retreats. He scratches the back of his neck. "Well… you used to say… you… mm, never mind."

"An attempt at humor?"

"No good?"

"The only one laughing is you."

He grunts, "We are still related." And walks off to join Tip.

The supper is not, of course, the high-spirited fellowship of that long ago meal when Tressa first visited, but it is peaceful and comforting. Mart and Tressa's deception of that other night is let go.

"We are in the business of forgiveness," her Mama says. But, in reality, denial is certainly preferable to pain.

News comes to hand that Ed Parsons and Luke almost came to blows over the fencing of Bear Paw Marsh, especially as the men set about fencing the dry land boundary either side and making good strides at it. Kelley takes advantage of the latest developments connecting her family and Luke's and rides out to Morgen to see him. They sit in the kitchen and drink coffee.

"Ed hasn't pulled out the fence, has he?" she asks.

"I wouldn't be sitting here if he had."

"I think if Ed destroyed that fence I'd punch him in the nose myself."

"Now you know how it feels."

"To have all your hard work thrown back in your face, yes. So, what has been resolved?"

"I ain't moving it."

"I never thought to look at the surveyor's map when we were there," she reflects.

Luke frowns at her.

She realizes her mistake. "I'm not doubting you," she says hastily. "More coffee?" As she is pouring, she ventures, "Have I proved that I can be your partner yet? We worked together; we accomplished something together…"

"K, it might be trampled down, even as we speak…"

"Up, down… it's still a symbol of teamwork. We can find who did this to Mart and Tressa…"

"Are you sure you didn't sign your name to John's Alliance papers, 'cause you sure talk like you have…"

She tries valiantly to govern her emotions but all too soon she is bursting. "I will never sign anything. Alliances are made in the heart, Luke…"

"A woman's perspective…"

"Your point?"

"I don't…"

"Otherwise there is merely political or financial expediency and the relationships between people mean little or nothing. Is that how it is with you?"

"Is that what you think of our Alliance, K? That your father, Ethan and I care for nothing else other than business? How can you think that?"

"You didn't answer my question."

"Mart and I both signed it. You think it was just business between Mart and me?"

"We said we wouldn't fight."

"Now you're changing the subject. Okay. Fine. I also told you we were too much alike. Right now we've proving it – again."

"You keep saying that…" she exclaims and then controls herself. "We don't even think alike, how can you say it?"

"Don't you know yourself, K?" he says, also controlling his fervor. "You want things to be done your own way. And so do I. One of us would always have to comply since we never agree on anything."

"It's something we would learn to do…"

"Compromise between us does not come natural. Someone would always have to yield and how long before resentment surfaced? We would have to trust one another completely."

"We could learn."

"K, admit it, you don't want to. You are crazy about your independence. You always have been. You want it more than anything. Same as I want mine."

"Why do you think about it so much? Make this so complicated?"

A thought occurs to her, one she should have had before. "Is there... is there someone I should know about? – I mean, a girl..."

He blinks. Frowns. "Do you see a line of women outside the front door? And no, I don't have a wife stashed away in another town. Look, what I need is someone who will make me never want to leave home. When I bring my saddle and place it at the feet of that someone it will mean something. But right now I got Wilson Cutter on my mind and that means gallivanting around and doing stuff and that ain't the place for a woman."

"Back to that again," she cries. "You have no idea what I am capable of when it comes to helping you with this... I believe I can do the job for Mart as well as you."

"Stop, K. Just stop," he breathes.

Her eyes begin to sting. From across the table his gaze is deep blue and scarily intense. Sara can be heard humming in another part of the house. Other silent minutes pass by. The tension shifts uncomfortably.

With surprising gentleness, he asks, "Is your alliance with me, K, in your heart?"

She must tell him so. "Yes."

He clears his throat. "You swear?"

"Yes."

"Then my alliance with you is in my heart... and no matter what happens to either of us, I won't break it..."

"Why do you always think that you have to do everything on your own?" she blurts out and he's shaking his head.

"My part, K, is that I will protect you, care for you, with my life if I have to. I swear it."

She knows she should say that she understands he must do what he feels is right, that in turn she will be patient, she will support him and she will wait.

What stops her she cannot fathom at first. She believes she loves him enough. Then all at once it becomes clear: her undying belief that a woman should not live her life dependent upon the life of a man.

"I do not believe a woman, any woman, should haunt a suspended reality until the man returns to restart her existence."

He frowns. "Neither do I, but...."

Her pride, her sense of self-worth that Aunt Edith drummed into her for five years, won't allow it. If Luke intends to uphold his principles, then she is entitled – obligated – to do likewise.

"I don't want to be that woman…"

She does not want to be a Liberty and Property woman.

Not Luke's, nor anyone else's.

She is her own woman. He needs to respect that.

The revelation tears her apart, and the urge to leave is so acute that she slips out of her chair…

"K, wait…"

And out of the house. She is running from herself, however, and an overwhelming love that has nowhere to go.

Ed

"So, Ed, our little problem just won't vamoose…"

Smart-ass Bodecker; he gestures with an exaggerated flick, watching it like he's launched something fascinating into the air; the sarcasm ain't lost on Ed, but he pretends he doesn't notice.

Whatever Bodecker may think, Ed treats himself as equal to his consortium partners, but he'll need to talk fast, jittery as they are over recent events. Sure, Keaton is dead and Cutter got away and is laying low. Nothing, however, is pleasing in terms of achieving their goal.

"The Alliance is effectively stalling our progress. We still want the pass, the land and the River. Hell, we want Bright River. And what do we have? – *nada*," says Bodecker, as if Ed needs it explained to him. "Your plan looks like it's turning sour, Ed. We need to back off now, re-think, before John Keaton, Benchley and Taylor start investigating what really happened to Mart."

Loren Bodecker. Tycoon. Railroad, mining, cattle. *Carve it up, dig it up, eat it all up*, is a famous quote of his. Operates out of Cheyenne, Omaha and Denver. Believes that the future of Wyoming belongs to the barons, so he favors Wyoming statehood as long as he's got a major stake it in. Has his own solution to the ominous over-crowding on the range and predictions on what that might mean – to force out most of the small to medium ranchers in the southeast. Irate because they won't sell, not without his own brand of incentive at any rate. Helped Ed buy out the district newspaper. Has part ownership in the Cheyenne Bugle and substantial shares in an Eastern syndicated newspaper. Happy, paunch airin'ly keen in fact, to talk about his friend the governor, who is also for Wyoming statehood. Ed's pretty sure the governor wouldn't be happy with his friend Bodecker if he knew what's been going on. But that's the point: nobody knows.

"Did you really think that intimidating and threatening young Keaton was going to work?" Donnelly asks while he fidgets with his striped silk tie. Business attire don't sit comfortable on him.

Donnelly. Thinks he's a businessman and a gentleman on the same level as Bodecker. He's deluded, but no one would risk telling him because he's got a mean streak deeper than the Grand Canyon. Face full of sharp angles; thin lips; shrewd, skinny eyes. Wrestles with his tie when things ain't going his way. One thing he can do right is provide backup in case Cutter fails to do his job or gets himself killed. And they need that, because Cutter is one crazy loon.

The connection between Donnelly and Bodecker is strictly back-stairs. The few that know are loyal without question; they are well paid. The governor doesn't even know Donnelly. On the surface Donnelly is just a Laramie businessman. But he's got himself rich – on cattle mostly, Ed thinks, but he knows better than to enquire, especially since he overheard the pair of them talking about something they operate out of North Platte.

Their consortium is odd to say the least, but they all want the same thing even if it is for their own reasons. When Ed met them some years back they were sympathetic to his plight with the Taylors and the Keatons. Said they could help. Gradually, everyone seemed to be getting what he wanted as they made steady progress on clearing out the small timers in the wider district. And their Association has consolidated considerable strength, something they worked on while Cutter kept Mart Keaton busy. Before they stake a major holding in the county, however, and claim the prize, they need to clean out the Alliance and those who shelter in its shadow. Unfortunately, the Alliance had had Mart Keaton and Luke Taylor. Fortunately, Keaton no more; but Taylor, always resolute and now angry and without Keaton's direct influence, still stands in their way.

"It worked good enough, but I didn't think Keaton would give his life," Ed says. "Who would? Thought he would have given up, backed down. That's what I expect any normal man to do. Mart ruined everything with stupid heroics. Had to fight the way he did and – "

"A martyr for the cause," Bodecker jeers.

"Shit, I hate that..." says Donnelly.

" – screw up the whole plan. Good thing the Alliance thinks that something personal between him and Cutter was the reason for his tragic end and haven't got a clue. We're gonna have to watch Taylor, though."

"Now what?" says Donnelly.

That's right. Leave it to him. Donnelly possesses no imagination. Goes with the lack of dress sense. Lucky Ed has something in mind. "I spied a rumor that Taylor and Keaton's daughter are likely to marry. Seen them together in fact and fancy it's true. If that goes ahead the Alliance will be even stronger than ever. And who knows what Taylor might resort to…"

"So what have you got in mind?" asks Bodecker impatiently. He exhales loudly, flipping his jacket open and setting his hands on hips. He lives the good life, Bodecker. Ed could be envious; Bodecker is younger too. But he is also paunchy, ruddy faced and in some ways looks older than Ed does.

"I think it's time to flush Cutter out of the willows and offer him an incentive to distract Taylor from his little romance, and get ourselves back on track," Ed says.

Bodecker and Donnelly exchange glances. The silent agreement.

"Sounds interesting," Bodecker says. "Look into it."

"Could be just the break we've been looking for," Donnelly contributes.

A break, Ed reckons, would be to lose these two sapheads. He wishes he could get the prize on his own, but he knows he can't.

"And if Cutter needs any help…" Donnelly's mouth curls unpleasantly as he finally leaves his tie in peace, "…only too happy to oblige."

"I'll let you know," Ed tells him.

Luke

He and Ethan head into town for mail and supplies. He's been thinking about K for several days now. Her impulsiveness and that demanding way of hers severely test his ability to say the right thing at the right time. Like that's ever gonna happen. He knows what's expected of him but…

"Hey! You awake?"

"Sorry."

"We're stopped, in case you hadn't noticed."

"I noticed."

"Mm. I'll meet you at the store."

Which leaves Luke to collect their mail.

Among the numerous letters, packages and journals, there's a telegram for him.

LUKE. CUTTER EVADED CAPTURE BY U.S. MARSHAL TWO DAYS AGO APPROX TWENTY MILES NORTH EAST OF CHEYENNE. REMEMBER WHAT WE AGREED ON. SIT TIGHT AND BE ALERT. CLIFF.

"Not bad news, I trust."

Luke refolds the telegram slowly, slides it into his trouser pocket and then turns to face McCurdy, who eyes him warily from beneath that slicked hair.

"Don't think, McCurdy, that I don't know what you're doing, and that you won't get what's coming to you…"

"Are you threatening me, Taylor?"

"…it may not be as soon as I want, but I'm a patient man. Now get out of my face."

McCurdy jams his thumbs in his gun belt. "Shame to have to put you in the lock-up."

"On what charge?"

"Making threats against an officer of the law."

"When there's an officer of the law present in this town someone should tell me. I'd like a word with him. Now I've got things to do, McCurdy."

"Well, you won't be doing them today, Taylor. I'm throwing you in the lock-up. Might teach you not to talk so high and mighty. And if you resist I'll have you charged and convicted of threatening me and resisting arrest."

A rush of blood threatens the patience Luke was just boasting about. McCurdy appears to be laughing while Luke restrains himself; since every move this lying skunk makes feeds Luke's suspicions, he needs to keep his sights fixed on the bigger picture, so he allows McCurdy to march him to the jail. The sonofabitch wears an irritating smirk as he locks Luke inside the cell.

"When can I get out?" Luke asks. The place stinks like its last guest hadn't washed for a month and the food disagreed with him.

"Well, I noticed Ethan about. He might like to pay the fine."

"What fine?"

"Fifty dollars, or two days in the lock-up. Now which do you think it will be?"

Luke grapples with the iron bars in front of his face as he grapples with a litany of retorts ready to spew from his mouth. McCurdy turns away laughing and slams the outer guard door shut, locking that as well. Luke squeezes his fingers around the metal and rattles the door furiously for several seconds. Then he sits on the old rickety cot, throws down his hat beside him, and takes out the telegram from Cliff. Reading it over and over, the idea of what has to be done and the conviction to do it comes to him. And the whole time he is thinking of that idea, he is thinking about K.

Sometime later, McCurdy unlocks the outer door and Ethan walks in. The wise old coot stands and stares at him as Luke looks on from his cot.

"So what's it gonna be, Ethan?" McCurdy smirks.

"Figured I'd be allowed time with the prisoner on my own."

McCurdy lets out a sneering laugh. "Guess it wouldn't hurt." He strides away, this time leaving the outer door ajar. Meanwhile, Ethan's stare is starting to become unnerving.

Raising his voice for McCurdy's benefit, Luke says, "I don't want you paying no fine, Ethan."

Ethan sighs.

"I didn't do nothing worth fifty dollars. Don't think I didn't want to."

"So you want to spend two days in jail? I know you have principles, Luke; know they're as stiff-necked as you, but…" He frowns. Lowers his voice. "Why are we yelling? – and why are you talking that way?"

Luke rushes up from the cot and pushes the telegram through the bars. In a hushed voice, he says, "Read this."

Ethan frowns even harder and takes the paper. Luke watches his eyes widen; Ethan rubs those eyes when he's finished staring at the words.

"We gotta work out what to do," Luke says.

Ethan glances up sharply. "You been sitting here. You went and worked out what to do."

"I admit it."

Ethan's eyes began to quiver.

"I'm going to Cheyenne, Ethan; it's time to keep my promise to Mart."

"Not behind these bars you ain't. Maybe I should pay a hundred and fifty dollars to keep you here till you come to your senses. You're gonna break that little girl's heart. She loves you – get it through your thick head!"

"You know I'm right."

"I know no such of a thing. You want me to tell you you're right. She's just a kid. Takes a woman to understand. She ain't that far along yet. You're used to Sara watching you go off and do whatever you get into your head to do like it was breathing. You gotta understand, Luke. It hurts, it…"

"Ethan, just tell me you wouldn't do it if you were me. It's time. Time to bring Cutter in and while I'm at it, take my file to Cheyenne. I want someone to look at it. Cliff will know who. I've told you there would come a time, and I've let it play out, but McCurdy's just forced my hand and that's a fact. No more coincidences, Ethan. From now on everything makes sense. We've done it John and Mart's way, it didn't work, now it's our turn. You and me, we trust our instincts. We believe in our suspicions. We make John believe it. Right or wrong, we make a stand. Ethan. We gotta do this."

Ethan pushes his fingers through his hair over and over. "Men have said that going off to war."

"Ethan…"

"It's true. I said it, your father said it. We picked up our rifles and we made a stand, right or wrong."

Luke swallows as Ethan looks him square in the eyes.

"If a man can see his path clear out in front of him, then his destiny awaits him," Ethan says.

"Red Sky… I remember, Red Sky said that."

"She always knew what to say, what to do… Had that calmness inside of her. She could see things, understand things…" A hard look surfaces in his eyes. "If you're planning on coming back you'll need someone to ride with you."

Not you, Ethan, I want a home to come back to.

Quickly, he says, "I'll be with Cliff."

"You're gonna get into trouble."

"I won't." Luke clutches the iron bars and plays his final card. "If you and Sara are so intent on me and K having a future together…"

"All right. I understand. The thing is, son… the thing is that Kelley won't."

McCurdy appears. "Time's up. What'll it be, gentlemen?"

"You want me to hand over what two of my prime steers are worth just for knowing the lousy truth about you, McCurdy?" Luke grinds out.

"Cash only. No bartering, Taylor."

"I wouldn't barter with you for my own life, you…"

"Ah, Luke's kinda in a hurry so you'll get your cash, McCurdy," says Ethan. "I'll just head on down to the bank."

"I'll be waiting," McCurdy sneers and walks out.

Ethan turns and says, "Son, you owe me fifty dollars."

Luke's eyes sting. *I owe you more than that, Ethan.* He nods in agreement.

Kelley

From her window, Kelley sees her Pa walking slowly across the yard with Luke. They stop at the slip rails and converse for some time. Back East, strategic Alliances discuss their next move in war rooms of leather and oak. Out West, it happens by the slip rails, fanned by the cool afternoon breeze, under a cloudless sky. Her Pa seems to be waving his arms a lot. He wouldn't be happy about McCurdy throwing Luke in jail. Not happy with McCurdy, or Luke. But maybe they are discussing the telegram. The reality is that Wilson Cutter has surfaced and the Alliance is back on alert.

Kelley paces a trail in her rug.

When she returns to the window they are gone. The meeting appears to be adjourned at last. She observes the space they left behind, where the wind spins dust into small, whirling flurries that rise excitedly and then drop into nothingness.

A short time later there is a soft tap on her door. She opens it to behold Luke.

"You look tired."

"Hello to you too."

"Come in then," she says and moves away from the door, returning to the window. She glances over her shoulder. He is watching intently.

"You should say what's on your mind."

"I will get to that," he says.

"How was jail?"

"How d'you think?"

"For you, just another brush with fate. It doesn't agree with you, you know."

He shifts his feet and says, "I've been speaking with your father."

"I know. I saw you together. From here."

"I have to…" he begins.

"Have to what?" She turns and faces him.

"There are things I need to do so we can all be safe."

"I see. And what would they be?"

"Find Wilson Cutter for one," he says at last.

Her stomach drops like a lead weight.

"Yet another brush with fate… what are you doing, Luke?"

"Brush with fate? K… you're not making sense."

"*I'm* not making sense!" she exclaims. She wraps her arms around herself.

"This is a job that finally – *finally* – needs to be done…" he says with feeling.

A woman's reaction, that's what she's having, she can feel it deep inside her, and she's not sure that she can stop it. She's not even sure if she'd ever have known it without the man standing before her. It's frightening, the depth of her feelings.

She hears him say, "It's the only thing to be done," which rouses her and then there is nothing vague about what she has to say to him.

"You mean it's the only thing that *you* can see to do. There would be no other opinion. Like mine, for example."

"I'm doing this for you."

"This is not for me," she cries. "You are *not* doing this for me. You are doing it for Mart. Without me – after I have begged you to let me help and proved that I could."

"Your father agrees with me."

"Oh, the mighty Alliance has spoken!"

"Can't you just wait for me while I do this? When it's all over…"

"Wait for you?" The job of the woman who loves him. He would likely be killed, just as Mart had been. Fear breaks out, mimicking hundreds of red-hot needles puncturing her skin. She swallows painfully. For several moments his face is a blur. "All I can see is a future tortured with endless days of coping with loneliness and worry, not knowing your regard in return for all of mine and what it cost me…"

Becoming a liberty and property woman.

"K…"

"Ask Tressa. Ask her what the cost is."

"I already know."

"And you ask the same of me? How can you do that?"

He stands mute.

He can't even make an effort to put his arms around her.

She shakes her head briskly. "You can't answer, can you? And I... what I can't do, Luke, is... I can't live my life dependent on your return for my health and happiness. I won't wait for you. I refuse to do it. And... and therefore I'm breaking our alliance..."

He flinches sharply and his dark eyes go wide. "You can't. You don't mean it."

"I do. I mean it. I mean it." Her throat is throbbing with lumps she can't swallow. "So you go and hunt down that madman, just like Mart did, and you can get yourself killed, just like Mart did, and I might even come to your funeral, but I won't have the feelings I have now. I won't. I won't."

"K..."

"I won't, I tell you."

"So you say. But my alliance with you stands," he says, his voice ragged. "Always be in my heart. Just like I swore to you. I swore it to you, K, don't you understand..."

She raises her chin and glares loftily at him. "That is entirely your decision but I won't change my mind."

He stares at her for some time, emotion quivering in his eyes. "You slam the Alliance Mart and I signed our names to, but not even death has broken it. Nothing will. So what does that say about your heart, K?"

She holds her tongue. He has no idea of the strength it requires not to throw herself at him and beg him to love her; her whole body quakes with the effort.

At last, he takes a step towards her. Afraid, she stammers, "It says my heart won't be broken by you..."

"I can give you everything you want, but not until I've done this."

"Go do it," she rasps, "for your precious Alliance, yours and Mart's, not the one which no longer exists."

"I haven't broken my part," he insists. "I will not."

"My heart wants love and peace, and yours is bent on your liberty and property. How can that be a true alliance of our hearts?"

"I don't have all the answers, K, I only know that what I s\
to you stays."

And then he leaves.

She turns to the window and presses her hands white against
pane, waiting. He rides into view; she catches her breath and h\
on until he has ridden away.

At breakfast the following morning, her Pa informs them t
Luke has departed for Cheyenne.

Her Mama is anxious. "I'm worried he'll do something rash."

"We agreed, Amy, that he would go to Cheyenne first and fet
the young sheriff," her Pa consoles her. "You liked him, remember

Kelley watches and listens in a daze as they discuss more deta
of Luke's intentions. In the meantime, Tressa returns to Morgen for
few days to visit with Sara. After all, Sara needs someone to condol
with her now that her precious son has gone to find a killer.

The days pass, tracking the path of her resistance.

She once heard an expression: love is a decision, not an emotion.
Luke has taught her what it means. So she switches off her emotions,
courtesy of Aunt Edith's life lessons and strategies, and doggedly
trains her mind to let Luke go, to comprehend that his destiny and
hers are no longer bound, that despite his adamant declaration, their
alliance is gone and was probably never meant to be. Each and every
minute of Life should be lived to the full. That is her decision.

Two days later, from out of the blue, Aunt Edith arrives.

SIX

In the world's broad field of battle,
In the bivouac of Life,
Be not like dumb, driven cattle!
Be a hero in the strife!

Henry Wadsworth Longfellow
A Psalm of Life

❧

Edith

I arrive at my brother's frontier home, for the first time ever, having experienced the worst coach journey of my entire life, only to find my dearest girl clearly in an unhealthy state of mind.

Waiting for Kelley to sort out her relationships is one of those things that cultivates parental patience even within a person not blessed with children. Her abject relief at my coming sets off my internal alarm.

"Auntie, I had no idea you were coming," she exclaims.

"Well, I did what you prefer to do, darling. I didn't tell anyone."

I hold my beloved girl close for several minutes in the first instance, and then keep her close while I reunite myself with my brother after more years than I have kept track of.

To see my dear Sean's expression as we face each other after so long is not something I will easily forget. He is bursting and hugs me with a ferociousness that warms my heart. We look at each other without words for an eternal moment, while years peel away and we remember.

Finally, I say, "I'm relieved to find you all coping so well with your grief."

Sean nods, but his face quickly becomes downcast. My tears start and I dab my eyes. "I'm so sorry, Sean. So sorry... You must miss him so..."

"Now, Edith, don't cry. We have Tressa, and soon a grandchild. And now you're here. We're gonna be all right."

"Sean, you are so hopeful and it does me good to hear it."

I like the younger Mrs Keaton at once. Without a doubt she has helped my brother's family cope with the shocking loss of Martin. I find Tressa to be a gentle, pure-hearted young woman – how could Martin have married any other kind – although she is obviously not blessed with the same kind of parents. Uncharitable, undeserving – I am furious with them even though I do not know them.

Reminiscing is the delightful – and distracting – activity I had hoped it would be. Amy still calls my brother 'John'. I smile as I recall their plan to outwit her father Willem Olufsen's almost irrational dislike for the Irish:

"If we call you 'John' and tell my father you are raised from plain American stock, he won't know the difference. But you'll have to dispense with the accent."

Sean had barely a trace of an accent because our Irish ancestry in America is two generations old. Our parents were Irish-born but raised from their youth in America. The elders of our family spoke as if they had just disembarked; those of us born here, and our parents Sean Snr and Keely – for whom my dearest girl is named – could turn the brogue on and off at will. (Sean was named after his father; and I after a character in a book to achieve some level of Americanization.) In those days, Amy did not want Sean to slip up, so he did exactly as he was told by his wife-to-be and watched his tongue. In time, Willem learnt to tolerate the Keatons, just as my Keith's family learnt, mixed bag of dreamers, social climbers and intellects that we were. Although, poor Willem never did discover that his son-in-law Sean has County Armagh cousins, who still correspond with me, who occasionally toy with the idea of leaving Ireland's shores to start afresh in the New World. They should come, I write, and often. They should all come.

"Your fair Amy is a treasure, Sean Keaton Junior," I babble, imitating our great uncle Taidgh 'Tim' Campbell, who played his part in the deception with enormous energy. "You must have found her at the end of a rainbow."

Sean sends me a wink and a smile.

"I heard that, Edith Edwards," says Amy from the kitchen where she is making tea.

"Well, he's not denying it, Amy," I continue.

She appears in the parlor threshold, sporting a grin appropriate for someone often called 'fair Amy', as delightful now as the day Sean married her, and clearly just as proficient.

"And I never will," says Sean gallantly.

We banter in a satisfying manner for some time, with a peculiar feeling that denies fifteen years of separation.

Their home is wonderfully comfortable.

My stiff muscles, my jarred bones and jangled nerves find relief in the softness of Sean's easy chair. And, mercifully, no one even hints at making me move. Instead, Amy brings a pot of tea and a tray of refreshments. Kelley pours.

"Everything is just how I pictured it," I declare. "Just as you described, my darling."

"I must have described it at least a hundred times."

"At least."

I wish to congratulate them on their success, but a wave of regret over Martin seals my almost tactless lips. Fortunately, the tea is hot and strong just as I relish it. My brother and sister-in-law sit side by side on the sofa opposite. I observe them over the rim of my teacup. They appear to be as much in love as they ever were; their relationship always had a tender quality. When they departed Philadelphia I wondered if their marriage would survive the legendary rigors of frontier life. It seems to me now that it would have survived anything. Indeed, the worst of all – the loss of their son. There is no bitterness, no recriminations. I see only determined solidarity, and that ever-present and poignant tenderness, which must be threaded with steel.

Evening brings their closest friends to supper. Sara Taylor and I take to one another in an instant. I believe we may be kindred spirits. Ethan is a drawling, engaging Texan; charming and just as Kelley described him. His son, Tip, a fascinating young man who is equally engaging, with a ready wit and young man's vitality, manages to shake the reserve out of Kelley. At first I thought that this might be her *l'amour fatale*, but over the course of Amy's scrumptious supper, my weary brain catalogues all the facts and I realize that the honor of stealing my niece's heart falls on Sara's son, who is absent. No one is particularly forthcoming about where he actually is, and from the expression on Sara's face I think it wise not to insist on knowing.

Kelley tells me herself later as we talk before bed. In fact, she tells me a great deal. I am very concerned, of course, but far too weary to have anything remotely wise to impart; we will speak more in the morning, I tell her.

I sleep without dreaming and wake feeling disoriented. It is fleeting, however.

Family, adventure, the fresh Wyoming air and beautiful country-side await me.

Me! – a Manhattan woman!

Mid-morning, Kelley leads me along a forest trail to her Meadow, a sun-drenched field surrounded by tall trees. She tells me about it. Always full of insects and tall grass and flowers. She snaps one yellow specimen from its stalk and uses it as a pointer. A sanctuary, she calls it. A retreat from the world. Surely, I say, this whole land is a sanctuary. The Shoshone, the Cheyenne and the Arapaho, she tells me with a smile, would be pleased with me.

"We loved this meadow," she says dreamily. "Me and Mart and Luke. When they outgrew it they gave it to me. It's sacred to each of us for different reasons. Every season is unique. In the spring – well, you can see the wildflowers stretched out like a carpet. So full of life. And the smell..."

"Fragrance," I correct her.

"Beautiful, isn't it?"

"Definitely invigorating."

"In summer the grass is so thick, like a mattress, soft and cool and very inviting."

"I think I could lie here for hours myself."

"In the Fall everything changes again. Leaves drift across from the trees and the ground becomes a crunchy sea of gold and brown. Then in winter it is purely white with snow..."

I study that dreamy young face and my heart aches for her. She has lost so much. "Luke will come back, my darling."

"It doesn't matter. I've made my decision, and I believe it to be right. You know, Auntie, far from giving my life direction, coming home took my direction away from me. Perhaps when you return to New York I should go with you."

"Misunderstandings and setbacks are just a part of life. I'm not in any rush to return, so we have plenty of time to think everything through."

She hugs me fervently. "Thank you, Auntie."

Luke

One week later

Luke engages his rifle and fires it twice; he hears the shriek as the bullets find their mark, and sees his quarry fall. Wilson Cutter is down; enough to keep him that way till Luke can get his hands on him and ride him into Cheyenne. Just like Mart wanted. Whatever had been in Mart's mind regarding Cutter, and Luke can imagine it had a lot to do with giving Cutter a chance to be a citizen, it was never going to work. Men like Cutter need a different type of persuasion. Luke could have told Mart that, if Mart had confided in him...

Luke gets up from his position; he moves forward slowly through the thick brush, attempting to put his memory of Mart dying in the bloodied snow out of his mind. Another shot is fired, but not from his rifle. Damn. The pain rips through Luke's leg so fiercely he thinks it has been shot clean off. He falls in agony.

Gasping, he struggles and fires a volley in Cutter's direction. Sweat breaks out all over his body, pushing through every pore like pins. And all that can be heard in the ensuing moments is the sound of his own groaning.

"No way is this finished, Cutter," he screams.

No reply. The mean bastard could be doing one of three things: fleeing, fainting, or nursing intentions of luring Luke to his death.

He breathes heavily through his burning agony; at the ghastly sight of the wound and his own blood oozing from it he almost passes out. But he must try and think. Cutter wouldn't get far with the wound Luke has inflicted on him; and Luke has no intention of dying. He staggers back into the thickness of the forest, whistles for his mount; the animal comes forth, nervous but obedient. He extracts a calico shirt from one of his saddlebags and does a clumsy job of wrapping his left leg, just above the knee.

With pain and shock draining him by the second, he heaves himself up on horseback, grateful for the animal's strength and temperament, and through a series of deep breaths gets himself almost upright in the saddle. In this condition, it'll take at least half a day's ride to reach town.

Cheyenne appears low across the flat horizon in the slanting afternoon light. The calico shirt is soaked with blood and the pain has just about numbed every other part of him.

As he rides into town about an hour later, his pressing need for medical attention overrides his intention to find Cliff. The streets are scattered with folk, but he ignores their curious stares and arrives at Jennifer's surgery.

He slides awkwardly to the ground, removes his saddlebags and drags them along behind as he limps into the building where the open door admits friendly afternoon sunlight.

Tall, robust Duffy is at her station. A sense of relief almost causes him to pass out. Instead, he clears his throat and gets her attention. He must look a sight because Duffy is speechless.

Jennifer breezes in and does a double take.

"Mr Taylor, what on earth have you done…"

"Can you help me?" he rasps, and winces with the effort of it.

"I repeat: what have you done?"

"Ran into a bullet."

"Duffy, Sheriff Ryan…"

"I'm on it."

Jennifer is by his side; she places one arm firmly around his waist. "Lean on me…"

"Too heavy, bloody…"

"I'm strong…"

He glances down at her; she appears determined and calm, steady, looking up at him with those emerald green eyes.

"Just let me help you," she says gently.

He understands what every man she helps must come to terms with – this woman knows more about them than they know about themselves.

He lifts his arm and places it around her slender shoulder.

"Which way are we headed?"

"Straight. The door beyond Duffy's desk."

Her surprising, steady strength keeps him upright until they enter a room with a scrubbed wooden table in the middle of it.

After she has helped him remove his coat, Jennifer has him lie on the table. Relief washes over him.

"Just what I need – " she chunters "– another bullet wound." She lifts his head and places a white pillow under it; drapes a warm blanket over him; soothes his head with her cool hand.

"Jennifer…" he sighs.

"Dr Sullivan to you," she says. "You are going to be my patient for some time."

He gives a helpless chuckle and then catches his breath as he feels those firm, cool fingers on his searing wound.

Next he hears her snipping his britches and immediately tries to sit up.

"Lie down."

"…wanna see…"

"I hardly think so. Anyway, it's very simple so far. I am sponging away blood. What happened to the person who shot you?"

"That's not your concern."

"He's not lying in a ditch somewhere bleeding to death, is he?"

"I hope so."

"I never took you for the heartless type."

"Ouch, that hurt."

"Probably because you have a very nasty bullet wound. It appears the bullet is deeply embedded in the flesh of the lower part of your thigh. Thankfully, it has missed the bone, but it has damaged the muscle and left a mess. It's a wonder you're not faint. The bullet will have to be removed and the wound requires extensive suturing, with you under anesthesia. That way I can take a thorough look at the damage. And then you'll need to rest for a few days. And, gradually, rehabilitate that muscle."

Anesthesia? Rest? Doesn't she understand that he has more important things to do?

"I don't have days," he protests, but she seems oblivious.

"This will hurt, but I need to slow the bleeding till I operate."

He feels her hands firmly bandaging his leg. The pain seizes him and burns deep and raw; he can't help but give voice to it – a few choice words.

Then it's over.

When he gets his breath back, he pants an apology.

She comes back into view.

Around her neck she has that instrument doctors use when they want to listen to your heart.

"I have heard worse."

Her hand is cool and reassuring on his forehead.

"You'll be all right," she says softly.

Predictably, Cliff is livid. The doctor stands back and watches wide-eyed as Cliff gives him a chewing out Ethan'd be proud of. Maybe she thinks he deserves it.

"Are you gonna go look for him, Cliff?" Luke demands, while his leg throbs and sweat breaks out again.

"Well, what do you think?"

The pain sends him reeling. "Sonofabitch… Sorry, doc."

Cliff pushes his hand through his hair several times. "You know, Luke, you can be the most exasperating human being."

A few minutes later, Luke finds himself helpless in the hands of the two women. Jennifer anesthetizes him before he has to endure the indignity, and time ceases to exist.

When he wakes, his head feels thick and heavy, like he's been boozing. And his leg hurts. He's lying in a bed in a different room, which is so quiet the silence buzzes in his ears. The light of the aging afternoon strays into the room from a thinly draped window.

Gradually, as the groggy sensation subsides a little, he becomes aware of two things. One, he is in the same room – the same bed – where Byron Sawyer died. And two, he is naked beneath the sheet and the blanket which cover him – at least he thinks so. Lifting the edge of the bedclothes, he checks. Hastily, he covers up again. The only thing he's wearing is a bandage on his thigh.

There ain't a situation more nervy than being hurt and naked and in a dead man's bed. How does he get himself into these things? Now he sounds like Sara…

As panic sets in, Jennifer appears at the door. "Excellent; you're awake."

"Where are my clothes?"

"Duffy took them. They need a wash and…"

"You took my clothes off?"

"They were dirty. You were dirty." She moves to his bedside.

"You washed me?"

"I don't like dirt when I operate," she says and sticks that contraption in her ears.

"Well, you had no right. Where are my long johns?"

"The red woolen underwear? Well, after I cut…"

"You cut them? They were new. Me and Ethan sent to Houston for those long johns." He is so incensed by now he can feel his heart pounding against his ribs.

"Calm down."

"I'm naked, my clothes are in shreds and I'm lying in the same bed as a dead man and you want me to be calm."

She peels away the top of the sheet to use her contraption on his chest. He pulls the sheet back and right up to his neck.

"I think you've seen enough of me for one day."

"Mr Taylor," she begins, "Duffy removed your clothes and washed you. I did not. Now, in case you were wondering, I am happy with the repair of your leg. It will heal satisfactorily. However…"

"*You* didn't?" he asks.

For the first time since she stepped into the room she looks put out. "…however, it is imperative that you stay in bed; not only have you lost a lot of blood, but there are the sutures and the risk of infection – unless you want to limp about for the rest of your life, something that is possible anyway." She reaches for his wrist, presses her fingers gently on his pulse and consults the bold-faced watch she has pinned to her waist of her skirt.

He half-watches her, coming to grips with a mixture of frustration and remorse.

"Your pulse is normal," she says.

"Don't know how," he mumbles.

"I took your protestations into account."

"I…"

Suddenly Duffy appears; he shuts his mouth. "Mrs Knox is here, Doctor. I'll see to the blue-eyed boy."

"Very well," Jennifer says. "He's a little clammy…"

"Infection?"

"I think it is the morphine. A sponge down will do wonders."

"Not a problem."

Jennifer walks out.

Duffy gives him a fierce look. "You've been giving her a hard time."

"Now how do you know that?"

"The sponge down. Don't think I don't know what it's all about. It might interest you to know, my boy, that while I'm around that young woman will never wash a naked man. There are some things I just won't subscribe to and she knows it. She'll tell you a few things that'll make your hair stand on end, and she's as clever as any Boston-trained doctor you'll ever find, but when it comes down to it, she's just a girl. Now, me – I've had two husbands. Number One was a little like yourself. Blue eyes and a smile that'd break your heart. He was grand…"

"What happened to him?" he dares to ask.

"Well, he was killed, wasn't he? Broke my heart all right."

"And number two?"

"Ain't you the nosy parker?"

He changes the subject. "I don't like being in the same bed where Byron Sawyer died."

"Be surprised if you did. But you're in luck, my boy, because around here we change the sheets and tidy the room up a bit. Even for the likes of you…"

He rolls his eyes at her. "Can I please have some clothes?"

"I believe we keep a nightshirt in your size."

"Nightshirt?" This is getting worse all the time. "I want some pants."

"All in good time."

"Duffy?"

"What is it now?"

"Gonna throw up."

"Jesus, Mary and Joseph, where's that basin…"

Kelley

When it is apparent that Sara has not heard from Luke in many days, Kelley visits her.

"I am more concerned about you than anyone or anything I can think of. You have shut yourself in here waiting for Luke to return and you don't even know where he is or what he is doing. I can't let you do that to yourself, Sara."

"Well, what else am I supposed to do? Life goes on…"

"Exactly. *Your* life. Yours."

"Kelley, you don't un…"

"So then, what do you want to do with it?"

"Do with it?"

Kelley smiles. "Tell me one thing you want to do, or a place you want to go. Something you dream about."

"Dream about? Now, that's just nonsense. And I must wait for some word from Luke."

"Ethan is here. Why can't he wait?"

She frowns deeply. "You are serious."

"We can go anywhere you want. Aunt Edith says she will come with me if I can convince you. The three of us together would be excellent, don't you think?"

"Yes, it would, but what about Tressa?"

"We would be back before the baby comes, I promise. And she has Mama at her every beck and call. They are great friends. She won't even miss us. Not terribly anyway. Now, you have to tell me. I can see it in your face – there is somewhere."

Sara fiddles with her handkerchief.

"You know, Kelley, I never saw my little girl again. I always wanted to go back. She is so far away… I couldn't expect you to, but this is what I've longed for."

"Katrine?" Kelley breathes. "How long…"

"I can still see so clearly Morgan burying her, the tears falling down his face. I never saw Morgan cry before. And Luke, his face rigid and defiant. The wind blowing constantly. The sound of sobbing. I can still hear it after all these years, the sound of my own sobbing in my ears..."

"This was on the trail, wasn't it?"

She nods. "But not on the Chisholm, which you probably think. We came north through the Panhandle. We crossed the Indian Territory and went straight into Kansas. Just over the border Indians attacked us. Morgan reckoned they must have been following us. Anyway, there's a bend in the Cimarron River. She is there."

"Do you remember, Sara, exactly where Katrine's grave would be?"

"I'll never forget where my little girl is. Pioneers and settlers buried loved ones all across the West in those days. Fallen and buried like soldiers in unmarked graves. But not Katrine's grave – there's a huge sandstone boulder near the river – Luke carved her name into it. I can picture the place in my mind very clearly. I know I could find it because I have refused to forget."

"Looks like we are heading south to the Cimarron River."

"You can't be serious, Kelley. We can't go there. It's wild country. How would we get there?"

"Well, I'd have to look into that. The train to Denver. Then the Kansas Pacific would take us at least to the Kansas border. Horseback, wagon, stagecoach, whatever. I'm game if you are..."

"What... what about your Aunt?"

Kelley gives a chuckle. "Auntie has caught frontier fever."

"Three woman alone on such a trip... Promise me that if either of us wants to stop at any time we will respect that wish and call a halt."

"Agreed."

Luke

Cheyenne

Now that Luke has a nightshirt (he's too scared to complain that it's better suited to a fourteen-year-old boy in case Duffy takes it back and not give him another), he rests comfortably while the two women take care of him. By lunch the day after his ordeal he's feeling a lot better, although his leg hurts and he can't stop thinking about Wilson Cutter's whereabouts. Unfortunately, Jennifer insists that he stay in bed, so thinking is all he can do. Then he keeps dropping off to sleep, or more accurately, waking up and realizing he's been asleep.

Jennifer changes his bandage again after lunch. Her manner is thoughtful and gentle; she regards his wound with what can only be described as clinical fascination and tells him details of its progress even though he'd rather not know. It's not infected; the sutures are perfect; she is monitoring his morphine; if he's in a little pain it's because she has him on a low dosage…

Once she starts talking medicine it is impossible not to be fascinated by *her*.

"How are you coping with the pain?" she asks.

He shrugs.

"Did you know that you are sensitive to opiates?"

He gives his head a shake. How does *she* know?

"Are you nauseous?"

He gives a shallow nod this time.

"Mm. It will pass soon. You won't be on morphine for more than another day or so. I'm watching it carefully. The drug will pass out of your system without any further side effects. For pain relief I can give something not as strong, but it may help."

"Why?"

"Why are you sensitive?"

247

He nods.

"Some people are, that's all. Just as some people are sensitive to certain foods. What is harmless to one is poison to another. So, is there anything I can get for you?"

"Need to send a telegram."

She opens a drawer in a small desk and takes out a notebook and a pencil which she hands to him. "If you care to write down what you want to say, Duffy will see that it is sent."

"Thanks."

"It hasn't been the right time to ask before, but I've been wondering... how is Tressa?"

"Better."

She smiles and says, "I'm glad. And the miles and miles?"

"Hired a buggy."

"You did?"

"Harry's Harry."

"And her husband's family?"

"Thrilled. Took her in."

"Really? What an excellent outcome for her. She told me that where you live is very beautiful. Forests, green pastures, rivers, mountains..."

If only it didn't hurt to speak more than three words at a time.

"You'd like it."

She frowns and turns to the bedside cabinet where she squeezes out a cloth in the basin of cool water. She arranges it across his forehead. "I want you to sleep as much as you can. Don't think. Rest."

"Sit'n talk to me."

"As tempting as that is, you are not my only patient. And I said rest."

He feels like the fourteen-year-old boy who once owned his nightshirt as she smiles her goodbye and leaves; once again he watches it happen.

"I swear tomorrow I'm getting out of this damn bed," he mutters shakily under his breath. Even if he is sick to his stomach and his leg aches like the devil.

The afternoon drifts by; he watches the light change in the room; he dozes and thinks about home. He writes his telegram.

When Jennifer returns again, he's doubly glad to see her; his leg is throbbing.

"In pain?"

He nods, grimacing at the thought of…

Another needle jabbed in the muscled flank of his behind to relieve his pain, to slow him down, make him sicklish and drowsy, force him to stay put and get better.

"Brave boy…"

"Just another side of beef to you."

"I equate none of my patients to a side of beef."

She fixes his damp cloth just the way he likes it as the pain relief takes effect. He feels himself relaxing. She sits beside him on the bed and takes his pulse, listens to his heart and lungs. She lifts the sheet at his knee and checks his bandage. His pain eases.

"You are doing very well, Mr Taylor," she announces as she stands over him. "I've been speaking with Cliff Ryan. He stopped by earlier but you were sleeping. As I understand it, you and he are good friends."

"Cliff and I go back a few years, to when he was a deputy here in town. I was arrested for something I didn't do and he proved it by catching the real culprit. We've been friends ever since."

"Arrested?" she says. "You don't lead a normal life, do you, Mr Taylor?"

He grins. "About as normal as yours."

Her green eyes widen, the color reminding him of meadow grass in June, but there's also a smile hovering about in them. "As I was saying, Cliff has offered to take you in until you are well enough to travel. I think I can discharge you to his care in a day or two."

"Bunk with Cliff? That's real nice of him. You know he…"

Before he gets to yammerin' some more about Cliff, there's a confusing noise coming from the door, and a ragged breathy voice that says, "I wanna see the doctor. I wanna see the doctor now."

Luke frowns; that voice sounds familiar, although he can't be sure…

Jennifer's reaction he finds curious; she tenses at once. He hasn't seen this expression before; sharp, protective. She swings around, blocking his view. After a long moment of looking at her back, he hears her say stiffly, "Have you made an appointment?"

"Stupid woman. Do I look like the kind who cares to make an appointment?"

"I'm not sure."

"Doctor. Now!"

"The doctor is not here."

"Who are you?"

"I'm his wife..."

"You can get me what I want, lady. Drugs and bandages."

"What's wrong with you?"

"You can see the blood."

"If you have been shot, we have to report it to the sheriff immediately. So if you wouldn't mind waiting in the chairs out front, I'll send for the sheriff and the doctor."

Suddenly, Jennifer flinches, although Luke can't see why.

"Cut the crap. I want drugs and bandages."

Convinced now it is Wilson Cutter, and that Jennifer's clever run of questions has been to determine just what kind of stranger she has on her hands, Luke struggles ineffectually through the morphine.

"Who's that?" the rough voice asks.

"A worker from the mining camps. He has a very contagious fever. He's dying. You'd better keep back."

"Just get me the drugs, doctor wife..."

"You can put the gun away. I'll show you where they are..."

Gun? Well, that's a giant tip off right there... Luke tries not to panic... Or maybe he should. Can a drugged person panic? Do something...

Jennifer walks towards the door, still blocking his vision. As she edges herself across the threshold, he finally catches sight of the disheveled figure. Indeed it is Wilson Cutter. Even in profile his face is drawn and pale beneath the unkempt beard. His clothes are smeared with blood. And he has not withdrawn his gun; he has it trained on Jennifer's back.

When they're gone, Luke sits up and gives his dizzy head a shake; his stomach imitates a butter churn; as he's about to throw his legs over the side of the bed, he hears a huge ruckus in the hall.

Jennifer rushes back into the room, flushed in the face and heaving air. "I've locked him in the medicine closet. What should I do next?"

"You did what? How?"

"I... I trapped him. What should I..."

"Gees, he can blast his way out. Time... we need some time... where is this closet?"

She blinks. "It's the closet under the staircase. There's only one way out. The door."

"Fix a chair... tight... under the door handle."

"Of course. Right." She grabs the wooden chair that sits by the door and disappears again.

He can hear shouting and swearing coming from the hall. She really did have him locked up. She reappears.

"Now what?"

An explosion in the hall makes her scream.

Breathing heavily, he says, "Just stay away from the door."

"Shall I get Cliff now?"

"Sounds like a plan. Where's my gun?"

"You're not getting out of bed."

"Well, Dr Sullivan, I'd like to be able to defend myself."

And her.

"Oh. Of course." She dashes to a low chest of drawers and from the bottom draw extracts his colt. Quickly, she brings it to him like it's contaminated, also releasing half a dozen bullets into his shaky hand.

"Thank you. Now you can go get Cliff. And keep Duffy away. Run."

"Yes..."

She is gone swiftly. Meanwhile, another shot explodes in the hall. He manages to get his legs over the side of the bed; another bout of dizziness takes some moments to clear. He is torn between staggering to that medicine closet, wrenching open the door and killing the bastard, and following the doctor's orders.

Jennifer returns to him before he can make up his mind. "I ran into Duffy. I can't trust you to stay off that leg."

He grabs her wrist. "Jennifer, that man killed my friend..."

"Then he also killed Byron Sawyer," she says softly. "Your friend...Tressa's husband... I..."

"It's all right," he reassures her. "I need to check he's secure in there."

"No," she says, the doctor again. "I'll do it."

"Bullets ricochet," he warns her.

She nods and steps cautiously into the hallway. He fumbles as he tries to load bullets into his colt. A lot of thumping, banging and swearing can be heard. Another shot blasts out. Jennifer almost trips back into his room, covering her ears.

"Right, that's it," he says.

As he is about to stand up, she cries passionately, "No! The door's locked, and I pushed some furniture in front as well as the chair. He's secure, I swear."

They are both surprised at her outburst and for a moment stare at one another.

"You did all that, Jennifer..."

"You shot him," she murmurs.

He can't deny it; he can't deny that he has put her life in danger...

"And he shot you..." She puts a shaky hand to her forehead, then walks out of the room.

"Jennifer... come back..."

He realizes she has gone in the opposite direction to where Cutter's locked up. He does the only honorable thing; he finishes loading his colt and waits.

Cliff bursts in minutes later. Luke points him in the right direction. Soon a parade of three deputies follows, all of whom see him in his small nightshirt.

The usual stand off and negotiation follows. Shouts, threats and the odd shot fired; before long the deputies march Wilson Cutter down the hall. Cliff stops by.

"Got him. Good work."

"Don't look at me," he says. "I ain't allowed out of bed."

Cliff eyes shine annoyingly and he gives a low chuckle.

"Serves you right," he says and leaves.

Luke lets out a sigh, places his colt on the bedside cabinet, lies down and pulls up the sheet. He feels sick and strange...

He closes his eyes. Enough for one day, even for him.

When he wakes it is evening. A familiar cool hand rests on his forehead. By lamplight he sees Jennifer's weary face.

"I suspect that your mother would have appreciated a vial of morphine on hand when you were a boy," she says as she removes her hand.

"That comment, Dr Sullivan, is unprofessional," he murmurs.

"Mm, perhaps… Supper will be here very soon…"

"What happened this afternoon?"

"You finally went to sleep as I asked."

"You know what I mean."

"Oh, that. Well, I patched up Mr Cutter…"

"You what?"

"… under the watchful eyes of at least four US marshals. They are queuing up at the jailhouse."

He is silent, digesting the information, and then for her sake says nothing more about it.

"I have been evading journalists all afternoon. They are all desperate to speak to you too. But I told them…"

"I'm your patient and I have to stay in bed," he drawls.

"Well, actually, I told them that you maintain a strict policy of not speaking to reporters in a nightshirt, especially one that short. Enjoy your supper, Mr Taylor…"

"It's Luke," he says to her back as she walks towards the door.

"That would be unprofessional," she replies.

"So you say. And how professional is it to keep me in this kid's nightshirt so I'll stay in bed?"

"It is part of my job to treat all patients according to their needs. Don't be bad-tempered about it. It's for your own good. We caught the outlaw – you should be happy."

"Mm. So we did. And I am. Lucky for us you possess the instincts of a Texas Ranger and the reactions of a mountain cat."

Her green eyes register full surprise. She gives a jaunty, "Thank you."

"You're welcome."

"What a strange and lovely compliment. I think."

"How does it feel to be a hero?"

"You sound like a reporter."

"Thank you."

"*That* wasn't a compliment."

"No," he smiles, "I mean, thank you."

"Oh. For… for…"

"Yes."

"I have a duty of care to you as my patient, and all my other patients."

"Above and beyond," he tells her.

"Well… I'll see what's keeping your supper."

And she crosses that threshold one more time.

The following morning Duffy brings him a crutch and teaches him how to use it.

"It'll be perfect for keeping those reporters away, too. Oh, I have another surprise for you."

She has a brown paper package on the chair by the door. She removes the paper and holds up his red long johns. Only they are long no more.

"I know a seamstress. My good friend Kathleen Quinn. She's a darlin' she is. She agreed with me that these are excellent quality and a shame to waste. So she matched the right leg to the left. A fine job, don't you agree?"

"Yep," he says, staring helplessly at the short red legs, "my partner Ethan is gonna be green with envy."

Ethan

That chilly January day twenty-six and a half years ago, when a boy was born to Morgan and Sara Taylor, the whole outfit celebrated with a feast. If they had known he was gonna be so much trouble they probably would have quit after a couple of beers.

They christened him Luke (Sara's favorite name) Daniel (after Morgan's grandfather) Taylor (because he was gonna carry the family heritage to the next generation).

"But the way you're going there won't be a next generation."

"Ethan, just try and focus on the outcome. Wilson Cutter is behind bars."

"Well, I've spoken to Cliff and four US marshals could have done that!"

Ethan holds Luke's defensive glare until the boy has to look away. "So, how long are you planning to bunk with Cliff?"

"Been here ten days and don't want to outstay my welcome. Cliff's a busy man. There's a boarding house I kinda like the look of…"

"You're not coming home."

"Ethan, I can't. This is where I need to be. There are hearings starting in a couple of days. Cutter will have to answer charges on a heap of crimes. Two of those US marshals are wanting to extradite him to Colorado and some other place. Meantime Cliff says he can get me in to see the chief prosecutor, take a look at my file. Because we're claiming a connection between Ed and Wilson Cutter he thinks this Faraday will be interested. We might even get help with further investigations."

Ethan sighs. And relents with a nod.

The boy looks relieved. "So how are things back home?"

"What? Oh…"

Ethan pulls his thoughts together; doesn't know how the boy's gonna take the news. "Interestin' development... Your mother is..." He stops and clears his throat.

The boy's dark eyes narrow. "Sara is what?"

"Well, you see, son, with you away and Sara being so worried..."

"Ethan."

"Okay. Sara went along with Kelley and her Aunt Edith to the Cimarron."

Luke looks blank for a moment. "Katrine..."

Ethan nods. Then he 'fesses up. "I didn't try and stop her. I warned her, though. Gave her a pile of advice. But I figured she's always needed to go back. Should've taken her a long time ago. I told her so. She said it wasn't up to me. But, well..."

"Who is Aunt Edith?"

"You know, Kelley's New York relation. John's sister. A fine woman, too. They'll be all right. Smart women, those three."

The boy starts rubbing his tender thigh. "How is K?"

"She's fine... Don't know how you're gonna go getting her back..."

The boy is silent, rubbing his thigh, his mind's eye seeing things no one else can see.

"So, how's the leg?" Ethan asks, brightening some. "Looks like it's giving you some trouble..."

"Reckon it's healed."

"Mm. You're a quicker healer. Had plenty of practice."

"Having these damn itchy stitches removed today. Last checkup. Least I hope so. You should meet the doctor."

Ethan's stomach squirms. "Me and doctors... you know how it is..."

The boy grins at last. "Think you'll like this one."

When Ethan shakes the hand of the green-eyed filly with the shiny chestnut mane, he kinda goes into shock. To stop himself from babbling like an idiot, he says, "Did Luke give you any trouble?"

"Not at all," she says and weaves a wavy forelock behind her ear. "This is my assistant, Duffy."

Now Duffy is altogether different. Tall. Direct. And Irish.

"Pleased, I'm sure." She gives his hand a firm shake. "Sorry about the long johns," she says and returns to her desk.

Ethan gives Luke a puzzled look.

The boy chuckles and says, "I'll explain later."

Ethan waits in the room with the chairs and several other people while Luke has his checkup. At last the boy appears with the doctor by his side and without the crutch. They're both smiling. Ethan scratches his head; he makes a close study of them in the moments before the woman Duffy voices a noisy remark about Luke dispensing with his crutch too early.

"Can't thank you enough for all you did," Ethan says.

"It's been a pleasure to meet you, Mr Benchley," the doctor replies with a heart-stopper smile. "Goodbye, Mr Taylor."

"Dr Sullivan," the boy says and then puts his hat on. They leave as Duffy is announcing the next patient.

Out in the street, Ethan says, "She didn't tell you to stay outa trouble."

"So?"

"So doctors always tell you that. Figure maybe she knows she's wasting her breath."

"Very funny."

"She's just a girl…"

"You noticed."

"You know, just looking at her makes a body feel better. When she smiles you might think you're cured, or maybe died and gone to heaven. I suppose you think you've fallen for her."

"No, Ethan. What would be the point of that? She's Boston born, bred and educated."

"Ah," he says and grins, wondering why that mattered to a boy like Luke. They cross the street, negotiating a muddle of wagons. "Well, she's looked after you real well. Maybe we should take her to supper…"

"No," the boy says, weaving with a decided limp. "I think we should visit Cliff. Find out when that attorney can see us."

"There's an idea. Tell me, though, about the long johns…"

Sara

Kansas

Sara sits up in bed and rubs her eyes – gritty eyes, after days on the trail. They have spent the night in the most primitive hotel room she has ever seen in her life, in a town aptly named Lamentation. There is a bed, a table with a lamp, a washstand and a fair layer of dust on everything.

Her mind is set out like a map. They are too far north to be near the grave, although in the sameness of the treeless plains anyone could be forgiven for thinking she is witless to be so convinced. Sara cannot forget, however, the landmark that is imprinted on her memory. She knows where Katrine is. There were no supply towns back then, and no railroads. There was just the rocky outcrop on a rise on the southern bank of the Cimarron, jutting out in the scrubby landscape, on a trail they had forged themselves through the wilderness to get to a better life. Life was better with Katrine.

They should have headed to Red River Station and set off north on the Chisholm Trail; Ethan wanted to, stay on the Chisholm till they made Abilene and then head northwest, and he tried to convince Morgan it was safer. Morgan said he wanted to take a more direct route north, that it was possible. Convinced and confident as he was, they agreed, albeit reluctantly, so they went north across the Panhandle. It is fair to say that something could have gone wrong whatever trail they took; there were no guarantees for a whole host of real or imagined dangers. The trick, Morgan said, was to stay confident and keep your mind's eye on your destination, on the dream… Sara forgave Morgan for the loss of their daughter because his grief was equal to hers. They went on whether it was good for them or not, because going back was unthinkable, the price of admitting defeat or folly too dear. But how many do you lose before you say enough?

Morgan answered that question with his death. Sara ferociously grounded herself and Luke on the Diamond-T, and Ethan, himself distraught, did the same with Red Sky and Tip. The result was probably what Morgan dreamed of all along: a place to call home.

The wagon trail from Dodge City has brought Sara and her companions here. In Dodge the railroad south terminates, swinging east to Wichita instead. So, they hired a wagon and horses from the livery stables in town, the owner of which seemed determined to either fleece them of all their cash or lump them with the worst of his stock. Sara watched in awe as Kelley and Edith proceeded to bamboozle the man, and they eventually came away with quite a serviceable wagon and a pair of fine and sturdy looking horses.

The wagon has served them well. The road to Lamentation is not much better than the road from Laramie to Bright River; it is also a longer and lonelier journey and takes them several days to complete. They had camped, wagon train style, for two nights and enjoyed each other's company and their adventurousness immensely. Soon she and her intrepid companions will set out in the dry June morning, once more in search of the Cimarron and Katrine's grave. This is a pilgrimage. And Sara reflects that their journey to the heart of her pilgrimage grows, as all pilgrimages should, more difficult and discerning.

With a distance of twenty to thirty miles to go in a south-westerly direction, the trail to their destination is – according to Lamentation's hotel proprietor – nothing more than a track through the scrub and a highway for bandits and Indians who like to wander off their reservation. Any women attempting such an expedition should have their heads examined. As for their destination itself, which is where the Cimarron dips below the border into the Indian Territory, it is isolated and wild, and not a place for three women alone. Kelley had thanked him sweetly and told him that they could hardly be alone if there were three of them. The man rolled his eyes and announced they'd 'been warned'. Sara clearly recalls Tip telling her that with Kelley you make suggestions – warning her only makes her more deter-mined.

Kelley is restless, in search of more than a grave. There can be no doubt she is driven; a person has only to look in her eyes. Perhaps she is proving something, either to herself or to Luke.

In any case, she is truly an extraordinary companion. She is fearless to be sure, and an excellent horsewoman. She has brought a compass, which Mart taught her how to use as a child. She carries a small pistol in the pocket of her dress or coat, which horrifies Edith, but which she has convinced them is a necessity. She can use it as well as she wields the compass.

Edith takes everything in her stride, with difficulties a curious and almost intellectual challenge. The dust and the heat of the past several days, traveling in the wagon, prove particularly bothersome. Edith, however, sits straight-backed, with her wide-brimmed hat low over her eyes and her sleeves pushed up to her elbows. A leafy branch serves as her swish as she fans herself and keeps the insects at bay. They have formed a firm friendship and talk on a great many topics, all of which Sara finds stimulating and an excellent way to pass the time. Once they have latched onto a topic and are in high discussion, Kelley lapses into one of her quiet moods for which they both share an unspoken concern.

After breakfast, Sara and Edith settle with the proprietor. He gives them a look of demeaning sympathy, which Edith tells him does little for his overall appearance. But he gives them something else, something extremely valuable. A map.

"It's on the house, ladies," he mutters. "Lord knows you're gonna need it."

Outside in the street, Kelley has brought the wagon and horses from the livery stable and has begun loading their gear into the back. Sara helps her, commenting that it looks like a hot, dry day ahead. Kelley agrees and they both set about filling their water barrels to the brim.

By the time they finish, Edith has returned with a pleasant-looking lad who carries two large boxes brimming with supplies. She gives him a generous commission. She comments that he is a nice young man for such a one-horse town. Kelley laughs and compliments her aunt on her quick study of frontier vernacular. It is good to hear Kelley laugh.

They consult their map carefully and then set out in high spirits for their destination on the Cimarron.

Kelley

The Cimarron River
on the Kansas border with Indian Territory

A hot drying wind springs up on the trail about an hour out of town. It is unpleasant, blowing dust in their eyes and rendering their dress impractical and uncomfortable. No one complains, however, such is their determination.

The hotel proprietor in Lamentation is correct about the state of the trail. Their progress is painstaking. But the map has proved an invaluable companion to Mart's compass and Aunt Edith can frequently be heard to exclaim, "God bless that dreadful innkeeper!" They are alert to hidden dangers, such as snakes, as well as the bandits and the Indians. So far, their worst nightmares reside solely in their imagination.

They take water regularly. Two dehydrated and dizzy aunts are not on Kelley's list of preferred experiences. The heat persists and intensifies as they traverse a particularly dry area. Then, in the shimmering band of heat on the horizon, they see clumps of trees hovering like green clouds. In these parts trees grow by rivers and creeks. The Cimarron lies ahead. They remind one another that distances in this huge expanse are deceiving.

The Cimarron cuts an impressive path through the expanse of wide-open spaces and drifting plains. Trees map its course into the infinity of the horizon. They reach it three hours later. On consulting the map there are three differing yet expert opinions on where they actually are, but they all agree on one point: how very much cooler it is by the river.

They make camp on the northern side and decide to look for an appropriate crossing in the morning.

"So, Kelley," Sara asks over supper, "what do you think of the Cimarron?"

"It's wild and beautiful, just as I imagined. When we cross tomorrow we could follow this northern bank and then cross where you did, Sara."

"I won't recognize the crossing from this side," Sara says softly. *Because you couldn't look back...*

"So we find a safe place to cross, then follow the southern bank."

Aunt Edith says, "And I think, darling, we should keep some distance away from the river. I suspect Sara might need a certain perspective to locate the approach. What do you think, Sara?"

"That would be very helpful, Edith. I remember the ground is sandy... a wide sandy stretch. There are large rocks just before you come to the riverbank. Must be ancient as the earth itself. There are thick trees on the other side, that's why we'd never see it from this bank. Morgan buried her; made a cross for her. My baby buried in unhallowed ground. Luke carved her name in the sandstone. I never took much notice of what he was doing, but there it was, as I said my last goodbye. Strange... He must have wondered if we would ever return ..."

Sara waits most of the following day for her certain perspective. The safest place to cross is miles downstream; a shallow, rocky wash which, although a little bumpy, is certainly firm under their wheels with an easy entry and egress. Cutting a trail through the thick grass and scrub on the other side is slow and difficult. Insects of an irritating and voracious nature attack them, a legacy of being too close to the river. So they head further south into the heat and leave the pests to their precious coolness. They actually sight the presence of life in the thickets by the river, and enjoy the lyric sounds of blue jay and scissortail chirping madly in the trees. They even glimpse human life traversing the hot plain, parallel to them yet so far off in the shimmering distance they cannot tell, nor care to know, whether they are Indian, bandit or cowboy.

They come upon Sara's perspective without realizing it at first. They distinguish a vague trail leading south into the heat of the prairie. They look north to see where it is headed. A large outcrop of yellow sandstone rocks and boulders skirted by a sandy dune apparates in front of them. From the direction they have come, a forest of juniper and cottonwood sitting proudly on a knoll obscures the landmark.

The trail sidetracks the rocks and obviously heads to the River. Although they know it is there, the Cimarron is hidden from them.

They sit in the middle of the plain looking south, then north. The road in and the road out.

Kelley turns the horses northward and spurs them on. She follows the trail and for a short time forgets that this is Sara's pilgrimage. She becomes enveloped by the enormity of what happened here.

Kiowa-Apache attacked the Taylor party further to the south. Assaulted the small wagon train with their chilling war cries, their deadly lances and arrows, and their fierce resistance to resolute white occupation. Morgan and Ethan, their fighting skills honed in war, fought hard and drove them off, only to discover that in the confusion Katrine had been taken. The Kiowa-Apache tore Katrine from her family and fled across this desolate prairie. Her terror Kelley can only imagine. She would have begged for her life. And how much she suffered before they killed her and left her in the manner which had Luke sleepless and sick for so long is an indication of their deadly resolve, and a grim warning to all who pass this way. The Taylors and Benchleys searched frantically, tracking the Kiowa-Apache warriors north to this place. And here they discovered her body. Her killers had fled back to the plains once more. These vast, eternal plains, surely not purposed for such grisly bloodshed and misery. More than once she can't help but look over her shoulder.

She draws the wagon to a halt a little distance from the edge of the dune. Sara is pale and solemn.

How did you live through this?

"Sara?"

"It's all right, Kelley. I just need time to take it all in. Keep on going and stop at the top of the trail. It's too dangerous to stop here and walk. Too many snakes." She pats Kelley's arm and looks ahead.

"Very well." The horses need little encouragement; they can smell the river.

They progress into the place, awed by the windy silence and the grandeur of the sandstone formation. The heat and glare off the sand and rock is harsh and uncomfortable.

Kelley pulls up the wagon, engages the brake, secures the reins, and surveys the whole scene. Aunt Edith is doing the same. Sara is climbing down from the wagon.

"Take it easy, Sara…"

"Don't worry about me, Kelley," she says.

Nevertheless, Kelley follows her to the ground. "Do you want us to go up there with you… I mean, we understand if you don't. It's just that it might be safer…"

Sara takes her hand. She smiles up at Aunt Edith still seated in the wagon. "We've done everything else together. Let's go."

KATRINE

…the letters had been hewn deeply into the rock, by blunt force and crude chisel. By profound love. By overwhelming grief. For all time. No one would ever forget her – not unless someone blasted away the sandstone. Flood and drought may come and go, the elements could assault it mercilessly, but Katrine Taylor will be remembered forever.

They walk together, stand in silence for a moment, and then leave Sara alone at her daughter's astonishingly beautiful tomb. Kelley and Aunt Edith sit quietly on a rock some little distance from where Sara stands staring at the ground and watch her. When she suddenly drops to the ground and clutches at the sand with her fingers, Kelley becomes alarmed.

Aunt Edith's hand steadies her. "Let her be, darling. She came here to do this, and do it alone. No matter how painful it is for us to watch her, we cannot enter into it with her because we cannot understand the depth of her anguish. Even you and I losing Martin and your Uncle Keith cannot compare. Her innocent young daughter. All alone. Killed in such an unspeakable fashion. One consolation, though, thank God Luke had the inspiration and the energy to effect that carving in the rock."

Kelley gives in to her own despair. Katrine's life was wasted, a life of promise cut down, and for what?

Wasn't liberty and property merely the kernel of what became a terrible propaganda of promoting westward expansion as though it was divinely purposed, as though land acquisition and nationhood are inseparable?

Even the Indians believe that the land does not belong to them personally; they are a part of the whole... Is that really such a crazy idea? She can hear Luke's voice in her head: *Ain't that what all of us want, to be connected to the earth?*

She stands up, feeling deeply agitated. *Some know how.*

"Where are you going?" Aunt Edith asks.

"For a walk," she replies. *And some do not.*

"Whatever is the matter, darling?"

Kelley looks out over the plain as it lies glistening like a blue-green jewel in the sun. "I want my life back... I wish you had stopped me from ever going home, Auntie. I wish I'd never come back. I wish I had stayed in New York forever. I would still have my independence, and my life with you. Why didn't you tell me that there is nothing better than what I had with you, the way I was?"

Aunt Edith stares at her. "Would you have believed me?"

"What was that voice then, in my head, day and night...?"

"The call for you, as a grown woman, to consciously choose, I suspect." Aunt Edith stands up and sighs. "Kelley, my darling, we have spoken about this so many times. Freedom, independence and such things each demand a certain responsibility. A person's freedom may well enslave someone else. Desire for independence may harden one's heart to the needs of others. You know all this, darling, but I suspect you can see a very dramatic example of it all around you at this very moment, and it's a little hard to take..."

"Yes. I despise what Luke holds dear. Even Pa maybe..."

Aunt Edith takes Kelley's hand in hers. "I know you're angry and hurt, but you can't hate people who act on their principles. Well, at least, you never used to..."

"And I have acted on mine."

"Yes," she agrees softly, "you have. Kelley, a woman's love for a man, if it is true, has a remarkable quality. It accommodates his principles while never compromising her own. And in time all the hardness of heart softens and the good things unite to become sound and solid."

"Luke thinks I am crazy about my independence. That I love *it* more than I could ever love him. I guess he's right."

"Insightful, perhaps," Aunt Edith murmurs. "And it seems he certainly knows you well. But circumstances change. People change. Love changes people…"

"Yes, but it didn't change me enough."

"Maybe not just yet… with a little practice."

"I couldn't tell him what he wanted to hear." The topic becomes too difficult to discuss any further. "Excuse me, Auntie…"

Kelley walks off in the direction of the prairie, keeping to the narrow trail. There are rocks scattered all about the area. As she stomps along she almost treads on a rattlesnake sunning itself. Stunned, they glare at one another for a split second. Then, threatened and afraid, it begins to rattle its tail. She is afraid also. Too close to move away without it striking her, there is only one thing to be done. She extracts the colt from her pocket and shoots the snake, the blast shattering the hot silence and throbbing out in endless waves of sound across the plain. She stares at its lifeless body, admiring the perfection of its markings. It retains the dignity its Creator intended, only now she has taken its life.

Aunt Edith and Sara come rushing up, breathless.

"Don't worry. I shot a rattlesnake. You're right, Auntie. If I hadn't been here, espousing my right to trample all over its home, it would still be alive, at least not dead by my hands and this gun." Kelley stops and takes deep breath. "I'm sorry. I think I need to be alone for a while."

She retraces her steps to where Katrine's name is emblazoned on the golden stone. In much the same way as she had done with Mart's tombstone, she traces her fingers in the carving.

Luke had made these letters. A boy who loved his sister. A defiant and tenacious boy. He hadn't changed; he never would.

Aunt Edith and Sara are waiting by the wagon.

"It's getting late. We should think about a place to bed down for the evening," Kelley tells them.

Aunt Edith looks around. "You know best about these things, darling."

"Maybe beside that forest over there?" Sara suggests. "I want to be close by just this one night. We've come such a long way."

Kelley smiles at her. "You wish is my command."

Sara returns her smile with one of gratitude and then hugs her. "You are the only person I know who could kill a rattlesnake and be grief-stricken about it."

The warm, motherly hug is indeed welcome. "I want you to stay here as long as you like, Sara. Aunt Edith and I will set up camp and see to supper. This is your day."

"Splendid idea, darling," Auntie says. "You are a good girl."

It is pleasing to have her say so because, for Kelley, trying and succeeding are totally different.

Edith

Being one of three women seated around a glowing campfire at night in the heart of frontier wilderness is not something I have ever pictured myself doing.

It is so far removed from my Manhattan home that I have to stop myself from laughing. Not only that, but the stories I am hearing around this campfire make my blood run cold and send the proverbial shiver up and down my spine. Sara and Morgan Taylor's expedition from the Red River in Texas across these wild and lonely prairies is the stuff of legends and now I understand how it once captured Kelley's imagination. But it is Sara's last memory of Katrine that breaks my heart.

"She had a determined streak in her, such spirit. I had already pulled her away, protesting, from the fighting after Morgan ordered us to the wagon. She'd been helping Luke. Red Sky stayed with Ethan, but Katrine and I crouched together beside our wagon, my arms tight about her, the attack raging all around us. Then Morgan called me to help him load. I told her to stay put but she said she would help Luke. He was just a boy, doing a man's job; he should have been taking cover with his sister. She didn't want to leave him. At some point after I left her, when she must have tried to get back to Luke, she was taken. It was utter confusion. I called for her amid the noise and fear. She was nowhere, and I will never, ever forget what that felt like."

Sara sighs, trembling.

"It has been a very long time since I have given an account of that day. This is the time and place, it was due, but for the rest of my life I never want to speak of it again."

"We won't," I say, barely holding back my sobs.

I look at Kelley, doing a double-take when I see the cold and brooding expression in her eyes.

What is going on in the mind of my niece is more than a rejection of the young man Luke, or even of her father's beliefs for that matter (after so long idealizing them); I believe that in her mind she is formulating her own life's philosophy, one that is somewhat severe upon herself and a little unaccommodating of human nature (a predictably youthful tendency). While the process is fascinating to observe, it is not the way to win Luke. She believes, however, she has abandoned that ideal for a higher one. I am becoming increasingly curious about the young man and wish I had met him at least once. If he is like most other men, he is bound to want a wife who at the very least pretends to offer some deference to his wishes.

"I don't know how you ever got through it, Sara," Kelley says. "All of it, any of it. I could not have done what you did."

Knowingly, wisely, Sara shakes her head.

"Kelley, you are only twenty years old. You don't know yet what you can and cannot endure. The human spirit wants to be tested by the unknown. Why else do we make these impossible journeys? Who would have thought the three of us would come here? I thought I was destined to stay in Bright River. I couldn't bring myself to venture any further. Journeys have only brought me suffering. But I am here, where in my dreams I've longed to come for so many years." Sara smiles at me. Kindred spirits, we two. Me in my Manhattan way. She in her frontier way. "Look at your aunt. I'll wager three months ago the last place she thought she would have found herself was out in the middle of nowhere – the Indian Territory and all."

"Amen to that," I say. "And I like it immensely. You always told me, Kelley, of how much freedom you feel out here in the West. In the wide-open spaces. Away from the city. Away from all its constraints. I believed you because it was plainly obvious you felt it. I never thought I would feel it too. I can see how it gets into your blood."

Kelley gives me her gentlest smile. She is heartfelt as she says, "I'm glad for you, Auntie. Everybody should know how it feels sometime in their lives. And I'm very glad we came here. To pay tribute to brave and spirited Katrine."

"Here, here!" I say softly.

"My sweet little girl, always in my heart..." Sara murmurs.

How vibrantly the fire dances in its hearth of prairie stones! I follow the column of smoke as it rises to the heavens and catch my breath. The black sky is awash with white stars.

A little later Kelley declares herself ready for sleep, and kisses each of us with warmth and affection.

"Enjoy the fire," she says sleepily.

When all is quiet in the covered wagon, Sara says, "I think this trip has been good for all of us, Edith. I just wish..."

I know what Sara wishes. "We won't give up just yet, Sara."

"Will she return to New York with you?"

"She has said as much."

Sara is plainly disappointed.

"But she turns twenty-one soon. And unless I am very much mistaken, all women from twenty-one years have the franchise in Wyoming."

Sara blinks. "Why, yes. We do."

I chuckle with delight. "She's not going anywhere just yet."

We proceed in a happier mood to prepare for the night.

The following morning we spend some time bidding farewell at Katrine's grave. Kelley and I pack, allowing Sara plenty of time with her memories.

As we secure our belongings in the back of the wagon, Kelley says, "You know, Auntie, I think we should return the way we came."

I take her meaning, and when we set out we do not cross the Cimarron at the point where the Taylors made their painful crossing so many years ago. Kelley turns the wagon and we head back the way we came.

The cornerstone of our pilgrimage, a young girl who died when her life had barely begun, and whose name gives dignity and beauty to a lonely prairie, has led us further into the heart of ourselves than we could have ever imagined.

SEVEN

Patient, courageous, and strong...
if ever
There were angels on earth,
as there are angels in heaven,
Two have I seen and known;
and the angel whose name is Priscilla
Holds in my desolate life the place
which the other abandoned.
Long have I cherished the thought,
but never have dared to reveal it,
Being a coward in this, though
valiant enough for the most part.

Henry Wadsworth Longfellow
The Courtship of Miles Standish

❧◆❧

Luke

Cheyenne

Luke thinks long and hard as he sits on the steps of the courthouse building, giving his leg a soothing rub. Since Ethan's return home four days ago he's had plenty of time for it. And in the process arose the intuitive notion that by now Ed would know about Wilson Cutter and be thinking that three weeks was a fair enough time to put between Cutter's arrest and doing something about it. With his file bundled up in a leather satchel and in the hands of Cheyenne's chief prosecutor for over a week, seeming to be going nowhere, he could feel disheartened, but he's not. He knows it will take time and he knows that only hard evidence turns the process of law into the deliverer of justice. While guilt about K often sneaks up on him, he doesn't need to rationalize her impulsiveness and lack of patience. Over the last four days he has committed himself to a period of vigilance; her presence, however well meaning, would not be appropriate. *Patience is a virtue*, Mart said. Well, it might be only a recent virtue, but it will be what powers him until something else is required.

He gets to his feet and sighs at the courthouse.

If he hadn't just talked himself into virtue he would be banging on the door of that prosecutor right now, only to get himself thrown out. They have met only once, at the time Cliff arranged. Luke found Cameron P. Faraday a little suspicious of him and quite unhappy about the circumstances leading to Cutter's arrest. And yet, at the same time, Faraday, an Eastern attorney in his early thirties, had a deliberate way about him that suggested he wouldn't toss Luke's file into a drawer and forget about it. He listened attentively, asked a few shrewd questions, which gave the impression he had caught on fast, and told Luke that without a witness to Mart's murder who could link it directly to Ed Parsons' activities he couldn't do much.

273

But he did promise that he would read the contents of Luke's file; and then he told Luke not to give up. As Luke shook Faraday's hand that morning, something in the attorney's expression gave him cause to hope, and so was born his understanding of what was required of him if he was to succeed; he needed to be on the case and ready for anything. Consequently, he sat in the back of the public gallery of the supreme court and observed Faraday trying a criminal case before a judge called Ambrose B. Callaghan and a jury that included two women; meanwhile, he convinced Cliff to lend him some law books; Cliff handed him a couple with a wry 'good luck'. He struggled with the convoluted expression and the legal terms but he persisted, and with generous explanation from Cliff, and despite Ethan's constant ribbing, he began to form a better than average notion of the law.

With the warm summer sun pouring down, he continues on his way, thinking about Wilson Cutter residing deep inside the jail beside the courthouse. Cliff told him they are trying to keep the cell either side of Cutter vacant. Keeping Cutter at all is proving a strain because those four US marshals are squabbling over who has first priority on extradition. The whole process has stalled. Something else Luke thinks Ed Parsons might find useful. At present, retribution for Mart's murder lies buried beneath a mountain of bigger issues. However, as Luke scans the midday hustle of down-town Cheyenne, he is determined to find a way to the top.

He strolls two blocks west, through the knot of churches, and turns on to 17th. The street is a maze of wagons and horses and people with business to transact. The buildings are made of timber, stone or brick, and their signs are fancy and eye-catching. Produce is visible in large windows or stacked in doorways or encroaching on the sidewalk. There is a raw truth in the pursuits of the common people, undisguised and sometimes unflattering, and he likes the feeling of solidarity it gives him.

He decides that lounging casually against a slip rail outside the saloon is a little too obvious, so he leaves the tinkering piano, muffled voices and the wafting smell of booze and heads up the street towards Jennifer's block. Nearby there is a barber, a fruit and vegetable market, a dry and fancy goods emporium, a tobacco store and an establishment built by the enigmatic Mr Wang who claims he can cure you with herbs and a mysterious kind of massage. Three women are picketing with signs outside his shop front for him to be closed down; he's been allowed to trade outside the Chinese quarter because he relieved the Mayor of his back complaint, Mrs Mayor of her rheumatism and a number of their friends of their woes. Now his business is expanding and he's also attracting Chinese, mostly from the mining camps, into town. Jennifer told Luke that she finds Mr Wang interesting and that a lot of people in Cheyenne are ignorant and yet to understand the meaning of tolerance. She fears Mr Wang will be forced out, particularly when the Mayor is seeking re-election.

Luke takes up his position on a bench on the sidewalk outside a gentleman's outfitters. The picketing ladies march silently up and down about ten yards away. Jennifer's place is just beyond that on the opposite side of the street, but he can see folks (he should probably call them patients) coming and going. He looks back the way he came. People weave themselves into a tapestry and he needs to focus more acutely. What is he actually looking for? Something… someone… He will know it when he sees it and that's about as concrete as he can be.

Minutes stretch. Why is this instinct so strong that what he waits for seems as though it's already here? So peculiar in fact that *day after day* he always finds himself waiting *here*, not at the train depot or anywhere else for that matter?

Jennifer appears at her door. She is seeing off two children, one older, one younger. Then, she looks up and down the sidewalk, steps to the edge and takes a deeper perspective of the whole street. Her hair shines bright in the sun. He smiles to himself… Taabe… What was she doing all those years ago when he was riding Taabe? A young girl with shiny chestnut hair in Boston… Read a lot more books than most other girls, he reckons.

She loops that wayward lock of hair around her ear and then raises her face skyward, taking a deep, sun-filled breath. He hasn't spoken to her in four days; not since Ethan wouldn't let up on the idea that they take her to supper before he left town and Luke had to give in… He hauls his eyes back to street.

Three riders move into view, a change from the tangle of wagons and buggies. They are still some distance down the street.

When he swings his eyes back to Jennifer, she has gone. He still couldn't extract from her the things he wanted to know, even after two hours over supper. She was reserved at first, until Ethan told her his jaded 'female company' jokes. Luke, knowing them all by heart, found the laughter they put in Jennifer's green eyes a refreshing use for them...

The riders move closer. He squints against the sun. He doesn't know them. They move on up the street.

Then there were Jennifer's jokes... Eventually Ethan asked where she'd got them. Medical school... *you don't think I heard them in polite society, do you?* Nope. She was different all right. Ethan was downright intrigued.

Luke lets out a laugh and attracts the curious attention of a passer-by, a middle-aged woman who glances back at him over her shoulder, which is when he notices two more riders moving in. These two immediately set his pulse racing. He is mesmerized for a moment, even as the blood rushes to his head; then he lowers his hat over his eyes and drops his head on his chest. Not until their booted feet (one pair in eagle beak taps) and the bay and white fetlocks of their mounts go by, does he raise his eyes. As he stands to watch their casual progress, he suddenly comprehends why he has needed to be here, near Jennifer's. It sends a shiver up his spine, and he crosses the street.

Luke

Harris and Richards dismount outside Jennifer's; Richards dusts off his eagle beak taps. Both men are wearing suits, which can only mean they have been here at least overnight. Luke observes them enter Jennifer's and close the door behind them. He thinks of the little bell... Swiftly, he moves down the sidewalk and gets to door. The shades are rolled up; a quick peak reveals the pair speaking to Jennifer. He takes a calming breath, puts his hand on the door handle and enters. As the bell over the door rings his arrival, Ed's men turn and see him. Jennifer, it seems, is so distracted by the affronting presence of them that she doesn't notice him. It's an auspicious moment, Ed showing his hand. Luke closes the door sedately in spite of his racing pulse. The waiting room is empty of patients.

"Well, well," says Richards, "look what the cat dragged in."

"Yeah," says Harris, "a rat."

"Thought you might show up," says Richards.

"Well, I've been waiting for you. A regular rat convention," Luke tells them and watches their lofty expressions fall a couple of notches. "I think you're lost; Ed's boy Wilson is in the jailhouse at the other end of town. The deputy can tell you visiting hours."

"We're looking for a doctor," Harris announces with hard, staring eyes that glisten with mean purpose.

"You don't look sick to me," Luke replies. "Now there's a saloon down the street. You could probably use a drink." Luke opens the door for them and the bell tinkles.

"What makes you think we're gonna let you talk that way?"

"Well, my reason for restraint ain't alive anymore. Cutter saw to that. So, you leave the young lady alone and get on with your own business. And don't think I ain't curious to see how the cat jumps. Good day, gentlemen."

Luke steps back from the door. They say nothing and stride out smelling of saddle wax and cheap aftershave. He pushes the door closed and watches them through the glass pane. They mount up and ride away in the direction they came.

He blows a loud sigh and remembers Jennifer. He looks around; she is standing still with one hand over her heart. She holds the other up to her forehead.

"Duffy?" he calls out.

"Right here." Duffy appears in the archway, wide-eyed. "I heard every word, don't you fear none about that, my lad. The gall of 'em..."

Jennifer, however, is glaring fiercely at him. "Life was so peaceful around here until you came along."

"Miss Jennifer! Is that any way for you to be talking to your guardian angel?"

"Angel?" Jennifer gasps, her eyes flashing. With her finger jabbing at the air in his direction, she says, "I want you to go the same way as those other two. Out. And don't ever come back." She storms off into her room and slams the door. He feels his head jerk back.

He and Duffy exchange glances.

"Ah, she doesn't really mean it," Duffy says softly. "They gave her a fright, demanding to know if she's the doctor who caught the outlaw and them not looking at all like reporters."

He swallows awkwardly. "What did she tell them?"

"God love her, she said she was and she'd do it again. So you see, she's afraid of her own courage more than those two men. Although only the good Lord knows what they intended. She should be thanking you."

"No... It's my fault. I should talk to her."

"Later. When she's cooled down, don't you think?" Duffy raises an eyebrow at him. "The plot thickens, so they say. Will you fetch Mr Ryan, or shall I?"

"No, no... I'll go," he says. "I'm gonna ask him to get a statement from you, Duffy..."

"I understand. And I'm sure Jennifer will oblige. When she's stopped being mad at you. Now off you go."

Later, he writes another page for his file. He includes what actually occurred and also outlines the implications just as he always does, but even more precisely and with that notion of law. He is tempted to rush over to the courthouse to slot the page in his file, but as he stares at the words they blur and his intuition cuts in once again. *Just wait.* All these insights are beginning to unnerve him. And he hasn't a clue where they're coming from. Something haunts his thoughts. At five o'clock that evening he heads back down to Jennifer's.

Luke

As Luke steps up to the door, Jennifer has her hand in position to pull down the shade. They stare at each other through the glass. He hopes he looks contrite enough so that she'll let him in. The shade comes down. He stands there nonplussed. Mm. He moves to the next door, she stares at him icily, he mouths the words 'I'm sorry' but the same thing happens; the shade comes down. No doors or windows with their shades up remain. In spite of himself, he starts to chuckle. He strides to the narrow alley that runs the side of her building and makes his way to the back entrance. (He has since discovered that the building itself used to be the town house of an Eastern businessman, who had made his fortune initially from the fur trade and then from cattle even before the boom of the last few years.) There is access on three sides of the building – front, side and back. Around back he goes. Her private entrance. Up a small stoop. Same kind of door, only the shade is already down. He raps on it firmly.

"Jennifer, open the door… Jennifer…"

No luck. He sits on the stoop with sigh. *Not a good idea to tick off your allies*. One of Ethan's sayings. He looks up and down a stretch of back entrances and across to their opposing neighbors, reminding him of people who refuse to speak to one another. The shade trees are pleasant.

He leans back against the door and remembers a time when Cheyenne wasn't like this. When this old building was probably one of the most sophisticated in town. Cheyenne was a wild town in those days. Decidedly woolly. With a string of travelers passing through pronouncing their judgment of a harsh and hellish place. Then came Gold! in Sweetwater and the Black Hills. And coal, tons of it, and the Union Pacific, with its territorial labyrinth of coalmines and troubled workforce of immigrant miners.

And enterprising men like Francis E. Warren, and Loren Bodecker. And, of course, the booming cattle industry, and the wealth of the cattle barons, who fatten their massive herds on the great prairies.

All have turned Cheyenne from a cow town and a 'hellish' stop on the transcontinental railway into a good-looking city with industry, gas and electricity, electric street lamps (new ones were going up every day) and telephones; with prosperity, law and order, culture and, above all, promise. But some day, progress aside, when there ain't a blade of grass left on the overstocked plains and the whole cattle business goes bust because of it, he and Ethan will still be raising first grade cattle on the Diamond-T. This territory will be grateful that there are cattlemen who envisioned the way it should be done.

Daylight becomes golden pink.

Dusk arrives, heralded by a parade of gorgeous colors. And then begins to fail.

Suddenly, the door opens and he falls backwards.

Lying flat on his back, he looks up into Jennifer's astonished upside-down face. "Nice evening, ain't it?"

"What are you doing?"

"Apologizing."

She actually crouches down beside him and attempts to help him up. "Did you hurt yourself?"

He gets to a sitting position. "Not sure..."

"You *would* know," she reproaches him and stands up again.

"I'm dizzy..."

"You're faking..."

He pretends to faint, muttering, "Forgive me..."

"Now you are making a joke of something that is extremely serious."

He opens his eyes. "Those men are no joke and them doing what they did is as serious as it gets."

"My point exactly."

"But I know, Jennifer, that you are..."

"What?" she asks suspiciously.

"Above it," he says and sits up again. "Jennifer, I'm groveling at your feet..."

"You know what this whole situation reminds me of? One of those popular novels you can buy back east. All about the Wild West. The *Five Cent Wide Awake Library* is popular. Or *Beadles Half Dime Library* will give you all the action of *Pawnee Bill...*"

"What are you talking about?"

"Oh, I beg your pardon. You don't need to read any Wild West novels. You are too busy providing the plots. They write them about men like you."

Intrigued, he squawks, "Do they?"

"The determined cowboy and the hardened gunslinger. I always thought they were abysmally contrived. And yet here you are – Cheyenne Luke!"

"If you say so," he says with a smile. Clearly, she's been doing some reading other than medical books...

"So what *do* you read?" she asks with sarcasm he finds amusing.

To mention that he's reading Cliff's law books seems kinda pretentious, as well as playing into her mood, so he shrugs and says, "Stuff. Just stuff... does it matter what I read?"

"No... I... no. I didn't mean..."

"What did you mean?"

"I...I am just... annoyed with you about before."

"I know," he says sympathetically. "I do that to a lotta folks. I don't want *you* to be."

She studies him silently, which has him both unnerved and intrigued. At last, she says, "I accept your apology. I think you should get up now." Her tone is flat and disappointingly aloof.

He gets to his feet favoring his injured thigh. "Thank you."

Grim and peaky she looks. She wraps her fingers around the door handle and avoids his eyes.

"I have work to do," she says. "So if you don't mind..."

"And you're sure you're all right?"

"I am perfectly fine."

"Well, don't work too hard."

"I won't," she says. She gets a determined look on her face.

He takes it like a man, says goodbye and leaves.

The door closes behind him.

Jennifer's peaked face haunts him right through supper and then afterwards as he strolls the streets, her block in particular, for any sign of Harris and Richards or suspicious after-dark activity. So, by the light of a waxing moon, he finds himself walking right up to her back door.

The shade is up and he can see golden light within, probably coming from the parlor since the kitchen is in darkness. He knocks softly and waits. The dark alley is dotted with spots of light from the buildings and backyards it divides. He hears a dog bark, then another. Someone a few doors down on the opposite side hollers; someone hollers back...

"Come on, Jennifer," he mutters.

He senses movement. Lamplight appears in the kitchen. She has electric lighting but is kinda quirky about how she uses it. She has a telephone too, located on the wall beside the front doors; in the Wyoming Telephone and Telegraph Company directory her number is 108. Duffy let him use it once, to tell Cliff he was being released and he would see him at home. But Cliff came and fetched him, they bought some supplies and got him settled in...

Jennifer opens the door.

"Luke..." she says, and adds in an arched tone, "More apologizing?"

"Making restitution. I'm checking up on you," he replies in a tone to match hers.

"Oh. I... I'm better, thank you."

He can see for himself that she looks brighter so his concern is already satisfied.

"I have some very good friends looking after me," she explains.

He nods. "That's just fine."

"Yes, there's no need to be concerned any longer."

"Well, it was my fault that it happened."

"That's true. But everything seems fine now."

"Then I guess I'll be getting back to my..."

"Don't tell me you are still watching out for those dreadful men?"

Before he can decide whether it is wise or not to tell her they ain't likely to give up, he hears a woman's voice. "Are you all right, Jen?"

Jennifer glances in the direction of the voice, then back at him. "Come in."

"No… thanks but…"

"I understand you've met Cam Faraday," she says with a raised brow and a slight smile. "He and his wife Meg are my very dear friends."

This ain't a great surprise when he thinks about it.

He narrows his eyes on her which she seems to find amusing. Trying to see Faraday is like waiting for Christmas.

"You're helping me; why?"

"To be honest, Cam and I were just talking about you. Unless I'm mistaken you need help, and considering I appear to be in the thick of *your* business…"

They stare at one another; and as fascinating as that is, he doesn't know what to make of the situation.

"Jen, do you need help?" That voice again. Young and full of life.

"I promise you'll like them," Jennifer says softly.

"Can you promise they'll like me?"

She opens the door wide. "Come on, shy boy."

He laughs a little and shifts from one foot to other.

"There you are, still in one piece…" Faraday's tall figure comes in contact with the yellow glow of the lamp.

"Cam, you remember Luke Taylor," Jennifer says.

"Yes, of course." Faraday extends his hand to Luke at once. "Taylor…"

Luke returns the firm grip. "Faraday…"

Almost immediately, a small pretty woman appears at his side. "What is going on out here?"

Faraday introduces her as his wife, Meg. She's young, at least ten years younger than Faraday, with dark, curled hair. She's cute; perky but soft. She lights up the back door as good as any lamp.

"I hope Jennifer has asked you in, Mr Taylor," she says.

"Don't want to intrude…"

"Not at all, Taylor. Give us a chance to talk. Jennifer and I have been discussing what happened today. I'm interested to hear your perspective."

"I'll make some fresh coffee," says Meg Faraday like it's a fresh idea.

A glance at Jennifer; she is pressing back a smile with her lips. She catches his eye and raises her brow again.

"Now why didn't I think of that," she murmurs.

Luke's perspective preludes a short discussion on the case he is trying to mount against Ed Parsons. The file is briefly touched on from time to time, but what unfolds is informal and friendly. For some time they speak about where they were born, where they have lived, should Wyoming become a State and related politics, and how they wished they'd been in New York last year for the opening of some bridge over the East River.

"They had fireworks that lasted for at least one hour," Meg Faraday tells him. "Can you imagine...?"

"I can imagine a very stiff neck," Jennifer answers and Cam Faraday chuckles.

"Saw some spectacular fireworks in San Francisco. Chinese New Year," Luke says.

"You've been to San Francisco?" breathes Meg.

"Mm. I was a longshoreman in the harbor. Struck up a friendship with a Chinese boy my own age. His father had worked on the transcontinental railway. We were loading a clipper one day and I told him I'd give anything to sail on her. He'd asked one of the crew if they were taking on any more men, and they were. He said they didn't care if you didn't have much experience. 'Why don't you, Luke?' he said. I told him I had promised my mother I wouldn't leave the country; I was young and I think she was convinced I would never return home. 'Very good thing to honor your mother,' my friend said, 'so you must be my guest at Chinese New Year, help you get over your disappointment.' Now that was some party..."

"Where was she bound?" Jennifer asks.

"The clipper? Hawaii."

"How old were you?"

"Twenty. And at the time I wished I'd never made that promise."

"No wonder you and Mr Wang find so much to talk about," she murmurs.

How does she know that?

"Well, he says you don't mind lending him your ear," Luke counters.

She looks a little sheepish. "In many ways Chinese medicine is very interesting. There is a lot to be learnt from it."

Meg lets out a small laugh. "Well, *a lot* of citizens in this town would like to see the back of Mr Wang."

"So you kept that promise to your mother," is Cam Faraday's observation.

Luke smiles philosophically. "Maybe when I'm through here, keeping another promise – to Mart – I'll go back and take that voyage to Hawaii."

"Oh yes… your poor friend," Meg murmurs.

"Trying to get Wilson Cutter charged with killing him with-out a witness is like that voyage… I can smell it, almost taste it…"

"You're not giving up?" Jennifer asks.

"Just feeling sorry for myself," he tells her. He hears then a distant tinkle of breaking glass; the sound matches the sudden intensity in Jennifer's eyes. She swings her chestnut head away in the direction of her surgical rooms, which of course are at the front of the building.

"Jen?"

"I'm sure it's nothing, Meg."

But as Luke gets to his feet, so does Jennifer.

"Well, if it's nothing why are you two standing there like that?"

"Because it ain't nothing," Luke says. And to Jennifer, "Stay here."

"It's my practice and my building."

"Fine."

"What is going on?" Meg asks.

Faraday is now standing and draws his wife to her feet.

"Stay with your wife, Mr Faraday," Luke tells him.

Faraday frowns, then nods. Luke follows Jennifer around her building. She takes him through a door to her operating room, which he recognizes, and then through another door which leads to the waiting room. He holds her back then; reluctantly she agrees to wait while he proceeds. In the shadows he can make out a moving figure; more importantly, he can smell kerosene. He stalks through the darkness only to topple over something. The sound of the crash (and his swearing) alerts the intruder who is now making for the front door.

Luke extracts himself and his tender leg painfully from the ruin of God-knows-what and dives towards the intruder. He catches him around an ankle and hangs on tight while the intruder squirms, kicks and cusses.

"What should I do?" Jennifer is shouting. "No, I've got it. Hold him. Hold him…"

He doesn't intend to let go. He tries desperately to subdue the intruder, who is wriggling and grunting like a crazy man and takes to wildly pounding Luke's hands with his other booted foot. All the while the smell of kerosene is overpowering. Suddenly, the electric light goes on, blinding him. He hears Jennifer's quick approach; there is a cracking thud and, to his relief, the squirming ceases. Only the sound of their heavy breathing can be heard for several moments.

"Oh, God, have I killed him?" Jennifer rasps.

"What did you hit him with?" he pants. His pounded hand is throbbing.

"This…"

He has no idea what 'this' is, but scrapes about for the intruder's wrist. "Still has a pulse."

More footsteps.

"Oh my," says Meg Faraday. "Cam?"

"Stay back a moment, you two," Jennifer warns. "Glass…"

Luke gets to his feet.

Jennifer is standing there with an umbrella in her hand. The handle is a substantial silver-cast head of a duck with a sizable beak; even so her placement must have been very precise. Her eyes are huge and glistening. He goes to her and puts his hand on her shoulder. She's trembling.

"Are you all right?" he asks.

"Perfectly," she replies with a quiver in her voice. "And you?"

"Still in one piece."

"I've never knocked anyone unconscious before."

He remembers the morphine and removes his hand. "Not with a hard object anyway."

Faraday joins them. "An interesting development. Attempted arson, it seems."

"And on the very day Harris and Richards come to town."

"Not a coincidence?" Jennifer asks.

"Violence is the name of their game," Luke mutters.

"Well, we don't know for sure yet," Faraday points out. "We will have to wait until our arsonist regains consciousness. I suggest you leave everything just as it is, including him, until Cliff gets here."

Wide-eyed, Jennifer exclaims, "Cliff! What will he say when he sees what I've done?"

"Mm, you know how Cliff is," Luke remarks. "He'll want a statement a mile long. We'd better get our story straight. And he'll want to weigh the umbrella, measure the beak..."

"I was just defending my property. He had kerosene. Cam?"

Faraday, plainly trying not to smile, puts his arm around her. "Don't worry, George. Luke is just teasing..."

"George?" Luke squawks.

Jennifer's eyes flash. "Didn't you say you were fetching Cliff?"

"Sure, Jennifer, I'm going." He glances at Faraday, who looks awkward as he slides his other hand in his pocket. "Going right this minute."

"And stop treating my welfare as some form of amusement."

Luke swallows hard. He tastes blood and wonders fleetingly if he's hurt. He holds fast to her eyes, still wide and unrestricted to his gaze. "I'm sorry. The danger's past. You're safe now. That's all it means." He smiles gently at her serious expression. "That's three apologies in one day. That doesn't happen very often."

She folds her arms. "Why am I not surprised?"

He turns away, chuckling.

As he picks his way over the intruder's body and shattered glass, he hears Faraday telling Jennifer that she handled herself 'commendably', followed by Meg's insistence that Jennifer is definitely staying at their house for the night.

When Luke arrives at Cliff's 16th Street branch office, Cliff is giving his night deputy instructions. As Luke approaches, he hears the deputy telling Cliff to go home and get some sleep.

Cliff's head swings his way. "Luke."

The deputy scrunches up his nose. "Pee-yoo!"

"Kerosene?" Cliff's eyebrow lifts.

Luke nods. "And a whole lot more. At Jennifer's."

"Let's go then. Clary, would you mind mopping up Luke's blood when we've gone."

Clary grunts. "Good thing that girl's a doctor."

Luke follows their line of vision. Blood spots pattern the floor. "What the...?"

"For a man who hates the sight of his own blood, you don't mind giving everyone else a good gander at it..." Cliff produces a folded white handkerchief from his pocket.

"Where?"

"Try your hand, chucklehead," Clary says with a grumpy *tsk*.

"Just who are you calling chucklehead?"

"Come on, Luke, let's go find Jennifer... 'Night, Clary."

Jennifer

Her arsonist is still out cold. She examines the damage she inflicted to his occipital bone while Cam stands guard close by. No blood, just a large swelling where she struck him.

Her once pristine waiting room reeks of kerosene; shards of glass lie scattered about and crunch whenever anyone moves.

"Will he live?" Cam asks.

"Yes," she says and stands up. "He's much younger than I thought. I just hope he doesn't wake up before Cliff gets here."

"He wouldn't get far; he's a little worse for wear, don't you think?"

"I'm concerned about that, Cam. I admit I struck him with force but not so hard that he should be unconscious this long."

"Come and sit here with me, Jen," Meg entreats her from the chairs, a safe distance from the body. So she sits with Meg while Cam keeps guard. Of course, as soon as she sits and does nothing, shock takes over. Her hands are shaking; she clenches them together and hides them in her lap. She makes a mental list of what must be done: knock out the remaining glass, board up the hole, sweep up the smashed window and scrub the floor. She wonders how long the smell of the kerosene will linger.

When Cliff finally arrives with Luke at his side, she expels a very deep sigh. She observes the men standing together; Cliff is a fraction taller. He wields impressive authority around town and the only thing she has ever known to really bother him are those four US marshals who seem intent on exerting greater authority.

Luke appears pale. His right hand hangs limp at his side wrapped in a bloody handkerchief. Hardly surprising with all the glass about, and if anyone is going to get cut it would be him – who else would wrestle with someone on a kerosene-soaked floor that's covered in broken glass?

She leaves her chair and crosses the room with glass snapping under her shoes. She stands at Luke's side. In his eyes, as they exchange glances, is a gleam of reassuring warmth.

"*You* did this?" Cliff asks her.

"All I did was take that...that... and then...the...the..."

Cliff holds up his hand. "Relax, will you?"

"I... I'm unrepresented and surrounded by..."

"Friends?" Cam supplies.

"Stop teasing her," Meg calls out from chairs. "She's had a very bad day."

"I'm sorry," Cliff says and looks directly at Luke.

"Okay, it's all my fault," Luke admits. "I apologized."

"You did?"

"A hundred times..."

"Three times," Meg interjects, "in one day, a rare occurrence."

In spite of herself, Jennifer suppresses a giggle.

"You," Cliff says to her. "Get your statement ready while I look this over." He examines the door, the room, the unconscious man, the deadly umbrella handle she used as a weapon and the container now empty of kerosene. She gives Cliff her statement, as does Luke.

"Somehow I don't think he intended to smash this much glass and alert you the way he did."

"Sloppy job," Luke remarks. "Think he stayed too long at the saloon."

"Maybe," Cliff concurs as he manacles the unconscious man's limp wrists. "What do you think, Jennifer?"

"An excessive amount of alcohol would account for why he collapsed so easily and remains unconscious. The combination of head injury and drunkenness is not..."

"Do you want to bring him around, or shall I?"

She goes to the top drawer of Duffy's desk. "We always keep smelling salts handy..." She finds the tiny bottle and hands it to Cliff, who rouses the perpetrator; the man groans.

"Perhaps I should examine him properly now that he is conscious," she offers.

"When I need you, I'll call you," Cliff says. "Okay, feller, what's your name?"

A blank stare.

"You are being arrested for attempted arson."

No response.

"He might be unresponsive for some time," Jennifer says. "And he really should lie down and be observed closely for a few hours at least…"

"He'll be fine, I promise."

"Keep him awake, won't you? There are certain symptoms you need to look out for. Dizziness, sensitivity to light, nausea, blurred vision… Cliff, I really think I…"

"Jennifer, listen to me, he was attempting to fry you and your livelihood."

"I know, but… yes, he was, so…so go on then, take him away. Charge him with attempted arson."

"Excellent idea. Thank you."

"But you will send for me if…"

"I will send for you," Cliff humors her.

They all watch mutely as Cliff marches the culprit away.

"Cam…" Meg clutches at his arm. "I didn't like to say before but I am feeling strange… and dizzy."

"It's the kerosene," Jennifer says. "With the fumes uncontained the way they are, it's no wonder. Home for you, Meg."

"And leave you with all this mess? I'll be all right." She half swoons; Cam wraps his arms around her.

"I'll help Jennifer clean up, Faraday," Luke says.

"Very well," Cam replies.

"Sorry, Jen," Meg sighs. "You will come over after though?"

"I think I should stay here and guard the place actually." Jennifer kisses her cheek. "Nice deep breaths on the way home, Meg. Really deep ones."

"Yes, Jen, I will, I promise."

When they're gone, Luke, looking around, says, "Guess we start on the glass first…"

"No," she says, "your hand is first."

Luke

By now Luke considers himself a very good patient. Jennifer has a special trolley table for sewing wounds; it's narrow and so clean reflections dance off the white enamel. She seats him at it in the quiet of her surgical room and shuts the door on the bulk of the kerosene. She thoroughly washes her hands. She fetches boiled water from the kettle and pours it into a bowl; to that she adds some pungent liquid from a brown bottle; then she takes a packet of cotton swabs from her cabinet.

"More sewing?" he asks.

"Possibly. I have to clean the cut first." Carefully, she unwraps his bloodied handkerchief; blood is leaking from the inch long wound in the fleshy muscle on the side of his hand. "This will sting."

"Of course," he quips. And it does. He grimaces.

As she cleans the cut her hands tremble, and considering he's the one bleeding and in pain, it's lucky for him he already knows how good a doctor she is. She brings a lamp as close as possible and proceeds to look for glass with her magnifying disc.

"I can see one small shard."

She picks her up her tweezers but her fingers won't stop trembling. As the pointy ends close in on his open flesh, he shuts one eye. Jennifer pulls away. She takes a shaky breath. He opens his eye. Jennifer makes another attempt. Again, the tweezers come towards him; he sways backwards. Then, he reaches out with his good hand and gently stops her. He clears his throat. "Allow me? You keep the magnifier; just guide me."

She looks on, stunned as he takes the tweezers from her.

"According to my mother, my father couldn't stand the sight of blood and that's where I get it from," he says jauntily, while he's screwing up his eyes and trying to locate the tip of the glass.

"No doubt predicated upon the fact that most of the blood you see is your own. A little to the right…"

"Am I close?"

"A fraction to the left. No, back. Yes, there."

Steadily, he latches onto the glass and extracts it. His stomach rolls. "Do I need stitches?"

Their eyes meet.

"I could use a drink."

"I have some brandy." She returns to the cabinet and takes out a near full bottle and a shot glass. Back at the trolley she half fills the glass.

He downs it at once. He says, "Couldn't we press both sides together, bandage it up and let the skin do the rest."

"It won't heal. And the risk of infection in your hand is high."

"You know, you're the cleanest person I've ever met," he remarks, pinching the sides of his wound together. Blood oozes freely. He winces.

"Dirt is overrated," she says. "Luke, I have to suture it."

She pours him another shot – which he tosses down the back of his throat – before she procures her needle and thread from her cabinet. As she sits down again, he says, "You're not used to hurting anyone, I mean the kind of hurt that doesn't help."

"I know what you mean. No."

"Even in self-defense."

She puts the needle to his skin and he tries not to shudder.

"I took an oath. The Hippocratic Oath. All doctors take it. You virtually live your whole life by it."

Her hand won't steady; he suspects this has never happened before; he wants to offer her the brandy.

"How does it go?" he asks.

"It's very long and…"

"I do solemnly swear," he begins.

She looks up sharply. "Yes."

"I took an oath once," he explains.

"I suppose all oaths do start that way…"

"So where were we – I do solemnly swear…"

She recites. And sows. Very slowly.

He focuses on her words and on her mouth as she utters them.

He listens carefully to the oath. Loyalty, uprightness and honor, aloof from wrong and corruption… Then she recites a particular line: *that you will exercise your art solely for the cure of your patients*, and he interrupts her.

"You knew exactly the right place to hit him."

"Yes. I used my medical knowledge to effect my assault."

"He looked all right to me."

"He has an egg-sized bump and likely concussion on top of an excess of alcohol in his system."

"That's what you get for messing with a doctor. You know, you had a duty to your patients not to let that jerk get away."

"Duty of care, you say. Yes, in an indirect way I suppose I did. But rationalizing is a dangerous habit to get into."

"Why?"

"I'd rather have a healthy conscience and be accountable for my worst decisions than constantly looking for excuses for everything I did or for what happened to me."

"That's some declaration," he says.

She slips the last of five sutures into place. They are knotted and surprisingly tidy. He observes her quietly as she inspects her work and then cleans dried blood off his hand. She applies a bandage.

"Keep it clean and dry," he quips, feeling fine and warm.

She looks up and locks onto his steady gaze. "That's right."

"How does the oath end?"

"*And now, if you will be true to this, your oath, may prosperity and good repute be ever yours; the opposite, if you shall prove yourselves forsworn.*"

"That's a lot to live up to. The last bit kinda sounds like a curse."

Her gaze intensifies. "Have I proven myself forsworn?"

She's asking *him*? He replies off-handedly, "Do I look like the kinda feller who knows about honor and uprightness and holding myself far aloof from wrong?"

"I don't know exactly what your oath was, but I think you swore it to your friend Mart, that you are in more trouble than you have ever known because of it, and you would rather suffer than not keep it."

Is he that obvious? Or is she that sensitive…

"And your answer to my question wasn't an answer at all."

"Will you take my answer and stop chopping yourself up into little pieces?"

She squirms a little. "Yes."

"Then the answer's no."

"That's all; just no."

"You have a gift for easing people's suffering. And that jerk was suffering from criminal intent."

"Thank you," she murmurs, "I think."

He smiles. "So put your cool steady hand on my forehead and tell me I'm gonna be all right."

"I think your oath and mine are not so very different."

"Cool hand. I'm gonna be all right..." he implores.

She reaches across the trolley table. Her hand, cool but not so steady, comes to rest on his forehead. A tremor passes through him.

She frowns delicately and whispers, "You'll be all right."

He closes his eyes and feels the peace and the delightful relief. A question forms in his mind. Is it right for a woman to make a man feel safe?

Kelley

"Home."

"Yes, God has been gracious."

"God, if he truly wants to be gracious, should do something about the state of this road."

Kelley looks at Sara and they start giggling. Aunt Edith's hat has slid sideways, her face has turned white and her gloved fingers dig into the meager upholstery.

"I feel like a horse that's charging for home," she adds.

"I hope God's graciousness extends to Ethan waiting for me at the depot," Sara says, feeling the small of her back.

"Do you think anything has changed while we were away?"

"Anything's possible. Just as long as Tressa hasn't had the baby early. And Luke is all right, of course."

But the baby hasn't come yet, her Pa tells them at the stage depot. Too early.

Ethan is there with him, as large as life and thrilled to see them. Sara promises to call by tomorrow to see Tressa. Ethan takes her home.

Her Pa returns them to a house that is entirely focused on the imminent birth. The progress of Tressa's condition is fully evident, and having never before encountered an expectant mother, Kelley is intrigued by Tressa's glowing health.

The baby is very active, Tress seems pleased to report, and restless to make an appearance.

"I hope it's a girl, Tress, a sane, sensible, thinking individual who'll grow up to be a credit to humanity."

"I was hoping for a boy," she says.

Aunt Edith pats her hand. "Take no notice of your sister-in-law, Tressa, my dear. So, Sean, what news from Cheyenne?"

"Thought you'd never ask," says her Pa.

In a gritty tone, he announces the capture of Wilson Cutter.

"Luke was injured but he has recovered. You know, this Wilson Cutter is wanted for so many crimes he's being held in the county jail while the authorities work out what to do with him. There's still no evidence to have him charged with Mart's murder, but Luke is working on it from another angle, and he has the chief prosecutor's help..."

Immediately, Kelley feels the urge to go to Cheyenne herself and investigate this 'other angle', but having just got home and with Tressa soon to give birth she shelves this idea for a later date.

"He keeps us up-to-date with everything," her Pa continues. "And he's assured Tressa he'll come back when she's due to have the baby. Ethan's annoyed with him on account of he keeps getting injured one way or another, but Luke was never a boy to go about things half-hearted. Anyway, he's staying in a boarding house in Cheyenne. I think he's done a fine job so far."

"Well, considering the length of time he's spent in Cheyenne, I'm glad Sara was away with us," Kelley says.

Her Pa's eyes narrow on her. "Ethan missed her, you know."

"She doesn't mean anything by it, Sean," Aunt Edith says. "We're very tired."

"Well, I got another surprise. I updated the plumbing."

"Oh, God bless you, brother. And there we were, tumbling about on the stagecoach, wondering if anything had changed. You did say the plumbing, didn't you, Sean?"

Her Pa chuckles. "Sure did, Edith. And Amy has a brand new, smooth-action pump in the kitchen. It's more compact, with the most up-to-date plumbing. The bathroom has the same plumbing and a new water heater. You know, they have this kind of plumbing in the White House. State of the art, they call it."

Her Pa (although he sounds like a general merchandise catalogue) seems as proud of his plumbing as Kelley is of her Cimarron pilgrimage.

Certainly, there is nothing like physical labor and ingenuity to keep the doldrums at bay. Each to his or her own.

For Kelley, the greatest change is that her parents have moved out of their large downstairs bedroom and into Tressa's upstairs, and she has moved into theirs.

In one corner of the room sits a crib (all tenderly kitted out for its soon-expected occupant), a small cupboard and a table.

The reason for the switch is obvious, although it will take some getting used to. This has been her parents' room since they moved here. She and Mart were up; they were down. The arrangement was fixed and preserved. Now it's askew. And it serves to remind her of how much she misses Mart. She takes a deep breath, nevertheless, and tells Tressa how wonderful the room is, perfect for her new baby girl.

"Boy, Kelley. A son."

"How do you know?"

"I'm his mother."

Kelley shrugs. "Then I suppose I should believe you."

"I wish you would. I haven't the energy to debate with you."

In the evening, Kelley helps her Mama with supper. They sit at the table preparing vegetables; her Mama takes the carrots and says chattily, "I'm glad your excursion was such a success. I'm relieved to have you home though."

"It's good to be home."

"Are you still angry with Luke?" she asks, working away.

Kelley looks up from her basket of greens. "I don't know how to answer that."

Her Mama glances at her. "That's an answer in itself. Tell me what you think about your pilgrimage as Edith calls it."

"You won't like it."

"I might surprise you."

She's already doing that.

"Womanhood has a power and an energy that prevails."

She picks up another carrot. "Go on."

"We endure."

Her Mama looks up with steady gray eyes. "Yes, we do."

"Our strength and self-determination is different to men, but no less potent. We do not need to *take* to be strong."

A hint of a smile. "Good."

"Mama, I'm feeling a restless urge to express my ideas."

Back to the carrots. "You must do what you must. Now get moving on those greens."

Kelley writes a letter to the Cheyenne Bugle a few days after their return.

The letter appears in the Bugle's Letters to the Editor column several days later, much to her amazement and Aunt Edith's delight, and while her Mama remains detached, her Pa and Tressa don't know quite what to make of it:

"SIR, On a desolate prairie in the Indian Territory along the Panhandle is a monument.

An eloquent engraving in sandstone bears the name of a girl who died as her family pursued their right for liberty and property. She died at the hands of a displaced people. What displaced people, you ask? Who would they be? There is no one displaced in this great democracy surely? Oh, but there is. And I beg to question the solemn notion of John O'Sullivan, the journalist who many years ago dumped the expression 'manifest destiny' into the minds and hearts of Americans. Exponents would have you believe that God has ordained it our right to plough down what he allowed so graciously to spring up.

We expelled the British from our shores for their imperial tyranny. Are we any better?

"It's big out here. I would have thought there was enough room for all of us. So, why does liberty have to mean the acquisition of property that was not ours to begin with? Why must we always take? Why can't liberty exist in the hearts of our citizens, to exercise justice for all of us who live here? We won't ever have true freedom in this country until we have justice and fairness.

> Freedom is first a spirit. Not a place, or a space. Am I the only one who tires of this need to destroy, impoverish, and discriminate? Freedom means responsibility. I put it to you, Sir, that we are an irresponsible nation."
> KD Keaton, Bright River, Wyoming.

If they think her letter is incomprehensible, they find the reply which features in the Bugle two days later even more so:

> "SIR, I reply to KD Keaton of Bright River, Wyoming. I am not sure whether to applaud KD Keaton, or suggest that we, as a nation, accuse him (or perhaps her) of treachery. In any case, he or she enjoys the freedom to write what he or she likes. Freedom comes in many forms. KD Keaton is obviously carrying the burden of freedom with commendable passion. Explain yourself, KD Keaton. You cannot write what you do without revealing your true intentions."
> C. Faraday, Cheyenne, Wyoming.

To have someone respond to her ideas in such a manner makes her fit to burst. She replies at once. It is published within days:

> "SIR, C. Faraday would have your readers believe that I am hiding behind notions and not expounding deeply held beliefs. Manifest destiny has been a disaster for the Indian nations in this country. We appear to have had too few scruples about wiping them out and none at all about taking what was theirs as if they have no right to it and we do.
> Meanwhile, is the blood of white Americans spilt in war to win freedom from slavery for Negroes forgotten? Ignored? Resented? It seems one war won't be enough; perhaps we need another, one without bloodshed and yet one that seeds a profound change

of heart to bring about equality; true freedom would see all Americans, no matter the color of their skin, accepted as equals. Or do we see discrimination as a freedom – free to do and think as we please regardless of the hurt we cause?

Both Indian and Negro are victims of inexcusable discrimination, but we are the ones who set them on the path they have traveled, and yet we blame them for taking that path. And what of the woeful state of the working and living conditions of migrant workers in industries in cities and towns? Relegated to camps and tenements to raise their families.

What is to be the fate of these Americans: the sacred ones who were here before us, the wailing ones who were brought in chains, the sanguine ones who trust the promise? They have given their blood and the sweat of their brow and their children to America, are they not Americans? What if the nation is great because of them – the lands we took from them, the labor we forced from them, the need we exploit in them? We take and we take. I say again, Sir, we are an irresponsible nation. Or perhaps we are just plain ignorant."

Miss KD Keaton, Bright River.

"SIR, All over this town people are beginning to say Miss Keaton has no right to call herself an American.

What say you, Miss Keaton? You believe in equality. Equal rights, equal opportunity.

What do you intend to do about the state of the nation?"

C. Faraday, Cheyenne.

"SIR, I live in the only territory or state in the nation where I have the franchise. As things stand, I have only just reached the age to exercise my right. What would Mr. Faraday have me do for the nation?

I resent this departure from the original discussion, Mr. Faraday. You are making a mockery of the call to true liberty – *Without* property, or 'fair property' for all."

Miss KD Keaton, Bright River.

"SIR, Miss Keaton brings us back to reality. She will not be distracted. I am impressed. However, she explores a hazardous philosophy.

Democracy secures our nation and our sovereignty. Come, Miss Keaton, tell us. Do you not believe in the great Revolutionary cause, which, as you said, expelled the British from our shores, and the men who fought courageously and single-mindedly for that cause under the banner of Liberty and Property? Do we not live in the heart of President Jefferson's 'empire for liberty'?" C. Faraday, Cheyenne.

"SIR, How much blood has been spilled across this continent in the last one hundred years, and now from one ocean to another we say we are free. A new revolution is needed, a peaceful one, a movement of courageous people who are prepared to cry enough! I say again, the acquisition of property has not given us true freedom.

And it is not I who is confusing democracy with the indulgent free market capitalism that is rife in this nation, or condones the arrogance of the great unwashed who mistakenly hold ignorance and cruelty as fundamental tenets of some hybrid democracy that, with rather sickening pride, Americans consider pure."

KD Keaton, Bright River.

"SIR, I believe that C. Faraday is getting nowhere with KD Keaton. She appears not to have understood the true meaning of 'property'. If she has held liberty and property as a purely romantic ideal and has now come to terms with what it really means, I congratulate her. If she intends to reject or has already rejected all that she once held dear, I feel sorry for her. She calls for justice and freedom to exist hand in hand. Make it happen, Miss Keaton. Don't just talk about it."

Liberty & Property, Cheyenne.

"I wonder who Liberty & Property is. Interesting, having someone else enter your discussion with this Mr Faraday," Tressa remarks, as they sit around after supper discussing the latest development. She has difficulty getting comfortable.

"Are you all right, Tress?"

"I think so. He certainly doesn't agree with your opinions."

Kelley takes a deep breath. "Liberty & Property is Luke."

Tressa fidgets some more. "How on earth do you know?"

"Tressa, you know your baby is a son, and I know that this letter is Luke's."

She rolls her eyes, and then suddenly clutches at her bulging stomach. "Oh…" She grimaces and lets out an alarming wail.

"Tress?"

"What is the date today?"

"Tress…"

"This baby is going to be early."

Luke

Bright River

How rare is it that when one precious life is taken there is another almost immediately to ease the loss… This child is a great gift.

Jennifer was right.

At the very moment Tressa lays her baby in his arms, Luke understands the greatness of the gift.

"Adam Taylor Keaton. He's perfect," he murmurs, marveling at the size of the infant. He looks up into Tressa's glowing face. "And you don't look too bad either."

"Thank you."

"You did a fine job, Tress. I'm proud of you."

Her wide grin softens. Gratitude shines in her eyes.

"He's the image of Mart," Luke continues.

"I believe so."

"Mart did all right."

"He did everything right, except for… well, you know…"

Before the melancholy sets in, he says, "If you reach into my saddlebags over there, there are presents for this character."

"Presents! Really?"

"Yes, really," he laughs.

Tressa unburdens his bags of the gifts; removes string and paper. She first opens the fine toy horse – a bay thoroughbred with a real mane and tail; then, the child-sized tin star with 'sheriff' emblazoned on it; and the box of wooden bricks painted on all sides with the letters of the alphabet and colorful pictures. She declares that she loves them. Then:

"What on earth is this?"

He takes his eyes off Mart's son to look. "From Mr Wang. Special ingredients for keeping evil spirits away from the boy. You put the stuff near his crib."

Tressa's face displays thorough distaste. "I don't know who Mr Wang is, but this smells exceedingly odd and I'm not putting it near Adam, at least until Amy can tell me what's in it." Then she smiles sweetly. "It *was* very kind of him."

He grins. "There should be one more."

"Yes. Here it is. Very neatly wrapped, so it can't be from you, cousin." She removes the brown packaging and then peels away another sheet of thin white paper. She lifts a fine white shawl from the inner wrapping. "Oh, it's lovely." As she is admiring it, a blue card drops onto her lap. She picks it up and reads: "Dear Tressa. My sister-in-law says you can never have too many of these! Congratulations on the birth of your son Adam. God bless you both. Jennifer Sullivan."

He and Jennifer shopped for the gifts together. She couldn't agree with him about the sheriff's star – 'not suitable' – but when he suggested that they take an oath on it on Adam's behalf, she started to think and enquired as to what kind of oath. That Adam will make his father proud all his life, he said. Her eyes kinda teared up as she said she had no doubt he would, and to tell Tressa not to let Adam play with the star until he was four.

"Oh, how very kind she is." Tress strokes the shawl; puts its softness to her cheek. "I can't believe she would even remember me."

"And all the time you were making a lasting impression."

A little later, when both mother and child are due for a nap, Luke sits at the Keaton table for the first time in a very long time. Amy wants to know why he still walks with a slight limp, and John can't ask enough questions about Wilson Cutter. Meanwhile, K is nowhere to be seen.

Luke asks about her. John stops his questioning half way and stares at him nonplussed.

"Your daughter, John," Luke says. "Where is she?"

"She and her Aunt Edith went on an errand for me this morning," Amy informs him while she studies the mixture Mr Wang sent Tressa. "I haven't a clue what that Chinese devil has put into this."

"Now, Amy, Mr Wang's harmless. Wouldn't hurt a flea. Just misunderstood I reckon."

"Oh you do, do you?" she says, frowning at him. "Well, harmless or not, this concoction is not going anywhere near that baby."

Close to an hour later a handsome, commanding woman walks in and John introduces her as his sister, Edith Edwards.

"Pleased to meet you, Mrs Edwards."

"Likewise, I'm sure, young man. I've heard a great deal about you."

Luke can only imagine what that would include.

"Kelley is seeing to the horses. That girl is obsessed with horses. They are nice enough, I suppose…"

"I think I should give her a hand."

"A fine idea, young man."

So, with Aunt Edith's blessing, he heads out to face K, feeling like it was easier to confront Wilson Cutter. She stands beside a horse securing its feedbag, with hair like spun gold. He's forgotten just how vibrant and pretty she is; if only he could forget that she once secured an alliance with him only to turn around and break it at their very first test.

He approaches softly and waits for her to see him. When she does, her bright blue eyes stir a long ago feeling. In that moment he thinks of how this meeting could have been. He would hold her and seek comfort from her. Gazing upon her beauty would lift his spirits, soothe his weariness. Her spirit would distract him from his worries. But the thought dissolves; he doesn't know if she is capable of comfort in the way he needs it. Shouldn't the understanding be there already, a natural thing? He doesn't want the disappointment that will come, but he must face it. And take some responsibility for it.

"I met your aunt," he says. "She's a fine woman."

"How long have you been here?"

"Long enough to hold Adam and speak with Tressa. A while, I guess…"

She strokes the horse's white starred nose.

"Your letters in the Bugle were interesting," he says. "Deep."

"I was under the impression you thought my ideas were romantic notions and that you felt sorry for me." She turns the horse and leads the animal into its stall.

"I think my letter was written in the same tone as yours."

She walks back to him with her arms folded. "You and I are never going to be the same, Luke, no matter how much small talk you make, whether it's sincere or if it's not. There is no use hoping that things will improve between us because I've changed and I don't doubt for a second that you have too..."

Changed? Why would he... "No. I'm still the same pain in the neck I've always been."

She sighs impatiently. His wounded leg starts to ache.

"It's just that some people can accept me the way I am," he says indignantly, "and some can't. I don't mind that. It's the same for everyone."

"I don't have to like your chauvinistic ideas about women," she bites back, her eyes flashing.

"I happen to think women should be loyal..."

"I *am* loyal."

"The same as men need to be loyal."

"I don't want your loyalty."

"So what do you want? And what do I do with the promise I made to you in our alliance?"

"We weren't engaged to be married, Luke."

"We had an understanding..."

"Relationships break down all the time..."

"Something you picked up in New York?"

"You said ours will never be broken, but it is. We owe each other nothing. I want you to accept it so we can both go forward and lead our own lives. Our paths crossed for a time but now we are traveling in different directions. Of that I am sure."

"You're releasing me from my promise to you?"

Her eyelids flutter. "I thought I already had."

"It didn't last long."

"There obviously wasn't much hope for it, was there?"

He holds his tongue.

"And when you return to Cheyenne I'm going with you. Not to be your partner – that was a naïve and childish idea that I've long since come to regret having. And, as I said, we have very different ideas about our futures. So I will do what I have to do for Mart in my own way. Pa won't like it, but I'm sure Aunt Edith will accompany me, and then he'll get used to the idea."

"Cheyenne is a dangerous place."

"Only if you put yourself in danger, which I'm sure you do often. But I don't intend to. Now, if there is nothing else I'd like to go wash up before lunch."

"No… there's nothing else."

He watches her go.

Over the next three days Luke maintains a hectic pace, dividing his time between the Diamond-T with Sara, Ethan and Tip, and the Keatons. He gives them a full briefing on the situation in Cheyenne; he spends as much time as possible with Tressa and Adam. Tressa arranges a thank you gift for Jennifer that smells a whole lot better than Mr Wang's evil spirit deterrent, and a note of thanks for Mr Wang himself. Then, when the time comes to leave, he is faced with the crazy situation of traveling with K and her aunt. And while K gives him a great big pain, he starts to warm to Aunt Edith.

Kelley

Cheyenne

The hotel in which she and Aunt Edith choose to stay is not the Cheyenne. Auntie prefers big hotels. The Inter Ocean Hotel is substantially larger and grander; it is sociable and friendly while lacking the cloying intimacy of the Cheyenne Hotel. When Kelley informed Aunt Edith that a black man named Barney Ford built and owned it, Aunt Edith declared that perhaps Kelley should revise her views on the treatment of black men, in the West at least.

"Many black men came to live and work here after the War and made a significant contribution. Still do. Frontier people respect that."

"I expected you to tell me the tolerance is measured at least."

Kelley gives her a meaningful glance. "It is."

As Aunt Edith surveys the view from her window, she says, "Well, I have just spent the better part of the day with that young man of yours and I can't find a thing wrong with him. He is perfectly charming and handsome. He is very intelligent, well read, well spoken, for which I think we should give the credit to Sara. He's witty. He has a wonderful smile and a hard-edge soft-heart, virile, confident sort of character. Dependable."

"For heaven's sake, Auntie! And do not ever describe Luke as my young man."

"No wonder you fell head over heels."

"Are you that desperate to make me laugh?"

"Well, I am in love with him, even if you are not!"

"So I see."

Auntie gives a smiling wink from her window. "Take comfort; he still has some growing up of his own to do." Then, "I'm curious, though, about his feelings for you."

"Why do you say that?"

"Well, I believe he has an attachment to you, that much is clear; and you are very special to him, I am certain of it, but…"

"But what, Auntie? Not that any of this conversation matters one tiny little bit…"

Auntie strolls across the room, takes up Kelley's hands and squeezes them gently as she looks carefully into her eyes. "As I said, he has feelings for you …"

Kelley withdraws. She proceeds to unpack her trunk. "It should come as no surprise that it didn't work out."

"I think it is complex between you. You told me you both made a special promise to each other."

"I don't understand why he made it. Probably out of obligation. Pressure from parents. For the Alliance."

"A little harsh, darling."

"Whatever, it doesn't matter anymore, Auntie."

"It's very difficult to just stop loving someone."

With a shrug, Kelley admits, "I have." Her thoughts drift for a moment to another time… "I guess there were moments…"

"Yes, well, there are always those… You know, it's very likely you might lose him to someone else."

"You can't lose something you never had to begin with. Auntie, may we please change the subject? This is not why we came to Cheyenne. Luke has his business to conduct and I have mine."

"Mm, certainly, darling. Just such a shame you can't work together."

"Well, don't blame *me* for that."

"Kelley, he lost Mart; he doesn't want to lose you too. Is that so hard to understand?"

"Yes, for me, Auntie, I'm afraid it is."

Aunt Edith frowns, pushes her lips forward and then pulls them back. "Well, then, what do we do next?"

Luke

"Glad to have you back," Cliff says, as Luke limps into the sheriff's county office located on Ferguson Street beside the courthouse. They shake hands. "Problems with that leg?"

"No. Not really."

"Mm."

"Really, it's okay."

"I believe you. Others wouldn't. And the baby?"

"He looks like Mart."

"Ah. That's fine."

"Yeah, but I can't help wondering if Mart knew he was…"

"You can't dwell on it, Luke."

"I know you're right, but…" A shrug to finish what seems to have no end: what would Mart have done if he had known about the boy?

"So… Tressa. How is she?"

"Obsessed with the kid."

"Excellent."

"Yeah. She's happy. So, what's new?"

"You'll want to hear this. Take a seat. The arsonist, Jake William Murray, is still with us. He's quite the songbird. Meanwhile Harris and Richards left town. That pesky deputy US marshal, Gates, decides he's had enough of getting under my feet and takes off after them. Tracks them down, brings them back. And now we have a perfect set in the lock up. Things are looking up. But Harris and Richards refuse to be interrogated without an attorney present. Twenty-four hours later a short whiny fellow shows up and claims to be their attorney. They still say nothing that I can tell is of any use, and they insist that Murray is lying, that we have no proof they paid him to do the job, but here is a copy of the transcript of the interrogation…"

Cliff rummages through several piles of papers on his desk and extracts a folio, which he hands to Luke. "See if you can make something of it. And any questions, another angle maybe. Their attorney wanted them released, but Cam stepped in; even so we're running out of time. One interesting point – the US marshal from Colorado, Dan Hummer, has become interested in your case. Even if the extradition goes ahead any time soon, he says we can have Wilson Cutter back on loan. Going on Hummer's reputation it could just be lip service, but you never know... Oh, Cam wants to see you."

Luke sits thoughtfully for a moment. "What's the name of the short whiny feller?"

"Kinrade. Did I leave that out?"

"Mm. If his first name is Lyle, then he is one of Ed's attorneys and there's a story on him in my file."

Cliff thinks for a moment. "Lyle Kinrade, he is. I'll check out his profile." He gives Luke a searching look. "You look beat, Luke. Get some rest. Cam can wait a couple more hours."

Luke gets to his feet. "Sure, Cliff. Thanks for the lowdown. Oh, I should tell you. Kelley came back with me."

Cliff absorbs the news. "What do you want her to know?"

"Whatever she wants."

He clears his throat. "Sure."

Luke is on the move. "Thanks."

"Rest!" Cliff calls after him.

There is something he has to do first.

Mr Wang makes a fuss about Tressa's letter of thanks, wants to know about the baby and then offers Luke a free massage.

"You exhausted. That leg slow you down. I fix."

"Well, Mr Wang, I'm gonna see the doctor right now."

"She is good doctor. Chinese not okay with female doctors, but she okay with Wang. I think she respect Wang and Chinese. Respect. Most important."

"Sure, Mr Wang."

"Go. She make you rest. Bye now." And Mr Wang shoos him out the door.

Duffy, ruling the waiting room as usual, welcomes him back and orders him to wait in Jennifer's parlor because she is with a difficult patient.

"Although looking at you, you could be her next," she says. "Go on with you. Make yourself comfortable."

When he sits himself down on Jennifer's sofa, he finally succumbs to exhaustion, so when she doesn't appear any time soon he slips off his boots and slides a pillow under his head; released from his burdens, he closes his eyes and slips away. And dreams… Jennifer, his refuge.

He wakes, momentarily disoriented. The room is dim; a lamp glows somewhere. He opens his eyes wider.

Curled up in the armchair opposite him is Jennifer, reading a book by the light of the lamp. He watches her eyes glide swiftly across the words on the page. Every so often, a tiny frown appears on her forehead and then smoothes again. Then, suddenly, she looks up.

"Hello," she murmurs.

"Jennifer…" He grins and says, "Everything under control? No outlaws in the closet, no madmen wielding cans of kerosene?"

"No. You were away."

While he laughs she closes her book and tucks it down beside the arm of the chair.

"Don't they sleep where you come from? Duffy said you were limping when you came in. Is there a problem with your leg?"

"It hurts when I'm tired, that's all." He stretches himself into sitting upright and pushes his fingers through his hair.

"Like an old war injury?"

"I guess."

"You walk on it too much. How do I make you understand that it is still healing?"

"I know, I know. I understand. So, will you stop lecturing me and come over here?"

Her eyes narrow. "Why?"

"I have something to give you…" he reaches for his saddlebags and rummages around for the parcel… "from Tressa."

"For me? From Tressa?"

He nods. "She loved the shawl. She was very touched. You know... the usual female stuff."

"And the baby? Is he wonderful?" she asks, her tone sweeter.

"He's small, and kinda cute," he says, handing her the parcel. "And he looks like his father."

"Oh, that's excellent," she murmurs.

"Sit."

She sits beside him on the sofa.

"Open."

She fiddles with the string. "What did Tressa think of Mr Wang's gift?"

"Well, it wasn't exactly gold, frankincense and myrrh, was it?"

She stops fiddling to laugh.

"And Amy said..."

"Who's Amy?"

"Mart's mother. She's kinda like a cross between you and Mr Wang. She grows herbs and knows a lot about that stuff, but she didn't like Mr Wang's concoction. I think she tossed it. Will you stop laughing and open the thing?"

"Why are you in such a hurry?"

"I'm supposed to see Cam."

"I know," she says, fingering the edges of the paper. "He called by looking for you. I told him you were fast asleep and he invited you to supper instead. Seven o'clock. It's only just six now."

"Are you coming?"

She shakes her head. "I have a procedure in the morning and I need to read up on it."

He considers her fidgety profile. "Tricky?"

"A little. I have to remove a tumor. I hope it's not malignant or the patient will eventually succumb to the cancer. Why don't I just open Tressa's present?"

He watches her peel away the paper from around a muslin bag of three fragrant palm-sized sachets of Amy's making.

"Oh, they are lovely," she breathes.

In fact, they bring her to life. Seems the tricky tumor patient is temporarily out of mind.

She inspects each one; smells each one; identifies each fragrance. Lavender, rose and pine.

He realizes he can't take his eyes off her; that he needs to look at her for a long time time. Every flicker of those long dark lashes, every green flash of her eyes, every tiny movement of her mouth, the pale freckles dancing across the bridge of her nose...

"Do you like these?" she asks, holding a sachet under her nose.

"Lavender's okay," he says.

"Yes, lavender is very good." She searches quickly for the lavender and holds out to him. "Here. Smell. It's wonderful."

The scent wafts under his nose. Clean and crisp yet so much nicer than the clinical smells of her surgery. But she is still busy.

"Rose petals..."

Sweet, like her. Rich and deep...

"Jennifer..."

"Mm..." she says, and looking up as she smells, her brilliant green eyes, full of warmth and feeling, go straight to his.

Unprepared, he has to swallow to recover.

"I didn't come back alone. Mart's sister and her aunt came here with me."

"She would be Tressa's sister-in-law."

He nods. "And the girl..." He hesitates.

She smiles very, very softly. "...of all Wild West heroes."

"Not exactly. She hates me," he blurts out.

"Well, you can be a handful," she says.

"Gee, thanks..."

Gently, she adds, "They always forgive in the end."

"There's a comfort. When do you think this story is gonna come to the end?"

Her smile broadens. "Only the author, the great controller of each character's destiny, knows that. I am but a secondary player. You, on the other hand, are the protagonist. You make the action happen, and you certainly do that..." She looks away and places the sachet back in its bag. "I'll make coffee, shall I?"

Secondary? She is indispensable to him. He couldn't have done any of it without her. He'd probably be dead.

And without her there would be no peace of mind.

No sanctuary.

"I should get out of your hair."

"No. I'd rather you stayed off that leg."

She walks off towards the kitchen with that graceful swing in her step, one of the sachets daintily held up to her nose. The lamplight catches her hair in its golden web. Maybe she's his angel.

When she has vanished, he falls back into the sofa and mutters, "Give me strength."

Cliff

Cliff decides that there is enough of interest in Lyle Kinrade's profile to submit the attorney to interrogation, with one peculiar strategy. He deputizes Luke, and gives him as much freedom as he wants in the interview. Kinrade objects bitterly in his high-pitched voice until Luke flashes his silver deputy's star at him.

"Why did Ed Parsons send for you?"

"Who's he?" Kinrade asks.

"And you know Harris and Richards, don't you?"

"Listen, cowboy. I am an attorney. I can represent myself and I don't have to answer any of your questions…"

"Ed sent you, didn't he?"

"What are you talking about?"

"Ed sent you. You are as good an admitting it…"

"I am most certainly not admitting to a single thing…"

"You might as well, Kinrade. I know who you are. I have you well documented in my file. Got a whole section on you. Just for you. Lyle Kinrade. Attorney. You're thirty-seven. Unmarried. You came into Ed's employ five years ago. He wanted someone unassuming, not too ambitious, but savvy enough to wash all of his dirty laundry."

"Sheriff, if you don't stop this right this minute…"

They do stop, but only because Miss Keaton appears at the door. "Mac the deputy said I should come right in."

"M'am," Cliff says. "Take a seat."

"Who is she?" asks Kinrade. "She can't just walk in…"

Luke laughs. "Come on, Lyle. You know who she is?"

Miss Keaton sits. She is quiet, her bright blue eyes darting between Kinrade and Luke.

"And how would I know that?" Kinrade persists.

"Do you know who this woman is, Mr Kinrade?" Cliff asks.

"No."

But Cliff is practiced at reading a man's eyes.

"Proceed," he tells Luke.

"My pleasure. So, Kinrade, you know what else is in my file?"

"I haven't the foggiest and nor do I care?"

"The story of two men. Let's take one of them: Howard Peters. Used to be one of Ed's smaller northern neighbors. I saw you and Howard Peters and Ed together in town on the morning before Ed's boys stampeded Howard's herd onto Ed's property. Howard's cattle were rounded up, ready for the drive. Ed has a rule: anyone else's cattle stray onto his property he keeps them. Ed kept Howard's cattle, Lyle. He branded over Howard's brand. Howard and all his men who were out trying to turn the herd witnessed the whole thing happen. Howard went to Ed and demanded his cattle back or he'd get the sheriff. Ed threatened Howard and his family with their lives. McCurdy turned a blind eye. They all felt powerless. You were there when that happened, Lyle. I know. It's all in my file. Howard, his foreman and a number of his men all gave me detailed accounts."

"You're making this up," is Kinrade's response.

Cliff places the relevant papers from Luke's file in front of Kinrade. Not only is the whole story written in Luke's handwriting, but the victim and the witnesses either signed Luke's version as correct or wrote their own. Kinrade's fidgety eyes scan the paper.

"This is basically hearsay," Kinrade says. "Not admissible."

"Well, it will be when I have it checked out," Cliff tells him. "Call in the witnesses. The district attorney will like it and the Judge will like it."

"I am not going to say another word," Kinrade declares.

"Pity," says Luke airily. "When you know so much."

"And get him out of my face," Kinrade demands.

Luke places his hands on the table and leans forward. "Do I make you nervous, Lyle? Well, here's a question for you; really make your palms itch and sweat. How did Wilson Cutter come to kill Mart Keaton?"

Cliff studies Kinrade's face. His palms might not be sweating, but beads of moisture break out across his forehead. He remains silent.

"Ed told him to, didn't he?" Luke continues.

Silence.

Sweaty silence.

"You know the answer to every question. Why Harris and Richards came to town. Why they threatened the doctor who captured Wilson Cutter. Why they hired that kid Jake Murray to burn down her place. You were there when Ed rustled Howard's cattle, took his land and threatened his family. And Howard Peters is just one Ed's victims, and you know that too. But you know what amazes me, Lyle? How Ed insults my intelligence. Does he honestly believe I am *so* stupid that I wouldn't put the pieces of his pathetic scheme together?"

Kinrade looks left and right. "Ryan, I asked you to get him out of here."

"I like him," Cliff says. "His words are illuminating."

"They're crap…"

"Mr Kinrade, you disappoint me. There's a lady present."

"Why is she here anyway?" Kinrade asks.

"She wants to know why Ed Parsons hired Wilson Cutter to kill Mart Keaton," Luke says.

Kinrade lurches to his feet, flipping his chair. As it crashes to the floor, he screams, "Get Taylor and the Keaton girl out of here now!" His eyes are bugging out of his skull; trails of perspiration line his forehead.

"So you do know the young lady?" Cliff asks.

Shaking, Kinrade spits out, "I don't have to tell you any-thing."

"It will go easier on you if you do. Eventually this whole business is going to be uncovered, Kinrade, and any help you can give us will see you in a much better position than if you keep this up. The district attorney likes sweaty witnesses. He gets them so mushed up they can't think straight. On the other hand, if you cooperate and get Harris and Richards to cooperate as well, then Faraday will take it kindly."

"You know what my mother used to say to me, Lyle, when I was a boy," Luke says. "She said, don't get mixed up with the wrong crowd. It'll only get you in trouble."

Suddenly, Miss Keaton speaks. "Mr Ryan? May I have a word with you? In the other room?"

Cliff gives Luke a steadying glance before he takes Miss Keaton into his office next door.

She comes straight to the point. "Now that Luke has gravely unsettled Mr Kinrade, I was wondering if you might care to try another tack."

"Now, Kinrade. Where were we?" Cliff says and takes a seat. "Mrs Taylor's advice to Luke as a boy. My own mother used to say when I was a boy growing up that if you do something wrong you should own up to it. People will respect you for it. Hard thing to come by, respect. You have to work for it."

Kinrade's eyes dart about as he tries to figure the new game.

Cliff continues.

"I think you want respect, Mr Kinrade. That's why you became an attorney, isn't it? To have people think highly of you. I think Mr Parsons respects you. He needs your excellent knowledge of the law. But as you can see, he's got trouble on the way, we will discover the connection between Mr Parsons and Mart Keaton's murder, and you won't want to be anywhere near him then, will you? You will be charged as an accessory or even with conspiracy. Conviction will give you six to twelve in the pen. You will have no one's respect then. You won't even have self-respect. Redemption is what it's all about, Mr Kinrade. You have now the opportunity to redeem yourself before that cruel and inevitable loss of respect."

Kinrade grinds out, "You won't respect me. All of you look down on me like I'm some kind of worm who dared to seek the light of day."

"On the contrary, Mr Kinrade," Cliff replies, "making good is part of this territory's unwritten creed and we all admire it. But I'm sure you understand that it's not easy to lose someone you love. Miss Keaton loved her brother. If you can help me convict her brother's killer, you will have her lifelong respect."

Kinrade's frown slides across to Miss Keaton; remarkably she holds his attention with a steady gaze of her own.

She looks neither sorry for him nor hateful of him. She is giving him a glimpse of her respect and gratitude for whatever he can do.

Her perfect skin, blue eyes and yellow hair don't go astray either.

Cliff's vague estimation of the feisty Miss Keaton registers a notch.

"And just how would Miss Keaton go about showing me that respect?" Kinrade rasps.

"The word we had in my office a moment ago…"

"What about it?"

"Miss Keaton wanted my assurance that if you cooperate the district attorney will show leniency in your case. She acted on your behalf, Mr Kinrade. And considering her loss… well, this is heroic of her, you'll agree. I gave her my assurance; as one attorney to another, Mr Faraday will be very grateful for your help."

Kinrade's eyes glaze over; he's shaking, struggling not to break down; he gasps, "Just let me think…"

Cliff motions to the others to leave Kinrade alone and they depart. He closes the door behind them; for a moment he watches the attorney through the glass pane.

"He's worse than a one-legged-man in a factory full of fire-crackers," Luke murmurs. "How long?"

"Hard to judge. Five minutes." Cliff looks at Miss Keaton. "Respect – very good, Miss Keaton."

Her eyes widen. "What will happen now?"

"He's going to talk," Cliff tells her.

"The district attorney will be lenient, just as you said?"

"He won't go overboard. Kinrade is not blameless. He stood by and watched innocent people suffer."

"I know. But he does seem such a sad victim of his own inadequacies, and so burdened by his wrong-doing."

Five minutes later Lyle Kinrade consents to giving a statement regarding his knowledge of Ed Parsons' activities.

It goes for five pages and validates everything in Luke's file including Parsons' harassment of the Taylor, Benchley and Keaton families with the intention of forcibly acquiring their land.

But nowhere in all those pages will he admit that Ed Parsons hired Wilson Cutter to kill Mart Keaton.

Kinrade insists that Ed never discussed it with him. He doesn't know. And that, he says, is the truth.

"He's lying," Cliff tells Luke later. "He knows Cam won't respect conspiracy to murder much at all. But we can still indict Parsons with this and all the stuff in your file. Cam will want to go ahead with the verification."

Luke, though, is miserable. "It's not good enough without the murder charge."

"Luke, someone in all this must be able to say that Wilson Cutter murdered Mart on Parsons' instructions. You're just going to have to be patient while we get through it all."

Luke lets out a weary sigh. "Patience. Here we go again."

"Think about it, Luke. Kinrade gives his statement after Miss Keaton declares her respect for him and her gratitude if he can help her convict Mart's killer."

"He was just trying to deflect some of the heat off of himself."

"Yes, that too, but there is a deeper motivation at work here. While Kinrade's statement lacks that crucial piece of information, the statement itself is a sure sign of it by the very fact that he offers it in response to her petition. This whole business is going crack wide open, believe me."

"There must be a money trail, something."

"There will be; an oblique one between Parsons, McCurdy, Harris and Richards, all his cronies. But as for Wilson Cutter's pay off, Parsons would be stupid to leave that in plain sight." Cliff clamps a reassuring hand on Luke's shoulder. "Stop worrying. You're doing fine. Oh, hand over the badge. Couldn't trust you with it in a million years."

Later, Cam looks over Kinrade's statement.

"Bribery and extortion, assault, harassment, threats, rustling, but not murder. Any chance he'll change his mind?"

"If you want to take a little more time bringing him before a grand jury, I've got a cell with his name on it."

"And he waived his right to counsel?"

"Could have walked out at any time. I guess he thought he wouldn't break. Or maybe he got tired of being a bad guy. Listen, Cam, I don't know how much more we'll get out of him. Parsons plays a rough game and Kinrade knows it."

Cam nods and folds his arms. "How did Luke take it?"

"Exactly as you'd expect."

Luke

Luke does his thinking at his favorite table in the Cheyenne Hotel dining room while he waits for Cam to join him for lunch; time for Cam to meet K. Her uninvited presence at the interrogation proved to him that she means what she says. She'd done a fine job with Kinrade for sure; only now he's plagued with doubt that he's misjudged her. Something of Ethan's often-voiced philosophy on women comes to him:

Every man knows what it takes for another man to make his decisions, and if it happens to be wrong there's still understanding for what it took, but it's easier just to apologize to a woman 'cause she ain't never gonna understand.

Well, he ain't ready to apologize just yet.

He notices Dan Hummer get up from a table on the other side of the room. The marshal walks Luke's way, spots him and acknowledges him. A strong, towering man, mid-forties, graying at the temples, Hummer wears every hard-earned moment of his success on his tanned face. Luke stands politely.

"Taylor."

"Marshal Hummer." They shake hands.

"All alone?"

"Just early. Thinking time."

Hummer gives a smile of approval. "Heard you had a breakthrough. Good work."

"Thanks."

"Word of advice. Accept Faraday's indictment like a good lad. These things have a way of working themselves out. Once that persnickity sheriff finishes his investigation Parsons won't have no place to hide. If he hired Wilson Cutter it'll come to the top. Seen it before. A hundred times. Lotta greed, but not much up here." He taps his finger on the side of his head.

Luke considers the experienced face of Marshal Hummer very carefully. "Thanks for the tip."

Hummer grins. "My pleasure. Now I know how gut churning this is for you, but you just gotta keep on holding your nerve. Pounce at the right moment. You'll know when it is. I reckon you got good instincts, son. Enjoy your lunch."

He takes off before Luke can ask him how the extradition is coming, although he gets the impression that Hummer don't mind in the least that it's taking so long. Luke still has the smile on his face when Cam appears at the table.

"Pleasant thought?" Cam asks and takes a seat.

"Not exactly. Dan Hummer just had a word."

"I saw him lighting up his cigar on the sidewalk a moment ago. What did he say?"

"To accept your indictment against Parsons with good grace."

Cam considers this momentarily. "What else did Hummer say?"

"To keep my nerve."

"Are you going to take his advice?"

Luke sighs. "I promised Mart I would get justice."

"Mm. I've been thinking about what you have told me about Mart, the caliber of man he was. Your Alliance exists to work for the common good, so Mart would not want justice solely for himself. I believe he meant justice for the whole Alliance and for the others who have become victims of Parsons greed. If we can take on Mart's mind so to speak, then I believe we will get the justice you promised him. It will certainly help our thinking."

Luke looks down at his hands. "*My* thinking you mean."

"I'm not criticizing you; sometimes it helps to…" Cam stops. Luke looks up to see Cam's eye on the entrance.

"Jennifer…" he announces. "She usually has that look on her face when someone has…"

"Passed on."

"Mm." Cam gives a discreet wave of his hand.

Luke's body releases the distinct pulse of energy it tends to do whenever Jennifer is near. Each seductive charge is stronger than the one before and there's nothing he can do about it. For now, he works hard to keep the sparkle out of his eyes while he's thinking if bits of Jennifer could do this much imagine the effect of huge doses.

As she arrives at their table looking pale and serious, and they both stand up, Cam says, "Who was it this time?"

"An elderly woman in room twelve. Heart attack. She was on her way to meet up with her sister whose husband died…"

She stops. Her eyes meet Luke's. There's a well of compassion in those lovely eyes, so it takes only a moment for him to catch on. Consideration for his grief over Mart. She understands that a little time and a lotta purpose only stave it off. That it hovers constantly, like a storm cloud that never breaks, that blocks the sun from ever shining the same way again.

"Water?" he offers hastily and reaches for the decanter on the table.

"Thank you," she says.

Knowing the canniness of Cam's observation, feeling mighty uncomfortable, Luke wishes he hadn't done it. Pouring is a major feat of coordination. The water tumbling over the rim and into the glass sounds like a twenty-foot waterfall.

"I was interrupting something…" she says before taking a sip.

"Well…" But again Cam's attention is sharply drawn to the entrance. "I think you are now."

"That's them." Luke excuses himself.

Edith's eyes twinkle as he greets them.

"Young man," she says. "How nice to see you again."

"And you."

"I don't like this hotel," K mutters.

Her eyes no longer sparkle when they meet; they used to, even when she hated him.

"The Inter Ocean gets kinda busy." It occurs to him that she finds being in the Cheyenne Hotel an uncomfortable experience, a place of grieving; for himself, though, the hotel is comforting, and he knows why. That reassurance gives him the grace to say, "Sorry, K, it was stupid of me and I won't ask you here again."

She merely looks at him as if he should have known better.

"Apology accepted, young man."

He knew he liked Aunt Edith.

At their table he introduces them to Cam, whose thoroughbred looks and impeccable manners appear to win Edith at once and put a dent in K's offishness; she manages a cultured smile.

Jennifer quickly introduces herself, without her doctor's title, and then promptly makes her excuses.

"I have an undertaker to see," she blurts out.

Luke coughs and politely covers his mouth; Cam clears his throat.

"Doesn't everyone eventually," Edith replies, pulling off her gloves.

Jennifer gives a soft, throaty chuckle. "Well, I hope we meet again. Mrs Edwards, Miss Keaton. Gentlemen."

"So, Miss Keaton," Cam says, when Jennifer has left and they are all seated, "it is a pleasure to meet you face to face."

"That's very kind of you, Mr Faraday. But on the subject of those letters I have nothing further to say. I am here in Cheyenne, as is my aunt, for my brother's sake."

"To be sure," murmurs Edith. "However, if my niece will permit me to say, Mr Faraday, the war of words, so to speak, between you caused what possible excitement could be had out here. I mean, it was no East River Bridge opening and fireworks, but since they completed the transcontinental railroad what is left for these hardworking people to get excited about."

Luke sticks his tongue in his cheek and holds it there.

Cam, deliberate as ever, eventually says, "So, Mrs Edwards, you were present at the opening of the East River Bridge?"

Edith's eyes twinkle some more. "Of course, Mr Faraday. Although I get the distinct impression you missed it yourself."

"Yes," Cam laughs. "Mrs Edwards, I hope you won't think this too forward of me, but my wife, who also missed the event, would be delighted if you wouldn't mind obliging her with an eye-witness account of it."

"Well, of course, I'd be happy to."

"If you and Miss Keaton are free for supper this evening…"

"We have no plans, do we, Kelley?"

"No, Auntie."

"Excellent. We have a comfortable home, and Meg is a fine cook."

Edith chuckles. "How charming you are, Mr Faraday, but hold no fears on our account about that. Has Luke told you about our trip down to the Cimarron?"

"I think he may have mentioned it…"

"I am quite used to roughing it, as they say…"

"Auntie?"

"Yes, Kelley dear…"

"May we please get on with why we are here?"

Edith shakes her head. "The youth of today, Mr Faraday, are always in a hurry."

Cam's smile widens.

"And so serious! My niece is very serious these days. Well, of course, you know that because of the letters. So, Mr Faraday, how may we help?"

Kelley

The picture Kelley had formed in her mind regarding Mr Faraday was that of a bald and stuffy old man who was more interested in his career and his own opinion than in people.

Nothing could be further from the truth. Aunt Edith raves about Mr Faraday's hospitable and charming manners and his impeccable attire, but there appears to be a great deal more to this intelligent and thoughtful gentleman. And while the idea of supper with him and his wife is appealing, she is unsure that she should allow herself to be attending a social gathering while there are more pressing matters.

Of course, Aunt Edith is walking so eagerly towards the Faraday's home in the warm scented dusk of Cheyenne's better district that Kelley struggles to keep up with her.

The young woman who greets them at the door appears barely older than herself. Mrs Meg Faraday. Vivacious. Petite. Dark, curling hair. Fine cherry brown eyes.

Above the hall stand where they set down their things is a framed cross-stitch of the finest embroidery:

Where we love is home
home that our feet may leave
but not our hearts

Oliver Wendell Holmes

Meg Faraday tells them her mother gave it to her the day they left Boston for Cheyenne.

Their house is outfitted with décor of the highest quality, elegant yet comfortable. Kelley admits she would be happy to be here except for one not so small detail.

Luke's presence.

330

This confuses her, although she did notice at lunch that Mr Faraday and Luke seemed on friendly terms. Mr Faraday appears to be the sort of man who plays his cards close to his chest, so she must go along with it for the time being.

When eventually they sit down to supper, there is an extra place setting on Meg Faraday's left.

"Are you expecting someone else, my dear Mrs Faraday?" Aunt Edith asks.

"Yes. Jennifer. But she often gets held up in her line of work. She won't mind if we start without her."

"You met her briefly today, Mrs Edwards," Mr Faraday explains.

"Oh, the young woman from the undertakers..."

The soup course is on. They are half way through it, Aunt Edith working up to her own spectacular with her narration of the fireworks at the opening of Roebling's East River bridge, when the absent young woman makes her entrance.

Kelley recalls her first sight of the young woman on that rueful visit to the Cheyenne Hotel in March, and thinks it a coincidence that she should have seen her there again.

Although her 'late' manners are faultless, her face is pale and a little grim.

Mr Faraday says, "Not another one."

To this she responds, "Mm. A five-year-old girl. Daisy Piper. Wagon accident."

Mr Faraday frowns. "I'm sorry."

Aunt Edith, who has finished with her soup, says, "Miss Sullivan, have you family here in Cheyenne?"

Miss Sullivan is arranging her napkin on her lap. "No, I don't."

"She is practically family to us," Meg Faraday offers, ladling soup into Jennifer Sullivan's bowl.

"How so?" asks Aunt Edith.

"Why I've known Jennifer since she was thirteen," Mr Faraday says with a grin. "I attended law school with her brother. We called her 'the brat of Boston' back then."

Aunt Edith wipes her smile very discreetly with her napkin. Kelley is not that quick; neither is Luke.

"So you were born in Boston, Miss Sullivan?"

"Yes. Please call me Jennifer."

"Very well, young lady. So you left Boston to work for an undertaker out here? What an extraordinary thing to do! You seem to me to be a very well brought up young woman."

Mr Faraday chuckles merrily. Luke takes a huge slurp of wine.

Jennifer looks from one to the other and presses her rosy lips together.

There's a joke to be had here and Kelley waits in anticipation.

"I, for one, certainly do not understand it," Auntie continues.

"Mrs Edwards, perhaps I should explain that I do not work for an undertaker, although I do see the man more often than I'd like. I was born and raised in Boston, attended medical school there, and also undertook my internship there and later in New York; I worked for twelve months in a teaching hospital in St Louis and then Cam and Meg persuaded me to come here where there is a shortage of doctors. And here I am."

Aunt Edith is openly staring at her from across the table.

"I apologize if you feel you have been misled," Jennifer adds.

"You are a doctor," Kelley says, to clarify things for Aunt Edith.

"And a fine surgeon," Mr Faraday chips in. "She has a special way with children, but also a peculiar talent for removing bullets. Ask anyone who has had the privilege..." His glance is aimed mischievously at Luke.

"Good heavens!" Aunt Edith declares. "What made you decide to become a doctor?"

Jennifer's eyes slip sideways. "That is a very long and boring story, Mrs Edwards. Not good dinner party material, I'm afraid."

"I find that hard to believe," Auntie exclaims softly.

Meg Faraday says, "Mrs Edwards, your narration of the East River Bridge fireworks spectacular was just coming to a grand crescendo. Would you mind finishing?"

"You were there?" Jennifer says. "Well, Meg, this is a treat."

"Precisely."

Later, after what proved to be a delicious supper, Aunt Edith corners Jennifer Sullivan, who will soon come to realize that Aunt Edith will not be denied information she is determined to have. Meg Faraday is an excellent hostess, Mr Faraday charming and affable. Luke is quite at home with them; there is but one moment that Kelley finds curious...

She is speaking with Jennifer about New York, and happens to glance across the room to find Luke watching them. His brooding gaze lifts and he acknowledges her with a sloping smile. Mr Faraday distracts him and the moment passes.

Aunt Edith joins them and wants to know if her hostess plays the piano.

"Well, I love to play, but Jennifer is the musician. She is quite the entertainer. You will play, won't you, Jen?" Jennifer, wide-eyed and nonplussed, is taken by the hand and led to the piano. "She is painfully shy, aren't you, Jen?"

"Er...well..."

"Nonsense," says Aunt Edith. "If you are talented, you should never be shy about sharing that talent with the world. Modesty is becoming to be sure, but let me assure you that you are amongst friends..."

A pretty speech, but Aunt Edith is an extremely curious woman.

Meg Faraday presses Jennifer firmly onto the piano stool.

"What would you like me to play, Mrs Edwards?" Jennifer asks.

"I'll leave that up to you, my dear."

"Then I hope you enjoy Liszt as much as I do."

From memory, with perfect precision, Jennifer plays Liszt. It is exquisite. Tender. Spirited. And yet she plays without the arrogance or conceit that such skill would normally exhibit. She is warm and graceful. It seems almost effortless; her cheeks grow pink and this is the only sign of effort.

Kelley glances around the room at the others; Luke is missing. She tries to pay attention to the music but his strange mood has piqued her curiosity.

She slips out of the room to a side porch and finds him standing there in the dark, looking out over a small courtyard. Out here, Jennifer Sullivan's music floats upon summer air thickly perfumed by potted gardenias, entrancing and somewhat exotic.

"What are you doing?" she asks.

"Listening." A wily glow from the house lights plays on his face. "You did well this morning. I've been meaning to tell you."

"Thank you. How do you think it's coming along?"

He lets out a sigh. "Quickly, considering how long it's taken to get this far."

"You have been very generous about this…"

"You expected me to guard every little piece of information like a jealous kid, did you, K?"

This is a fraction too insightful and she chooses not to answer.

The piano stops; gentle applause follows. An inscrutable smile curls Luke's mouth. Then a different melody, lyrical and a touch poignant, slips along the summer evening.

"Pa hums this sometimes," she murmurs. "A beautiful Irish tune. Makes you homesick for a place you've never even seen."

He says nothing.

They listen some more.

"Jennifer saved your leg, didn't she?"

"Mm. K, is there a point to all this small talk?"

"I realize now that we have to work together even if we don't want to, and I am trying to make an effort to put our differences aside."

There is a stumble in the music and laughter breaks out. She thinks she hears Jennifer declare that she is too tired to play any longer.

Aunt Edith's strong voice follows on with, "Yes, well, that is a very timely reminder. It's time we were leaving, my dear Mrs Faraday."

Inside, leaving preparations are under way. Luke doesn't appear until Aunt Edith and Kelley are almost at the front door.

"I'll see you back to your hotel, Edith," he says.

"Oh, thank you, dear boy. Such a beautiful night for walking, I must say."

Their goodbyes are said; the evening with Mr Faraday and his wife has been surprisingly enjoyable.

"So," says Auntie as they stroll, "what do you think of the Faradays now?"

Hard to answer with Luke right there.

She says, "Meg Faraday is much younger than I imagined."

"Yes, but you imagined Mr Faraday to be…"

"Yes, Auntie," she says quickly. A glance at Luke, but he is nothing more than a remote figure walking beside them.

"That Mr Faraday adores her is evident in every glance, certainly."

This, too, is unexpected. He should be someone who keeps his distance, aloof, humorless. Instead, he stealthily finds the way to the heart of a person. His calm disposition allows him the luxury of powerful observation and she admires this immensely.

Her deepening feeling is that the man is entirely trustworthy.

Ed

Bright River
ten days later

...is distracted from his paperwork by the commotion coming from the hall.

A booming voice carries clear through the house until a big-faced man in a worn slicker and with an unlit cigar in the corner of his mouth appears in the doorway.

"Are you Edward Parsons?"

"Who wants to know?"

"Ah, that's easy." The man strides forward. "Dan Hummer's the name."

"What do you want? And how'd you get in here?"

"Good question... well, two questions."

"I don't know how you got in here, Hummer, but I'm sure you remember the way out."

"No can do." He stands up straight, blows out his chest some, hands clasped behind his back.

"What do you want?"

"Are you Edward Parsons?"

"Yes, now what do you want?"

"Good. Now we're getting somewhere. Charges."

"Charges?"

"You know – Charges." Hummer reaches into his coat pocket and extracts a piece of paper folded in three sections. "Some of the citizens reckon you've been a bad boy, Ed. Ah, doesn't the thought of it just send a tingle of excitement down your spine? I love the smell of a courtroom. Here's your list."

Ed refuses to take the document. "Get lost."

"Can't do that. Sheriff of Laramie County..."

"No sheriff outside of this county's got jurisdiction here."

336

"There's a point. Only that's why I'm here, United States marshal an' all. Hell, you've been invited to take a seat before a grand jury in the territorial seat of Cheyenne; hell, Ed, the chief prosecuting attorney of Wyoming territory's got your measure. Why, just your money trail winds clean around three counties. But you already know about that, don't you? Now, I'm sure the grand jury will be done with you in no time. So where was I... Yep. Got it. The Sheriff of Laramie County has charged me with this errand because, you see, Ed, I just got so sick and tired of waiting around looking at that no-good Wilson Cutter while someone decides he can come back to Denver with me, well, when Mr Ryan asked for volunteers my hand was first in the air. I'll go, I said. I know where Bright River is. Been out this way once or twice."

"Show me your badge," Ed grinds out.

"Be my pleasure." Hummer opens out his slicker and a silver shield engraved with US Marshal hits Ed square in the eyes. Hummer bares flashy white teeth. "Got a fine bunch of witnesses waiting."

"What witnesses?"

"Didn't you ever wonder why your faithful attorney never came back, Ed?"

"He wrote me, told me he had everything..."

Hummer's eyebrows go up expectantly. Ed clamps his mouth shut.

"Fine boy Taylor," Hummer rambles on. "Fine instincts. All a man needs really..."

"What are you talking about?"

"Why, Ed, you should read the warrant. His name's mentioned. Now, are you ready to leave pretty soon? – I had a good night's sleep and I'm keen to get back to that sheriff. He's got more to do than he can handle and I'm a real help to him."

"I ain't going anywhere with you, Hummer."

"Ed, you disappoint me. I thought we were on first name terms. It's Dan." He gives a low, growling laugh and peels back his slicker further this time. On his hip sits a colt, from his belt hangs a pair of wrist manacles. His laughter rings louder. The tingle that goes down Ed's spine is not one of excitement.

"Ain't it a grand feeling, Ed, when you love your work?"

EIGHT

So these lives that had run thus far in separate channels,
Coming insight of each other, then swerving and
Flowing asunder,
Parted by barriers strong, but drawing nearer and nearer
Rushed together at last, and one was lost in the other.

Henry Wadsworth Longfellow
The Courtship of Miles Standish

❧⚬❦

Faraday

"Mr Keaton... a pleasure to meet you, sir," Faraday says, as he shakes the hand of the powerfully built rancher.

"And you, Mr Faraday."

"Please, take a seat."

"Don't mind if I do."

"And how is Mrs Keaton?"

"Waiting back at the hotel. She's fine. Nervous about everything..." Keaton gives Faraday's office the once over; the wood panels, law books showing through the paned doors of several cabinets, leather furniture... "Nice place."

"Thank you."

"I hear a lot of good things about you, Mr Faraday."

"That's very kind of you to say."

"Can't tell you how happy me and Amy were when Luke told us Ed Parsons had been indicted for trial by the grand jury. And how quick the trial was set to begin."

"Judge Callaghan is very eager to dispense these matters."

"We did as you instructed. We went through our son's things and I brought whatever we thought might be useful."

Keaton places a wrinkled paper sack in front of him on the desk.

"As you can see, there's not much. My son wasn't the record keeper that Luke is."

"Sometimes it only requires a single piece of information."

"You're the expert, Mr Faraday. And we are in your hands."

A jury would be hard pressed not to believe John Keaton.

"Then let's start. From the very beginning. And tell me everything you can remember. I'll ask questions when I need to. Oh, by the way, have you ever read Luke's file, Mr Keaton?"

The man gives a chuckle. "Just the first piece he did. He was young and full of big ideas. I told him he was crazy, and that it would never come to anything. Even Mart told him it might be dangerous if Ed found out. Luke just said Ed was never gonna find out. So we kept it between ourselves. On occasion we'd make a joke about it. Or if Ed had paid us a visit, Mart would joke, 'Hope you got all that, Luke.' Always knew Luke was smart, but I never thought his file would amount to much…"

"Fortunately, that's not the case."

"Ah, that boy is always one for surprises."

"Indeed. So, Parsons' plea of not guilty merely prolongs the inevitable. And, conversely, gives us an advantage – time wise. Because the only evidence we need and don't have is…"

"The connection between Ed and Wilson Cutter and my son's murder."

"Mm. But I believe it will come from this trial."

"You believe that?" Keaton asks, his bright blue eyes fixed. "I sure hope so, Mr Faraday, 'cause my son died in my arms saying that Wilson Cutter shot him. He might have kept secrets but he never told a lie in his whole life. Now, I'm gonna tell you what the Keatons know and you are gonna ask me questions…"

One hour later, when John Keaton has left, Faraday opens the paper sack and tips out the contents. A few inconsequential letters, that's all, mostly from Miss Keaton in New York.

Faraday sighs deeply.

"I need proof, Mart," he murmurs. "Give me proof."

Kelley

The presence of her parents in Cheyenne gives Kelley more reassurance than she cares to admit.

But Aunt Edith doesn't mind voicing it. And adds, "Your mother certainly has her hands full keeping Sean calm for the week until the trial commences."

Her Pa is being called to testify and he strides around his hotel room like a caged animal.

"I prefer that we are all together during this difficult time."

Yes, the Alliance is back together again. While Luke and the Keatons face the rigors of an impending trial, Ethan, Sara, Tip and Tressa prevail at the Diamond-T, although they expect Ethan will make an appearance at any time.

Her Pa regards Luke as some sort of hero; she overhears him raving to her Mama and Aunt Edith.

The hero himself works extremely hard on the case and assists Mr Faraday as if he is born to it. But, when he is not on the case, he is pale and restless.

His leg is a curiosity. Some days he limps and some days he walks normally. When she suggests he should see the doctor, he tells her to mind her own business.

"The strain must begin to rear its head sooner or later," Aunt Edith remarks.

"Well, he would take things on himself…"

"Compassion, darling…"

"As I said, he would take things on himself."

Mr Faraday takes her through her testimony for the trial.

She is staggered at the bulk of evidence he wants her to present, the effect being that she feels of some importance, that she has something to contribute after all.

"Miss Keaton, I am going to be frank," he says. "Have you any idea how you would look to a jury? Everything from your appearance, to the manner of your speech – the jury will pay very close attention to whatever you have to say and you are going to say a great deal."

Meanwhile, Ed Parsons, under the watchful eye of a deputy, has ensconced himself with his defense attorney. In the jailhouse Jake William Murray, Harris and Richards, and Lyle Kinrade also wait for the trial to commence. And in the middle, apparently, resides Wilson Cutter.

The newspapers are beginning to show an interest. One reporter accosts her in the street asking if she is the same Miss Keaton who said – quote: the acquisition of property has not given us true freedom, unquote; demanding to know the name engraved on the rock and has she always been a friend of the Indians. She replies, 'No comment,' to the abrasive young man as per Mr Faraday's instructions and rushes away.

However, the exchange provokes the memory of an incident from long ago; the day Tip at the age of seven is taunted ('half-breed' is a mild taunt compared to others that she vowed never to repeat; at the time she pestered Mart to explain what they meant and then wished she hadn't), and mercilessly beaten by much bigger boys. Just a little older but smaller than Tip, Kelley manages to help him up out of the dirt only to have the same boys taunt *her*: Indian *lover*! – and again expressions Mart later needed to explain. She is outraged, but Tip, who is badly hurt and bleeding, suffers deep humiliation.

With great difficulty, scared that the boys will return, they trudge homeward. Before they get far, Luke finds them; he is so angry he is shaking. 'Are you gonna get those boys, Taylor?' she demands to know. He tells her to shut up, and then he carries Tip in his arms all the way home. Nevertheless, those boys never came near either of them again; she had to guess that Luke challenged them and put them in their place, as Luke himself would not speak about it.

There are many other incidents involving Tip, and even Red Sky, but that particular time was the first in her life when Kelley questioned why, considering the brutal slaughter of Katrine, Luke held no resentment towards Indians.

He wasn't vengeful or angry or prejudiced like most people. He understood, unlike those vicious, ignorant boys: human beings, regardless of their color, whatever their situation, depending on their motivation, are capable of unspeakable acts.

Suddenly, all these years later, it occurs to her that her first awareness of intelligent, non-prejudicial thinking came courtesy of Luke. For years she had unconsciously observed him, and now it seems he had influenced her in ways she has never acknowledged, and led in her ways she would never have attributed to him. So, after a life honed by practicing justice and fairness, it would appear that Luke is adequately equipped to carry out his promise to Mart.

The morning after her session with Mr Faraday she is called back to his office, and when she arrives Luke is present. While they eye one another warily, Mr Faraday has Luke's file and appears to be dividing it. Sure enough, he places one half in Kelley's hands, with the letters her Pa brought with him slapped on top, and he gives the other half to Luke.

"What is this, Cam?" Luke asks.

"I would like the two of you to sit together and look at…"

"Not again, Cam…"

"Humor me. Think hard. Test one another. You're both shrewd and intelligent. Try looking at the same evidence from another angle…"

"Cam, I know this stuff as well as I know my horse…"

"*Together* this time. It will surprise you what can…"

"I thought we decided to wait for the trial."

Mr Faraday stands up straight, slides his hands in his trouser pockets, takes a deep breath and exhales. He gives Luke a hard look. "I know. But I also said we were going to put on the mind of Mart. Let's use that, hmm? Now I'm due in court. Get to work the pair of you."

After Mr Faraday leaves, Luke mutters, "Waste of time…"

Kelley puts Mart's letters to one side momentarily and takes up Luke's file. She has never seen it before.

Mr Faraday has given her the second half; the date on the top of the first page is February 17, 1883. The pages consist of journal-type entries, eye-witness accounts or simple statements. There are signatures everywhere. And there are sketches. Indeed, very good sketches, of differing size, full page drawings, right down to detail squares. She recognizes Ed Parsons, Sheriff McCurdy and other people from their district against familiar backgrounds – Bright River town and buildings, scenery and landmarks. In a way they are like photographs; a moment in time captured by a deft hand. The figures are labeled; the circumstances are precisely explained; the page is dated and signed by Luke. Some sketches are co-signed. Luke has included the exchange he had with a particular witness and, amazingly, trusting him, defying fear of repercussion, they have signed it. No wonder the file carries so much weight with Mr Faraday. This is an extraordinary and unique set of chronicles. And it touches her deeply. It brings Mart close, raises him out of the dirt and places him in their midst. The past comes to life.

"Luke, this is… I can't find the words…" She looks up to where he stands by the window. He is not on task, however; he stares out of the window, his half of his file clutched by his side. "Luke, you're not working…"

"Cam says to put on Mart's mind like it's just a shirt or a coat. I can't do it anymore." His eyes swing around, swollen with anguish. "How many times does he expect me to relive this?"

"But it's wonderful. You're an artist. I remember how you used to like to sketch horses…"

His whole body stiffens. He crosses the room and thrusts his half towards her. "Here. You like it. You find what Cam is looking for, and you can be happy about it."

She stares up into his eyes as they glisten with unshed tears. Hesitantly, she takes the papers from him. "I am happy to take the load from you, Luke. If that's what you want. My mind is fresher than yours."

His smile is glib. "That's what I want." He wipes one eye with the heel of his hand. "I'll be at the boarding house if you need me for anything."

"Mart would be so proud of this," she tells him. "Luke, *I* am proud of it…"

He swallows noticeably. "It's too late, K."

Feeling utterly puzzled, she watches him stride out; for a little while the room bears a frazzled, melancholy silence. Carefully, she places the two halves back together to start at the beginning. She won't be able to do as Mr Faraday instructed, she needs Luke for that, but that doesn't mean she isn't entitled to examine the file and be familiar with what it contains. It could prove to be very useful.

Faraday

Faraday reaches the door of their home and breathes a huge sigh.

Another day such as this one…

Right at this moment he needs Meg.

He'd waited a long time for the woman who would balance his passion for the law with a passion for life.

Despite her youth, Meg was a smart woman; although when she turned down his proposal, twice, he wondered what was wrong with her – she wouldn't marry a man, she declared, who was already married to his ambition. So, if he really wanted her, he had to win her.

It made him rethink long and hard his life, and turned his head around. He resigned his political aspirations and then directed his ambitions with fresh integrity.

Different yet meaningful opportunities presented themselves.

Margaret Louise Wiltshire married him. He never looked back.

By the time he walks through the door he is aching with weariness.

He drops his satchel on the hall table. "Meg."

He removes his coat and tie. "Meg."

He wanders through to the kitchen to encounter cooking aromas and a pot of supper sitting on the stove, but no Meg.

The back door bursts open. "I'm here! I'm here." She rushes up to him and kisses him. Panting, she says, "I was behind you up the street. I couldn't catch up."

He holds her tight against him. He studies her soft pink face and mirror bright eyes; breathes in the scent of her dark curls; savors the feel of her body pressed against his, and kisses her with tender passion.

"You've been at George's. You smell like that brown stuff she keeps in the tall bottles."

She grins her *so you think you know where I've been* smile; his heart skips at the delight of it, because he can't imagine a day when she wouldn't have him guessing.

"Make yourself a drink," she says. "Supper will be on the table in five minutes."

Eventually, the intensity of homecoming eases; while she lays the table, he washes his hands in the sink, fixes and sips his drink, and looks on in anticipation as she ladles a hearty beef stew, fragrant with wine and herbs, onto their plates. She tells him often they should eat in the dining room, but when it is just the two of them the kitchen is warm and intimate.

"I don't know what to do with Jennifer. The Mayor's birthday party is tomorrow night..."

"I know," he says.

"And she is behaving as though I'm dragging her to her execution. And when I tried talking to her about it today she got very annoyed and said she would... you know that thing she says she's going to do, the thing that I refuse to say in this house..."

"I know," he laughs.

"You have got to do something about it."

"No."

"But, Cam..."

"No."

"Please?"

He appreciates the cherry brown intensity in his wife's eyes; she is adorable whichever way he looks at her. But: "I won't interfere, Meg."

"She is miserable." Her expression changes and he is supposed to feel guilty. "All she does is read those dreadful medical books. She knows them back to front anyhow."

"Let her work it out for herself."

He picks up his fork.

"It's not our place, Meg. And none of our business."

Casually, as if she's changed the subject, she asks, "So, how is Luke?"

At this he sighs. "I feel like I'm losing him."

"*Are* you losing him, Cam?"

"Not likely... but he's definitely feeling the strain."

She excavates her stew with her fork. "The strain of what, Cam Faraday?"

He chuckles. "You tell me, Meg."

"Speaking of Miss Keaton, it was she who changed things."

Were they speaking of Miss Keaton?

"Don't go blaming her. Besides, I thought you liked her."

"I do like her. She's smart and says what she thinks; she just changed things, that's all I'm saying."

Caused Luke's remoteness – an unusually brooding, almost melancholy Luke – is what she means. Complicated what seemed like a perfectly agreeable situation. He covers her free hand with his, caressing her fingers. "Meg…"

She stops him with a tender smile. "It's all right, Cam. I won't say anymore." But she sighs to good effect.

Luke

The following evening

Light streams from nearly every window of the mayor's house into the darkness of the street, and there is music and the sound of voices, laughter mostly. Every so often neighborhood dogs bark and howl. He doesn't want to be here, but his feet conveyed him without any help from his brain. Besides, he spends most evenings walking. Walking until his leg can't take it anymore. Then he falls into bed and it throbs through his dreams.

His walks usually take in the Cheyenne Club. In high summer the grand house – said to be as opulent as any of its kind, with its rooms for billiards and cards, another for reading, a lounge and a spacious dining room – is busy enough to intrigue him, while the spectacle of its electric lights blazing out into the night amuses him.

He'd asked Jennifer about the Cheyenne Club.

"The members never come to me with any of their complaints," she said. "No surprises there. But their 'women' often drop by."

"With plenty of gossip I guess," he said.

"I turn off to anything that doesn't concern their condition."

"Their condition?"

"Luke, I never told a living soul what we talked about when you were my patient. Or Tressa either."

"That's okay," he teased. "She told me everything."

"Oh, of course," she laughed, "she told you how she expected to give birth."

"Getting back to the Cheyenne Club…"

They were both at the Faradays. A few nights ago. And found themselves alone together in the parlor. Cam got called away. Meg went to make coffee. Luke sat on one end of the sofa, Jennifer on the other.

"What fascinates you?" she asked. "Their wealth?"

"I don't know," he said.

"You must be cashing in on the cattle boom yourself."

"I guess. But I have to admit I don't believe in the way these men go about it."

"Well, of course you don't, no one least fits the profile of a capitalist better than you. Still…"

"Still what?"

"Have you ever inquired about membership?"

"I'm not a millionaire and I speak English."

She chuckled. "The members speak English."

"Scottish."

"With European accents," she laughed. She turned towards him. "I dare you to walk into the Cheyenne Club and ask for membership. With an accent."

He turned towards her.

"Go on, shy-boy. You can't refuse such a dare."

He laughed, entertaining the notion that he should take the dare just to amuse her. He found himself staring at her. With her green eyes twinkling mischievously, the Cheyenne Club and its electric lights seemed very dull. And millions of dollars couldn't buy how he felt…

"Well?" she asked. "What do you say?"

"I would never want to need a club like the Cheyenne to make me feel like I owned the whole world."

"How does anyone feel like they own the whole world?"

"Don't you know?"

She stared back at him. Peace settled inside him like a full and vast sea. Like he could live on its shore, contented, forever. Then Meg returned. Luke came to his senses. Jennifer looked away.

For days that exchange played over in his head until he found it impossible to concentrate. He was miserable and edgy. Tonight, however, his restlessness is consuming him.

He leans against a well-grown cherry tree by the sidewalk, cloaked in darkness, and imagines the scene inside. But not having been to a mayor's birthday ever, he can't come up with much.

Saphead, you have to get a grip, pick up your feet and walk away.

Just at that moment, a figure runs towards the mayor's front gate.

Under the welcoming lamp Luke spies an adolescent boy panting and pushing back his mop of dark hair.

Luke squints into the glare of the lamp and thinks he has seen him before.

The boy looks up at the house and groans. Then he takes a deep breath and enters the property.

Luke walks to the fence but stays out of the lamplight. The boy, now at the front door, thumps his arrival.

The mayor's doorman is huge, like a moving rock, and he towers over the youngster who cowers at first. The doorman pulls the door ajar and speaks to the boy outside, but enough light has been shed for Luke to finally recognize the boy.

"What do you want?" the doorman growls.

"Please, sir, my mother needs the doctor."

"There ain't no doctor here, kid, now get lost. This is the mayor's birthday party, your kind ain't wanted here."

"You don't understand. Dr Sullivan is in there and she is my mother's doctor. My mother is going to have her baby. She needs the doctor…"

"Tell someone who cares, half-breed."

Luke speaks as he limps into the light of the lamp: "Excuse me. Is this the mayor's birthday party?"

"Who wants to know?" a voice booms back.

"Well," Luke says, as he hobbles up the front path, "I heard Dr Sullivan is a guest and I need a doctor. I'm a patient of hers."

The doorman looks at them in turn. "What is this?"

Reaching them, Luke says, "Hey, I know you, kid. Saw you at Doc Sullivan's one day. With your mother."

The boy brightens. "I remember. I'm Josiah. We talked while she had her check up."

Luke grins. "Yeah, helped me get my mind off *my* check up."

"Bad leg, I remember. You're Luke."

"Yep."

"Listen, you two, skedaddle. Now."

Luke raises his eyes to the doorman who is standing two steps higher. "Josiah here needs the doctor. His mother is gonna have her baby. Mind going inside and fetching Dr Sullivan?"

"I mind. Get outa here."

Luke steps up and gets himself level with the doorman. "Well, since you don't have a mind to be fetching her, be happy to do it for you. She knows me. In fact, a lot of people in there know me. But *you* don't want to know me if you don't do as I ask."

"Tough guy, eh? Listen, the kid ain't nothing but a dirty stinking half-breed…"

"None of us turn out perfect. Me, I'm nothing but a dirty stinking cowboy. How 'bout you?"

The man glowers at him. "I could crush you like a bug."

"But you won't. Mayor's birthday an' all. Now get the doctor. And hurry. Babies like being born when you least expect it."

The doorman screws up his face. "Who *are* you?"

"Josiah's waiting. There's a life at stake. And I'm getting a hankerin' to see the mayor's birthday cake…"

The doorman grabs Luke by the collar. "If I ever see you again, I'm gonna scrape you off my shoe…" He lets go with a shove, and when he opens the door again to return inside, internal light floods out onto the porch.

Josiah's shiny black eyes make Luke smile.

"Something to look forward to, eh? Well, I'm gonna wait back over there in the dark where I came from. I'm gonna be watching though, to make sure he brings the doctor. Okay with you?"

"Sure," Josiah grins. "And thanks. Thanks a lot."

"Don't mention it," he says, and rights his collar.

He hobbles back to his position under the cherry tree.

A few minutes later, Jennifer appears on the front porch. "Josiah! What a brave boy you are! That doorman is alarming to say the least. How is your mother?"

"I am to tell you that the con… her pains just started."

"Then we better get moving. Did she happen to say if her waters broke?"

"Er… water? Gosh, she didn't mention that…"

"Good." They move quickly down the front path, Jennifer fixing her cloak around her evening gown. "I need to fetch my bag and some other things first."

"I left the wagon outside your place, Dr Sullivan. That Mr Wang heard me hammerin' on your door and told me where you were, and I ran here – sorry."

"No, it's fine; a brisk walk will do me good. Strange, I left a note on the door so urgent patients could find me…"

"You sure look nice, Dr Sullivan," the boy says. "I bet the doctor when I was born didn't look near as pretty as you."

Luke glimpses her smile before she steps out of the light.

"What a lovely compliment. Thank you, Josiah."

Sunday morning in Cheyenne is peaceful. Church bells peel melodically. Folks heed the call to worship.

The widow Donahue, his landlady, knocks on his door to tell him that she has left his breakfast on the stove before she herself joins the flow of worshippers heeding the call.

He gets up, eats half of what's on the plate, washes it, and then sits in his room reading the last two chapters of one of Cliff's law books.

Mrs Donahue makes a traditional Sunday spread which they eat at one o'clock precisely. Her boarders, eight in all, gather round her large dining table and consume the epicurean ritual, the kind which makes up a good deal of Mrs Donahue's existence. The best part is the smell of her cooking, which wafts up to his room goading his appetite. Despite this, he only eats half of it, even though she'll want to know why.

"I'll clean up for you, Mrs Donahue," he offers, to deflect the public inquisition.

"You are a sweet lad, Luke, but I can't have it. A man in my kitchen!"

He only intends to roll up his sleeves.

One of the older male boarders, who often has his eye on Mrs Donahue, leans towards Luke and whispers, "Tried that."

Luke retreats to his room. He stands at his window and observes Mrs Donahue's seven-year-old daughter and a son he thinks is nine playing in the yard with their small yapping dog. A sketch of them would make a nice gesture to thank Mrs Donahue for all the trouble she goes to, but he can't risk that being taken the wrong way either.

So he sits down at the small table that comes with the room and begins a new sketch anyway.

He can't make *her* hair yellow or her eyes bright blue, but whatever he does surely it must get his thinking straight. He walked out on her and he shouldn't have done it; he should be spending *more* time with her, making things better between them, trying to get his thinking straight...

She'd liked the sketches in his file. A pleasant surprise that. Something to build on maybe. He has a box of horse drawings at home; maybe he should give her one.

He never thought the hours of practice Sara forced on him (because it was a sin to waste his talent), even if he did kinda enjoy it, would ever amount to anything until he needed to record Ed's activities. And then he was grateful for Sara's persistence.

The sketch of K is unfinished when Mrs Donahue calls him, but he signs and dates it anyway and heads downstairs.

With a sparkle in her eye, Mrs Donahue tells him he has a visitor in the parlor; so he prepares himself for K with some annoying question about the file, except that the face in his sketch is not the face that waits for him.

"Jennifer..."

Standing over by the hearth.

"I'm sorry to disturb your Sunday, but I want to thank you for what you did last night. It was all Josiah could talk a..."

"How is his mother?" he interrupts, moving into the middle of the room.

"The baby has been in breach position for months and would not turn no matter what we tried and was always going to be born breach. And there were serious complications. Without a doctor, Grace Smith and her baby would have died. Josiah is a resourceful boy, but who knows how long it might have taken before that doorman would have helped him, or if indeed he would have. Timing is everything in these matters. But because of you, mother and child are doing extremely well."

"You delivered the baby, Jennifer," he says, trying hard to ignore the details...

She strides right up to him with her green eyes flashing and he's a little taken aback.

"Don't do that. You did something good and kind and decent last night and I'm proud of you. Josiah's family is so very grateful; they asked me to bring you back with me when I check on them today, so they can give you their thanks in person."

"You're proud of me?" he echoes in disbelief.

"I will be leaving for their place in approximately three minutes; they live on a farm about an hour or so north of town, so if you think you can actually admit that you need to escape from the confines of town for one afternoon, I'd be happy to take you."

"A farm?"

"Yes, shy boy, a farm. Horses, cows, chickens…"

"Horses? How many horses?"

"Well, how do I know? I delivered a baby, not a foal."

"Point taken."

"Finally," she exclaims, "I win one! Are you coming?"

"What d'you mean *finally*?"

"Luke…"

"All right, all right," he concedes. "I'll come. It would be rude not to."

Silence.

No retort? Crackling flecks of amber in her eyes have gone to green, and for a moment, while he observes this, he's tongue-tied.

"Very," she demurs.

The curves of her face soften, like a painting…

Finding his voice, he says, "I'll need to get my coat."

"No gun."

He gives his head a shake and repeats, "No gun."

"Let's go then." She starts moving towards the door.

Did he just say he wasn't taking his gun?

Then she suddenly turns, walking backwards as she tends to do, saying, "Would you mind driving? The livery stables gave me a horse that doesn't like me…"

Like a horse that likes her altogether too much, he follows in her steps. "The mayor's birthday – how was that?"

"Deadly," she says as he draws level with her, and they walk out of the room side by side. "Delivering Grace Smith's nine pound baby boy was by far the best part of the evening. Why were you out walking that way instead of resting your leg?"

He thinks fast. "I like the music."

"Why did you leave?"

"Er… my leg was hurting and Josiah had a handle on…"

"Would you have really gate crashed the party if the doorman hadn't fetched me?"

A sidelong glance at her and he wonders if she would have liked that. He says, "Never thought he wouldn't."

Jennifer

Trying to quell stirrings in her chest, Jennifer watches him from the corner of her eye. He doesn't help her into the buggy like most men would; instead he goes straight to the horse.

Stroking the animal's nose, he says, "No wonder she's not happy with you, Jennifer, she's as old as the hills and ready for retirement. Gonna have to have a word with your stable boy."

"Well, that explains it then," she says. But he is not listening. He is talking very softly in the horse's ear, stroking its neck. Ears twitch; head moves slightly; soft neighing ensues. Finally, he gets into the buggy with a smile on his face.

"Will she go the distance?"

"She will," he says simply, and takes up the reins. He clicks his tongue and after a sprightly snap of the reins, they move off smoothly. The horse looks confident, with a swish in her tail.

"And did she tell you where she would like to retire?"

He grins. "A female horse is like any other female – age ain't the subject of choice for conversation."

She almost believes him.

"For instance, if I was to ask you how old you are, you would reply…"

"I'm twenty-five," she says.

They exchange glances. He lets out a soft laugh. "And very young to be such an accomplished doctor."

"So why do you like horses so much?"

"Are we changing the subject back? Okay, we can talk horses. They're a fine animal. Noble, loyal…" So he speaks about horses and she listens. She needs to hear the sound of his voice; the Wyoming via Texas drawl that tickles her ears like it does the mare's. When he stops speaking, she asks him another question.

"What made you help Josiah?"

He is slow to answer, uncomfortable with approval.

"Well... remember Ethan told you he has a son?"

"Yes. He has an uncommon name... Tip."

"He's the grandson of a Comanche chief. His mother, Red Sky, was Ethan's wife. She was the sole survivor of a raid on her band by Texas Rangers; Ethan found her wandering in a daze on our ranch in Texas when we still lived there. He married her. And eventually Tip came along."

"And you looked after him, protected him from..."

"Now Josiah, he's half Shoshone..."

She lets the interruption pass. "How can you tell?"

"On one cuff of his coat there's a special pattern. Shoshone. Long ago the Shoshone and the Comanche were once brothers. What did they name the baby?"

"They haven't far as I know."

"He'll get two names, one American, one Shoshone; like Josiah. Ever read anything on the Plains Indians?"

She shakes her head.

"Like I said, seems the Shoshone and the Comanche were related way back. Same language family."

"Would you teach me to speak Comanche? I should think you speak it very well considering you grew up with it..."

He gives her a sidelong glance, probably to check she is sincere in her request. "Okay. Just a few simple words. When you greet someone, 'haa'. How are you: 'unha haki nuusuka?'"

She practices the sounds and he encourages her.

"Now we say: Fine, and you – 'tsaatu, untse?'"

"I thought you said simple words." She tries anyhow. "I think Latin and Greek sounds are easier."

"I guess it's what you're used to. Come on," he says, putting the reins in her hands. "Let's be practical. You need a lesson in how to drive a one horse buggy."

"But..."

"No buts. Hold the reins just like I was... Concentrate... Better... Too tight... Jennifer, you've gotta relax with horses..."

But it is not the horse that's bothering her.

Luke

About an hour out of town they are traveling beneath tall, voluminous clouds the color of lead that are moving rapidly into a variety of thunderhead formations, all meaning just one thing. Their matron horse is making good time, spurred on maybe by the scent of the approaching...

"Storm..." Jennifer murmurs. "Well, we certainly could use rain. Precipitation in these parts tends to be very low. I blame the wind; you could blame anything on the wind in Wyoming..."

Luke chuckles. "Well, if that means what I think it does, that's because the mountains to the west shadow the rain. So we sit high and dry. It rains a lot in Boston I guess... being on the coast an' all."

"The Smith's farm is down this road coming up on our left."

"And in St Louis?" he continues. "What's the precipitation like there?"

"It's wet," she says.

He takes one look at her poker face and bursts into laughter.

"Ask a silly question..."

"A searching question," he corrects her and takes the road on the left.

For some miles now, he's been prodding her for information about herself; she gave well-practiced and impersonal replies and then asked him something in return; his full and frank answers made way for several discussions that revealed more of her character but nothing of her life.

Okay, maybe it's better that way, although it's kinda amusing – he's still pleading with her through windowpanes and she's still pulling down the shades. He gets the feeling a person could know Jennifer a long time and still be doing exactly the same. Or maybe she thinks that even though they're good friends, they won't know each other all that long, so... maybe it's better this way.

361

They travel the picturesque road in silence until the Smith's ranch house comes into view.

"There's the house," she says.

"I see it. Pretty place."

"Yes, it's lovely."

A dog starts barking frantically as soon as they pull up.

He starts chuckling again as helps her down from the buggy; even though she is visiting a *farm*, she looks like she should be stepping down from a carriage. But she always wears a *sensible* wide brimmed, low crowned Stetson that looks incongruous with her dress, but with which she defiantly *denies the wind.*

"You really should stop laughing," she says, "or the Smiths will think their hero is addlebrained."

"Yes, M'am," he murmurs.

He catches her eye; she's smiling.

Josiah comes running out of the house.

"You came," he beams at Luke. "My parents will be very pleased. Hello, Dr Sullivan. Please come in. My mother is feeling better today."

"Good to see you too, Josiah." Luke tosses him a quarter and like all boys Josiah's age, he knows exactly what it's for.

"Don't worry, Luke, I'll take good care of the old girl."

Josiah jumps into the buggy and gets busy.

Jennifer lets out a huge sigh as she watches the kid.

Luke blurts out, "You know, just because you're smarter than most people on the planet, it don't mean you're expected to know everything. You're a people doctor, not a horse doctor."

She turns to him, releasing another sigh. "Horses..."

"Sorry. I..."

"Luke, we are friends, aren't we? You can say anything to me, you know that?"

He does, up to a point. There are still a few eggshells of significance, such as quit being so beautiful and kind and good to people and tell me what I want to know about you. At this point it's best not to mention the eggshells... anyhow, she didn't mean them. Although she should. Because they've been though a lot together and she should trust him. Now his head's in a spin and he's so damn fascinated he wouldn't notice an Indian attack.

"Harris and Richards," he mutters instead.

"Oh. That. I was just mad. And frightened. Besides, I..."

"You what?"

"I... I couldn't let you know I'd forgiven you five minutes later, could I? You would have thought..."

She comes to a dead halt.

Thought?

An involuntary look comes over her face that he'd have to be a complete and utter chucklehead not to comprehend. His heart starts galloping to make sure that he gets it.

He gets it.

Although he never got it before. When did she... Maybe she just... Or did she... Didn't they just...

If that don't beat all.

Her eyes are uncertain.

He begins to feel the need for confirmation.

To hell with it. He takes a step towards her.

"Dr Sullivan," says a strong voice from beyond them.

They both start. Her doe-eyed expression slips into a frown and then is quickly transformed. Dr Sullivan turns and smiles.

"Mr Smith, how is the family today?" says she.

"Couldn't be better."

"This is Luke Taylor. Luke, Mike Smith."

Smith holds out his hand. "May I call you Luke?"

Luke takes his outstretched hand and says, "Sure."

"I can't thank you enough for what you did."

"It was nothing, Mike. Congratulations on your new son."

"Thanks." Mike Smith is beaming. He's about forty, shorter than Luke, but solid, with a crop of curly brown hair and blue eyes. "Come this way..."

They follow. "Nice place, Mike. How long have you been here?"

"Long time now. Grace and I settled here before Josiah was born. Cheyenne was a different place then. I was in the army for a while; you know, it got me out here and then I just fell in love with the territory, and Grace. Found her on the Wind River reservation northwest of here where I was posted for a time. Left the army so I could marry her. My Pa bred horses. Decided to follow on. Breed and train quarter horses mostly. Make a good living. We need to be fairly self-sufficient. Lotta folks don't accept Grace and me but we manage. They don't mind my horseflesh though, and you get kinda determined. I couldn't be with anyone but Grace. Happy to show you round later. But come in and meet Grace, Luke. And my new son. We have two daughters, too. Lorena. She's ten. A big help to her Mama. Loves the baby. I guess she's female through and through. And then comes Marybeth; she's five."

Mike takes them through the house while he's talking. It's comfortable and neat, the kinda place that makes a body feel right at home, with pieces of Grace's colorful Shoshone heritage scattered throughout the furnishings.

A little girl with hair like Mike's darts out into the hall and runs straight to Jennifer.

"Marybeth!" Jennifer lifts her and holds the child on her hip. "How's your new brother?"

Her small fingers tickle the neckline of Jennifer's dress. "I want to play with him and he won't quit sleeping."

"Well, he has just arrived and still getting used to his new home. He will need you to show him how to do everything one day, but he is going to sleep a lot until he is ready."

"Okay, Dr Sullivan…" A cherub grin. "Down please."

"Certainly."

The kid rushes off down the hall. And they all follow.

Grace Smith's eyes are shiny and black like Josiah's, the shape of large almonds. Her long hair, the color of raven's wing, falls like a thick satin drape over one of her shoulders. Her bronze skin is smooth and unlined over her high cheekbones. She sits up in bed with a simple woolen shawl around her shoulders and her sleeping baby son tucked into the crook of her arm. A broad band of worked leather and woven colored beads is wrapped around her wrist. She is radiant with the Shoshone understanding of life; Luke, suddenly nostalgic for Red Sky, her proud beauty and the extraordinary woman and mother that she was, is tongue-tied by Grace until Mike introduces them.

Luke greets her…

"haa, grace smith. unha hakai nuusuka?" Hello. How are you?

Her eyes light up.

"tsaangu yeyeika." Good afternoon.

She also tells him – from what he can glean of the similarity between Comanche and Shoshone words – she is extremely well and no longer surprised that he helped Josiah last night. He replies that it was an honor to help and a privilege to meet her family.

"Thank you," she says in American. "You speak…"

"numu tekwapu."

"numu. Comanche."

"My brother is half Comanche; his mother was the daughter of the chief of her band, nakoni people."

"Our languages are similar."

"I can understand you pretty well."

"But *your* people are American."

"That's right."

"I see. There is, how Mike would say, a story there. With your Comanche brother."

"There is. Congratulations on your new son," he says. "What name have you given him?"

"Well, that's why we wanted you to come today, Luke," says Mike. "We were hoping we could name him 'Luke', after you, if you don't have any objections. Grace sure would like it."

Luke stares at him, lost for words.

Grace starts to giggle.

"I think he's very pleased," Jennifer says.

He clears his throat. "I am. And I don't have any objections. In fact, I'm honored. He's a fine boy. "

"Yes, indeed," Mike says enthusiastically.

Grace tells Luke that she wants the baby's Shoshone name to be 'kettaa pihyen'.

Her eyes rest on the one for whom the child is being named. Jennifer's expression sharpens at the attention she doesn't understand. Mike grins; murmurs his agreement in Shoshone.

"What does that mean?" Jennifer asks.

"I think it means 'strong heart'," Luke tells her. "The baby's Shoshone name."

Grace nods serenely and says to Luke, "jennifer tsaa' kettaa dai'gwahni-a."

"puhu," he replies.

"What was that?"

Grace's smile broadens. "My son, Jennifer, has been named for the one who had the courage to defy her own people and bring him into this life. You. It was not easy. You would not give up and so I could not. And we are both here. I told your fine-looking friend that you are a good and strong leader. He says you are powerful medicine. And I agree. Your skill is great. And your heart is very strong. My son, I pray, will have this heart." She removes the band from her wrist and holds it out to her.

Jennifer, wide-eyed, takes it. "Grace, I don't know what to say..." And she doesn't for a moment, as she lightly fingers the unique and colorful beadwork. Then, "I am very honored..."

Without warning, thunder explodes over the house and they all jump. Lightning flashes, followed by another boom. The baby jerks awake and Grace fusses over him. Josiah rushes in and screams for help getting the yearlings into the barn. Outside, the dog is barking wildly. The older girl, Lorena, pushes herself passed Josiah, yelling, "Papa, I can't get Whisker tied up. She's gone crazy."

Mike throws up his hands.

"I'll help Josiah, Mike. You stay with your wife."

"Sure, Luke," Josiah shouts enthusiastically. "Let's go."

Luke

For the next twenty minutes Luke feels like he died and went straight to heaven. He rides an alert and responsive piebald called bo'nai, to help Josiah wrangle eight storm-spooked (and highly valuable) yearlings before that black cloud unleashes its contents.

Josiah is a natural rider; Luke watches him tear across the field with a couple of spirited young horses streaking ahead of him. Reminiscent of Tip at work, it is a sight that Luke hasn't seen for some time and does his heart good to behold.

They meet in the middle of the corral where Josiah confirms that all the horses are now stabled. As thunder booms over them, they walk their mounts to their stalls; they talk about the ranch while they give bo'nai and daa'bu a rub down.

"I'd better get up to the house, Luke, see if Pa needs me," says Josiah. "Thanks for your help."

"Hey, I should be thanking you. I haven't had that much fun in months."

Josiah flashes a grin and takes off.

Luke continues the piebald's slow grooming, but eventually the animal wants to be left in peace.

A shadow falls across the barn door and he looks up from shelving the grooming brush. Jennifer is sauntering towards him. As usual, his body reacts to the sight of her, while his brain lumbers along behind warning him she's a valuable friend and to keep it that way.

Except that now they have some unfinished business…

"Hello," he says.

She stops beside the piebald's stall. "Hello."

Her chestnut hair is splattered with raindrops.

He steps out of the stall and closes the gate.

"I came to tell you that there is a naming party about to start in ten minutes," she says.

"Food?"

"Yes," she grins. "I watched you ride. I sometimes hear a saying out here: born in the saddle. I think it may apply to you."

She watched him?

"You make it look incredibly natural and easy."

Maybe she's just admiring a skill she could never acquire.

"That's because it's not hard."

"It looked exhilarating. Like flying perhaps."

"When you really put the licks in you almost catch up to who you are."

Her eyes widen. "Do you? I was wondering about that. Like losing and finding yourself at the same time."

"I reckon."

Thunder rumbles ominously overhead. A couple of horses stir. She looks around, unsure about them.

"Storm's shaping up," he remarks.

"Indeed."

"Do you like storms?"

"Mostly. You?"

"Better in town where you don't have stock to worry about."

There's a lightning flash, followed at once by thunder.

"It's directly overhead," she says, looking up at the roof.

He removes his gloves. He stuffs one in each pocket, saying, "I want to thank you for bringing me here."

"Don't mention it," she replies distractedly.

"Did I look that lost in town?" he wonders out loud.

Her eyes come back to his face.

"Not at all," she murmurs. "Well, maybe just a little."

He grins.

She smiles.

"What is his name?" she asks.

"The piebald? – bo'nai."

"Shoshone?"

"For 'mouse'. I'm sorry, I should've introduced you…"

"I like the way you treat horses with the same respect as people."

"Well, you know by now how I feel about horses."

Yet another pretty smile says she does.

An over-bright flash of lightning blinds him temporarily. The thunder crackles and rumbles deep into the earth. Reverberates around his body, almost stilling his heart. Every horse and pony in the place objects until the last of the rumbling goes away.

He turns to Jennifer to find her staring at him. He stares back for how long he doesn't know, and mutters, "You're not scared."

"No. I'm with you."

His heart is racing but he's got to remain calm.

She breaks her gaze with a glance directed at the stable door. "I should go... now..."

She turns and walks away.

At first, confusion cements his boots to the floor. "Where are you going?"

She mumbles something.

"We..." he starts after her, "... we weren't finished."

He swiftly overtakes her and blocks her path. She pulls up before she cannons into him.

"We have unfinished business."

She starts walking backwards slowly. "Unfinished business?"

He follows slowly in her steps. "Icebergs."

"Icebergs?"

"They have tips that sit above the water but underneath..."

"I *know* what an iceberg looks like," she says.

"We must've read the same book."

She rolls her eyes and checks behind her. She's clear, for the moment.

"Like I was saying. There's a lot more going on with you and me than meets the eye."

"You have a vivid imagination."

"For a long time now I've imagined holding you in my arms. Ah, you're running out of space back there."

"I am not. You... you stay back because I think that there may be something wrong with you."

"Maybe. But I ain't the one acting addlebrained right now."

She stops suddenly; puts out her hand to halt his advance; it lands on his chest, right atop his heart. "Are you..."

"What?"

"Are you or are you not promised to Miss Keaton?"

He stares at her, taken aback.

"You see," she says gently, "not so addlebrained."

No. He's the one who has to pull his thoughts together. And he hesitates. How does he explain something that confuses *him* day and night?

"Just tell me the truth…" she says, even softer.

Be honest. Take a stand. Make a decision… End this now.

"Luke."

"I was once but I'm not now. She has totally, absolutely given me up. The agreement between us broke down. She won't have me."

"And you? You won't have her?"

Again, he hesitates; when it comes to the Keatons he has never said that one all-important little word:

"No."

"Are you certain there is no chance that you will reconcile?" she asks, her eyes penetrating his.

These questions are just, he reasons. They reveal her integrity, and challenge his. But there is something more that needs to be said. Words he has uttered in his dreams but now need to be said in reality. And somewhere in the back of his brain is a tiny voice, *what about our alliance, Taylor?* that needs to be silenced.

"Luke, I understand…"

"You couldn't understand this. Jennifer, beneath your hand is my heart. Can you feel it hammerin' away in there?"

"Yes. Your heart rate is elevated."

"That is for you. It does that for you and only for you. No one else."

A smile pulls at the corner of her mouth, but she tries to bite it away. "Certain… things can get pushed aside if a man with a sense of duty as strong as yours needs to do it."

"The first moment I saw you, the very sight of you… You went straight to my heart, the same heart going like a train under your hand."

"You never said a word."

"Neither did you."

"A man like you couldn't possibly want someone like me."

He wants to break apart with incredulous laughter. Instead, he steps up to her and takes her face between his hands. He touches his forehead to hers. Looks into her eyes.

"Jennifer," he sighs.

A shaky sound escapes her lips.

"Scared?"

"We're supposed to be too different," she says.

"Somehow we're not."

"What do we do now?"

"No more pretending."

"Luke, wait…"

"For what?"

"You have to understand… if we… How do I hand you back to… someone else?"

"I do understand, Jennifer. But you ought to know by now that nobody hands me anywhere."

"My blue-eyed boy… *you* should know it is dangerous to believe that you are the master of your own destiny."

"Say that again," he mutters.

A nervous, tender smile. "My blue-eyed boy."

"I love you, Jennifer."

She almost gulps. "Luke, I…" Seems it is her turn to hesitate. Her eyes, however, have taken on a sultry luster.

"Say it," he urges softly. "You won't ever find a man who wants to hear it more."

"Luke, I… I love you back."

He takes her in his arms, his head swimming with delight, and a touch of triumph, and kisses her soft-red lips.

Faraday

Just before supper, as Faraday is examining documents, Meg shows Miss Keaton into the parlor with the offer of a hot cup of tea. Miss Keaton looks both a little buffeted by the inclement weather and gravely resolute.

"I am sorry for intruding, Mr Faraday."

"Not at all, Miss Keaton. What brings you here on such an evening? Come. Sit down."

"Thank you, no. I don't think I can sit at the moment…"

Faraday raises his eyebrows.

"What I mean is that I have here one of Mart's letters; it was not in the pile you gave me to check with Luke's file. My mother had it and she finally gave it to me, and…"

He frowns and she stops speaking. "Go on, Miss Keaton."

"There is something very odd about it. I was wondering if you know where Luke is. I need to talk to him about it…"

"Well, no. I haven't seen Luke. Perhaps if you can tell me what you've found…"

"Well…" She reaches into her purse and takes out a folded letter. Handing it over to him, she says, "I don't think it will strike you as strange, Mr Faraday, but some of the things Mart has written are not right."

Faraday unfolds the paper and reads:

My dear Kelley,

You have always believed in me. Always made me believe I could do anything. I always appreciated it. I have always loved you for it. You tried to make me tell you the problem I carry with me everywhere I go. You tried to relieve me of it, but I couldn't tell you. I still *can't tell you. Just believe I have done nothing wrong. I am still loyal to the Alliance. I am still working and putting all my efforts into it. My efforts are just different to Luke's. Believe me, Kel, when I tell you I am fighting for us not deserting you. There are things I need to do to ensure the safety of you all.*

I know what freedom and truth and all that mean to you. Never stop believing in these. It makes you the extra ordinary person you are. When you search for the truth dig and dig till you find it. Remember when we were kids and we dug up crocus bulbs from the meadow for Mama. We would plant them in pots and place them in the sun on the porch. Truth can bloom where you least expect it so never give up. And while you are doing all that believing, Kel, just don't stop believing in me. Always your loving brother Mart.

"A meaningful letter," Faraday remarks... indeed, a much needed piece of the man that he intends to dissect like a scientific specimen.

"One that I have not seen until today, which I find very hard to comprehend as it is addressed to me. It should have been given to me a long time ago. But it was with Mart's things and it took my mother some time to go through them and when she did she... well, if you knew my parents... they hadn't opened it, so..."

"I understand their grief, certainly. Now, your concern is?"

"As I said I need to confer with Luke about it, but of this much I'm sure: there were never crocuses in the meadow until we planted them there. Saffron crocus corms, and we planted them all over the place. Mart asks me in the letter to remember digging them up. We never dug them up, Mr Faraday."

He studies her excited expression for some moments. "You're right. I think we should confer with Luke."

"But I do have my own theory, Mr Faraday."

"Mm... And that would be?"

Jennifer

Although the storm is spent, the streets of Cheyenne are awash after the great dumping of rain. The wheels of the buggy smatter through one moonlit puddle after another until at last Luke draws the old mare to a halt in front of her building.

Oh, that moonlight…

The Smiths insisted they wait until the rain had completely gone. They were made to feel completely at home with the family. The baby was brand new – a family renewed. The storm and the rain saw the earth renewed. And certain feelings, once contained and now freed, began to expand, fill the once-empty spaces, deepen, and strengthen. This was also altogether new.

When he barely strayed from her side all evening her feet didn't seem to touch the ground.

What had happened to her good sense?

The wisdom that restrained her feelings for him for so long got washed away with the rain, and now something truly wondrous had bloomed by the light of the moon.

On the day they met she had made a serious pact with herself that she would not let this happen; assured herself that she could keep him out of mind and at arm's length. But he kept returning to Cheyenne, and to her; he sought her out, she never turned him away. The natural feeling between them made them friends. Her pact kept it that way, until her guard slipped. And something she didn't expect got uncovered.

She wasn't the only one who had made a pact.

When the clouds parted, the night sky was fresh with stars. It was no ordinary journey home, not for her at any rate.

Over the years she had watched others in this condition and wondered; and it was so blissfully different when it was reciprocated.

It had tenderness and it had power; a life of its own. It was good.

But Luke *is* goodness, she is convinced of that, albeit a complicated and adventurous kind; he is also somewhat unconventional compared to other men, so he doesn't realize yet how good a man he actually is. She wants him to know it, but what truly frightens her is that she wants to be the one to help him come to the realization. That was definitely not part of the pact.

"The livery," she reminds him.

"No. I'll take her back in a minute. See you inside first."

"You don't have to…"

"The streets are soaked."

She sighs. "They are at that."

"Stay put. I'll see you down."

The street feels deserted as they walk quietly to the door.

"People tuck any urgent messages in between the doors," she whispers as she rummages in her pocket for her key. "Or under it…"

"How kind of them," he replies. "Oh, darn. No messages."

The key turns in the lock. "Well, it's very late and we were gone for a very long time."

"Not long enough."

"You had your holiday," she teases him.

"Why are we whispering?"

Once inside, he snaps the door shut, and in the cool darkness of the room, he puts his arms around her. "Any messages?"

"Difficult to see in the dark."

"I'll light a lamp."

"No, I'll light the lamp, you had better go home."

"Not until I know you're safe."

"But there's been no trouble since…"

"The arson attempt, I know. But Cam sees you home safely at night?"

"I usually stay over if it is late."

"Very sensible. Where are the matches?"

She keeps a lamp table by the door; she goes to it and lights a match to reveal his figured presence before her; she gazes at him in the glow; that he loves her fills her with wonder, makes her heart resemble the match… she has to shake out the flame before it burns her fingers.

"There's something I want you to know," he says, "so that you know you can always feel safe."

"What do you mean?"

"There are people watching over you at bedtime."

"What people?"

"Cliff for one. At night he'll walk around this building and check out the alley. If not Cliff, one of his deputies. Every night."

"Oh my. How do you know this?"

"Because... because, Jennifer, it's what I do every night. I see them, but they don't see me. And, thankfully, none of us sees anyone with bad intentions."

"How on earth does Cliff not see you? He has eyes in the back of his head..."

"I learned a lot more than how to speak Comanche from Red Sky. Just don't tell Cliff. I'll be in trouble. He hates the unbadged doing his job."

"The unbadged? Luke, I don't know what to say. Except..."

"Mm?"

"Thank you. And, now I know why your leg aches."

"It only aches when I'm not with you."

Suddenly, she's aware of a match scratched to life and illuminating the space between them. His smile is soft; in his eyes a sultry glow. The match dies. His arms draw her meltingly into the leanness of his body.

"Tomorrow?" she smiles.

"First thing."

"tsaa," she says.

He laughs gently. "Very."

Even so, her heart is beating a warning: *Don't do this, Jennifer.*

And her drowning common sense, which has been gasping for air from the moment he kissed her, is desperately trying to get her attention: *Dr Sullivan, you cannot be serious.*

Luke

The following morning

Since he is late by fifteen minutes, Luke has a mental picture of Cam standing beside assistant prosecutor Josh Bridger's desk, studying his pocket watch. Sure enough, as he gets to where Bridger sits at his desk pouring over a pile of papers, Cam is standing there consulting the famous watch.

"Very sorry," Luke offers. "Prior appointment."

Before long Cam is studying *him*. "Mm."

Luke wonders if Cam can read on his face that he's been with Jennifer this morning as well as he can read the time on the face of that pocket watch.

"Something the matter?" Luke asks.

"What a difference a day makes."

"Sorry?"

"Storms must agree with you."

"Your note said K's found something."

"She has. Very interesting too. She has a theory and needs to confer with you."

"Well, here I am. She's in your office?"

Cam steps aside. "After you."

When he sees K standing by Cam's window, he pulls up short; some of the morning's glow fades; his sense of having at last regained some control of his life slips: he must deal with something he hadn't anticipated – guilt, a pile of it. Has he been unfaithful to her; or has he merely done exactly as she wanted and moved on with his life?

"Where have you been?"

"Well, I…"

"I need to talk to you about this…" She holds out the folded paper she's been clutching in her hand.

"What is it?"

"A letter to me from Mart. The date indicates he wrote it just before he left…"

Kinda bewildered, he takes the letter, unfolds it and reads. After the first paragraph he needs to sit down. He glances up at K. She is watching him with a look that pretty much expresses how he feels.

"I need a drink," he mutters.

"You told me Cheyenne is a dangerous place; I understand what you mean. Now read the rest."

He swallows and braces himself. "…when you search for the truth, dig and dig… truth can bloom where you least expect it… don't stop believing in me."

"So," says Cam. "What do you think?"

"To be fair to Luke, Mr Faraday, the letter is… it is difficult."

"Of course; my apologies."

They are quiet while Luke reads the letter a second time. He stands up and paces. Thinks till his brain hurts. Mart's obsession with the crocus makes no sense. He glances up again; K's eyes are fixed on him.

"I don't recall Mart digging up crocus bulbs. I only remember us planting a whole bunch of them. When we were kids. Those saffron things your mother uses for cooking and making dyes. I recall she wanted to see if she could grow them and we were cheap labor. "

He is rewarded with a smile from the K of old.

Cam circles close by him with a wry grin on his face and a sharp glint in his eyes. Luke tries to ignore him.

"Very good," he murmurs. "Your powers of concentration this morning amaze me. Anything else?"

"Well, Mart's explaining his motivation. His intent. Whatever he was doing in that forest with Wilson Cutter, this letter explains his motivation for doing it. The second paragraph reads like a clue in a treasure hunt. And the last line is like…"

"Like?"

"A warning."

Cam narrows his eyes. "Interesting."

"I agree," says K spiritedly. "Luke, see where Mart says 'when you search for the truth, dig and dig till you find it'?"

"Sure."

"I believe that Mart has left us some record of the truth of what he was doing."

"What record? He hated my file, why would he…"

"I am certain Mart is telling me in the letter that he has hidden important information back home. Not only because he thought we would need the information for our survival, but because he knew we would want the truth."

"Hidden?"

K's eyes blaze like points of blue fire. "Think back to the day when we planted the saffron crocus in pots on the porch. I think I was eight. Mama said before we put the corm in the earth we should say that we are burying our sins, and that when the green shoots came up we would know we were forgiven. I asked her, what if we bury good things accidentally and they die in the dirt? Mart said the good things never stay hidden, things like the truth always come out, like the green shoots will."

"That's Mart for you. Straight as they come. He should've been a preacher."

"To save your miserable soul he probably would have."

"Yes, K, my miserable soul…" he says gruffly.

"Well, you said that if I wasn't careful I would never be a green shoot. I threw dirt in your face and I had to wash the supper dishes for a week."

"At least the dirt made it memorable."

"Oh, I forgot for a moment you have no sins…"

"Ah, the story is very nice, Miss Keaton," Cam breaks in. "Even the dirt… Perhaps we could move on?"

As Luke eyes K sorely, she composes herself.

He asks, "Where do you suppose Mart hid the information?"

"The clue is in the line where he says 'we dug up crocus bulbs from the…'"

"Meadow. Your meadow. I'll be damned. He buried it…"

"Are you sure, Miss Keaton?" Cam asks firmly.

"Mr Faraday, you were keen to find something amongst Luke's file and Mart's letters and I have; now I intend to follow it through whether you do or not."

Cam studies K for a long moment.

Then he says, "Well, we had better send for Sheriff Ryan."

NINE

There is a mountain in the distant West
That, sun-defying, in its deep ravines
Displays a cross of snow upon its side.
Such is the cross I wear upon my breast...

Henry Wadsworth Longfellow
The Cross of Snow

❦

Kelley

Bright River

Underfoot and all around, her meadow.

Green, alive.

Overhead, the sun.

White hot.

The songful cheep of meadowlark and the wind moving in large swells through the tops of the pines.

If she stands here long enough she can almost forget that her life is not *the most exciting adventure she can imagine.* Aunt Edith got that wrong. But, as she searches the long grass for signs of crocus, she admits that her selfishness, her self-absorption, has charged her with a set of consequences with which she must redeem herself.

And Luke. Who almost fell in love with her… She stares at her soiled fingers. Where he slipped through. She must learn to cherish, because so many things fade.

"What are you doing, K?"

He looks hot and fed up. Two hours of searching, digging. It's all wrong.

"We need to rethink," she tells him.

Mr Ryan joins them. And the court clerk. What's his name? He's young and hard-working, but even he seems to be lagging.

"Take a break?" Mr Ryan suggests.

She nods. She moves into the shade, sits on the old log seat and pulls out Mart's letter. Surprisingly, Luke sits beside her. He hands her a canteen of water. She takes it and then asks him to leave her alone to think. He seems hesitant but leaves without a word. She observes him; with his shirtsleeves rolled up to his elbows and the fabric clinging in places to his lean body, he looks just as Aunt Edith described. Her hero. Always there. Always ready to do what must be done. Never shirking his duty.

She admires it. All of it. And yet... and yet their minds never seem to meet. He joins Mr Ryan and the clerk in the middle of the meadow. They talk, they point, they gesture their bewilderment.

The cool water on her dry throat makes her cough.

Mart, where have you hidden... it?

She must think. Forget all her mistakes. And concentrate on being a little green shoot. Her sins are buried; she is waiting to be saved. She rises up from the dirt to show her fresh green head to the world... She's missed a step. Burying her sins and hoping for the best is not enough. She must repent and seek forgiveness. Mart the preacher used to say to know you're forgiven just look to the Cross... yes, the most powerful symbol of forgiveness is a cross.

She quickly gets to her feet and walks out into the meadow. Frantically, she looks around for a cross; in the trees, in the grass...

She hears Luke behind her. "K?"

"What is the one sign you would use above anything else to symbolize forgiveness of sins?"

"Come again?"

"What sign, Taylor? Even you know the answer." She twirls around looking for the sign.

"All right. It's a cross. Mart was determined I would know that much." And now he's looking too. "Is that what we're searching for – a cross?"

"I believe so."

"Where?"

"Well, it can't be on the ground, otherwise we would have seen it by now. I mean look at this meadow; it looks like gopher city."

"A tree then?"

"Mm. But which tree? You know, if Mart was so determined for you to know what a cross meant, then maybe we should look at the tree with your initials on it."

As she starts walking he has his arms up in a gesture of frustration.

"You know... the heart with LT and EM..."

"Oh," he says and his arms come down.

"Emily McIntyre. How old was she? Fifteen. You, I clearly remember, were sixteen. I wonder what happened to her; she had such a crush on you it was pathetic."

"She was a lovely girl," he argues.

"Well, I'm sure you'd know…"

Suddenly, he grabs her shoulders and stops her. His grip is a little firm.

"Say one word, Taylor, about the deficiency of my character and…"

"Mart was the best of the three of us. I just don't understand why he's gone and you and I are still here."

"Don't think I haven't asked myself the same question. But we don't hold the plan." She shoulders herself out of his grasp and signals to Mr Ryan.

They all converge on the tree, one in a stand of old leggy conifers on the perimeter of the meadow. Mr Ryan reads the initials aloud, much to Luke's chagrin and her satisfaction.

"Is this where we dig now?" the young clerk asks.

"There's no cross," Luke points out.

"Just a very sweet heart," Mr Ryan says.

Kelley catches the expression of mock disdain Luke gives Mr Ryan as she looks around at the other trees close by.

"Here's something, Miss Keaton," says the court clerk.

Indeed it is. Roughly made on a near tree.

Her heart is beating so fast she is breathless. She places her fingers in the carving; her fingertips seem to visualize Mart with hammer and chisel, chips of bark falling to the ground as he works… his cross.

"Mart… what have you done…"

She becomes aware of frantic movement around her. Luke has a shovel and is digging near the base of the tree.

"What are you doing… slow down. You're flicking dirt all over me."

"I'm just returning the favor," he replies. "Now stand out of the way."

Dirt flies fast. "Why are you so mad?"

"All this talk about a cross. Forgiveness. Next you'll be trying to save me. You as you're standing there and Mart from his grave…"

Mr Ryan calmly wrestles the shovel from Luke's grasp. "Come on, Luke. I think you and Miss Keaton should just watch like the Judge said."

Luke stands back, panting, agitated, wiping dirt off his face with his cuff.

"You can't blame him for one last attempt," Kelley says.

"I never blamed Mart for a damn thing except for not telling me about Wilson Cutter." He steps back, off-balance, and with fists clenched, exclaims as if he is expecting Mart to answer him, "Why didn't you tell me?"

Her heart leaps. A shiver passes through her.

Mr Ryan hands the shovel over to the court clerk. "Keep digging." Then he takes Luke by the shoulders and urges him further away. "Stop doing this, Luke. It's not your fault."

"It *is* my fault. I could have saved him," he agonizes, "and instead he's still trying to save me. He never gives up…"

"No, he doesn't. And neither do you. How do you think we got this far? Now let's just dig and find whatever it is we're supposed to find."

Luke

With each blow of the shovel, condemnation rings in Luke's ears. Cliff has taken over digging from Bowen; is it the shovel that his boot strikes, or Luke's gut? Meanwhile, a mound of earth grows steadily, and soon a substantial pile of guilt and regret is removed from the ground.

A lifetime passes by. K watches each strike as if it will be the final revelation.

Cliff's coat and tie hang over the branch of another tree and his sleeves are rolled up; he has excavated the spot thoroughly.

"That's it," he murmurs.

"Are you sure?" Luke asks.

Cliff straightens and wipes his brow. "I'm sure."

"You see...it?"

Cliff nods. "It's there." He turns to K and says, "Good work, Miss Keaton."

It's obvious that she can't speak; her eyes just stare at him as if validation is the last thing on her mind.

"Are you paying close attention, Bowen?"

"Yes, Sheriff," the clerk from Cam's office says.

Cliff reaches down into the hole and pulls out a leather package.

"My God," K breathes.

He brushes soil off and then carefully undoes the leather wrapping, which is stiff, washed out, and weather-beaten. But beneath this layer there is another, this one folded in the opposite direction and in better condition. He peels back the tucks and folds with great care to reveal a hard-covered book resting inside the inner wrapping. They all stare it.

"Open it, Cliff," Luke breathes.

Cliff lifts the book off the leather wrapping, which he hands to Bowen.

He inspects the outside where the edges have yellowed. The cover sticks a bit as he cautiously peels it back. Then Mart's handwriting can be seen flowing clearly across the first page. Luke gasps, as does K.

Her voice trembling, K asks, "What does it say?"

Cliff turns the book around again. "Let's see. It reads: *To the greenest shoot that ever rose from dark earth — my sister Kelley. And the bravest soul that ever lived — my friend and brother — Luke. We will always be free in our hearts. We will always love the land that sustains us and gives us life. We will always be together. Mart.*"

Luke slumps back down again in the dirt feeling as though something has just sucked the life out of him.

Cliff says, "There's more at the bottom. *Hopefully by the time you read this Ed Parsons McCurdy and Wilson Cutter will have dug their own graves and you know the truth. But if what I fear becomes reality you won't ever hear from me what truly happened so I have written down as much as I can. I also fear for all of you because Ed will not stop until he has seen us gone from our homes and our grass and the River are his.*"

"Sweet Jesus," Luke mutters.

He looks at K; she is dumbstruck, staring at the page, then tears flood her eyes and she rushes off into the forest.

"Will she be all right?" Cliff asks him.

"I'll go after her in a minute," he says, unsure of his own emotions. "So, what else is in there?"

With care, Cliff flicks through the pages. "Journal entries, lots of them."

They look at one another for a long moment.

"What do we do now, Sheriff?" Bowen asks.

"Take this back to the Diamond-T, be ready to leave as soon as possible."

Luke nods wearily. "Pack up the tools and we'll meet at Morgen. K and I'll be along. Don't let Tressa see the journal without Sara being there."

"See you at Morgen then." Cliff gives him a sympathetic smile as he takes his coat from the branch. "Okay, Bowen. Grab that shovel."

Luke watches them for a minute, then turns his eyes to the forest where K ran off. He is unsure of her and even less of himself. Without too much effort, he finds her leaning against a tree; she has been crying pretty hard.

"K, we need to get moving. That book of Mart's is a journal full of entries."

Her teary eyes meet his. She is still the prettiest girl he's ever seen, even with a tear-stained face and dirt smudges. Guilt for falling in love with Jennifer and not with her causes him to break his gaze.

So, maybe not that kind of love, but he does love her. He reasons it as friendship, that cares and comforts and supports, and expects nothing in return. Maybe it's more, or something different, or maybe she's a Keaton and that's a standing peculiar all unto itself, but he certainly can't explain it better than that.

"You were right, K," he says, looking at her again. "I thought I could do it all on my own but Mart needed both of us. I... I should have listened to you. Mart gave you...no, entrusted you with something and I had no right to..."

"What is this, Taylor? My consolation? If you could have shown just one ounce of faith in me..."

He takes her by the shoulders and pulls her away from the tree. "I'm sorry, K. I'm so sorry. I was wrong."

"It won't bring him back..." Tears drop onto her cheeks. "And it won't bring back the person I was before. I lost myself when I loved you, and that girl who had so much faith and hope in life never came back."

"It ain't easy to take the licks... it never is. But I still see her... determined and clear-thinking..."

"Mart believes I am still that person, doesn't he?"

He swallows. "Yes. That can never change."

"Because he said so. Because he's gone and can never take it back."

"He knew you better than anyone. He knew and loved the greatness in you, K."

Her eyes blaze briefly. "Then I suppose that will be enough."

Only Mart can give her the consolation she needs. And only now does he comprehend how painful his lack of belief in her must have been, because he knows how much *he* needs Jennifer's belief in him, how freely she gives it out of love for him and the strength he draws from it. But it's too late for him to give K the same consideration. The damage has been done; for him to try to repair it he would have to turn his back on Jennifer. If only they had known about the journal sooner! Discovered it after Mart died! All these months... All this time it's been lying there, waiting... For the decision to withhold the letter, for fear of facing its unknown contents, they are paying the unholy price. He shivers as another stab of regret rips through his insides. This one brings tears to his eyes that burn deep into the sockets.

"I'm so sorry, K."

"The sorrow never seems to..." She sighs. "We should go."

He nods.

"I think the truth will be hard to take."

"Let's just not do it alone." He starts them walking back.

After a bit, she says, "I accept your apology."

"Thank you. It won't ever be enough."

"I know you are sincere. That you care about me the way you care about Mart. I accept responsibility for my part in what happened to us. You and I have to start somewhere, and there is already too much pain."

They return to Cheyenne the following day.

Ethan accompanies them.

He clamps his hand on Luke's shoulder and says, "Don't worry, son, things are gonna be all right. I swear to you."

Luke is relieved to discover that there is room in his aching heart for gratitude.

Mart

3ʀᴅ SEPTEMBER 1882: One of Ed's men bailed me up on the Bright River road this morning and took me at the point of a gun to see Ed. At the time I went along thinking that Ed was joking. He threatens Luke and me all the time — just more of the same I thought. This morning I was not laughing. The threat was serious in every way. I must convince Pa to remove the fencing and renew Ed's water contract or else we would find ourselves at the mercy of a hired gun. When I told Ed he couldn't be serious he said that his hired gun would see to me first. Again I told him he must be joking — that this was all just one big joke. His reply was that if I told Pa or Luke or Ethan anything about this there would be bloodshed.

Ed warned me not to bother with the sheriff because McCurdy was on retainer. I immediately thought of going to Laramie for help. But Ed was one step ahead of me. He warned me not to go to Laramie because his hired gun would do anything he was asked to do including shooting any lawman I managed to convince. Who would make the connection he said. And that would mean the end of my life also.

I left Ed's place and was half way home when a mean looking character blocked the road and introduced himself as Ed's man. He had an ugly grin and a scar and a black beard and he threatened me.

I finish this entry in a state of disbelief. I know that in revealing any of this to Pa and Luke at the moment would be disastrous. Ed wants bloodshed. He wants us off. If we start the bloodshed even by an innocent protest all the better for him. I can't let that happen. I must fight Ed myself in my own way. A start would be to keep an eye on Ed's hired gun. I pray that God will guide me in all this and that somehow it will all soon be over that Ed will back off and come to his senses. It hardly seems real.

4TH OCTOBER 1882: There is no sign of Ed's hired gun these past few weeks. Perhaps it was all a dream. Luke told me this morning though that Ed called on him yesterday asking him weird questions. I knew where the questions were leading – Ed wanted to know if I had told Luke anything. I pretended I didn't understand what Luke was talking about. Luke was frustrated with me.

10th OCTOBER 1882: First time I have seen Ed's hired gun today since the first meeting. He was on the ridge overlooking the herd in the south section. I spotted his figure and rode up to get closer. He fired a shot at the ground a few yards in front of me. I pulled up quickly. Lucky I was the only one around. I called out to him to give the whole damn business away. He laughed at me and rode away. I wished I was more like Luke – he would have shot him in the leg and dragged him off to Laramie come hell or high water. But I am not like Luke and Ed knows it. Ed has another way of dealing with Luke.

9TH NOVEMBER 1882: In the past three weeks I have encountered Ed's gunman twice. The first time he issued the same threat as before. The second time he told me Ed was running out of patience and I should have convinced the Alliance of Ed's wishes by now. He said that he had his eye on Mama and Sara. I warned him not to hurt them in any way. He just sniggered. I paid Ed a visit and told him to back off. He said he would if he got his water contract back. I warned him I would hunt down his hired gun and bring him to the sheriff in Laramie. Seems Ed don't take me seriously. We'll see.

19TH DECEMBER 1882: I took two weeks from the ranch and went looking for Ed's man. Found out his name is Wilson Cutter. He is wanted in numerous places. No luck this time. I WILL find him. I found someone else though. Tressa. In Omaha. The crazy thing is I walked into an office building called Taylor Mining. I knew if Kelley was with me she'd say "let's see if that Taylor is Luke's uncle". It always was a standing joke between us – would this or that Taylor be Luke's long lost uncle? But what do you know – it IS Richard Taylor's company. Tressa is his daughter. I still think it is crazy falling in love with Luke's cousin. I can't tell anyone about Tressa or that we are married. She would be just one more pawn in Ed's game. Tressa's folks ain't happy about me – I ain't good enough. But we are married and she is safe with her folks in Omaha. I'll see her whenever I can. We're both miserable about it. Won't give up.

18TH JANUARY 1883: Got a message from Ed yesterday. Told me to get Luke to back off. I asked Luke what happened when he went to see Ed. He told me Ed was planning to challenge the bill of sale in court. Luke was furious. You know how he is about the bill. How he is about anything that was his father's. Anyway he got real hot under the collar with Ed and grabbed him and pushed him back. Ed demands I get Luke to just let him have the bill. I told Ed that I was getting closer to Cutter. If I can take Wilson Cutter alive then I am sure I can get the truth about Ed out in the open without bloodshed.

22ND FEBRUARY 1883: Ed lost his challenge to the bill. Luke is quietly triumphant. Ed can never win. He is just trying to wear us all down. Well we just won't give up. Pa and Luke are showing concern for my behavior. I know how strange it must seem but I have to keep thinking and being one step ahead of Ed. This Wilson Cutter is like a ghost. He slips through your fingers and disappears before your eyes. I need to stay alert. It is all part of Ed's game to wear me down but the Lord strengthens my spirit daily. There is no Keaton or Taylor blood staining the River!

25TH MARCH 1883: I am becoming very practiced at this charade. We are like cat and mouse. Sometimes I am the mouse and sometimes Cutter is. We no longer need words to communicate. We know one another well. I am determined. I pray constantly. But when will there be an end? I am so tired. They know there is something wrong with me. They haven't spotted Cutter. I manage to drive him away by stalking him at every opportunity. I am not sure any more what is real. If this is real. It feels like a very long dream.

10TH APRIL 1883: I must write that yesterday on my return I saw McCurdy and Ed in town. I saw Ed hand him a wad of money. McCurdy pocketed it right away. They talked briefly and then broke up. I walked up to Ed and said I thought he was getting careless but brazen is a better word. He asked me where Cutter was. "You don't know?" I asked him. He cursed me and walked off. I followed McCurdy into his office and reminded him that bribery was a serious crime. I asked him how much Ed paid him to be his messenger boy between him and Cutter. He grabbed me by the collar and said it wasn't my business. I removed his hand and reminded him it was very much my business and that the law would go easier on him if he owned up. He just told me to get out. The law is in a dangerous condition in this territory if McCurdy is anything to go by.

29TH APRIL 1883: Luke keeps saying that Ed and McCurdy are doing deals. I know they are but I can only say they probably are. If we could get into McCurdy's bank account we could prove it. But how can we do that? Luke tells me he has been faithfully keeping his file on Ed and that every time he has a suspicion he notes it down and follows it up as far as he can without breaking the law. There is a lot I could give him for his file but I cannot risk it. As things stand the file is a risk because if Ed ever found out about it he might think I had been leaking information to Luke. I pretend I do not know about Luke's file and I certainly do not want to know what is in it.

16TH MAY 1883: I have spent the last week in Omaha seeing Tressa. Cutter spent some time in Colorado. He took a shot at me this time. Think he is frustrated. My ultimate aim is to get him in alive and talking. Ed's tactics ain't working. He expects me to tell the Alliance everything and force a showdown. He won't have his way while I am alive. I told Tressa about Kelley this trip. I know they would like each other. And also told Tressa about Luke. She was upset with me at first because I had not told her my best friend was her long-lost cousin. Now she is very curious and I am scared she will try to contact him. Her interest is unexpected. In this I thought she would be like her father. Richard Taylor is an unhappy man.

16TH JULY 1883: More of the same. The heat makes all this riding and stalking uncomfortable. McCurdy is making my life hell at present. He likes to tell me that he has got Wilson Cutter right on my tail all the time and I haven't got a chance. When I am dog-tired this kind of harassment really bites.

7TH AUGUST 1883: Luke backed me into a corner today and demanded to know what was the matter with me. I tried to convince him that there was nothing and to let it drop. He asked if Ed was bothering me more than usual. I said that it was no more than Ed bothered him. Then he told me Ed was mounting another challenge to the bill in two weeks. I told him I would help in any way I could. He just wanted me to help Ethan keep an eye on the Diamond-T – which means Sara – while he was in Laramie. What Luke does not know is that my eye is always on the Diamond-T.

20TH AUGUST 1883: Ed did not win his challenge to the bill – again. He constantly harasses Luke and me. He has two cronies called Harris and Richards with him now who like to stop us in town and push us around. It was hard but I made Luke agree that we will not push back. Ed will step up his harassment in other quarters if we do. Surely Ed will soon see in light of our reasonable treatment of him that he is wrong.

27TH AUGUST 1883: Pa received a telegram from New York. Kelley will be home on 4th September. I will be happy to see her but fearful. Yet another life to protect and such a dear one at that.

4TH SEPTEMBER 1883: Kelley is home. I am glad to see her but surprised at how beautiful and sophisticated she has become. Her spirit is unchanged. She witnessed the incident in town between Harris and Richards and Luke and me. Typical she asked her questions. She cannot know anything.

20TH SEPTEMBER 1883: Cutter is playing games. He has rustled fifty of the herd and driven them north by the looks of it. He obviously had some help. Pa insisted I stay home while he went. I needed to go after Cutter myself.

21ST SEPTEMBER 1883: Tressa succumbed to her curiosity and arrived today. My anger with her is almost overwhelming me. She came to the house wanting directions to the Diamond-T. Kelley took her over and now Tressa is staying at Morgen. I know Luke will take good care of her but I wish she were back in Omaha. My life is complicated enough.

24TH SEPTEMBER 1883: Cutter was here today! He came to the house while Kelley was there alone demanding to know where I was. Kelley wouldn't tell him. I wish she had. She and Luke and Ethan drove him away without anyone getting hurt. The ground is shifting beneath my feet. I cannot be everywhere and I need to be. I just wish Tressa would return to Omaha and Kelley to New York. I love them too much to have anything happen to them.

26TH SEPTEMBER 1883: Pa returned unharmed with the cattle. He is jubilant as Kelley likes to call him. I am relieved. I rode the ridges today and there is no sign of Cutter.

14TH OCTOBER 1883: I meet Tressa secretly all the time. My life is bittersweet. Kelley has taken upon herself to get me to talk to her about what is troubling me. She is very sweet. She always believes in me no matter what.

17TH OCTOBER 1883: Kelley was badly hurt today in the Shoshone forest. She has suffered a severe concussion. Luke found her as usual. I searched the area myself and got a glimpse of Cutter. I chased him but he has gone deep in the willows.

28TH OCTOBER 1883: Luke and Kelley. An interesting situation. Something is developing. Though they have the same spirit and much in common including a deep feeling for this land we all love I always pictured Luke with someone who would be a steadying influence because he really needs a woman who can settle his restless soul. Kelley stirs him up like she does everyone else! He DOES have a unique way of handling her and that is fun to watch. But I would not like either of them to be hurt.

8TH NOVEMBER 1883: Everything is happening at once. Tressa's uncle in Boston has died and her mother wants her to go home. I want to go for her own good. Ed's line-riders have fired on our line-riders without any provocation and McCurdy is gloating. I need to track Cutter down in the next few days and this will settle things down again. I understand how desperate everyone is to know my problem. Their concern is nearly my and their undoing. But Tressa needs to go home and Kelley needs to return to Aunt Edith.

15TH NOVEMBER 1883: I have my wish. Tressa and Kelley are gone. Life is empty but I feel more in control. Saying goodbye to Tressa broke my heart. I will never be the same I know it. Saying goodbye to my sister was hard because she thinks she has failed me. But she never could. I know she will always love me. I saw Cutter today when I was line-riding. He was talking with Ed and McCurdy. First time I have seen all three together. Money exchanged hands. They talked for about ten minutes and then separated. Time to take Cutter on another trip.

3RD DECEMBER 1883: I thought things were a little too quiet. McCurdy was rather talkative in our weekly chat. He told me that

Ed had given Cutter instructions to fire me up some by scaring Kelley – her bad fall from Dancer last October. He stalked her and fired a shot and spooked Dancer. I will never understand how a parcel of grass and water can mean more than people. Pretty sure Ed would be unhappy to know McCurdy told me all this.

2ND JANUARY 1884: I am ready to go. I write this the evening before I intend leaving. I have what Luke calls a gut feeling I am not coming back and this is the final chapter. If I am wrong then no harm done. But I do not want this journal to fall into Ed's hands so I will hide it and leave a message Kelley will understand. I know she will take good care of it.

I do not know what the future holds. Maybe *more of the same. Maybe not. I want my family to know I love them and I respect them and I am grateful to them for a full and privileged life and for the Faith they handed down to me and that I have fought for them the best way I knew how. I want Luke to know he will always be my brother and the Diamond-T and his father's heritage were things I cared about. I want Tressa to know I love her and the time we spent together was the best of my life. I believe my journey takes me east. How far I do not know. It will be cold and lonely but I have the memories of a life of love to keep me warm.*

I swear on the Bible that this account is the truth.

'Then you will know the truth and the truth will set you free.' John 8:32.

Martin John Keaton.

Faraday

Cheyenne Courthouse
August 28, 1884

"Thank you, Professor, you may step down."

Professor Rowe nods politely at the Judge and removes himself from the witness box.

"Call your next witness, Mr Faraday."

"Your Honor, the prosecution recalls Miss Keaton."

Reporters know that when Cliff Ryan leaves town in search of something, one way or another he will return with it; and so he did, with Luke and Miss Keaton, and Ethan Benchley.

Once the newspapers discovered and reported that the new evidence in the Parsons trial was a mysterious journal kept by murdered Alliance member Mart Keaton, public interest soared. And now the whole of Cheyenne seems hell bent on being in court. Judge Callaghan taps his gavel in a preemptive move to quiet the ever-humming public gallery, but there doesn't seem to be any need; a hallowed hush comes over the room as Miss Keaton makes her way.

McKinnon had protested the journal, but a grand jury was shocked by its contents and the Judge would not be swayed. And despite Mart Keaton wanting justice for all Ed's victims, a conviction of murder is the one the Alliance truly wants. Faraday was granted a motion to add conspiracy to murder and murder for hire to the true bill of indictment before the start of the trial.

Faraday casts the stifling courtroom heat, the dissonance of periodic coughing and the swishing fuss of ladies fans far from his mind. This auspicious moment has been a long time coming and Faraday intends to savor it. It is tantamount to Mart Keaton's presence in the courtroom, a ghostly one, a voice from the grave; no wonder they are hushed.

After two days of solid testimony, from Miss Keaton, and her father, from Howard Peters (who presented an inventory of Ed Parsons' other victims in the district), from various witnesses regarding the money trail and records thereof, and from Luke, with his file painstakingly verified by Cliff to Judge Callaghan's and a grand jury's satisfaction, the Territory's case against Ed Parsons appears to be firmly established. It had all been done according to Mart Keaton's fervent wish – lawfully.

And now this. The journal is going to breach what is left of McKinnon's line of defense: that Ed, needing water for his livelihood, which was under grave threat, was driven to desperate and necessary measures by the malicious actions of the war-mongering Alliance.

Faraday smiles slightly. Miss Keaton appears ready.

"Miss Keaton, you hold in your hands your brother's journal. Correct?"

"Yes."

"Would you open the cover please?"

"Certainly."

"Thank you. Is this your brother's handwriting?"

"Yes, it is."

"Where did you find your brother's journal, Miss Keaton?"

"In the ground, under a tree, in the meadow back home."

"How did you know it was there?"

"I didn't know that it even existed until I read one week ago the letter Mart wrote me before he left home last January."

"What did the letter tell you?"

"The letter, in part, was cryptic. After careful thought and a lot of remembering, I realized that Mart was trying to tell me that he had left a record of his dealings with Mr Parsons, Sheriff McCurdy and Wilson Cutter buried somewhere back home for me to find."

"The letter contained the clues as to the journal's whereabouts?"

"Yes."

"Your Honor, I place into evidence this letter to Miss Keaton from her brother…"

"So noted. Continue."

Faraday encourages Miss Keaton to relate the clues very clearly and slowly.

He observes the jury absorb the clarity of her speech, her sincere and polite delivery that tells them she knows they understand and believe her. Over the next few minutes, interspersed with his questions, she relates the whole story of the discovery and retrieval of Mart Keaton's journal. Faraday remembers John Keaton's comment that Mart wasn't the record keeper that Luke is; what superb irony.

"Miss Keaton, would you be so kind as to turn to the last page of Mart's journal, and in a loud voice read for the court the first sentence of the final paragraph."

She recites: "I swear on the Bible that this account is the truth."

"Miss Keaton, return to the very beginning, the prologue as it were, and read the entry on the bottom of the page."

Miss Keaton reads the paragraph.

"So Mart fears that Mr Parsons will not stop until he has your father's ranch and the Diamond-T in his grasp?"

"Yes."

"Read if you would the first entry which is dated September Third, 1882."

Miss Keaton obliges.

"So Mr Parsons threatened bloodshed if Mart told anyone?"

"Yes."

"Even a seemingly innocent protest would have been out of the question?"

"Yes."

"Would you read the entry dated October Tenth 1882?"

Very calmly, Miss Keaton turns the pages and reads. An edge has found its way into her tone and the words begin to leap out nicely.

"So Mart asked Wilson Cutter to stop the whole business, give it away, and come clean?"

"Yes."

"Objection!" McKinnon finally calls out. "Your Honor, Miss Keaton is not her brother. This questioning is prejudicial to my client. Mr Faraday would like us to believe…"

"Overruled, Mr McKinnon. I will allow Mr Faraday's line of questioning. And you will get your turn in due course."

Walter McKinnon resumes his seat.

"Miss Keaton, would you read the entry dated November Ninth 1882?" The entry is read.

"So Wilson Cutter relayed the message that Mr Parsons was becoming impatient to have his own way, and had widened the threat to include Mrs Taylor and your own mother?"

"Yes. He did."

"In the entry dated December Nineteenth 1882, please tell the court what Mart wrote about his wife."

Miss Keaton shuts her eyes momentarily before she reads. "I can't tell anyone about Tressa or that we are married. She would be just one more pawn in Ed's game."

"So Mart was fearful for his wife's safety?"

"He was."

"So much so that he didn't tell anyone he was married?"

"No."

"Not even you?"

"No."

"Not even his best friend, who is his wife's own cousin?"

"No."

"When did you discover the relationship between your brother and Tressa Taylor?"

"Tressa herself told us after Mart's death."

"And why did she disclose the marriage?"

"Because she was expecting Mart's child."

"So the threat to the lives of Mart's loved ones had become so real and frightening that his life became one of secrets and solitude?"

Her eyes flash. "Yes."

Faraday eases the tone of his voice. "Would you read for us the entry dated January Eighteenth 1883?"

Miss Keaton turns the page and reads the entry with a catch in her voice.

"Four months on and Mart is still determined to take Cutter alive and seek justice rather than bloodshed, is that correct?"

"Yes."

"And from this entry we also see that Mr Parsons threatens Mart even further, in order to get Mr Taylor to back off, as he says, when Mr Taylor is unhappy about having his bill of sale challenged in court. Is that correct?"

"Yes, that is correct."

"Would you read the first paragraph of the next entry?"

Again she obliges.

"Mart shares Luke's triumph at holding off the challenge to the bill of sale. If the bill of sale is legally tight, why was Mr Parsons determined to challenge it?"

"Mr Parsons is determined to see us quit our lands by any means possible, including wearing down our resistance. This type of harassment is common."

"Please read the next entry, Miss Keaton."

She does so in a tight, determined tone.

Faraday echoes her: "There is no Keaton or Taylor blood staining the River. Mart expected bloodshed, didn't he?"

"I believe so, yes."

"And why wasn't there bloodshed?"

"Because he worked tirelessly, at great cost to himself, to prevent it."

"Would you find and read the entry for April Tenth 1883?"

Miss Keaton's eyes hold onto his face for a moment before she turns the page. Then she reads. "I must write that yesterday on my return I saw McCurdy and Ed in town. I saw Ed hand him a wad of money…"

However history might judge it, Faraday admires the way Mart stood up to McCurdy in his own quiet and self-assured manner…

"I removed his hand and reminded him it was very much my business…"

…the way he kept offering both McCurdy and Cutter a chance to get out by lawful means.

"…that the Law would go easier on him if he owned up. He just told me to get out…"

"Did your brother ever do anything unlawful to bring about an end to this whole business of bribery and conspiracy?"

"No, he did not."

The slight inflection in her reply intimates she wishes Mart had. After a moment she lowers her eyes, confirming it.

"In fact, he tried to help these men to a lawful exit from their unlawful actions. To help the very men who were egregiously hurting him and his family."

She looks up, her eyes full of pain. "Yes."

"Please read the next entry, dated April Twenty-ninth 1883."

Her voice wobbles this time.

"If the court pleases, Your Honor, let the records show that this entry verifies the existence of Luke Taylor's file, the nature of its content, the manner in which the information was collected, the approximate date it was begun and for what purpose."

"So be it, Mr Faraday. Continue."

"The following entry, if you please, Miss Keaton – the first paragraph."

Miss Keaton reads the first line, which pertains to Tressa Taylor-Keaton, and stops. She swallows and continues. She reads the second and third sentence, then stops again.

"I'm sorry," she says, "this is difficult."

Judge Callaghan clears his throat. "Are you fine to continue, Miss Keaton?"

"Yes, I think so, Your Honor."

The passage is read, not particularly well, but Faraday continues his questioning.

"So, it seems that Mart was in a situation he could not win?"

"Yes. His only hope was to take Wilson Cutter alive so that Cutter might be persuaded to reveal the whole conspiracy."

Faraday continues to draw out one incident after another while Miss Keaton continues to speak for her brother and verifying with her own experience. The fight in the street the day she returned home. Her spill from her horse, Dancer, and her concussion.

"Miss Keaton, from the entry dated November Fifteenth, would you please read the third paragraph?"

"I saw Cutter today when I was line-riding. He was talking with Ed and McCurdy. First time I have seen all three together. Money exchanged hands."

"So, Mr Parsons, Mr McCurdy and Wilson Cutter were altogether. They had a short discussion. The wealthy cattleman, the wanted outlaw and the sheriff. And money was pocketed. Miss Keaton, please read for us the fourth sentence of the first paragraph of the entry dated January Second?"

Her fingers slide over the page. "I have what Luke calls a gut feeling I am not coming back and this is the final chapter."

"Your brother, Miss Keaton, really believed that he might be killed in this final attempt to apprehend Wilson Cutter?"

"Yes. He was killed trying to protect us, trying to get the truth about Ed Parsons and what Parsons was doing to us and to himself with this threat to his life."

"And finally, read for the court the very last line of the final entry which is dated January Second?"

"Then you will know the truth and the truth will set you free. John 8:32. Martin John Keaton."

"Thank you very much, Miss Keaton. Your Honor, I have no more questions for Miss Keaton at this time."

"Very well. Your cross-examination, Mr McKinnon, will follow after a one hour recess."

Kelley

The lunch recess, it seems, has done very little to improve Walter McKinnon's irritable disposition. He has asked her to describe the nature of her relationship with Mart, and as she is telling him he is cleaning his spectacles.

"A close brother-sister relationship. Commendable indeed. Miss Keaton, this court has heard you present your brother's journal almost as if you were present when he wrote it and know all his secrets..."

"Objection..."

"If you can attach a question to this, Mr McKinnon, I will allow you to proceed," says Judge Callaghan.

"Yes, Your Honor. There is a question."

"Make it a good one, Mr McKinnon."

"Yes, Your Honor. Do you expect this court to believe, Miss Keaton, that in spite of this extraordinary relationship between you and your brother, he never told you about his journal?"

"Your Honor..."

"Objection overruled."

"Miss Keaton?"

"My brother never even hinted that he was keeping a journal about anything, let alone documenting the criminal activities of Mr Parsons."

"Move to strike."

"Members of the jury, you will disregard the witness's comment relating to the defendant's activities."

"Thank you, Your Honor. So, Miss Keaton, why wouldn't your brother tell you he was keeping a journal – surely something that is supposed to be so important?"

"My brother states in the journal that he can't tell anyone for fear of reprisal by Mr Parsons."

"But surely this concern he has for his family, for the Taylor family and the Benchley family would translate into at least telling you secretly about the journal and indeed swearing you, his beloved sister, to secrecy also? Did he think you couldn't be trusted?"

"My brother entrusted me with finding his journal."

"Ah, so he did. We have heard from Mr Faraday how you are here today to represent your brother in the courtroom."

"I am here to give testimony regarding his journal."

"I beg to differ. Mr Faraday would have us believe that you are the only one who can present the journal with conviction equivalent to your brother's very presence. That's a hefty responsibility, yes?"

"Yes, I suppose it is."

"But it is not the same, is it? Yes or no?"

"No."

"And yet the temptation to make you the keeper of all your brother's secrets is hard to resist. Indeed, Mr Faraday thinks you are. Therefore, Miss Keaton, I am curious to know why your brother didn't reveal the existence of his journal in the last moments before his death. Can you, the keeper of his secrets, the light of revelation, enlighten the court about this?"

"Objection, Your Honor. Miss Keaton was not present when her brother died. Counsel is asking the witness to speculate."

"Your Honor, Miss Keaton is supposed to represent her brother here; she should know…"

Judge Callaghan looks thoughtful for a moment. "Overruled, Mr Faraday. Miss Keaton, please answer the question."

"I don't know why he didn't mention it, but he *was* dying."

"The knowledge of the whereabouts of this 'weapon of truth', as Mr Faraday calls it, went to the grave with your brother?"

"He left the letter for me so we would find it."

"But in those last moments of his life, when all hope was fading, he neglected to mention the letter for you and his so-called 'weapon of truth'?"

"Yes."

"Why?"

"I don't know."

"You are either the keeper of his secrets or you are not, Miss Keaton."

"He entrusted me with finding his journal, not keeping secrets…"

"Miss Keaton, why didn't your parents show you the letter your brother left you before he went to Missouri, the letter that you say contained the clues to the whereabouts of the journal?"

"They didn't know it was there in Mart's things for some time and then they withheld it from me because they thought a letter from Mart would upset me."

"Well, when did they think the time was right for you to read it?"

"I don't know what they thought. The time came though, didn't it? – the time they believed was right."

"When your parents finally got to read it, did they under-stand the so-called clues?"

"No."

"Did Mr Taylor know of the letter?"

"No."

"Did Mr Taylor understand the letter?"

"Some of it."

"Ah. But basically you had to explain it to everyone – the clues, etc?"

"Yes."

"Why is that?"

"Because of the connection the content had to an incident in our childhood. I remembered it and Mart knew I would."

"Miss Keaton, this relationship with your brother is quite extraordinary. The clues in the letter are obscure to say the least."

"Not to me."

"In your testimony on how you found the place to dig, it seemed Mr Taylor didn't know where to dig, but you did – correct?"

"Not at first. I had to think about it."

"Miss Keaton, how long have you really known about your brother's journal?"

"As long as everyone else."

"I think, Miss Keaton, you have known about it a lot longer."

"No."

"Your brother didn't mention the journal before he died because you already knew about it."

"No, I didn't."

"Didn't you help your brother bury his journal before you left for New York?"

"No, I did not."

"Didn't you help your brother write the journal?"

"No."

"Write a whole lot of libel about Mr Parsons which, because of you and your brother's close relationship with Mr Taylor, the three of you found it a simple exercise to put together the journal and the Taylor file?"

She stares at Walter McKinnon deeply shocked. "That is the most ridiculous load of drivel I have ever heard in my life."

"Your credibility is under a cloud, Miss Keaton, and yet Mr Faraday seems to think you are the expert on your brother's journal, so let's find out shall we?"

Mr Faraday springs to his feet. "Your Honor…"

"Mr McKinnon shall have his day, Mr Faraday. Proceed, Mr McKinnon."

"Miss Keaton, the first entry of your brother's journal contains the line: 'It hardly seems real.' Is this another clue, Miss Keaton? A clue which tells us, the realists in this courtroom, those of us who can tell the difference between fiction and non-fiction, that the whole story is contrived, a fabrication?"

She denies this adamantly.

"There was no use in bringing in a lawman, Miss Keaton, because a lawman would have seen through the whole charade, wouldn't he?"

"There was no charade," she says fervently.

"Your brother kept his marriage a secret, Miss Keaton, not because he was worried about his wife's safety, but because as it says in the entry of December Nineteenth 1882: Tressa's folks ain't happy about me – I ain't good enough."

"That was a secondary concern only."

"Was it? Your brother spent a great deal of time separated from his wife. Surely he didn't need to if his parents-in-law approved of him – fine, upstanding young man, mm?"

Mr Faraday interjects. "Your Honor, Miss Keaton has not met her sister-in-law's parents. None of us have. We cannot speculate on what kind of a man they would have approved of for their daughter, even one as upstanding as Mart Keaton. And I doubt the relevance of us knowing at all."

Mr McKinnon is smiling. "Your Honor, I believe I was asking the witness."

Judge Callaghan addresses her. "Miss Keaton, please explain for the court why your brother kept his marriage a secret from his wife's parents?"

"Your Honor, I object to the relevance of this testimony."

"Yes, Mr Faraday, but I want to know," Judge Callaghan retorts. "Please, Miss Keaton. And don't regurgitate what your brother said in his journal. *That* we already know."

"I can only tell you what Tressa, my sister-in-law, related to us of her experience."

"This will be hearsay, Your Honor."

"Your Honor, if Miss Keaton is Mart Keaton's voice in this court, she must be able to speak about what went on in his marriage."

"Your Honor…"

"Enough! I want to hear Miss Keaton."

She swallows hard under their scrutiny. Her only strength is Mart's belief in her; he wasn't afraid of the truth and neither should she be.

"From what I understand, Tressa's father is a very stern man and a strict father, who said that he would cut her off from the family if she married my brother. Tressa said she didn't care what her father said or did. But Mart insisted that she never allow herself to be cut off from them. He was adamant and she had to agree to it. Later, after he'd been killed, she understood that in the event of his death she would still have her family, her life."

"Mrs Keaton knew her husband was hunting down Wilson Cutter?" Mr McKinnon asks.

"It came out in one of their arguments that Mart was trying to apprehend Cutter for the purpose of protecting the Alliance."

"So your sister-in-law's parents weren't such unreasonable people after all, were they? They are respectable citizens. They wanted to protect their daughter, didn't they?"

"They prejudged my brother, because they didn't even know about Wilson Cutter, about our troubles."

"Do you know that for certain, Miss Keaton?"

"Yes."

"No, you don't. You have never met them, or spoken with them. You have only the word of your sister-in-law, who isn't even here in court. Your brother wasn't acceptable to them. And they were gravely deceived."

"No, that's not how it was. They shouldn't have cut her off. It wasn't reasonable at all."

"It was their loss and your gain. You got their daughter and their grandchild. And they have nothing."

In the pause that follows, Kelley glances at Mr Faraday. He gives her a wry smile that tells her to let it go.

So she endures Mr McKinnon's self-satisfaction and waits for the next question.

"In the entry of January Eighteenth 1883, your brother supposedly writes that my client asked him to get Mr Taylor to back off. Mr Taylor, in fact, pushed my client spitefully."

"Your client, sir, was not the victim of that encounter and you well know it."

"My client has had his water contract withdrawn, his stock is thirsty, he can't sustain his herd, and looks very much a victim to me, so much so that he has to challenge the so-called Bill of Sale to try to regain access to the River he desperately needs."

"That's not true."

"I put it to you, Miss Keaton, that the many references to your brother chasing away Wilson Cutter are collectively just another clue to your brother hunting down Wilson Cutter. You are good at clues, Miss Keaton, are you not?"

"There are consistent references throughout Mart's journal which indicate his aim was to bring Cutter in and have him face the Law, so that the truth could be extracted legally. My brother faced death each time he tried."

"Yes, it makes thrilling reading. In April 1883, your brother begins to allege that my client is engaging in bribery. Isn't it just a little coincidental that Mr Taylor has his file up and running at the same time as your brother is writing his journal? They were like brothers, were they not, how easy for them to concoct the elements of a crime that never happened?"

"Yes, they were like brothers, but it seems to me that the coincidence lies in the premise that your client had become very careless, even arrogant, about the way he conducted his business with Mr McCurdy. My brother specifically states in his journal that he cannot give Luke anything for his file."

"You know your brother's journal very well, Miss Keaton," McKinnon says sneakily.

"You know my brother's journal very well also, sir, and you have no emotional attachment to it."

The Judge makes a strangled sort of noise and she looks across at him. His eyes are merry and his hand and long fingers are spread across his mouth. Hastily, he straightens up and says gruffly, "Continue, Mr McKinnon."

"Miss Keaton, you and Mr Taylor and your family would have us believe that your brother took it upon himself to carry the enormous, incredulous, *un-be-lieve-able* burden of this alleged extortion because he thought that if he didn't there would be bloodshed?"

"Yes."

"In his journal your brother related the enduring of incredible hardships. This is not normal behavior."

She is growing tired. She longs to stuff something into Mr McKinnon's mouth. He goes on; she goes on. For Mart's sake.

At last, Mr McKinnon says, "I have no further questions, Your Honor."

"You may stand down, Miss Keaton. Call your next witness, Mr Faraday."

Mr Faraday calls Sam Pike.

Faraday

"Mr Pike, on the day before Mart Keaton was murdered, two men transacted business at your establishment. Who were they?"

"Luke Taylor were one, the other John Keaton."

"What did they want?"

"Food, warmth and information."

"What kind of information?"

"They were looking for Keaton's son. They described him and I matched it to a young feller who came through my place the day before. I told them he were asking after a black-haired man with a beard and a scar on his cheek going by the name of Cutter. According to this young feller Keaton, they had business out Sedalia way. I didn't recognize the name Cutter, but a mighty unsavory type going by that description had been through. *This* feller were bragging. Going to Sedalia, he reckoned. Who cares? I told them it all happened yesterday and Taylor gets all fired up."

"So Mr Keaton and Mr Taylor cared?"

"Yep. They got their information and they left."

"Now, Mr Pike, a few days later this same bearded man with the scar on his cheek appeared again at your establishment, is that correct?"

"Sure he did. My daughter refused to stay in the bar while he were there."

"And what did this same man who goes by the name of Cutter want?"

"Wants a drink to celebrate."

"Celebrate?"

"He reckoned he killed two men."

"Are you the only person he told, Mr Pike?"

"My establishment were full that day; the word got around."

"And what did you do, Mr Pike?"

"Like I said, this character said he wanted to celebrate. I give him whiskey like he wanted. When he were gone I contacted the sheriff."

"Thank you, Mr Pike. No more questions."

"Mr McKinnon?"

"Thank you, Your Honor. Mr Pike, was there anything unusual about this character? Something that stands out perhaps?"

Faraday catches Pike's knitted glance.

He knows what's coming but lets it come to pass.

"Well, he were downright unusual, main thing were he had wounded his thigh."

"Gunshot wound?"

"Might have been…"

"Objection. The witness is being asked to speculate."

"Objection sustained."

McKinnon looks put out. "Did you see the nature of the wound, Mr Pike?"

"Hec, no. He could've fallen off his horse. I only saw him limping. And I weren't gonna ask a character like that where he gets his battle scars. He were already bragging about killing two men. I didn't intend being his next victim."

"Mr Pike, did this character ever tell you his name?"

"No."

"He never identified himself?"

"Didn't have to. I recognized him as the man Mart Keaton were asking about few days before; it were Wilson Cutter – beard, scar an' all."

"Do you drink, Mr Pike?"

"Objection!"

"Overruled. The witness will answer."

"If you're insinuatin' because I'm a barkeep I drink so much on the job I don't know Adam from Eve, then you got it all wrong. I run a business, a good one, honest, a lot of people depend on me, just ask that young feller Taylor. You don't run a business if you drink less'n you want it run into the ground."

"Did you drink on the day that Wilson Cutter allegedly announced he had killed two men?"

"Too busy that day for nothing but work. And that's a fact."

"That is all for this witness, Your Honor." McKinnon sits.

"Call your next witness, Mr Faraday."

He recalls Luke.

"You are still under oath, Mr Taylor," the Judge reminds him. Luke nods once; if anyone is going to lie under oath, it certainly won't be Luke. "Proceed, Mr Faraday."

"Yes, Your Honor. Mr Taylor, we have already heard you testify to many things regarding the activities of Ed Parsons. Some of those things, without your knowledge, Mart Keaton was recording in his journal at the same time you were recording them in your file."

"Yes."

"You suspected a connection between Ed Parsons and the black-haired, bearded man with a scar on his left cheek?"

"Yes. The day Wilson Cutter threatened Miss Keaton while she was at home alone was the first time I laid eyes on him."

"And did you see him any time after that?"

"Yes. Once back home on a hill, as he watched Miss Keaton and me driving to the Diamond-T. And then again, when I cornered him with the intention of bringing him to Sheriff Ryan."

"And you were successful?"

"Not exactly. I disabled him, but he shot me as well, so I couldn't bring him in. He was caught when he came into town looking for a doctor. Dr Sullivan locked him in her medicine closet and Sheriff Ryan came and arrested him."

"And then, three weeks later, two men arrive in town; they are familiar to you…"

"Yes. Harris and Richards. They are Ed Parsons' minders. The same men who constantly harassed us back home. I saw them go into Dr Sullivan's place and I followed them. We recognized one another immediately. We had a brief exchange of words and I convinced them to leave."

"What did Harris and Richards want?"

"To know if Dr Sullivan was the doctor who caught Cutter. She admitted it. Later that night, her surgery was doused in kerosene by a boy named Jake Murray working for Harris and Richards."

"Jake Murray was later charged with attempted arson?"

"Yes. Dr Sullivan and I managed to stop Murray from setting the place alight."

"Therefore, from the moment you discovered and wounded Wilson Cutter, a string of events connect the capture of Wilson Cutter to the activity of Ed Parsons' men."

"Objection, Your Honor…"

"Your Honor, it is vital that this association is established."

"I will allow it. Overruled, Mr McKinnon."

"Mr Taylor?"

"There was never any doubt in my mind that at some point Ed Parsons would send someone to Cheyenne once Wilson Cutter was in the lock up. I remained here in Cheyenne waiting for it to happen, for Ed to show his hand, and I was right."

Faraday moves slowly towards the jury and draws Luke with him. "Mr Taylor, you and John Keaton found Mart Keaton dying in the snow in that forest near Sedalia…"

There is an immediate reaction in those dark blue eyes; Faraday wants the jury to see what he sees – Luke's narrative skill and the raw honesty of his story.

"Can you describe the scene for us?"

"With Mart a day ahead of us, John and I didn't stop from the moment we left Pike's saloon and we made up the time. We had been following the rail line for miles and came to a solitary carriage on the track. The guard was unconscious on the floor inside when we got there; he'd been bashed and we couldn't bring him round. There were fresh footprints in the snow which we followed. They led to a clearing in the forest. That's where we found Mart lying in the snow. All around him the snow was red with his blood. He had been shot in the stomach and it was a mortal wound."

He stops; whether deliberately or out of necessity, his timing is perfect as the jury forms a picture in their minds for what is to come.

"John takes Mart's body out of the snow and he… he kisses him. This is his son… and a son of whom he is understandably proud. And he's dying."

"What did *you* do?" Faraday asks.

Luke clears his throat. "I pushed John back and tried to bring Mart round. John kept saying it was no use, but I had to know who shot him. Maybe it was cruel to have him endure so much pain at the end, kinder to let him bleed out into the snow, peaceful, quiet, but I couldn't let him go without knowing, for his sake and ours…

415

"So I stem the blood with my shirt... Finally, Mart's eyes open and I start to ask him: Who did this? John starts to ask: Can you tell us, son? I take his hand and I promise him that I will bring to justice the man who shot him. I give him my word."

"Did Mart tell you who shot him?"

"His answer to my asking him was: Wilson Cutter. You have met him. You and Ethan and Kelley."

"That would be on the day Cutter came to the Keaton ranch house when Miss Keaton was alone?"

"Yes. I checked with him – the stranger with the black beard? Mart said yes. Then he made a plea for justice. He asked John to pray for him. And then he... Then he died. John... wept and he prayed."

"And what did you do?"

"I stood there with Mart's blood on my hands and my clothes, in disbelief that he was gone; wishing to God it were me lying there, that John still had his son; it was overwhelming. Mart was gone."

After several respectful moments, Faraday asks, "And what happened to the train guard, Mr Taylor?"

"The train guard? Oh... when we got back to the car he was dead. Knifed in the heart, a wound he didn't have when we first discovered him. He'd been killed since."

Faraday takes a deep breath. Luke copies him, the aim of the exercise. "So. Mr Taylor, what precipitated your decision to go looking for Wilson Cutter this past May?"

"I received a telegram from Sheriff Ryan telling me that Cutter had been sighted some miles north-east of Cheyenne."

"And your reaction was to do what?"

"To do what I promised Mart. Get justice. I take my file and head to Cheyenne hoping someone will listen to me – understand that the contents of my file and the murder of Mart Keaton by Wilson Cutter all come down to one person: Ed Parsons."

"Along the way you decide to capture Cutter yourself. Some would say a rash act considering the Alliance code of non-violence."

"Before Mart died I promised him justice – a new promise written in his blood this time. Mart would have realized that if Ed Parsons had turned Wilson Cutter on *me*, I would not have put up with it. That's why Parsons chose Mart and *not* me."

"And this is what you believed Mart expected of you?"

"When Mart asked me for justice he would have known how I intended to handle it. Finish what he had started, what he gave his life for. Bring Cutter in, but my way. No killing, but no need to help Cutter redeem himself either; just persuasion of a different kind to Mart's. And then this trial, this justice."

"How did the discovery of Mart Keaton's journal affect your campaign to do just that?"

"Mart's journal proved the connection between Wilson Cutter and Ed Parsons."

"Thank you, Mr Taylor." As Faraday returns to his seat, he looks directly at Ed Parsons. The old man is glaring fiercely at Luke; there is alarming hatred here.

McKinnon is on his feet. As Faraday sits down, he notices Luke's eyes narrowed on Parsons with defiance in equal measure.

Suddenly, Parsons says in a loud, gravelly voice, "Don't bother asking the liar any questions, counsel."

Judge Callaghan almost explodes with indignation.

"Mr McKinnon, instruct your client to remain silent at once."

"The truth, Ed, is just too hard to take," Luke hisses back.

Faraday cringes.

The Judge swings his wide, shocked eyes across to the witness stand. "Mr Taylor!"

Luke faces the Judge squarely. "I apologize, Your Honor. It won't happen again."

Judge Callaghan blusters a little, fidgets with some papers and finally settles down to look most unhappy.

In the end, Parsons instructs McKinnon to refrain from cross-examining Luke. Faraday is flabbergasted. McKinnon can barely mask his frustration; he jotted down notes all through Luke's testimony. After the Judge dismisses him, Luke steps down and takes a seat.

"Call your next witness, Mr Faraday."

McCurdy is to be his last. The Bright River sheriff has been charged with bribery and corruption, but in giving testimony against Parsons, he is claiming immunity under the Fifth Amendment. He is a hostile witness and through him Faraday intends to bring his case to its ultimate conclusion.

Luke

Luke takes a seat, his blood stampeding around his body. In the row of chairs alongside him sit John and Amy, Edith, K, whose blue eyes gleam just a little as she exchanges glances with him, and Ethan… he dare not look at Ethan after his outburst before the Judge. *Concentrate…* Then he feels Ethan's firm hand on his shoulder, reassuring, affirming.

"Mr McCurdy, I understand that you do not wish to incriminate yourself and prejudice your own trial, however, you are not granted immunity from telling the truth."

"Yes, Judge."

"This will be brief, Your Honor."

"That will be a blessing, Mr Faraday."

"Mr McCurdy, how long have you known Mr Parsons?"

"Since I came to Bright River in May '82."

"Just over two years in fact?"

"Yes."

"And what kind of man would you say Mr Parsons is?"

"Hard working."

"And what kind of neighbor is he?"

"Attentive."

"Have there ever been any disagreements or upsets between Mr Parsons and any of his neighbors?"

"He… that is, Ed wanted the Taylors, the Benchleys and the Keatons to renew his water contract and they refused."

"Why wouldn't they renew his water contract, Mr McCurdy? I assume that you being the law and order at the time you would know why."

"It wasn't any of my business."

"They believed they were being extorted by Ed Parsons. You didn't think that extortion was your business?"

"Objection. Your Honor, Mr McCurdy is not on trial and under the Fifth he is not required to answer..."

"Withdrawn," says Cam. "Mr McCurdy, how would you describe the Taylor, Benchley and Keaton families?"

"The alliance they formed caused Mr Parsons inconvenience and hardship."

"Mr McCurdy, I only asked you to describe the families, not give your opinion on something else entirely."

Stiltedly, McCurdy replies, "Very close friends."

"Mm. And are you friends with Mr Parsons?"

"Objection."

"Overruled."

"Mr McCurdy?"

"Yes."

"Then you would know well the relationship between Mr Parsons and Mart Keaton, wouldn't you?"

"I might."

"Yes or no, Mr McCurdy."

"Yes."

"Was Mr Parsons' relationship with Mart Keaton friendly, such as you would expect from a man whom you yourself describe as an attentive neighbor?"

"Not particularly."

"Mr McCurdy, did Mr Parsons have a problem watering his herd these last two years? Were his cattle suffering?"

"How do you mean?"

"Well, you being a friend of Mr Parsons, he probably shared his ranching interests with you, correct?"

"Yes."

"So did Mr Parsons have a problem watering his herd?"

"He wanted to renew his contract..."

"That is not what I am asking you, Mr McCurdy. Did you ever see Mr Parsons' land drought-stricken or short of grazing pasture?"

McCurdy shifts about and looks downright uncomfortable. "No."

"And yet he was desperate to renew the water contract with the Alliance. John Keaton, Miss Keaton, Luke Taylor, and Mart Keaton in his journal, all testified *under oath* that Mr Parsons harassed them for renewal of the water contract, expressing the firm belief that Mr Parsons wanted their lands and would stop at nothing to have them. What say you to that, Mr McCurdy?"

"I have nothing to say."

"You have nothing to say, Mr McCurdy, because you cannot bring yourself to tell this court that your friend, Mr Parsons..."

"Objection. This insinuation of guilt by association has gone on long enough, Your Honor."

Judge Callaghan gives a sharp nod. "Sustained."

"You have nothing to say, Mr McCurdy, because you cannot bring yourself to tell this court that Ed Parsons is a greedy land-grabber who will stop at nothing, and that includes extortion and murder, to get what he wants, isn't that so, Mr McCurdy?"

"Objection."

"Overruled," the Judge snaps.

"Mr McCurdy?"

"I... I don't know."

"Yes or no, Mr McCurdy."

"Objection. Mr Faraday is harassing the witness."

"Overruled. The witness will answer Mr Faraday's question."

"I can't say," McCurdy answers pathetically.

"Can't? Or won't, Mr McCurdy?"

"Objection. Badgering..."

"Overruled."

"You knew Mr Parsons' business, Mr McCurdy. It was bad business, wasn't it?"

"I don't know," McCurdy persists. His hands are shaking, his eyes water.

"Yes, you do. You said you were friends, and that he told you about his affairs. Yes or no, Mr McCurdy?"

"Objection. This is blatant harassment. Mr Faraday still hasn't got the point, Your Honor."

But Cam is relentless. "Mr McCurdy, it will be a shame for this court to find you have perjured yourself for a man who is *supposedly* your friend."

"Objection!"

"Your Honor... "

"Sustained!" Judge Callaghan booms.

"But, Your Honor..."

"Mr Faraday, you will cease and desist!"

"Yes, Your Honor. Mr McCurdy, why did Ed Parsons send for Wilson Cutter back in May, just before Luke Taylor received a telegram saying that Cutter had been sighted again?"

No one, not even McKinnon, is prepared for the question.

"To break up the alliance," McCurdy replies.

"Move to strike."

"Overruled," the Judge says quietly.

"How would that break up the alliance, Mr McCurdy?"

"Objection."

"Overruled," the Judge repeats, intently. "The witness will answer the question."

"There... there was a rumor that Taylor might marry the Keaton girl. Ed didn't want that to happen. So he sends for Cutter ...to lure Taylor away and deal with him..."

"Deal with him?"

"...have him killed."

"And the Alliance?"

"...would be broken up, the Keatons without Taylor and left on their own would be..."

"Would be what?"

McCurdy trembles. "Easier to break..." His voice dies away to a pathetic mumbling.

Cam stands there staring at him. The jury stares at him.

The whole room is suddenly still, even the ladies fanning themselves in the stale summer heat.

"Do you know who killed Mart Keaton, Mr McCurdy?"

Sweat has broken out over McCurdy's entire face. "Yes."

"Who killed Mart Keaton?"

"Wilson Cutter."

"And was Wilson Cutter instructed to kill Mart Keaton?"

McCurdy is almost sobbing. "Yes."

"By whom, then, was Wilson Cutter instructed to kill Mart Keaton?"

"Objection, Your Honor. Mr Faraday shows so little respect for this court that he dares to ask Mr McCurdy to violate his own immunity. This question is in contempt of court."

Cam is appropriately indignant. "Your Honor, these are delaying tactics by counsel. I have no intention of endangering Mr McCurdy's immunity. The question simply relates to who gave the order to murder Mart Keaton – a fact of knowledge – and I believe Mr McCurdy knows. His telling will not affect his own trial."

Cam is right; McCurdy is to answer charges of bribery, aiding and abetting extortion and being a totally corrupt sheriff.

In exchange for his testimony against Parsons, Cam excluded accessory or conspiracy to murder from McCurdy's indictment. So far Cam had established McCurdy and Parsons were friends to give credibility to McCurdy's testimony.

But being a friend of old Ed comes at a price.

"Your Honor, I move to declare a mistrial on the grounds that Mr Faraday has violated this witness's rights under the Fifth Amendment."

"Motion denied. Gentleman, I will decide who is in contempt of court. Mr McCurdy, whatever you say next in answer to my questions, will not affect your own trial. You must tell me the truth, is that understood?"

Pale-faced and trembling, McCurdy nods and says, "Yes, Judge."

The Judge looks straight into McCurdy's eyes. "Is the person who instructed Wilson Cutter to murder Mart Keaton sitting in this courtroom?"

"Yes, Your Honor."

"Point him or her out, Mr McCurdy."

McCurdy is shaking so violently now that it takes him some time to get his finger pointing in the right direction. People watch the finger and draw back from it as it approaches them; relief as it passes by them.

With his eyes rimmed red, and sweat dripping down his face, eventually McCurdy aims at Ed. His head droops, leaving his finger to face Ed's stony expression.

Luke feels the blood drain from his head... at last... and then rush back again... at last!

"Let the court records show that Mr McCurdy indicates the defendant, Ed Parsons, in response to my instruction," says the Judge, and the court recorder answers the Judge accordingly.

Luke wants to jump up and shout. But from out of the sticky silence, K beats him to it, springing to her feet. "Ed Parsons, I hope you rot in a prison cell for the next fifty years!"

There is commotion. Luke is tempted to join K until he feels Cam's needle point gaze on him. Luke grins; Cam rolls his eyes and fixes his attention on K, whose magnificently raised chin and blazing red cheeks are certainly worth it. Needless to say, the Judge is not pleased. After the commotion dies down, under the persuasion of Judge Callaghan's gavel, Ed again declines his right of cross-examination. McKinnon looks ready to strangle a cat. Cam tells the Judge that the prosecution rests.

As Luke is leaving the courthouse, Cliff stops him. "I have news concerning Wilson Cutter's extradition. It's going ahead tomorrow. Hummer's got first bite of the cherry and he's moving Cutter to Denver in the morning."

"What, now? Who decides these things?"

"It got complicated and the governor called in the Justice Department to sort out the mess. I'm afraid you got relegated to the bottom of a very tall pile."

Kelley

She moves impatiently with the stodgy flow of the dispersing courtroom; nervous exhaustion threatens to overwhelm her sense of triumph. She spots Luke speaking with Mr Ryan and observes some kind of disappointment wash Luke's own sense of triumph away. She is so curious about what that might be that she neglects to watch where she's walking, and steps straight into a middle-aged man with a large stomach and a ruddy, deeply-lined face; he is well-dressed, a businessman. She apologizes at once; he removes his expensive-looking topper slowly, his eyes penetrating as he stares into hers.

"No, Miss, it is I who should look where I am going," he says. "I offer my sincere apologies."

Instead of flattering her, his exaggerated gallantry annoys her and then piques her curiosity. She has never met the man, yet his face seems familiar; she has looked upon it before, somewhere.

"Is there a problem?" Aunt Edith inquires from over her shoulder.

"Not at all, I assure you. Good day."

She watches him as the waning crowd takes him away.

"Who was that?" her Pa asks, his eyes narrowed on the large man's back.

"I can't say," she tells him. "But... I..." As she watches that back disappear, the cogs of her memory turn quickly. Luke's file flashes into her mind. She turns to her family. "I need to see Mr Faraday. I'll meet you at the hotel later."

424

"Miss Keaton, I know I've been demanding, but I think now you can relax. We have presented our case. The day went well." Mr Faraday picks up Luke's file from the pile of documents that he has undoubtedly just put down.

"Mr Faraday, I know this is an imposition, but you told me…"

Mr Faraday raises his hand to stop her. "I know."

Sighing something about bringing it all on himself, he hands her Luke's file.

"Sit down and take your time. Judge Callaghan requested to see me in his chambers about another matter; I will be there, when you are ready."

Mr Faraday closes the door behind him, and in the silence of his office, she proceeds to turn each extraordinary page until she indeed finds what she's looking for.

Faraday

Miss Keaton has been and gone like a rush of Wyoming wind.

Faraday stares at the penciled face on the page she had eagerly shown him. Beside the sketch are the words *who is this man?* written in Luke's hand. Faraday wishes he didn't know it, but that is Loren Bodecker's face looking back at him. Hatless – which is unusual.

"So," the Judge squawks. "Miss Keaton saw Loren Bodecker in the courtroom and has identified him from Taylor's file."

"Yes, Judge," Faraday murmurs, looking up. He hadn't been entirely honest with Miss Keaton, a woman he greatly respects, and it is not sitting well in his stomach.

"So," the Judge says again, this time pursing his lips and then drawing them back into a thin line, "now we know – when you tell Miss Keaton to be vigilant about any little thing, she is exactly that. Suspicious types, these Alliance people. "

Faraday closes the file. "This doesn't affect the outcome of this trial. Going on all the evidence I didn't think it would."

"I know. We agreed there were no reasonable grounds to connect the governor's good friend Loren Bodecker with the likes of Ed Parsons on the basis of that sketch."

"Bodecker's been out of town the whole time Luke has been in Cheyenne…"

"Mm. Except for today at least. Are you telling me he would have identified him?"

"I don't know; Loren didn't run into Luke, he ran into Miss Keaton."

They stare at one another for what seems like an age.

"Carefully, Mr Faraday," the Judge murmurs.

Faraday sighs and nods.

"What will you do?" the Judge asks.

Bring the territory to its knees.

426

"If I'm wrong…"

The Judge exclaims, "Ha!" and tosses his spectacles on his desk. "The governor will want cold, hard evidence and lots of it. There's no room for being wrong, Mr Faraday. Being seen with a man is not a crime!"

"It appears Bodecker has been in Bright River."

"Perhaps. It is only a sketch after all. Mr Taylor may have seen Bodecker right here; we don't even know if Parsons was with Bodecker when Mr Taylor saw him to draw the infernal thing. Besides, businessmen like Bodecker move all over the territory. And didn't Mr Ryan say that there are several other articles in Mr Taylor's file that have no bearing on this case?"

Faraday shifts his feet. "Yes, there are just a few. Bodecker's secretary dismissed Cliff Ryan's inquiry, as to whether Bodecker knew Parsons, as someone he thought Bodecker might very likely consider as a cattle supplier."

"Old ground this, Mr Faraday. A grand jury will have nothing to do with it. The young Keaton woman is playing on your conscience. You told her that Loren Bodecker is a respected businessman in the territory and that is correct. You have no legal grounds to signal him out as in some way connected to Parsons because his face is in that damn file; to do so would produce an outcome you don't want to think about, for yourself or this territory."

"Good of you to spell it out for me that way, Judge."

"I believe that's what you want of me."

"The way I see it …"

Judge Callaghan narrows his eyes expectantly. "Yes, Mr Faraday?"

Faraday wants to express his firm conviction that the sketch in Luke's file has no bearing on the outcome of the trial, and that unless he is very much mistaken, Mart Keaton and the Alliance will get justice; Parsons will be punished and his career as a murdering extortionist finished. Correctly, however, he says, "I don't see a problem."

Judge Callaghan exhales loudly. "Thank you, Mr Faraday. That will be all."

Jennifer

As Jennifer turns into the back alley she spies him with his head down, lost in his thoughts, sitting in the shade of the neighbor's elm that generously overhangs the fence. He has an amazing effect on her; there is place inside her that he reaches without even coming near her, a place that dreams of life's possibilities and toys with the idea of giving life to them.

They spend time together every day (usually in the late afternoon, as now) but they keep their relationship extremely private; not so private that she can keep it from Duffy.

"You know he's the best thing to ever walk through your door, don't you?"

"Yes, Duffy, I know."

"Mm. And do you know what you're doing, Miss Jennifer?"

"No. I have no idea."

"Good. It's about time."

Duffy may think so, but when it comes to time, Jennifer takes their romance on a strictly day-by-day basis. She cannot comprehend for one moment how it can continue beyond the time it will take Luke to extract his justice. His sense of duty to his family is remarkable, and there is Miss Keaton and her family...

Her approach disturbs him. He looks up with those tired blue eyes; the life that springs into them is her doing and it makes her heart skip. He reaches for her hand and plays with it gently. A gentleness that is for her.

He loves her, even knowing she keeps secrets from him; he has stopped trying to tease them out of her because the trial has overtaken him. She is his Cheyenne love. Love for a time and a place when love is sorely needed. She never says as much, but as the days go by, as their hearts learn to love more than the day before, each day's farewell is more difficult to perform.

Even when he says her name, uttered tenderly in his drawl, her toes curl and her day-by-day resolution gets chipped away. She is fooling herself in so many ways. And all Duffy can say is *good*.

"I heard you had an excellent day in court," she says. "I was with Meg when Cam came home. He seemed pleased."

He grins. "He should be. He did fine. Cracked McCurdy like a nut." His smile fades. "And we heard what we knew all along. Only the whole world heard it for a change."

She squeezes his fingers. "I'm glad. He said you were particularly fine yourself. So, you look perfectly at home; are you going to sit there all evening?"

"No, I have to meet Ethan and the Keatons for supper." He unravels his lean body and stands. "Will you come? You helped after all. "

"No," she says. "I…"

"Come on, Jennifer."

"How can I pretend I'm not in love with you for the whole of supper?"

"Well, don't pretend. Just be in love with me. Like I'll be with you."

She shakes her head. "We agreed."

"Jennifer…"

Not that.

"We agreed."

"Jennifer…"

Just once she wishes she could be strong so that when the end comes, and he goes back to Miss Keaton, it won't hurt quite so much. Annoyed, she snaps, "Don't do that…"

"What? Say your name?"

She turns and crosses the alley towards her back steps.

Looking over her shoulder before she puts her key in the lock, she sees him standing with his hands on his hips and a grin on his face. In a few strides he has caught up to her, saying her name over and over, very softly, until they are both inside standing in the kitchen and the back door is firmly closed.

Luke

Through her open window the late sunshine, filtered by a thin drape, pours in over them. The beauty of an upstairs bedroom; it is almost like being outside. A breeze blows the curtain, moves her hair, and cools their skin. Tenderly, he strokes her flushed cheek. They stay in each other's arms as they wait – oddly silent – for the sun to set.

... when they first began meeting every afternoon he discovered something about them – the friendship they thought they'd been having had been a way to express their hidden feelings. With the truth came the revelation of why they had always wanted each other's opinions, why he had wanted to help her as much as he could, why she had always made him coffee, why she had always found another odd job for him to do when he said he should go and stayed to talk while he did it, why if he got desperate and made up some excuse to see her she always made him feel like it was good that he had come by, and why running into each other somewhere was not always a coincidence. Now it all made sense. Now it was obvious they couldn't have gone on like that forever – it had to break.

Now was better.

All the small things still mattered.

But the big things, like difficult trial days, got soothed away. He could put his arms around her, look at her face, kiss her lips and feel all the life and the strength that had been sucked out of him that day being restored. Knowing that she would be his reward at the end of a long day gave him a kinda energy he had never known before. As the days went by fewer words were needed. Often just a look was enough. The feeling between them came into its own.

He began to share her world more than ever. 'Details' could be expected daily. She was interested in everything he did or planned on doing. They talked about the trial. They discussed the newspapers.

He loved how confused she got when his imagination challenged her intelligence. Except when she talked music: 'Music simultaneously transcends the world and makes sense of it; you escape to it only to have it reveal the deepest truths, it cushions and under pins your emotions as your discoveries are brought to bear.' He understood that because he realized that's how drawing made him feel. 'I thought as much,' she said. 'I think you have a creative soul, Luke.' If she said so; he only knew that certain things centered him, one was drawing. Music was hers.

They laughed a lot more too. She would say 'I heard a good joke today', tell it to him and laugh at it herself. She liked to laugh; he realized he made her happy. Almost as if this warm and funny character had been waiting for him to come along. Her secrets were still off-limits, but as he tried to unlock them, he got the feeling they belonged to a past she wanted to forget; if he pressed her, she would make a joke, but the mood shifted and it felt forced when he changed the subject.

He was shaken by Mart's journal. She steadied him. When the trial began and he was nervous, she calmed him. As it got hard, she eased his mind. Cajoling her secrets out of hiding was shelved. He wasn't worried because one day he would succeed in gaining her trust and she would confide in him.

It didn't stop the increasing attraction between them. That had a life of its own. Each day he seemed to stay longer than the day before. Their parting grew strained. He would hold her and not want to let go. Just the thought of leaving her made him feel lonely. His walk back to the boarding house was downright lonesome; a couple of times he stopped on the sidewalk with the urgent need to go back to her and he had to force himself to go home.

This power she had over him felt new and strange in his life, a life that always had the same people who commanded the same importance to him since he could remember: Sara, Katrine, Ethan, Tip and Red Sky; Mart, the Keatons; and his father. He realized that Jennifer was starting to occupy that same level of importance.

Then yesterday he found her on the sofa in her parlor, crying. She is the bravest of women. Since when does his Jennifer cry?

Two important people had died during the day. One, a patient who she had tried to make well for a long time and couldn't; the other the wife of an influential couple, the first people to trust her when she arrived in Cheyenne. She owed this woman a great deal. And they had become friends.

431

The first died before Jennifer could get to her; the second as Jennifer was still at the home of the first. The grief was too much for her. 'Sometimes I just can't help it', she told him. He comforted her. Let her talk it all out. He looked into that tear-stained face, green eyes bright with tears, and realized she needed him as much as he needed her, that he was important to her too. She looked back with the same intensity as he and mumbled, "I am not good company just now."

"You want me to leave?"

"No… I mean, perhaps you should."

"You didn't go to Meg. You waited for me."

"I… Yes."

"Because you knew I could make you feel better."

"Yes, but…"

"Then I ain't going."

They snip-snapped back and forth stubbornly until she put her hands firmly around his face and in doing so knocked the breath out of him.

"Say what you mean," said she. "And don't say icebergs."

That intensity seemed to burst into flames.

Words didn't cut it; so he didn't use any. Except her name.

Until someone needing a doctor knocked on her door…

Gradually, the light begins to pale; the breeze freshens. Pink and gold colors fill her room.

He thinks she has drifted to sleep, but she stirs against him. He places a kiss on her forehead.

"The sun is going down," she says.

"Only in the sky."

She gives a gentle laugh and turns her head to look at him more easily.

"Changed your mind?" he murmurs.

"No," she frowns. "When are you going?"

"You know, I was thinking emeralds, desert sands and heat… exotic, uh?" He gives her a teasing look.

She looks away, trying to hide her smile. Her fingers begin to play with the edge of the sheet.

"Jennifer…"

"What?"

"You don't know, do you?"

"Know what?"

"That you are the most wonderful creature in all creation."

"I was thinking that you were."

He takes her into his embrace. "You're serious?"

Her answer is to gaze at him with the tender eloquence of her beautiful eyes.

His heart begins to beat fast and strange.

"I don't know how this happened," she says.

"There was a moment on the stairs."

"You would have left."

"Jennifer, don't you know how hard it is to leave you."

"The house feels so empty when you're gone."

"Lonesome."

"Achingly so."

"Just the house?"

"No. Not just the house. All of me."

"And all of me. Now you won't be at supper it's gonna feel mighty peculiar."

She goes to say something, but kisses him instead.

"I'll miss you," she murmurs.

He holds her closer and says, "I think I'm gonna be late."

Ed

…thumps the table and watches with satisfaction McKinnon's involuntary flinch.

"What are you gonna do about it, Walter?"

McKinnon folds his arms. "What do you suggest?"

Ed leans across the table and glares into McKinnon's face. "I don't think you have my best interests at heart, Walter?"

McKinnon sits back and gets that irritating look in his eye. "We have four witnesses. Four people, Ed, who said they would stand up for you. After what Faraday pulled today, you want me to win this with four miserable sons of bitches?"

Ed grabs his collar. "Don't push me, Walter."

McKinnon brushes Ed aside and stands up, his chair crashing backwards to the floor. "You won't let me cross. And I needed to cross Taylor and McCurdy. If I can't win this, you know why."

"Anyone would think you don't want to win, Walter. You are obliged to do…"

"My best, I am well aware of that. I can't help it if I don't have a shred of innocence or one mitigating circumstance on my side."

McKinnon walks out then.

Ed strides around the table and picks up the chair. Innocence. The word reminds him of Keaton's sister and he loathes Keaton's sister. Her performance in court made him sick. She made the jury believe her. Everything after that was pointless…

Anyway, he has plans for all of them; with Wilson on the move again, it feels like a good time to execute those plans.

He knows Taylor has a secret; his spies have done their job. Bodecker had caught his eye in the courtroom today. And not long ago Donnelly had been itching to help any way he could. Taylor's world is about to come crashing down around his ears.

Meg

Meg is preparing coffee when the back door opens. The sight of Jen so uncharacteristically pale and fragile-looking, eyes red and blotchy, arrests Meg with the spoon in the coffee canister. They stare at one another.

"Tell me what to do…" Jen says, finally.

"About…"

Silence.

Meg tells her to sit. "Men are not that hard to work out."

"Oh, this one is!"

"Men only want two things, Jen. First, that you make them the center of the universe; and secondly, that you let them make you the center of their universe when it suits them. It doesn't get any more complex than that."

Jen gapes at her. "Cynic," she mutters, and Meg grins.

"One minute we were fighting criminals together and the next we were… we were…" A distracted look comes over Jen's face.

"You were what?" Meg asks.

"We… Er. Never mind."

Meg laughs softly. "So, it's not Luke that's hard to work out, it's the situation in which you find yourself."

Jen nods.

"He's the one, isn't he?" Meg says gently. "The one who has surmounted all those impenetrable walls and unassailable fences. And yet all he had to do was walk right in."

Jen looks at her hands. "Yes."

"No wonder you're terrified."

Jen's eyes shoot up. "I… don't want to be."

"I think he loves you, Jen."

"Yes. But…"

"Miss Keaton."

"I think he might love her too."

"From my observation, you make him happy and Miss Keaton makes him sad – if you were him which one would *you* keep?"

"If only it were that simple, Meg."

In a timely fashion, Cam breezes in.

"Hello, George, you're back. Coffee? The Petersons from next door are here if you care to join us."

Jen is staring straight through him. Well, an evening with the Petersons who outright refuse to consult a female doctor might not be the best incentive.

"Are you all right, George?"

Jen looks away, hides her tear-stained eyes.

"I see," he says, even though it's doubtful.

"Better not leave the Petersons alone, Cam."

"Well, I just left them a second ago, Meg. I'm sure they'll survive another minute… George, is this about what I think it's about?"

"No," she and Jen say in unison.

Cam grins. "Just when I thought this trial already had everything, we have romance."

"Oh, Cam, how could you?" Meg says and places her arm around Jen's wilting shoulders; Cam chuckles naughtily.

Jen throws up her hands. "I just don't seem to be able to do anything wrong. How is that possible?"

"Dreadful to be so perfect," he says, shaking his head.

"I'm not perfect," she exclaims, "I'm flawed, seriously flawed, like a… a chipped vase, a cracked windowpane… like a doll with one eye missing…"

"How can you say that," Meg interjects.

"Nothing chipped, cracked or missing that I can see."

"You know what I mean."

"We are all flawed," Meg says.

"Exactly…"

"Look at Cam; he only thinks he has perfect hearing. He'll be using an ear trumpet before the year is out…"

"Uh?"

"Well, you only ever hear half of what I tell you, what else am I to assume?"

Cam blows a disgruntled sigh, but Jen manages a smile despite the tears in her eyes.

"Petersons, darling."

"Just leave the Petersons a moment longer. George, there's no escaping the human condition. But you have made an extraordinary life out what should have been no life at all. That is an achievement if you would only look at it another way. Tell Luke about it. If you can do no wrong, what have you to lose?"

Two large teardrops roll down Jen's cheeks. "Him."

"Oh, Jen, you don't know that; we've already established he's not like other young men."

"His perfect opinion of me, gone forever. I half-dreaded half-hoped that if I told him nothing then... Oh, nothing makes the slightest difference. Not even Duffy. She adores him."

"That's a telling statement on its own," Cam says, folding his arms.

"And it's true," Meg says. "Kathleen Quinn told me that Duffy told her that Luke reminds her of her first husband."

Cam blinks. "Well, there now. How many people does Duffy adore apart from you, George, tell me!"

Jen shrugs, at a loss to answer.

"Besides, when you think about it shrewdly, a woman with a touch of mystery is like live bait on a fishing line."

"Cameron Faraday!" Meg exclaims.

A look of desperation contorts Jen's face. "Oh, it wouldn't work."

"Well, how do you know that? I think it would. So does Cam."

"Look at me! I am not a frontier, ranch, horse... person. And that doesn't bother him either. He just gives me lessons."

Meg has to press her lips together.

Cam catches her eye, smiles and slides his hands into his pockets. "Who locked Wilson Cutter, an outlaw and murderer wanted in two states and three territories, in her closet?"

He eyebrows the question, but Jen is silent, staring at him.

"Who stood up to two thugs and then hit an arsonist over the head to protect her property? – or was that Luke you were protecting? Who delivers the babies of mixed American and Indian marriages and makes no discrimination between peoples of every race? Who removes bullets from rowdy cowboys when the herds come in and then agitates for the sheriff to reform the town firearms ordinances? Sound like anyone we know, George? For heaven's sake, you move with perfect ease within his world."

"It won't work, I can't do it," she says; she springs up and wrenches open the back door.

"Jennifer," Cam says in his courtroom voice, detaining her, "you haven't even tried to walk away from this, have you?"

"I don't seem to be able to."

"An honest answer…"

"But he will go back to Miss Keaton and where will I be then, Cam?

Cam frowns at this. "Are you sure about that? Or are you merely using it as an excuse for not taking the next step?"

Too shrewd, Mr Prosecutor…

"How could you, Cam," Jen mutters and then she's gone into the night.

Meg lets go of a huge sigh and closes the door. "Didn't want coffee with the Petersons then."

"No," says Cam, rubbing his chin. "Well, now we are getting somewhere."

"She's scared, Cam, truly…"

"I know." They look at each other and grin. "I believe George has finally met her match."

"I believe so."

"And there is nothing wrong with my hearing, Mrs Faraday."

"Petersons."

"Oh, very well. Where's the coffee then?"

"Oh, dear, I'm sorry; I was interrupted."

Ethan

Ethan raises his glass and declares, "Well, this has been a great day." He tosses the whiskey down the back of his throat and lets it warm his appreciative insides. As he sets his glass down, he realizes Luke is still staring into his drink and hasn't moved a muscle.

"You're not drinking, son."

"Ethan…"

"I'm listening."

The boy glances at him with a smile. "In Mart's journal he writes about me and K…"

"Interesting comment that. You know, Sara just doesn't agree with him…"

"Ethan, Mart was right and I know who that someone is." Now he swigs his whiskey in one gulp like a man twice his age.

Ethan smiles to himself. "That's why you said two words at supper and…" Across the bar and through the cloud of wafting smoke, a vision of pure loveliness appears at the door. She is searching the room careful-like. "This ain't the place to ask a woman to meet you, son. Thought I taught you better than that…"

"What…"

Luke looks for himself. Ethan watches the change that comes over him. Oh boy…

Meanwhile, the rest of the saloon sees her.

"Evenin', doc," say voices from the cloud.

"Evening, gentlemen," she says, reserved, self-contained, but kinda warm at the same time; hard not to be with all that chestnut red hair, tender green eyes and face all aglow.

"Catch any outlaws lately, doc?"

"Not unless you are volunteering, Clay," she responds. A round of good-natured laughter follows. She is one hundred percent at home in a room full of whiskey swillers.

He watches Jennifer's eyes find their mark. And he watches Luke find his. Oh boy… They smile across the room, in a world of their own.

Then, without taking his eyes off of her, Luke says, "You knew…"

"You tend to forget how long I've known you, Luke."

"You knew I'd fall for a female doctor who looks like she just stepped out of a painting?"

"And get into a heap of trouble doing it."

"I asked her to supper, she wouldn't come. I told her you and I'd be here after. She still said she wouldn't come."

"Well, that's a woman for you," Ethan sighs. "Or maybe she likes me."

The boy gives a laugh. "Reckon she trusts you, too."

While Jennifer walks towards them, the boy straightens from his lean against the bar. Ethan plays odd man out while they gaze into each other's eyes; he can almost remember how that felt with a woman. Oh, boy…

Suddenly, she's smiling at *him* and holding out her very genteel hand. "How are you, Ethan?"

Someone should hold up a warning sign before this woman smiles: not for the weak-hearted. That aside, there's goodness in her, and it goes deep. Kindness, to all kinds of folk in their pain and suffering, even if they're different, or done wrong. She could be bitter about being an unconventional woman, but she ain't. She's lovely, and it's right there in her eyes. No wonder the boy's head over heels.

"Why, Dr Sullivan, I'm mighty fine and it's always a pleasure to see you."

"And you. Do you drink tequila, Ethan?"

He gives a chuckle. "Does an old-time cowboy miss the days of the long drive…?

Sweet as candy, she looks to Luke for help. The boy grins; then he nods. Ethan laughs louder and calls the bartender over.

"Bottle of tequila."

They consume near half a bottle at a table in the back of the room. He never knew a woman of Jennifer's caliber who could drink tequila. Conversation flows; he enjoys their company.

And he watches them. He's always known Luke is tender-hearted; just ain't always obvious. Known he could be serene about life, if given the chance. Believed he could mature into a self-assured and contented man Morgan would be proud of. Such is the man he is seeing tonight. And such is the power of this unique young woman; she's fascinating. And grand. Ethan don't need to be here; but they keep drawing him into the conversation like he's important. Anyway, it's kinda nice to sit back and watch something special happen before your eyes.

All of a sudden, a large man with a big face, bearing a fat unlit cigar between dazzling white teeth appears at their table. Luke gets to his feet.

"Marshal Hummer."

"Luke, m'boy." They shake hands.

"Meet my partner. Ethan Benchley, Marshal Dan Hummer."

Ethan extends his hand. Invites him to take a seat. Hummer obliges. But not before he addresses Jennifer.

"Dr Sullivan, M'am. A delight as always."

"Marshal," she says.

Ethan is amused to see her smile has the same effect on the marshal as it does on him.

Hummer clears his throat and takes a seat. "Saw you over here. Thought you might be feeling a bit low about Cutter's extradition going ahead tomorrow morning."

"Mighty thoughtful of you, Marshal," Luke says. "Tequila?"

Hummer chuckles. "Never touch the stuff."

"I don't suppose there's any way you can hold off on that extradition until Parsons' trial winds up," Luke says.

Hummer chortles this time. "You know, son, that's what I like about you. You never miss an opportunity. But I wanna tell you something. Permission to be indelicate, Dr Sullivan, M'am…"

"Of course, Marshal," she says, her face as charming as a pale pink rose, which is kinda fascinating when you know she's game enough to catch outlaws.

"You're a gracious woman, M'am… Now where was I…? Yep, Wilson Cutter. He's gonna hang for his crimes. Now I know that you want him hanged for murdering your friend, but he's gonna hang regardless. So now you got bigger fish to fry, m'boy, 'cause the mind that's sets about plotting and scheming the killing of another human being, he's the one you really want. Cutter's brains got mashed when he was a young'un – ain't excusing him, mind – but he'll kill anyone you tell him to. Now Parsons, you gotta watch him. You can't underestimate him." Hummer draws closer to Luke. "Do you hear what I'm saying, Luke?"

Ethan knows the cogs inside the boy's head are spinning, although his face looks as cool as you please.

"Now Ryan tells me Parsons stopped his counsel from crossing Faraday's witnesses all day, yourself included. So what is that telling you?"

"That he knows he's going down."

Hummer lets out a loud, nerve-jerking *ha!* "And what would you do if you know your enemy is a-bringing you down?"

"Strike back."

"Doggone, that's two out of two. Like I told you, I seen it before. I'm telling you, friend. Don't underestimate him."

"Do you know something that I should know, Marshal?" Luke asks.

"Only what I just told you. Good question, though."

Jennifer sits forward. "So, Marshal Hummer, what time will you be leaving?"

"Well, I'm an early riser myself, but that sheriff... he goes by the book. I can't have Cutter till nine o'clock, so nine o'clock it is. Well, I guess I better get some decent shut-eye before the big day arrives. Check that my traveling companion is tucked up in bed." He chortles at his own joke. To Ethan, he says, "Benchley. Always a pleasure to meet a friend of Luke's."

"Good luck, Hummer," Ethan says as the big man gets to his feet.

Luke stands with him. "Marshal..."

Hummer removes his cigar from his mouth, a sign of respect in any man's language. "You take care now, son."

They shake hands; the cigar is put back where it came from; he bows politely to Jennifer, who says goodnight, and he strides away, drawing curious attention from nearly every hombre in the room.

"Well," Ethan says, "it's late and he makes good sense. You two gonna stay here and drink the whole bottle?"

"You're leaving?" Jennifer exclaims.

He looks at her steady-like. "Jennifer…"

"Yes, Ethan?"

If she ain't one of the most intriguing women he ever laid eyes on, aside from Red Sky, who was a fine-looking and intriguing woman herself.

"Once upon a time I would have finished the bottle, but that was a long time ago."

"Not that long, Ethan," says the boy.

"Watch it," he replies. "And do you have to make friends with every blue belly in this town? How am I supposed to get you back on the ranch?"

"You'll think of something, Ethan."

"I ain't that smart."

The boy starts laughing pretty hard.

"What is a blue belly?" Jennifer asks.

"A Yankee," Luke tells her, still chuckling.

"Goodness," she says.

"Don't worry, Jennifer. Ethan's a friendly Texan; just forgets sometimes how long it's been since he lived in Texas."

Ethan chuckles himself. "True enough. Mighty good of you to come, Jennifer. Look forward to seeing you again soon."

She says goodnight; says it in that warm way he's coming to know.

After he's left them, Ethan looks back from the door to their table. Oh boy…

Someone's heart's gonna get broke. Might even be Sara's.

Luke

"I just realized something," she says when Ethan has left. "*I* am a blue belly."

"Let's see… Boston, New York and St Louis… anywhere else I should know about before I give my ruling? …relatives, close connections…?"

"Nothing south of the Mason-Dixon line."

At that snappy retort he can only grin, and then chuckle; she continually outwits him when it comes to digging for information about her.

"So, if you have never been south of St Louis and I've never been east of it, then I guess if we were gonna meet it had to be here."

"Such gallantry," she teases.

"You out-drank Ethan," he retorts.

"I did not."

"Did too."

"Ethan is…"

"Impressed with your capacity for tequila."

"Wise."

"Wise?"

"And… and…"

"And?"

"Dear."

"Never heard him called that before."

"I've seen his wisdom in you."

He doesn't know what to say. In fact, he didn't think wisdom – Ethan's or anyone else's – was actually on her mind.

"He has taught you many worthwhile things."

"Like a father, you mean?"

She seems unsure. "I suppose so. Yes…"

"I don't know where I'd be without Ethan. Guess you could say he stepped up after Pa died when I was eleven, but Ethan... well, Ethan's always been there. I remember fishing with him, throwing lariats, roping calves and riding horses together when I was three years old. That's when Sara finally let me out of the house."

She shakes her head, smiling. "Oh, yes. Your long-suffering mother."

He observes her playful tequila smile and is tempted to take advantage by asking fast and furious questions about her life until she got head over ears and accidentally answered a few. But he loves her something fierce, and even with tequila soaking his brain, he knows he has to wait patiently for her to give up her secrets.

He blinks and notices her smile has faded some.

She asks, "What are you thinking?"

A brave question.

He gives a lazy shrug. "What are *you* thinking?"

She has the kinda brain that thinks about a dozen things at once. So right now she could be thinking about all the things she ain't gonna tell him and why, all the things she can and why, her patients and all of their ailments, and...

"Walk me home?"

Precisely.

Along the dark streets side by side they stroll, every so often passing by a streetlamp which illuminates her and brings to life his image of her as his angel guarding him from the shadows of his life. In the side alley of her building, she reaches for his hand. His insides begin to riot. As she finds the lock with her key, he puts his hands around her waist. By the time he has locked the door behind them, they are in each other's arms.

"You smell like roses and taste like tequila," he says.

"Luke...What is happening to us?"

"We drank a bottle of tequila."

"No, I mean..."

"I know what you mean. I'll tell you later. Between you and the tequila I can't think straight."

Sometime later, as he dreams about her, he stirs. He reaches for her and a murmur tells him she's awake.

He opens his eyes to deep moonlight falling across her face. Propping himself up on one elbow, he gazes down at her restless eyes.

"Something else I have just realized…" she says, her tone sleep-soft. "The T in Diamond-T doesn't stand for Taylor at all. It couldn't, when you think about it. It stands for Texas."

"Diamond-Texas Cattle Company."

"A legacy."

"Mm."

"Why 'diamond'?"

"Our ranch in Texas was on a river, like the Diamond-T. Ever seen sunshine on water?"

"Like diamonds."

"Like diamonds," he smiles.

"The river is precious… *water* is precious."

"Folks don't tend to gather in places where there ain't any."

"Mostly true. But a great many people take it for granted – especially in towns and cities. But you don't.

"Well, no…"

"You are a river man," she says.

"Because I know I can't raise prime cattle without a reliable water supply?"

"Some men can only be content in the city. The hustle and bustle. Everything the world has to offer at their fingertips, and they need to feel they live at the center of the universe."

"Go on," he says, wondering if she's had any sleep at all.

"And some are men of the sea or the coast, and they live on salty air, the constant swell of the waves beneath them, the smell of fish and the sight and sound of the ocean waves pounding the shore. A sense of timelessness, grandeur, and at the same time contest and humility."

"I like the sea."

"I know. Rivers flow to the sea. Shall I go on?"

He nods, hanging off every word.

"Some are men of the land: the earth, the mountains, the woods and the plains are for them, and luxuries are definitely not essential.

They need to ranch, farm, grow, hunt, chop, harvest and do it tough, because working with the earth and her seasons to produce or procure what people need makes them content. One with nature."

"And?" he murmurs, wondering why, since she just described his occupation, he's a river man.

"And some are river men."

"Jennifer, I make my living off the land. Ranch, grow, chop... tough..."

"Luke..."

"Okay, I'll ask. *Why* am I a river man?

"You're restless."

For a long time now, but...

"You have deep, still pools, but your life needs to be fluid... moving, creating, finding a way."

"Is that good?" he asks.

"I like it."

That's good enough.

"What about Ethan... is he one?"

"Ethan is..."

"Wise and dear."

"Mm."

"Do I snore?" he asks.

"What are you talking about?"

"I kinda figure that if you can lie awake thinking even after all that tequila and what came after that I must snore..."

"Shall we go on?"

"There's more?"

"Luke..."

"Okay, it's my turn, I know," he grins. "Matthew Taylor, my great great grandfather, settled on the Ohio River, raised beef and rafted them down the Mississippi to New Orleans back in the days when that was the frontier."

"I love your stories, you know."

And he'd love to know hers.

"Daniel Taylor, my great grandfather, became a frontiersman and the story goes there wasn't a river or a mountain or an Indian nation he couldn't tame. Then my grandmother, Lara Proulx, her folks came from Quebec City on the St Lawrence River. She and my grandfather never strayed far from the Ohio River. My father and Ethan's ranch – Diamond Bend – was on the Red River. I was born there."

"On the bend of the river."

"The ranch spread ten miles along the river and thirty back from it. It took weeks to round up the herd. In the furthest reaches you were always on the look out for Indians…"

"You must have hated leaving."

"Downright inconsolable. Ethan and Red Sky sat me down. Looked at me like they understood how bad I felt. Red Sky said: Luke, when you are older you will understand that life is like the great river, sometimes we are still and sometimes we flow where the current takes us. And Ethan said: I swear to you that you'll love our new ranch by the new river. We're gonna call it the Diamond-T, T for Texas. The Red River will always stay in our blood 'cause this is where we come from. Now be proud, 'cause what we and folks like us are doing is somethin' special."

"I knew it."

"Just Ethan rattling on…"

"Ethan doesn't rattle on; and I've seen how you listen to his every word. *And* how much Red Sky meant to you. It must have helped a great deal."

"Gave me something to hang on to. Katrine scolding me for being a baby helped too."

"You should write down your stories."

"I will… if you ask me."

Silence falls between them, a stretch of some minutes, of perfect meeting of minds and realizing it, of mutual longing as waxing as the moon through her window.

He caresses the side of her face with his fingertips.

A smile tugs at the corner of her mouth. "Luke… tell me now."

"If anyone had told me I'd meet you in Cheyenne in the middle of all this… I've been here a heap of times and I never saw you until that day…"

"We loved each other a long time before we finally told each other. How did we ever manage it?"

"I don't know. The feeling between us is getting stronger, so things are gonna change. How we feel, what we want… we can't just expect life to be the same. I never have imagined this for myself: you; how I feel about you; that as long as I have you I will be happy for the rest of my life."

Suddenly, that body beside him tenses. She sits up, her figure silhouetted, detailed in the moonlight. His breath catches at the silvery beauty before him.

Keep talking, he tells himself.

"I... I wouldn't make love to you this way if I didn't know that."

His hands might not be touching her, but his eyes are. Soon an easy lick of desire unwinds from deep inside his gut. He is unable to keep his hands off her any longer. He sits up and cradles her shoulders with one arm and smoothes his other hand across her belly. A shiver, an echo of ecstasy, grips his body. He sighs and drops his head into the hollow of her shoulder; nestles his face in that fragrant spot between her neck and the curve of her jaw. Jennifer...

"I know you think I'm hard to handle..."

A soft, nervous sound. "I like you just the way you are, and you are the most honest man I know besides..."

Besides? He knows better than to ask and does he need to know? The compliment has already been paid and he likes it.

"You see inside my heart the way I see inside yours."

"We love what we see."

"We want more."

"Yes."

"If I could win your trust, Jennifer, as well as your love..."

"I do trust you."

"There's something holding you back."

She doesn't reply.

If her silences were to put him off then he wouldn't be the one for her. He caresses her shoulder, her throat, her cheek with kisses. "What do you see in your future, Jennifer? Just making sure every-one else has one, mm?"

She surrenders and kisses him back. What she loves is his steady patience. For her, he has a lifetime of it.

"There'll never be anyone else," he says. "You are the one."

"Luke..." She takes his face into her soft warm hands and cool tapered fingers. "You are the one."

He quivers and sighs. "Now do you see how a person gets to feel like they own the whole world?"

"Yes..."

In the dark hours before dawn, while she sleeps, he leaves her. Even in this temporary separation there is a welcome pain. He knows when he returns to her the pain will disappear. And his mind and body will long for that moment. He slips into the boarding house, changes his clothes, grabs his coat and heads to Ferguson Street.

TEN

Listen to their words of wisdom,
Listen to the truth they tell you,
For the Master of Life has sent them
From the land of light and morning!

Henry Wadsworth Longfellow
Hiawatha's Departure

৵৻৶

Kelley

In the dark gray gloom before dawn, Kelly lets herself out of the Inter Ocean Hotel. In her step is a confidence she has not felt for a long time. She is confident that Ed Parsons will be convicted of orchestrating Mart's murder. After yesterday even Ed himself must be confident about that. No, this confidence is about herself. It is not just the dawn of another day that hovers beyond the eastern horizon; the dawn of her new self approaches. And just like the sun, which must first broach the horizon before it can shine, she has one more hurdle.

The extradition of Wilson Cutter.

As she passes the courthouse and approaches the sheriff's building next door, she spies a shadowy figure reclining on the bench beside the door. Typical; he couldn't sleep in his bed till it was time. Oh, no: Luke has to keep a vigil. Still, she doesn't really mind. It's not as if she didn't expect him to be here. In fact, it makes her smile. Neither of them is going to let anything stand in the way of doing the utmost in Mart's memory.

She gives his shoulder a nudge.

He rouses himself. "What's happening?"

"Nothing. You fell asleep."

He blinks several times. "K… I wondered when you'd turn up."

"Here I am."

He gets himself upright, trying to stretch those lean muscles. He makes her wonder what it's like to be tall. "Take a seat."

As she sits she can feel his eyes on her.

"Thank you. You're not cold?"

"Now that you mention it …"

"I'm glad you're here."

He smiles through the gloom. "What's got into you?"

"Oh, very funny…"

"No, I'm serious. You seem different. Last night I thought so."

"Last night? At supper you barely ate or said one word, you looked totally distracted, and you still noticed that I seemed different?"

"You were quiet, too, only a peaceful kind of quiet."

"Mm," she murmurs and looks up and down the street resting tranquilly in its gray cocoon. Their voices sound strange in the still morning; raw, transparent, maybe like the first voices ever heard on earth once did. "Perhaps we've both worked out at last what we want."

He doesn't reply; curious, she turns her eyes back to his face.

Gently, he says, "What is it that you want, K?"

She sighs. "You'll laugh."

"Try me."

"It's so obvious. Aunt Edith's been hinting at it for years. Mr Faraday told me that he believes I have the ability to express myself and ever since then I've had this feeling growing inside me that I can do it."

"Do what, K?"

"Write. Be a writer," she tells him. "I may have to write under a man's name... but, well... maybe not."

He's the first person she's told. It feels weird to speak her heart out loud to someone for the first time, but for that person to be Luke after what happened between them is entirely peculiar. She once fell in love with the confidence she felt in him. The love suffered a painful demise, but in spite of herself that confidence remains and will probably firm into a close and lasting friendship.

"You were right about me. I do love my independence. When I was growing up I never understood that about myself. You forced me to see it. I believe I should write about that."

She hears his sigh; he takes her hand in his and a tingle floats up her arm. "Don't leave out the part about how much blood has been spilled across this continent in the last one hundred years and now from one ocean to another we say we are free."

He remembers that? Deeply touched, she swallows awkwardly and says, "I won't. And, I don't want what you and I and Mart and the others did here to be forgotten. So – in time – I will return to New York with Aunt Edith."

"I'm proud of you, K," he says.

They exchange sidelong glances.

Since the Cimarron she never imagined she would have this moment with him; she withdraws her hand before his sensitivity makes inroads on her vulnerability.

"There's just one thing…" he adds.

"What?"

"Why did you give up on us so soon?"

"Sooner than you, you mean?" she responds.

He coughs, which amuses her.

"I will concede that your sense of duty is admirable, Luke, but you and I know how hard living here can be, and only the very deepest love and commitment makes for success. Look at my parents. And Sara; she still loves your father even after all these years; she could have remarried, moved on, but she continues to live his life. As for us, you weren't in love with me and I… I am not a liberty and property woman."

Quietly, he says, "There's no such thing as a liberty and property woman."

She smiles boldly at him, feeling her newfound confidence. "She is everything I am not. She will be calm and sweet… brave… and find all your irritating traits endearing, just like someone who loves you should. She's out there, somewhere…"

His eyes widen, their pupils deepening in hue.

"…and in her own way she will fit right into the legends with Elizabeth and Roberta, Lara and… oh, dear… Sara, who won't be too pleased with us."

He looks away. "No, you'll be off the hook – it'll be all my fault. Don't worry about it. Ain't like it's the first time."

She studies his handsome profile wishing it *were* all his fault. Then, suddenly, her ears pick up the gentle neigh of horses and the jangling of livery.

"I hear it," Luke says. "Round the back. Let's go."

Faraday

Faraday buttons his watch securely and tucks it into his vest pocket. In the dim light, he caresses Meg's long tousled curls as they spill across her pillow. He is grateful for all the time she selflessly gives him without her, including the eternity he'd spent with the governor last night in an eleventh hour and unsuccessful attempt to revoke the extradition of Wilson Cutter. He would make it up to her, as he always did.

Faraday strides out into the cool pre-dawn air; it blows away the cobwebs of sleep deprivation and makes him shiver. With the streets of Cheyenne still asleep, it takes him only half the time it usually does to reach the jail.

Jennifer

Jennifer wakes feeling chilled. Beside her the sheets are bare and cold; he has been gone for some time. She knows where and she knows why.

Meg's assessment of her was correct; she is terrified. Terrified of this never before experienced ache inside her. Of these lonely morning hours. Of the longing to turn herself into his arms and place herself against his warm body every day for the rest of her life. She puts his pillow to her face and nestles into it. After last night she is uncertain she can live without him. And right at this moment, he might not think so, but he needs her.

She washes and dresses quickly; brushes her hair and fastens it simply. From force of habit she collects her satchel, then steps out into the alley as the early morning gloom begins to brighten.

After some minutes of brisk walking, she passes the front of the sheriff's building and the jail, and rounds the corner to the yard. At once she sees Luke looking across the yard from the gates, but he is not alone and she stops in her tracks. Miss Keaton stands closely by his side; he holds her hand.

Perhaps Miss Keaton is the greatest terror of them all. Jennifer's life plays like a bad tune by a poor musician on a defective instrument every time she sees Miss Keaton. And Miss Keaton looks like a symphony to her. She doesn't understand Luke's choice, which only makes her love Luke more, and trust the future less.

Before she is seen, she backtracks and enters the sheriff's building.

Cliff looks up from his discussion with the night deputy. "What are you doing here?"

She steadies her breathing. "I... Checking."

Cliff frowns. "Checking what?"

"And being on hand."

"For what?"

At that moment, Dan Hummer brings forth his impressive frame from the doorway of the lockup. "Ah, Dr Sullivan, M'am. Had a feeling last night I didn't have you folks fooled for a second. But you got no cause for alarm. Everything is under control."

"I do not doubt you, Marshal; I just prefer not to underestimate Wilson Cutter."

"Well, Dr Sullivan, M'am, you were the one who caught him, so you know how he can be, but you rest assured that after your stupendous efforts to get him behind bars, I got no intention of letting the weasel out of my grasp." He almost champs his unlit cigar in half, so she should be convinced. "Now, if you will excuse me, I got some things to take up with the good sheriff here."

Cliff

After he coaxes Jennifer into a chair and out of the way, he dismisses the night deputy and tries to tell Hummer for the hundredth time that moving Wilson Cutter is like playing with fire in a woodpile in the middle of July.

"I know you mean well, Ryan," Hummer says through his chewed up cigar, "and you're a good sheriff, one of the best, but you gotta learn to accept your limitations – you ain't the governor."

Cliff sighs; the Silver Star pinned on the left lapel of his coat suddenly feels like a lead weight. The worn engraving reads 'sheriff'. There are even nicks and scratches in the silver. He resists the urge to glance at it or touch it in front of the marshal. Hummer is right; he's absolutely right.

"And neither am I," Hummer continues. "Now have the prisoner ready soon as you can. I wanna be outa here before the citizens wake up."

Outside in the corral the prison wagon is being prepared. The morning light has yet to shine. Cliff feels like he's preparing to move a load of nitro. And the thought of letting Cutter out of his cell for even one minute makes him shudder. Only that one shudder could set off an explosion, so he pulls himself together and gets back to work.

The two prison wagon guards trudge in carrying thick iron manacles made specifically to secure the prisoner inside the fortified wagon. Noisily, they proceed to put them in order.

Cliff opens the outer door to the jeers of Cutter's inmates.

Luke

At the rear of the jail, backing onto the jail wall, is a large stockade-like corral where the transfer of prisoners takes place. The walls are made of double stone; they are chest high on Luke but from the center rise long iron bars with spiked ends. The gates are tall and also made of iron bars.

An armed deputy stands guard on the other side.

He and K are able to observe the growing activity, which includes the loading of provisions and weapons under the driver's seat of the prisoner wagon.

And in one corner there's a gallows; it's morbid and sickening and he doesn't want K to see it.

But not only does she see it, she says, "Is it wrong to want to watch Cutter hang from there?"

"I'd say it was normal," he tells her. "Go beyond that and you reach another level of humanity."

"The level where people are able to imitate the Divine?"

"Wouldn't know about that, K."

"Yes, you do. You do it everyday. You just don't know it."

Coming from K, it's a quite a compliment; more than that, for just a moment he gets a flash of insight into her beliefs, and Mart's, but it is fleeting and he can't hold onto it. Frustrated, he takes her hand and grasps it securely. She's far too impulsive and he has no intention of letting her out of his sight.

"Why don't they just put him on the train?" she asks.

"Pretty sure they want to keep his travel plans unknown, keep him away from folks. But I'm with you on this; I think it's a risky idea… and I think I know why."

Footsteps approach from behind; they swing around to see Cam.

"Can't say I'm surprised," he remarks dryly.

"Good morning, Mr Faraday," K says politely.

460

"Miss Keaton," he replies. The pleasantries stop there as Luke receives a cautioning frown. "I am going inside in order to speak to Marshal Hummer. Do not, and I mean do not, follow me in."

"Of course not, Mr Faraday…"

Cam asks the deputy to admit him; they watch as he strides across the stockade and disappears inside.

K says, "Do you ever feel that the sun shouldn't rise on some mornings?"

Wilson Cutter

"Keep your eyes to the front," the deputy snaps at him.

Wilson can hear Faraday and Hummer arguing in the outer room – again.

"Give it up, Faraday," Wilson mutters to himself.

Hummer gets the upper hand and soon appears in the lockup. Wilson snorts. As if he's scared of these assholes.

"Keep quiet," the deputy snarls like a dog.

"Don't tell me what to do," Wilson snarls back.

Hummer starts walking up and down in front of him. "You got a heap of folks who don't want you to leave, Wilson. In fact, me and the governor are the only ones who want you gone." Hummer stops directly in front of him and glares at him. "Don't you give me no trouble, boy…"

Wilson flexes his wrist a fraction. Excitement dances along his veins; his skin tingles. "Trouble's in the eye of the beholder… Marshal."

Luke

When the shabby figure of Wilson Cutter emerges from the dark doorway and into the light of day, hands and feet manacled, Luke shudders. He hears K gasp; her hand tightens in his.

"He looks restrained enough," she says.

"I'm gonna have to stop this, K."

"I know."

Luke bides his time; he observes Cutter being maneuvered into the back of the fortified wagon. With its checkered iron bar walls riveted to an iron plate base, a team of four collared draft horses pulls it. Hummer calls the deputy on guard duty at the gate over to help and Luke is presented with his chance. At the precise moment that Cliff, Hummer and the deputies are focused on securing Cutter to the wagon, Luke slips inside the corral and steals his way to the driver's bench. He lifts a fully loaded Winchester from the seat.

"He's secure," says one of the deputies.

"Just the way I like it," Hummer prattles.

Luke engages the rifle and five startled faces appear.

He trains his weapon on Cutter.

"Cutter ain't going anywhere today or any other day," he announces.

"Hey, Hummer, you didn't tell me we were gonna have a party," Cutter declares.

"Shut your face," Hummer tells him.

There is a strange kind of peace floating through Luke's veins. He knows he's breaking the law, but he and Mart didn't get this far to see it all go to hell, and he can't let go of it.

"Luke, what are you doing?" Cliff asks.

"Take Cutter back to his cell and I won't shoot him."

"I'm sorry. I don't think I heard you right."

"Sure you did."

"*Shoot* him?"

"Tuck your surprise back in, Cliff. Yours too, Marshal."

Hummer removes his cigar. "Now, son, I know how you feel. But you can't do this, you know you can't. Sheriff Ryan here will tell you that you can't interfere with justice."

"Well, that's just fine, Marshal; Cliff can talk if he wants, but no one is leaving."

"Luke, you're a fine young man, so I'm gonna pretend this never happened if you just hand over the rifle and leave the yard."

Luke aims just that little better at Cutter's head. "Take Cutter back to his cell and I won't shoot the headline feature of your circus of justice."

"Luke, don't do this," Cliff urges.

"Sorry, Cliff."

Hummer glares at him through squinted eyes.

"I'm disappointed in you, son."

"Not interested, Marshal."

Hummer clicks his fingers and the deputies train their rifles on Luke. "Hand it over and you won't get hurt."

"I don't care if you shoot me stone cold, Marshal, cause I'm gonna shoot this bastard first. In fact, it should have been me that died in the first place. Not Mart. He never did one bad thing in his life, not like me. And I won't allow the bastard who killed him to go free. Now I ain't afraid to die, but Wilson here... he's looking a might pale, wouldn't you say? You scared, Cutter? You should be. Cause you're going back inside or I'll shoot you."

"Go free?" Hummer shouts. "What are you talking about?"

"You surprise me, Marshal. Wasn't it you who told me not to underestimate Ed Parsons? Do you think that for one moment he's gonna pass up an opportunity like this?"

Hummer has a think about this. Still, he says, "Far-fetched, son."

"Well, I don't know what you meant then, Marshal. But I ain't taking risks. The lives of my family and Mart's family are at stake. Cutter goes back inside or I kill him. One way or another, he ain't leaving."

"Hummer, call off the rifles; I will not permit you or your men to shoot Luke," Cliff declares. "Not now, not ever. Besides, if anyone is going to shoot Luke, it'll be me."

At any other time, Cliff's frustration with him would be a source of amusement.

"Hec, I don't mind that, Ryan. Time is short. Me and the boys'll just stand back and egg you on."

"Luke is obviously emotional and needs persuasion of a different kind."

"He's acting like he wants to be shot."

"Come on, fellers, search the bastard," Luke exclaims.

"The prisoner's already been searched, Marshal," says one of the deputies.

"Well, do it again," Luke suggests.

"Hang fire, Deputy. He don't take orders from you, Luke," Hummer says.

"What are your terms, Luke?" Cliff asks.

"I'll be happy to see the governor. I'll wait. All day if I have to."

"We're not negotiating," Hummer declares.

"We can end this now, Hummer," Cliff persists.

"Nope. Now bud out, Ryan, before I... aw, let it go, Ryan."

"Cutter stays or Cutter dies," Luke declares, "so, which one is it, Marshal?"

"Son, you're obstructing the path of justice and that's a serious crime."

"What's it to be, Marshal?"

"This stinks, son," Hummer declares petulantly. He throws his cigar down and grinds it into the dirt.

Luke tightens his aim. "Now we understand one another."

"Get him off of me, Hummer," Cutter screeches meanwhile. "Get me inside..."

Kelley

Kelley feels some relief now that she has heard Mr Ryan's adamant declaration that no one will shoot Luke.

Nevertheless, there are three rifles trained on him and she cannot become complacent.

Crazy warrior. Yes, that's him.

And she can't help feeling they are like children who should be telling their parents they are in terrible trouble. That, however, is a long time ago. They are no longer children.

And no longer innocent.

And what of Red Sky? Is this the day she knew would come?

Suddenly, Jennifer Sullivan of all people is beside her, a little breathless, her brilliant green eyes shiny as though she saves unshed tears.

"Dr Sullivan…"

"Miss Keaton…"

"Where have you come from?"

"Inside. Miss Keaton, last winter I treated the governor's children for scarlet fever. They recovered with no complications and to this very day they are extremely healthy and the apple of his eye."

"What are you saying?"

"He *will* see me, and he *will* listen to me, but with you there we have a greater chance…"

"I can't leave Luke out here by himself."

"I understand how you feel, but Cliff will look after him – and Cam, too, I promise you, and if we wait until Hummer decides that Luke really means it when he says he wants to speak to the governor, it could take hours. As the day goes on he will try and wear Luke down. And then Luke really will be in serious trouble. We must act now."

Kelley stares at her, bewildered. "What is this to you?"

"I caught Wilson Cutter," she says simply. Unexpectedly, she takes Kelley's shoulders in her hands. "Miss Keaton, I strongly suspect you believe as I do that women, with a few exceptions, have underestimated their own power since the dawn of time. And I would dearly love the dawn of today to be an exception to the rule. Will you come with me to see the governor?"

Kelley turns her eyes back to the stand off. Luke is strong, but how long can their crazy warrior prevail?

Jennifer releases her shoulders. "Will you trust me, Miss Keaton? I believe it is the only way to help Luke and stop the extradition from going ahead."

Kelley remembers that Luke seems to trust her, and nods her consent. A smile dripping with relief softens the desperation in Jennifer's face.

Thirty minutes later – they had to wait for what seemed like an eternity – the governor of Wyoming is being bombarded with the most persuasive spell of advocacy Kelley has heard outside of the courtroom. He clearly respects Jennifer because he listens without interruption.

"My dear Dr Sullivan," he says finally, "if Mr Taylor has got himself into trouble then it is up to Mr Ryan to handle it. I will not renege on my agreement with Denver."

"Governor, I think his demands are very reasonable. To speak to you personally and have Wilson Cutter searched. He is not a man given to irrational behavior, but this is a matter of life and death. I was present when Marshal Hummer himself said that Mr Taylor should not underestimate Ed Parsons, and I understood, as did Mr Taylor, that this could very well mean that when Cutter is transferred at this very crucial stage of Parsons' trial, Parsons' would use it to strike back. Now, I know Cutter and I know Mr Taylor, but I believe Miss Keaton should tell you about Ed Parsons…"

The governor, a dapper man with a substantial and well-coiffured moustache men of his position seem to prefer, turns his eyes on Kelley. "I've seen the trial transcripts. Mr Faraday made sure of it. Well, Miss Keaton, what have you to say?"

They are standing in a lavish house, with French doors that overlook pleasant gardens. Fresh sunshine glistens on a bed of dewy roses, a manicured lawn and a row of simple topiaries. If ever she had dreams of advocacy, reality is now upon her. Mart's undying faith in her spurs her on; words fill her mind and clamber to be spoken.

"I...I believe, governor, that very soon Ed Parsons will be convicted of the murder of my brother. But it's not an incident that stands alone. Ed Parsons has tormented my family and Taylor's family and numerous others since I was a little girl. I don't think you understand what's at stake here. Don't you ever put yourself in someone else's place? What if someone was trying to extort and kill you to get his hands on this beautiful house, hurt your family, destroy your position? And believe me, that's what has been happening for many years with Ed Parsons. Our land, our livelihood and our people. Your citizens, governor. And now you are telling us that the people of Colorado are more deserving than your own citizens?

"I bet the extradition was music to Ed Parsons' ears. Help Cutter get free en route to Denver and back to doing what he does best – killing people. Governor, it may be Luke standing in that corral with three rifles pointed at him and defying the law, but the Alliance stands with him. We need you to come to the jail, and we need you to call off the extradition until Ed Parsons has been convicted and sentenced and imprisoned, and we need you to order a search of Wilson Cutter to prove that Luke was right to disrupt the extradition because you would not listen."

The governor inhales and exhales. He rubs his eyes. "Very commendable, Miss Keaton, but I've heard many arguments. Mr Ryan, Mr Faraday... my God, that man was here till one o'clock this morning..."

"But you didn't hear from the Keatons or the Taylors, did you, Governor, when we are the ones whose lives are at stake and who plead for your sympathy."

"No," he says solemnly.

"Governor, I am begging you. Are we not worthy of your consideration?"

Luke

Judging by the movement of the sun, Luke estimates an hour could've passed. His eyes are starting to water. The sun grows warm; Hummer grows sour. Cutter will not shut his mouth for even a minute. It doesn't bother Luke; but Hummer is fed up and orders one of his deputies to gag him. While this is happening, a familiar voice reaches his ears.

"Need any help, Luke?"

Relief *almost* causes him to lose focus. "No, Ethan. I'm fine."

"Would've been here sooner, but I guess I can't handle tequila as good as I used to. Say the word and I'll take over…"

"Stay put, Ethan. John's with you?"

"We're here," comes John's firm voice. "Me and Amy."

Hummer rages, "Sheriff, you'd better get ready to charge those three with obstruction as well."

"I'm not charging anyone with anything," Cliff says, his tone taking the sting out of the sun. "Why can't you just call off your deputies, let's go back inside and discuss this – rationally?"

"Skedaddle, Ryan."

"*Skedaddle?* Listen, Hummer, this is my jurisdiction. You've had your fun, made your point, now call off your deputies…"

"I got one word for you, Ryan. On my badge the President of the United States gave me. *US Marshal*… hell, that's two or three… and don't try nothing cause I swear on my mama's grave you're gonna regret it." Hummer tucks a fresh fat cigar into his mouth. "I refuse to be dictated to. The law is the law. This man is scheduled to be extradited this morning and he is gonna *be* extradited this morning."

Out of the corner of his eye, Luke sees Cliff stride around on the spot in sheer frustration. He also sees Cam bringing down a consoling hand on Cliff's shoulder.

"Cliff," Luke calls out. "No hard feelings?"

Cliff jams his hands on his hips and looks hard at him for a spell. Then, calmly says, "No."

Relieved, Luke checks his aim.

"Hummer," Cam says, "why can't you listen to reason in this matter? You know Luke has a good head on his shoulders."

"I thought I knew it. Stay out of this, Faraday. This prisoner is leaving..."

"You move him out of here, Marshal, and I kill him," Luke reminds him. Meanwhile, he spies Cliff and Cam whispering together...

"You gonna deny justice to a heap of folks cause of a whim, 'cause you can't take one loss? Hell, you're gonna win your case, Luke."

"I'm gonna *die* winning this case if it means Cutter stays here till Parsons is incarcerated, because you see, Marshal, if I don't do this, I'm probably gonna die anyway. And so will my family and my friends. So don't preach to me about justice because right now I don't see much of it happening."

"Oh, bullshit!" Hummer explodes. "Do you think I'm gonna let this good-for-nothing loose once we hit the prairie? What's the doggone matter with you?"

"I thought a man's reputation was everything. Wilson here has one; you know it and I know it. Now, I appreciate your confidence, but I hope you'll forgive me for saying that when it comes to Wilson here, I don't share it."

Hummer throws up his hands. "Fine. FINE! Deputy, go get me a chair."

"Hummer...."

"Shut your trap, Ryan."

Cutter starts squirming and carrying on, making muffled pro-testations that stop abruptly when Luke tightens his aim.

"Are you gonna search the weasel, Marshal?" Luke asks.

"Already been done," Hummer says. "Watched the night deputy do it."

He's composed himself, not something Luke wants to happen.

Kelley

The governor studies her for a very long time and her nerves feel set to burst.

"My father, Miss Keaton, taught me that a man should never lose face, and in my position people respect that."

"The Alliance has gained many friends in recent months, many right here in Cheyenne. You would be a hero to your own citizens."

"Huh! You think so? Define hero!"

Kelley swallows; her throat is parched. She quickly finds an answer. "Someone who acts bravely."

"Mm. And you, Dr Sullivan, can you define hero?"

Jennifer doesn't seem to be able to compose her quivering intensity. But, after a moment, she says rather coolly, "There are people, governor, who aren't afraid to sacrifice themselves..."

"Go on," the governor urges.

"They act with integrity..."

"Not bravery, Doctor?"

"... and courage in the face of opposition whether it be hardship, danger, uncertainty or ridicule."

The governor, staring at her, says nothing for a long moment. Then, "Your own definition?"

"In a manner of speaking," she says. "There are a great many people in this territory who have helped create it, and every day I witness them give new depth to the meaning."

Surprisingly, a genuine smile softens his expression, and in a more gentle tone he says to her, "You believe in this man Taylor."

"He is a man of integrity. Like Mr Faraday and Mr Ryan and yourself. I stake my reputation on it."

If the governor isn't shocked by this, Kelley certainly is; it must have taken Jennifer months to get the town to trust her, let alone gain a reputation worth the price of this negotiation.

"A rough diamond?"

Luke? That crazy warrior?

Kelley casts her glance at Jennifer's pinking face.

"Not so rough," Jennifer says, adding, "besides, a diamond is a diamond, sir."

The governor grins broadly.

Apparently, he speaks the language of diamonds.

Luke

Sometime later, when Luke's aching arms have stiffened to the point where he thinks they will break off, a man with a grand moustache, and wearing a well cut suit, strides up to Hummer.

Hummer jumps off his chair. "Governor."

"Marshal Hummer, I understand there is a problem with the extradition."

A master understatement. This man has to be a politician.

"Well, governor…"

While Hummer is waxing lyrical about his beloved extradition, Luke comes to the realization that this man truly is the territorial governor. Very soon, he walks right up to Luke and asks him to put down his gun.

"Governor, it's a pleasure to finally meet you, but I have to tell you that when Marshal Hummer finally comes to his senses and searches the prisoner, he'll need my gun as well as his deputies' as a precaution."

"Young man, you've had some very persuasive people speak on your behalf and that's why I'm here. Now tell me what you want to say. You can lower your weapon; no one will do any-thing…"

"Sorry, governor, but I can't do that. So if you don't mind…"

The governor sighs and shoots a disagreeable glance at Hummer. "Go ahead, Mr Taylor."

"Thank you. This prisoner needs to be returned to his cell inside the jail and then searched for a concealed weapon."

"Young man, you are breaking the law…"

"Wilson Cutter is a mortal threat to me and I'm defending my life, my property and my rights."

"A fan of John Locke, I see. You are claiming self-defense?"

"I am."

"Well, that's an argument I've not yet heard."

"What have people been saying about me, governor?"

"That you are a man of integrity. Are you, Mr Taylor?"

Cutter decides to have his say; thankfully, no one can understand it.

The governor studies him. "You say this is the man who murdered your friend, Miss Keaton's brother?"

"Yes, sir."

"And you claim Ed Parsons employed him to commit that crime?"

"Governor, yesterday in court the whole town heard what Mart Keaton knew for two years before he died. Ed Parsons paid Wilson Cutter to torment him; and he finally killed him. Ed Parsons then brought Cutter back to try to kill me, his objective being to bring my family and the Keaton family to a state of capitulation so that he could go ahead and realize his obsession – our land and our river. Do you know what that feels like, governor?"

"No, but someone has already asked me that question this morning, Mr Taylor, and again I find myself in your shoes. Hummer, I want you to carry out Mr Taylor's request at once."

Luke's heart quickens.

"Governor?"

"Immediately, Marshal."

Hummer slams yet another cigar into the dust.

"Governor, I whole-heartedly object…"

"So noted, Marshal Hummer. Sheriff Ryan, would you be so good as to send a wire to Denver and let them know that there will be a delay in the extradition of Wilson Cutter on my orders."

"Certainly, Governor."

Luke doesn't have to see Cliff's face to know he's smiling.

"Carry on, Hummer. I will wait with Mr Taylor while you do whatever it is you have to do. You understand, Mr Taylor, that if the search reveals nothing, you will have to be charged with obstruction of justice."

Luke squeezes stinging moisture from his eyes. "Yes, sir."

"Hummer, tell your deputies to train their weapons off Mr Taylor and then he can lower his at the same time."

Hummer gives the direction.

"In good faith, Mr Taylor…"

Luke lowers his rifle. Dizzy, arms aching, he looks around at last and sees Cam standing there to the side with his hands in his pockets, his face troubled.

But Luke cannot relax; very soon Cutter has been unchained from the prison wagon and the deputies are pulling him out. He is protesting wildly despite his restraints. Cliff orders an armed deputy back to the gates.

Inside the jail, Luke's eyes have trouble growing accustomed to the dingy light. The other prisoners are yelling and jeering as Cutter is shoved back into his cell. The governor directs Hummer to carry out the search of the prisoner.

"I want him stripped naked, Hummer, and his clothes turned inside out. I want Mr Taylor here to be thoroughly convinced. Understood?"

While one of the deputies gets to strip Cutter, the other keeps the barrel of his Winchester at Cutter's head.

The gallery of men watching the proceedings is quiet; and, strangely, so are the inmates. Quietly pacing, quietly waiting. Quietly expectant? Luke senses it at once. He catches Cliff's watchful eye. Cliff has already sensed it; he gives a small nod.

Luke calls out the warning.

Hummer reacts. "Haven't you said enough for one day?"

"Look at the others, Hummer," Cliff says.

Hummer stops and looks around. "Right, you boys, stop pussy-footin' around in there and strip that shirt off of him…"

Cutter hurls muffled abuse. The deputy rips the front of his shirt in two. He moves to Cutter's back and grabs both sides of the shirt, stripping it to Cutter's waist. Still his arms are half covered. The deputy yanks the left sleeve down to Cutter's manacled wrist. Nothing. The deputy grabs the right sleeve and wrenches it also.

A knife, shaped like a small Bowie but large enough to effect a disarming injury, sits knotted to the inside of Cutter's lower arm. There is a collective gasp from the men watching; Luke stares at the knife, kinda numb but relieved, mostly because it is there, but also because Cutter is not out on the plains with it. He feels a hand come down on his shoulder; it's Cam's.

"Well…" Hummer murmurs, "where did this come from?"

Cutter scowls through his gag.

"Oh, you'll talk, Wilson…" Hummer says. And to Cliff, "How did this happen?"

"Well, if I knew that, *Marshal*, then we wouldn't be in this predicament."

Hummer grunts and barks, "Strip the rest of him, and make it snappy."

Wilson Cutter naked is enough to give a man the willies, but the revelation provided by his butt ugly body, covered in the scars of old wounds and the bloody scabs of recent ones, is thoroughly beautiful to Luke. A small pistol is similarly knotted inside his thigh.

"It's loaded," says the deputy after he's confiscated it.

"Taking a risk, ain't you, Wilson?" Hummer says.

"That night deputy was one of yours, Hummer," Cliff says in Hummer's face. "I want answers."

Hummer grunts at him.

"Mr Faraday, there will be no prosecution of Mr Taylor for obstructing justice," says the governor. "He was acting in self-defense and in the best interests of this extradition."

"Yes, sir. I agree."

"Good. Now maybe I can get some sleep…"

"You and me both, governor."

They begin a slow walk into the front office.

"I am mighty grateful," Luke says. At the door, the governor accepts his handshake.

"Well, I didn't work alone," he replies with a smile and looks across the room. Luke follows his line and sees Jennifer and K standing nervously by the chairs at the front of the office. "You must count yourself lucky indeed to have them on your side, Mr Taylor. Charming, aren't they? No one would suspect for a moment that they too conceal weapons. Oh, just a small point, the charming one with the dark hair, who staked her rather considerable reputation on your integrity, likes diamonds. Perhaps you should buy her one…"

Cam chuckles; and so does the governor.

"Oh, a warning for you, Mr Taylor. Don't ever try this again. If this territory is ever to become a State, we must prove that Wyoming citizens have healthy respect for the law and work to uphold it. Since Mr Faraday took up his post here things have definitely been looking up, but there is still much to be done. It's up to all of us."

"Well, I couldn't agree more, Governor," Luke says. "Only you'll pardon me if I tell you that if the Alliance didn't have a healthy respect for the law as you call it, there'd have been a range war up in Bright River a couple years back. Parsons was itching for it. Mart Keaton didn't die because he was a bad shot, Governor. He was trying to bring Wilson Cutter in, get the truth, and some justice. The Alliance between the Diamond-T and the Keatons was founded on being law-abiding, we worked damn hard at it, and it's cost us more than you'll ever know."

As Luke speaks, the governor's eyes widen, then narrow. "You've made your point, Taylor, and you don't seem backward about doing so. We also need that in Wyoming." His mood lightens, and with a flourish he announces, "And now I must go and be a hero to my people," and departs.

Suddenly, Ethan, John, Amy, Edith, a string of trial witnesses and a throng of journalists burst into the building.

"The extradition won't be going ahead today..." the governor declares. The crowd gasps and starts talking all at once.

"Don't think the town thought about sleeping in, do you?" Luke murmurs.

"And miss the best thing since the completion of the transcontinental railroad?" Cam quips.

Some of the journalists have trapped the governor near the door. A rabble of questions spews forth and the governor, with his hands waving in the air, directs them all outside.

Luke strains to see through the crowd. At last a pair of shining green eyes meets his. His body tingles from head to toe. The strain of stopping the extradition eases.

"Now how do you suppose our Dr Sullivan knew? And knew what to do?" Cam speculates.

At the door, Jennifer takes a couple of small backward steps, smiling at him as she leaves. She's gone. For now.

"Well, you know how smart she is, Cam," he says.

"Oh, I do. And is Miss Keaton as smart, do you think?"

K is surrounded by family, but she looks up and catches his eye.

She smiles, too. A deep river summer sky smile, beautiful, that touches his memory, gentle at first, then grasping. It takes his breath away, and then floods that memory with regret.

Walter McKinnon

Two days later

"Proceed with your closing remarks, Mr McKinnon."

Judge Callaghan sits back in his chair. Walter gains eye contact with the jurors.

"Two years ago, my client suffered the cruelest of deprivations. The water he so badly needed to sustain his cattle and his livelihood was denied him. The two sources of this vital component are the two families you see here in court today, calling themselves the Alliance. Their cruel and mean-spirited action, in which they refused to renew my client's water contract, drove my client to the brink of desperation.

"Their Alliance is a mangled mess of lies and desperate strategies. The Keatons lost their son in the process of this mess they created because of their own stupidity and malicious intent, and now you are supposed to believe that it is the fault of my client. All Ed Parsons wanted was the water to keep his cattle from being wiped out in the heat of summer. All he wanted was the assurance that the water would be there when he needed it.

"You have heard that my client is a well-respected rancher and a neighborly man, a man with good connections: the doer of good in the Bright River community, a man who has brought undeniable prosperity to the whole district. And yet this Alliance sought to bring him to his knees: this Alliance who foolishly lost one of its members and seeks to blame my client for their own pitiful misjudgment and deceit.

"Let me ask you this. If you were faced with a crisis that struck at the very heart of your being, what would you do? You would fight. Oh yes, you would. You wouldn't allow a mob of bullies to have their way without a fight. You would not succumb. Am I right? Of course, I am.

"Mart Keaton died as a result of the chaos caused by this so-called Alliance of which he was a member. When it all goes wrong, it is so easy to blame someone else.

"As you deliberate on the innocence of my client, I would urge you to remember what it means to be a neighbor, what it means to live out here a frontier life, its difficulties and trials, and that neighbors need each other. The Alliance between the Keaton, Benchley and Taylor families caused my client abject grief and despair. They were *not* neighbors as we understand the term. My client has lived the last several years at their mercy. All he wanted was a share of the water. All he wanted was fair and just neighbors. All he has received is accusation and condemnation. It is in your power to save him from further detriment. Thank you."

Faraday

"When you are ready, Mr Faraday."

"Thank you, Your Honor. Members of the jury, there is in the Bible, in the Gospel according to John, the scene where Jesus Christ comes before the Roman governor Pilate, you probably know it, and Pilate and Christ discuss, one-sidedly, Christ's innocence. Pilate demands to know if Christ is a king. Christ answers that he is right, he is in fact a king, that he was born to come into the world to testify to the truth, that everyone on the side of truth listens to him! Everyone on the side of truth listens to him...

"Pilate asks the right question, an eternal question, a burning question: What is truth? But, Pilate doesn't wait for the reply. He proceeds to allow the crucifixion of an innocent man. Had he really desired it, he would have heard the truth.

"Since you have listened to the defense's testimony and closing argument, I ask you to listen *now* to the truth, because what you have heard from them is anything but the truth. Remember, using the definition you have just heard, the genuine leaders in this world are those who know, keep and live their lives in truth. They have our hearts, not maintain our fears."

Faraday strides across to the witness stand and picks up the Bible; he turns and holds it up for the jury to focus on.

"When, in the last two years of his life, Mart Keaton chose to write down what was and what did happen to him and his family and the Diamond-T families, he concluded 'I swear on the Bible that this account is the truth'. And then he quotes John 8:32 – 'Then you will know the truth and the truth will set you free.' Mart Keaton wants us to ask the question 'What is Truth?' and then he entreats us, urges us to listen to the answer, unlike Pilate.

I, for one, will not allow his entreaty go unheeded, because if we ignore the truth, pretend it is something else entirely, there is no

480

justice. And justice demands that we right the wrongs of unfairness and injustice and allow freedom to flourish."

Faraday places the Bible back on the rail of the witness stand and approaches the jury. He stands directly before them and studies them quickly. They have followed and he has no intention of losing them.

"The facts are these. In September 1882, Ed Parsons, who you see over there, forced Mart Keaton before him and threatened him and the families with bloodshed if the water contract was not renewed. Mart Keaton specifically states in his journal that he dared not tell anyone, not his father, John Keaton, not his best friend since childhood, Luke Taylor. No one; because the slightest protest would make it very convenient for Ed Parsons to initiate bloodshed. The instrument of this threat was a hired gun, the outlaw Wilson Cutter, whom Ed Parsons paid handsomely to intimidate and threaten not only Mart Keaton, but also members and employees of the families. The fact is that Wilson Cutter, under the direct orders of Ed Parsons, murdered Mart Keaton.

"And, there was a middleman, whom we have heard about, particularly from the file doggedly compiled by Mr Taylor and painstakingly verified by Sheriff Ryan. This middleman was a sheriff – an officer of the law. Ed Parsons colluded with him in the harassment of the families. Ed Parsons bribed an officer of the law.

"We heard from Mr McCurdy, under oath, that at no time in his friendship with Ed Parsons did he notice that Ed Parsons' ranch was in dire need of water. So, for all this desperation, grief and deprivation supposedly suffered by Ed Parsons, I would ask you to ask yourselves *what is the truth*?

"And as for all the chaos the Alliance families supposedly caused themselves: we know that several other ranchers in the same district suffered grievously at the hands of Ed Parsons. They were threatened and driven off their land by Ed Parsons, and their cattle stolen. Extortion, theft, cattle rustling – the defendant is nothing short of a pirate. He takes what he wants, plunders the livelihood of others and then flaunts his ill-gotten gains while he greedily prepares his next raid. His next raid, members of the jury, was right into the heartland of the Keaton, Taylor and Benchley families.

"Remember – Ed Parsons was not in need of water.

"These families formed an alliance to protect themselves. They dared to defy this pirate and have been paying the price ever since. These families have a fine and noble heritage on the land that they intend to pass down to future generations. And not just the land itself and the business of raising and selling cattle, but also an integrity, the likes of which Ed Parsons over there attempts to push aside with scornful arrogance. Integrity, with its backbone of truth, cannot be pushed aside.

"Mart Keaton has proved this, with his life and his death – and with the triumph of his journal which he wanted his sister to bring to light because he saw her as the brightest, most fervent exponent of the truth. We should not treat the honor Mart Keaton bestowed on his sister lightly. In her hands you will remember that Mart Keaton's journal became like a sword to carve up the web of lies camouflaging the crimes of Ed Parsons. From her mouth came his words; from her heart came the strength of those words, and from her soul, the spirit of them. The truth.

"The truth is that Ed Parsons is a land grabber of the worst kind. He is quite blatantly prepared to lie, cheat, steal, threaten, bribe, conspire and murder to get what he wants. When will he stop? It is in your hands to stop him right now. Then our community will be free of Ed Parsons and the danger he presents to us. Then these families, who have had their courageous son, brother, husband, father and friend so brutally taken from them will once again be free to live and work on their land, without the threat that Ed Parsons has inflicted upon them for many years.

"Members of the jury, the laws of this territory and of our nation exist to ensure justice and protect the liberty of all its peoples. If these laws, founded upon our Constitution, are to remain the standard by which we live and work together, then you must find Ed Parsons guilty."

Judge & Jury

Approximately three hours later

"Mr Foreman, has the jury reached a verdict?"

"Yes, Your Honor."

"The defendant will stand. Mr Foreman, what say you?"

"In the matter of the Territory of Wyoming verses Edward Donald Parsons, we find the defendant as follows:

"On the charge of extortion, guilty. On the charge of bribing an officer of the law, guilty. On the charge of cattle rustling, guilty. On the charge of conspiring assault causing grievous bodily harm, guilty. On the charge of conspiracy to murder, guilty. On the charge of murder for hire, guilty."

"Thank you, members of the jury. Your unending patience and attention to the details of this trial are commendable. You are dismissed from your duty. I will now hand down the sentence of this court.

"Mr Parsons, you are a grave threat to this community. Assault and murder are not an acceptable or lawful means of achieving one's goals. Your actions were calculated, brutal and callous and I am outraged at the suffering that the Keaton, Taylor and Benchley families have had to endure at your hands and your cohorts. You instituted the death of a fine and upstanding young man, who had much to offer his community and this territory. And we are a lesser people for his passing. Edward Donald Parsons, I hereby sentence you to thirty years imprison-ment for conspiring to murder Martin John Keaton and hiring a gunman to commit it. For your other crimes of extortion, bribing an officer of the law, conspiring assault and cattle rustling, I sentence you to twenty years imprisonment, in which you will be submitted to solitary confinement. This, in effect, constitutes at least two life sentences, Mr Parsons, and should indicate to you the extreme gravity of your crimes.

"I hope you spend your time wisely contemplating on the salvation of your soul. You are to be incarcerated at the Colorado State Penitentiary and expedited from this city's jail tomorrow morning to begin your sentence immediately.

"Anyone who attempts to interfere with these arrangements will be charged with obstruction of justice and incur a severe penalty. I hope I make myself clear.

"Thank you, Mr Faraday... Mr McKinnon. These proceedings are concluded. This case is closed."

The conclusion of McCurdy's trial
Several days later

"The defendant will stand. Mr Foreman, what say you?"

"In the matter of the Territory of Wyoming verses Vincent Robert McCurdy, we find the defendant as follows:

"On the charge of accepting bribes, guilty. On the charge of extortion – aiding and abetting, guilty. On the charge of not upholding the office of sheriff, guilty."

"Thank you, members of the jury. You are dismissed from your duty.

"The court will now hand down its sentence. Mr McCurdy, the office of law enforcement in this territory has been brought into serious disrepute through your unlawful acts, which are despicable in the extreme. Bribery, in particular, is always to be regarded as one which strikes at the very heart of the justice system, and must be severely punished whenever it is detected. I can't help feeling deep regret when I recall the passage in Mart Keaton's journal where he says the Law is in a dangerous condition in this territory if you, Mr McCurdy, are anything to go by. I am grateful to that young man for the sufferings he endured to bring this unacceptable situation to the attention of this court. And before these proceedings close, I wish to publicly convey my deepest sympathy to the Keaton family for the loss of son, brother, husband and father. Vincent Robert McCurdy, I sentence you to twenty years imprisonment at the Colorado State Penitentiary.

"This case is closed. Mr Faraday, I will see you in my chambers in five minutes."

Faraday

Judge Callaghan's chambers

"Yes, Judge?"

"An update on Ed Parsons' incarceration, Mr Faraday, if you will."

"I have received a wire from the prison governor. Parsons is settled as well as can be expected."

"I see. Tell me, how long do you intend to wait before Marshal Hummer can re-attempt Wilson Cutter's extradition? The outlaw has been indicted for the murder of Mart Keaton."

"Yes, Judge. The hearing is tomorrow morning."

Judge Callaghan flips a page in his desk diary. "So it is. What has Marshal Hummer to say about this?"

"Well, now that he and Mr Taylor are back on friendly terms, Marshal Hummer petitioned both governors for a delay in the extradition so that we can try Cutter for Mart Keaton's murder. They have agreed. I believe, Judge, that if this comes to trial, it will be short and conclusive."

Judge Callaghan nods his head pensively. "Not dangerous, I hope."

Faraday slides his hands into his pockets. "After what happened at the attempted extradition, I am confident that Wilson Cutter will not present a danger."

"Good," he says, nodding some more.

"The only complication is that Wilson Cutter is ill."

"And what is the matter with him?"

"It seems that the stale air and constraints of jail life don't suit him, on top of recent wounds that won't heal, while the prison yard stalemate and the strip search resulted in some sort of nervous collapse."

"I assume a doctor has been dispatched."

"I asked Dr John Mackay from Laramie to assess if he is fit to stand trial, and he assures me that despite a little melancholy Cutter is fit. Cliff Ryan and his deputies confirm that Cutter is despondent, but then he's never been in such dire circumstances before. Reverend Jamison has been calling on him regularly. Cliff seems to think that the visits are contributing to Cutter's melancholy."

The Judge's expression sharpens. "Remorse?"

"That doesn't seem realistic," Faraday replies.

"There are different kinds of remorse, Mr Faraday. Acknow-ledgement followed by a sense of futility is as remorseful as some men get. Of course, all Cutter's friends are in the same position as he. So now he has no friends and that can bring reality home with an almighty thud. And when Jim Jamison starts preaching hellfire you need to duck... only Wilson Cutter is not to know that. Probably never saw the inside of a church in his life. *And* he's a captive audience. Won't do him any harm to see the error of his ways."

"Of course not, Judge."

Judge Callaghan sighs and picks up his spectacles.

The meeting is all but concluded; Faraday knows the Judge well enough to sense he has a final remark to add. "You know, Mr Faraday..."

"Yes, Judge?"

He places his spectacles on the end of his nose and then peers at Faraday over the lenses. "I don't know what we are all going to do with ourselves when Mr Taylor leaves town."

Faraday suppresses a grin. "Neither do I, Judge."

One hour later, Faraday joins a healthy celebration taking place in a large corner of the Inter Ocean Hotel reception room. The Alliance is there, of course, and so are all the trial witnesses for the prosecution.

Champagne is flowing and some surprising guests appear to be enjoying the occasion as much as the victors themselves. Mr Wang is one, and Duffy another. And Faraday has never before seen Dan Hummer at a post-trial victory party, but there he stands as large as life and raising the noise level considerably.

Faraday pauses outside the perimeter of the group and savors the moment.

The grin on Luke's face is for the first time dancing in his eyes. Miss Keaton appears to have put the serious side of her nature out of mind and is drinking champagne at Luke's side – although he would not want George to see how naturally compatible they look together. Even Amy Keaton seems light-hearted. Hard not to be when you have won for yourselves a comprehensive victory. Besides, Dan Hummer's witty rejoinders are failsafe.

Suddenly, Miss Keaton is taking his arm. He looks down into her clear blue eyes.

"We've saved a whole bottle of champagne for you, Mr Faraday," she says archly. Then she announces his arrival to the whole group. He is applauded, back slapped, thanked, afforded numerous accolades. Although he enjoys their revelry, he prefers to think of their win as a team effort. When they demand a speech, he says as much.

After a little more speech making, principally by John Keaton, Faraday draws Luke aside. "So, what are your plans?"

Luke shrugs. "Back to the ranch I guess."

"Mm. You and the quiet life... I'm struggling to picture it."

Just then Dan Hummer's voice booms, "Ah, look, folks, our persnickety sheriff has decided to come join us..."

They look up to see Cliff and George walking towards the group.

"And Dr Sullivan, M'am. A delight as always."

Faraday chuckles. "Well. Maybe things are looking up, my friend."

"What d'you mean by that, Cam?" Luke asks.

However, as Faraday observes the burning intensity of Luke's gaze on George – and the delightful way she's trying to ignore it – it is obvious that Luke knows exactly what he means.

Cheyenne

The following day

The fairest of mornings.

Sunshine warms the streets and gleams on freshly washed store windows. It is cool in the shadows though. Fall comes quickly once it decides to come. And winter will be close on her heels. At the station, the morning train from Laramie puffs itself to a halt. Citizens and visitors alight.

Welcome to Cheyenne.

At the other end of town, prominent amongst a sprinkling of citizens going about their business, is Miss Keaton and her sun-gold tresses. She strolls down 17th Street towards Dr Sullivan's building with a pleasant smile on her face. She recognizes a citizen and stops to talk. After a few moments she moves on and soon traverses Eddy Street to Dr Sullivan's block. The women are picketing outside Mr Wang's establishment.

High on the roof of the building on the opposite side of the street, where the barber and the tobacconist work, crouches a man unknown to Cheyenne. He is a stranger who holds a rifle. No one can see him. No one knows he is there.

Mr Taylor once used to keep vigil in this precinct, but even he would not see this stranger. Particularly now as he dismounts and removes the saddle from his hard-ridden horse, another older animal the livery supplied and for whom long distances should be a thing of the past. Dr Sullivan stands smiling on the sidewalk outside her building, watching him care for the horse. He lets the animal dip its nose into the water trough close by.

Miss Keaton's dainty boot negotiates a discarded newspaper.

Mr Taylor drops the saddle close to the feet of Dr Sullivan and looks into her face.

Miss Keaton lifts her eyes from the sidewalk.

She sees them and freezes. Sees the saddle at Dr Sullivan's feet. For a brief moment, Cheyenne's new autumn air offers the eye unique sharpness and clarity, as though gazing through the finest crystal.

Miss Keaton frowns ever so sweetly.

Dr Sullivan's smile breaks into a lovely grin…

The stranger on the roof takes his aim.

…with eyes only for her blue-eyed boy, whose adoration brings a pretty blush to her cheeks.

The stranger on the roof fires his rifle. The sound explodes into the fine crystal air and shatters it to pieces.

The bullet finds its target.

The pickets spill into the dust.

Cheyenne shudders.

The stranger scrambles across the roof and down a rain pipe. A horse waits, stomping at the ground. As confused citizens are crying out for Sheriff Ryan, the stranger rides off, weaving his way east through the back alleys of Cheyenne until he is gone from sight.

Cheyenne is speechless before the wailing begins.

Luke

With his heart thumping from the shock of the unexpected gunshot, Luke peels back layers of onlookers who have swarmed on the sidewalk.

Someone is shrieking, "Get the sheriff, get Mr Ryan at once…"

The onlookers are alarmed and weeping. One woman cries, "It is your friend, Mr Taylor…"

Panic grips him. His friend?

He is a little too rough with the next person who stands in his way and they fall aside. Then he sees.

He feels the blood drain from his face. He drops to his knees onto the sidewalk beside K's motionless body.

Jennifer appears. Her face is white and she is shaking, but she has K's body under her hands as she examines frantically. She is doing everything she can; he has seen her do all this before, yet he instinctively knows. He can smell it, taste it in his mouth. But this is K. He promised to keep her safe, he swore to her… Jennifer gently turns that golden head towards him. There is a precise red-black hole in the side of K's head. He hears the trembling words, "She's gone, Luke."

He gapes helplessly at her face, its beauty marred only by that hideous mark and its tail of blood.

"I'm certain that it happened instantly," Jennifer murmurs. "She wouldn't have known or felt anything… Luke, I'm so sorry…"

He cannot think, or form words, or even breathe. There is only one thing to do. He takes K into his arms. He strokes her cheek. This can't be happening. He's gonna wake up now, gonna wake up… K is gonna stop this, and laugh at him, taunt him…

But she is still. Limp in his arms. Those summer sky, deep river eyes are wide open, and he stares into them, entranced, as the morning sun catches facets of their jewel-like brilliance.

Snapped like a photograph, in their piercing expression, is the last thing she saw and what she thought. Only she knows what that is. And before he's ready, before there's an answer, Jennifer's trembling fingers gently close K's eyelids. He will never know. He will never, ever know.

A rush of terrifying emotions. Roaring in his ears.

Excruciating pain everywhere in his body, like needles, a thousand needles. He wants to scream and howl and fight but the pain is too great. All around him the world seems to move out of focus, shifting away from him. He looks up, searching for Jennifer's face, but can't see her. So he holds K tight to him, and weeps.

ELEVEN

All are scattered now and fled,
Some are married, some are dead;
And when I ask, with throbs of pain,
"Ah! When shall they all meet again?"
As in days long since gone by,
The ancient timepiece makes reply, ~
"Forever~never!
Never~Forever!"

Henry Wadsworth Longfellow
The Old Clock on the Stairs

৵৽৹

Wilson Cutter

Wilson stares out on his bitter world hoping someone, anyone, will show him an ounce of mercy. He shifts his gaze from Ryan's cold, hard face to Jamison's blazing eyes. What does this reverend want from him? What does anyone want from him?

"Answer the sheriff's question, Wilson," Jamison says.

Wilson can't feel the anger anymore and without that there's nothing. "I... I don't know who killed her. How should I? I don't see no one, only you, Jamison."

Jamison's eyes get a burning look to them; he says 'the eyes of the angels burn with righteousness to guard against men burning in hell'. Wilson's never sure if Jamison ain't in fact an angel because his eyes sure can burn.

"You're lying, Cutter," Ryan says. Wilson's never seen Ryan like this. He ain't even wearing his coat; he's got his sleeves rolled...

Jamison clears his throat. Talks stern. "Wilson, it's time you made peace with your Maker. The only way is to face the truth. Hell is whole lot worse than a jail cell. A whole lot worse. But God won't let you set foot there if you can make peace."

"Peace," Wilson snorts. "You don't care about my soul. The sheriff sure as hell don't care about my soul. You just want all your loose ends tied up..."

All of a sudden Ryan grabs his collar, choking him with an angry strength that Wilson wishes he still had.

He don't want to die this way... he fights to suck air... splutters a plea to stop...

Ryan says, "Let's make a deal. You tell me who killed Miss Keaton and I'll ask God to forgive you."

"It don't work that way, Sheriff," says Jamison.

"Shut up, Jamison..."

"God heal you of this anger, Mr Ryan..."

Ryan lets go; Wilson heaves what breath he can into his lungs and then has a coughing fit. They watch him while his chest rattles and the shaking worsens. He feels sweat break out all over his body.

This sickness is hell.

Jamison gets up and lays a blanket around him kindly. From a brown bottle he pours out a spoonful of liquid.

Wilson opens his mouth like an obedient child and receives the bitter tasting medicine. He shudders, wishing there was a whiskey chaser. Drops of it run into his beard, so not only do the vile taste linger in his mouth, the smell of it hangs like fumes in his nostrils.

Ryan, meantime, sighs over and over.

Jamison says, "Sheriff, has it occurred to you that Wilson doesn't know who killed Miss Keaton?"

Wilson is mighty grateful. In a raspy voice, he says, "Listen to him, Ryan, cause it's true. I don't know."

Jamison's eyes blaze even brighter. There's a hint of approval as they crinkle in the corners. Wilson kinda likes it, someone approving of him for a change.

"God hears every murmur of our hearts, Wilson."

"Old man Parsons never told me stuff like that. I had partic'lar responsibilities and that's all. Don't go nosin' into my employer's business. Just did my job."

Ryan is looking like he's thinking, as well as angry. Wilson thinks maybe he's beginning to believe him.

Wilson pushes on. "Why don't you ask Parsons or McCurdy who killed the Keaton girl? I don't know. I don't wanna know. That's the truth, Ryan. Whether you believe me or not, it's the truth..."

But Ryan glares at him with the coldest eyes Wilson ever saw.

Jamison says, "I think we must accept the fact that Wilson is being truthful. I believe, Wilson, you might finally understand what truth is and why it's important. Right now it's determining your guilt or innocence."

Wilson observes Jamison's glowing face. Not once has the man condemned him for his crimes; he only talks about God, about truth, about peace, how bad hell is and how mighty nice heaven is. Wilson's never known nice that way. Jamison's made him curious. 'Course, there's a catch.

Wilson's lived a brutal life and he's gotta be sorry for what he's done. Making amends, Jamison says, is the best way to be sorry. And this sickness – Wilson's never been this sick in his life; bullet wounds, sure, but he was always strong from the thrill of the fight, invincible. But now he's got crushed, humiliated; he's scared of this rheumy illness, and he's never known fear before.

Jamison says God takes away fear when a person asks him for help. Jamison tells him a whole bunch of stuff no one ever bothered to tell him before. Wilson never imagined he has a chance to know 'nice'. Jamison means 'goodness'. Anyways, Wilson always believed that 'nice' made a man weak, like Keaton – that's what he was taught. But he is weak now because things went sour and Jamison says when a person's weak God can make them strong – the right kinda strong. Jamison understands that Wilson's been angry all his life; says it's time to stop being angry and start being sensible.

Wheezing, Wilson says, "I wanna be sensible, Jamison." He flicks a look at Ryan whose eyes squint at him mean-like. "If God's watching, is he looking at me like Ryan?"

"The sheriff is a man, Wilson. He's hurting and he's angry about Miss Keaton's death. God's upset too, but if you honestly don't know who killed her, God believes you, Wilson. Justice is best served in heaven, I heard a man once say, because only God knows what in men's hearts."

"God believes me," Wilson mutters, amazed someone besides Jamison does. "Jamison, I hated God all my life 'cause I got a bad deal. Why did he let that happen?"

Ryan blows a sigh and Wilson is scared to look at him.

"In truth, only God can answer that, Wilson. When it comes to your life he knows best what he expected of you. No doubt you had your choices. Only if it were me, I'd rather go to heaven and have the chance to ask him personally. Maybe even chew him out about it – friendly-like o'course."

Wilson is shaken by this thought. "Yeah, I could do that, couldn't I?"

Jamison smiles and gives a nod. Then Wilson is tortured by another coughing fit. Jamison and Ryan look on, in their different ways probably thinking he deserves his suffering. Wilson can't worry about what people think of him no more.

When the torture stops, and he's just wheezing again, he knows he has to lie down. "I wanna say something, then I need to sleep."

Ryan says, "What do you want to say, Cutter?"

Wilson appeals silently to Jamison: how does he go about this?

Jamison's eyes glow. "Why don't we make it a prayer? Ask for forgiveness for all the things you did in your life. I can help with that. The sheriff won't mind, I'm sure. God sure would like to hear what you've got to say."

Ryan picks up his notebook, and dunking his pen in a bottle of ink, mutters, "He's not the only one."

Faraday

The next morning

As Faraday takes his seat behind his desk, he invites Luke, John Keaton and Ethan Benchley to sit also. John accepts; Luke and Ethan remain standing behind, hat in hand. Their unshaven faces are expressionless; their eyes, ringed red, stare out... how do you hold fast to your principles when your hearts are bled dry, when the world around you has fallen into confusion and chaos... The rule of law? Common decency? Integrity? Faith?

Faraday places Cliff's notebook in front of John Keaton. "I believe you need to see this."

"What is it?"

"The reason why I asked you to come. Read it."

It takes some time for John Keaton to absorb what it is he's reading.

"What is it, John?" Ethan asks.

John clears his throat; suddenly, there is a little color in his cheeks. He looks up at Faraday, his eyes coming to life.

"I believe, John, that this is what Mart wanted," Faraday says.

"Cutter's confessed," Luke deduces flatly.

"Let me see that," Ethan mutters, and takes the confession from John's hands.

"Yes, he has confessed, not only to Mart's murder but to every other charge he's been facing. To all his crimes." Faraday lets that sink in for a moment. "You'll be interested to know that every state and territorial governor, every US marshal and deputy, every sheriff that wanted him have all agreed to his sentence being carried out here in Cheyenne. Judge Callaghan will pronounce his sentence at ten o'clock this morning. Cutter will hang tomorrow – but he has been granted a final request, that the hanging be at dawn, not a public execution."

Ethan hands the confession to Luke, saying, "You reckon he deserves a final request, Mr Faraday?"

"It's a matter for debate, I agree, but Reverend Jim Jamison has been working with him..."

"Which is why it reads like a prayer," Luke murmurs, his eyes quickly running down the page.

"Yes. The request was basically Jamison's."

John Keaton clears his throat a second time. "I think Mart would agree with the Reverend. Doesn't matter what we think." His eyes fill with tears and Faraday recalls another pair of eyes of similar hue that shone so intelligently and with utter sincerity.

"So who killed my little girl, Mr Faraday?"

"We don't know, but we will find her killer, John, I swear to you."

John nods feebly, looks down, covers his eyes with his hand.

Faraday swallows awkwardly. The oath he swore before the governor and Judge Callaghan when he took this position is very much in his mind. Fervently, he mutters, "I swear."

At home later that evening, Cliff calls on him. Their devoted sheriff looks physically and emotionally exhausted.

Faraday pours him a drink.

With a directness born of that exhaustion, Cliff says, "Any ideas on where we start on Miss Keaton's murderer? I thought Parsons should receive a visit. And McCurdy. Soon as possible."

Faraday examines that weary face. "Take a day off, Cliff."

"A trail can go cold in a day, Cam."

Cliff swigs a mouthful of good Irish whiskey.

Faraday considers his colleague thoughtfully. From his desk he lifts Luke's file, and sliding his fingers between the pages he's marked, he opens it. "By all means, you should give Parsons and McCurdy the pleasure of your company. But this... this is where we truly begin."

Cliff frowns; he places his glass on the desk and carefully takes the file out of Faraday's hands. Faraday watches Cliff's eyes roam over the page; they stop exactly where he intends. Cliff stares at the spot and practically gulps.

He meets Faraday's eyes with understandable surprise.

"I'll lose my job," he says.

"As will I."

They stare at one another for several moments.

"But," Faraday says, taking the file back and closing it, "not before we have brought this territory to its knees."

Rueful amusement mitigates the fatigue in Cliff's face. "I thought you and I were aspiring to more than one horse towns and circuit courts."

Faraday reaches for his whiskey and picks up Cliff's as well. Handing him his glass, he says, "Let's drink to that."

Luke

Daybreak

As he strides down Ferguson Street towards the jail, Luke buttons his coat against the damp. A dense gray mist blankets Cheyenne, delaying its awakening, saturating the ground, and cheating Cutter of the backdrop to his glorious salvation.

When he arrives at the gallows, John and Amy and Ethan are already there, along with Cam, and Judge Callaghan, Marshal Hummer and his colleagues. Nobody speaks. They stand silently as the mist swirls passed them and retreats into the streets as if it wants nothing to do with the execution of Wilson Cutter.

The gallows, its gruesome splendor towering defiantly in the mist, stands ready with its noose hanging motionless. The executioner and his assistant are muttering up on the platform. With dispassionate application, they test their masterpiece and are rewarded with perfect precision. The sound of what is to come echoes across the compound and into the street. They reset their contraption.

He and John stare wordlessly at one another. John's face is as white as the mist is gray. Amy stands by his side. Ashen, gaunt, she seems brittle suddenly. She shouldn't be here, but who could deny her if this is what she wants.

He has never seen them so fragile; one more blow and they would smash into a hundred unrecognizable pieces.

This is where their Alliance has brought them.

In the face of such desolation, scratching around for something to anchor himself to, he thinks of home. Tressa is there, and Adam. Mart's son: a bittersweet consolation, once again a point of hope for a future where hope is thin. A baby to replace Amy's babies. For a bleak moment he hangs his head; oh, how he had loved Amy's babies...

From the silence comes footsteps and shuffling. Then Cutter's hacking cough.

Cutter – escorted by Jamison, two armed deputies and Cliff – steps up to the base of the gallows.

"I leave you here, Wilson," Jamison tells him. Cutter is looking into Jamison's face as if he is salvation itself. Jamison croons, "Even though I walk in the valley of death, no evil shall I fear."

Cutter nods and looks up at the flight of steps leading to his death. The deputies escort him to the top, then stand guard on the platform. Cutter refuses the black hood; when the executioner insists, Jamison intervenes: *do as he wants.*

The executioner stands Cutter on the trapdoor. His wrists are already manacled, so the executioner straps his legs together tightly. Cutter's frail body almost collapses. The executioner cuts some slack and steadies his victim. The executioner takes the noose and loops it around Cutter's head, positioning it precisely on the left side of his neck. Meanwhile, Jamison's trumpeting voice can be heard.

"For he will command his angels, they will lift you up in their hands..."

Cutter holds up his head like he sees those angels. For a second that ugly face almost looks human. The executioner proceeds; trapdoor becomes aperture and Cutter's noosed body descends. A distinct crack, as his neck snaps cleanly, sounds above every other noise. As Luke's stomach lurches into nausea, he hears Amy's gasp.

For several vile moments, he witnesses through the wooden beams that bear the gallows above, the body rocking on its pendulum while the last traces of mortality leak out of it. As the minutes tick by, it steadies to sway a shallow creaking knell in the remains of the silent dawn, its pathetic head crooked on its neck.

"You will tread upon the lion and the cobra..."

Enough.

Enough death.

"... you will trample the great lion and the serpent..."

If Jamison only knew...

Luke turns and walks away.

Jennifer

Jennifer wakes with a start and is disoriented. So heavy her slumber, she cannot remember why she is lying on the sofa and not in her bed. Her mind swims in a thick soup.

Suddenly, a jolt. She hurries to sit up only to become tangled in a blanket that she can't recall tucking around herself. And what of the fire in the hearth? – she certainly did not light it. The living room is warm and cozy, whereas it was cold and dark when she threw herself down about an hour before dawn, fully clothed and utterly spent after a night of delivering twins. There can be only one explanation. He has been here. Left his love to warm her.

She turns her bleary eyes on the mantle clock. Twenty-seven minutes past eight…

The hanging! She has missed it. After she promised.

As she rolls the blanket aside, something catches her eye.

Perched between the two cushions she'd used as pillows is a white envelope. She snatches it up. Her name is written on the front in Luke's hand. She stares in wonder at it, and then becomes confused by it. She should tear it open in excited anticipation, but instinct and then logic preclude this. He would never write to her what he could say to her face, and if he cannot say it to her face that means only one thing.

Shakily, she takes the chair by the hearth; she stares at the gentle flames and then at the letter. Nothing hopeful could come from his present state of mind.

Her fingertips detect a hard object wedged into the corner of the envelope. She opens it quickly and unfolds the notepaper; it's her own stationery, so she attempts to piece together what has occurred.

He came to look for her after the hanging and found her deeply asleep. Whether he couldn't bring himself to wake her or face her, he lit a fire and warmed her.

He went to her desk and wrote her this letter, and then placed it between her pillows… All the while she never woke.

She takes a deep breath, and considers the flow of his script; it is unusual, individual, imperfectly skewed because he is left-handed. Where Jennifer attended school a left-handed pupil was forced to abandon his or her natural instincts; she doubts that Luke would have succumbed to a cane-swatting martinet… She blocks that at once and disciplines her thoughts to the present and to the letter.

My darling Jennifer, how is it that we can love each other apart as intensely as when we are together? Remember the day we met? You took me into your office, gave me coffee and I told you about Mart, all the while wondering how any woman could have perfect freckles, perfect green eyes, make perfect coffee and be perfectly understanding.

How hard it is to love you and write this letter. If I were any kind of gentleman I'd be letting you be the one to break my heart — although I think, Jennifer, you always intended to. Maybe this is the best way or maybe there is no excusing my behavior. You be the judge. You do not have to forgive me.

I am leaving on the seven o'clock train with the others to take K home. Then I think I will go west again, San Francisco, and probably Hawaii. A long journey on a hard trail to cleanse the soul is what Ethan calls it. K deserves to be mourned properly and I need to mourn her. I am so sorry, Jennifer, but I cannot burden you with my grief. It is agony; I have no control over it. It controls me and it would control us. I will try to explain.

K and I made a pact with each other some time ago; she broke it pretty much right away when it got hard to keep and then released me from it. But I never broke my side of it with her — which was that I would look out for her, protect her with my life if I had to – and I failed to keep my part. I guess there's a lot of breaking been going on. We reconciled our differences just days before she died.

Sometimes I think I am going insane. How did I lose both of them, Jennifer? Why am I left? Ethan keeps the story about men during the war who felt guilty about surviving when their brothers-in-arms were killed. He and my father were at Vicksburg and from the hundreds that were slaughtered they survived and were captured. They eventually got paroled because at that time the North and South exchanged prisoners. Later the Yankees weren't so inclined and left men to rot in prison. Either way, those who survived never forgot, and Ethan says it took a long time for him reconcile the whole thing. But K wasn't a soldier. She was just a girl, an innocent girl. If only I could be sure that she is happy and peaceful at last.

Don't try to be understanding. I'm not asking you to understand, Jennifer. I know I'm hurting you. Be angry. Hate me. Whatever you want. I deserve all of it and more.

A few days ago I felt like anything was possible, now I realize how naïve that was and I am downright humbled and on my knees. Time goes by and steals each breath from me; that is how I survive. My world has become a hard place. You are my bright star and my love, but it wouldn't be right to presume that you would want to make my world livable. Not right to test our love with such bitter grief.

I get to wondering sometimes if you would have trusted me completely. In a way, by giving you and taking from you in this short span of time what I wanted for my whole life, I gambled our future and I lost. I know Mart would say so. I have no right to expect more from you than you have already given me and for that there could never be enough gratitude in the whole world.

But there is one last thing.

There is something I want you to have. The enclosed ring. My great great grandfather's ring. You remember Matthew, the Revolutionary. The ring has always reminded me that freedom is hard fought and won, that it is more precious than precious gold – or diamonds for that matter – but in what other way can we represent its value. When my mother gave me the ring after my father's death she said that freedom is eternal, and that it lives on in the hearts of those for whom so many have fought and died in its name generation after generation.

I don't know about your family, Jennifer, and what has influenced you, but you make peace and tolerance and compassion a large part of freedom, the kind that Mart and K valued so dearly and gave their lives for. The kind that makes the world a better place. I hope that Matthew's ring will remind you of what you will always mean to me. Luke.

She retrieves the solid object from inside the envelope. The wide gold band is scratched and somewhat dull, worn by time and hard work; but clear runs an inscription on the inside that reads: *We will not be slaves. Sons of Liberty.*

In that moment, her life rears up in her face like a panicked horse; she gasps, and understands with terrifying clarity.

She stares at the ring until it disappears behind a wall of unshed tears. "I love you back, my blue-eyed boy…"

January 1885

River Man

You are a river man...

An icy wind whips around the bay and hammers at the windows of the shipping office.

"Well, are you going to sign on or not? We could certainly do with the likes of you, and she's a fair voyage, but we'll be gone a long time and you don't want to be leaving nothing important behind."

With pen and ink poised over the crew's sign on log, Luke looks for a decision in the experienced eyes of the *Pacific Treader's* first mate. Eventually, the older man smiles cannily.

"Son, if she's that grand that you need to put an ocean between you, maybe you shouldn't be putting an ocean between you at all."

Luke sighs. Straightens up. "She's an angel."

"Got you any idea how missing a woman makes you feel when the ship's rolling in bad weather and you're heaving your guts over the side?"

"Can't say that I do."

"Not – any – better!" The first mate snatches the pen away. "You can't love a woman and the sea at the same time, my friend. Believe me, I know. It don't work. Now get out of here."

...you have deep, still pools

Two days later in cold blustery conditions under a struggling winter sun, Luke watches the *Pacific Treader* sail on the afternoon tide, her graceful form dipping and shuddering on salty, white tipped waves.

Overhead the cry of a lone gull sounds above the moaning wind; the bird alternates between riding the squall and flapping against it on its way across the drab, cheerless sky. It comes to rest on the rocking mast of a moored sloop.

My blue-eyed boy, you should know it is dangerous to believe you are the master of your own destiny…

"I miss you, Jennifer," he murmurs.

He works too hard. Walks too much.

It hurts *so* damn much.

Ethan warned him and warned him good.

"You love that woman and she's good for you. Like Mart said. Are you gonna turn your back on that?"

"I'm not good enough for her, not this way…"

"You're plenty good enough. You're gonna regret leaving her. Will you listen to me?"

He couldn't hear a thing except for the last words K ever said to him… *We did it, Taylor, just as Mart wanted. I could dance for joy about it. Couldn't you?* …playing over and over inside his head.

But something had happened at the shipping office; there was a stronger voice inside him – his heart, sounding oddly like Ethan, screaming to be heard over the torment: *You love Jennifer more than anything or anyone else in your life. She is your true direction, not the point on a compass or a distant land.*

He'd made a decision. He was going back to her.

He'd made another decision:

From now on, pay attention to Ethan's voice.

And come to a conclusion:

It was time to get some perspective.

Right now there's a powerful need inside of him; a yearning – as strong as he has for Jennifer.

For insight. To know his destiny… know the path of it… now that he accepts his life is truly at a crossroad.

Mart used to say, "Luke, if you wanna know what's going on inside your head you gotta be still… put all doubts aside, let your thoughts flow and don't be scared. You'll handle it."

A man couldn't have two better people in his life than Ethan and Mart… and as for Jennifer, he tried to go back to living his life as it was without her and realized it couldn't be done.

There are serious things he needs to face and understand about himself and his life. They've been there all along and they hold him back. When he finally faces Jennifer, even if he's on his knees, he needs to be strong in the deepest part of him.

He wants to live an honorable life so she will be proud of him.

And there are two people to whom he owes an honorable life.

His guilt cannot change the past, but he can live a life worthy of their sacrifice; and his actions can shape an honorable future in which they live as a proud memory.

The idea is right but how does he make it work?

He remembers when he was a boy Ethan used to tell him not to run from what ails him, but stop, turn around and run right back at it, waving his arms, ranting like a 'crazy warrior'; but Luke always ran away from the fear he felt when his father died, he never turned around... and he carried it with him.

He ran from Cheyenne too.

He succumbed to despair. Like he did when his father died.

He turned his back on the very thing he had been given to help him.

His angel. His Jennifer.

He has an image of Ethan smiling at him. Good son, now you're listening...

Suddenly, a strong wind swirls around him. The sea salt pierces his nostrils; his chest rises as his lungs fill; the rawness sends tingles up and down his spine. Another gust, laden with salt, hurls itself at him, taking his breath away. He wrestles the wind for control of his lungs. Then, with a great sweep, the wind departs, retreating to the sky above the bay.

The space around him stills. His breathing calms.

Strange clarity follows. Like someone lit a lamp in his head. Like that moment he burst through Jennifer's door and broke her bell, only much stronger.

Things about himself he has never understood take shape in his mind.

The shadows.

They lurk but never identify themselves. They keep a man stumbling and he doesn't know why. Make a man run when all he wants to do is know how to stay put.

He sees them, exposes them, and he understands. When they can no longer hide, they flee.

His grief and guilt for K was so crippling it prevented him from doing for her what he'd done for Mart, and drove him away from the only woman he will ever want.

And where did that despair come from?

From a shadow fortressed by another even deeper fog of grief for his brave father and innocent Katrine.

So thick with fear, it has prevented him from ever securing the deep down peace he craves and sampled with Jennifer. Feeding on his soul since he was a boy.

Now he can sense its hold slipping because he has turned around. Facing it, not fearing it, just like Ethan said.

He recalls the day his father died. The men brought his body back to the ranch and wouldn't let him see it. Not fit for a boy, he heard someone say. They didn't know what he knew about Katrine. He imagined his father like that; his brave Pa like that. He never questioned Sara about it and he never allowed himself to be rational. He's seen a man crushed in a stampede, it ain't pretty, it's grim, but it's not what Apache do to you and he should've known better, he should've turned around. Instead, he let a dark shadow come over him, and it stayed to torment him.

His father died trying to save his herd and that was a rancher's business. His Pa loved him; left him his ranch and a man called Ethan. It's time to be grateful.

He recalls the day they fought the Kiowa-Apache. He fought as hard as any man in the outfit; he fought hard to protect Katrine, but he was only a boy and that was a man's job. The guilt didn't rest with him and yet he carried it, and a shadow came and stayed to torment him. Katrine was his sister and he loved her, looked up to her. He was a good brother; he knew it because she fussed over him and endured his antics and hugged him on his birthday and he let her. She was affectionate and he liked that about her. She was kind and funny and nearly always did as she was told. She didn't deserve what happened, but she was also brave and somehow believed in God. Mart once said that God sends angels to deliver the faithful ones from the horrors of death. How did he know these things? Probably all that praying he used to do.

Luke is starting to believe in angels, beginning to see beyond death because it felt good to have hope for a change. Katrine was in good hands. *So long, Katrine. Rest in the arms of those angels.*

Life sure turned out to be complicated.

Red Sky told him that a life where you rise refreshed in the morning, do a day's hard work, be kind to your neighbor, retire to bed satisfied and sleep well is a good, simple life. *Yours, Luke, will not be like this, but you are strong, you will find your way.*

Good of her to warn him, only he never understood what she was getting at until now.

Holding out his right hand, he studies his finger where Matthew Taylor's ring used to be; the mark has faded some, but it's still there, the groove it long and silently etched still obvious. He gave it to Jennifer because he was too scared to give her his whole heart. At least it was a symbol of what is close to his heart.

Freedom.

K was right: true freedom lives in the hearts of people. He gets it. *His* heart. At last.

He feels the need to get back to Jennifer and share these insights with her. She would understand. She had been a gift to him all along. She showed him deep down peace, so that he could recognize what it was he'd longed for and how to get it. She'd gone deep into his soul and sealed the entrance behind her. The contentment, no matter how complicated things get, is to be had with her and that's just the way he wants it. Now all he has to do is think of a way to get her to take him back.

He hopes that she would understand one other thing...

He'd left it to others to get justice for K, but it is his responsibility. It strikes him all at once that at the moment Mart died, everything he was he charged Luke with being. It is time to live up to that for Mart and for K. Ethan wrote that the investigation goes slow: unhelpful people, bad weather, dead ends and a cold trail. Luke decides to wire Cliff when he gets back to town.

This will be a new chapter in that story he and Jennifer once spoke about; by the time he has returned to Cheyenne he'll be ready.

He heads back to the pier to collect gear he'd left behind and take one last look at a world he'd come to think of as sanctuary.

The gull, releasing a series of hawking cries, takes off and this time executes a perfect sweeping circuit of the bay. K always longed to be free. Free as a bird. He believes that she is finally happy.

but your life needs to be fluid...

Jennifer twists and turns through towers of crates, some clustered into enormous nets of stout rope. Longshoremen in woolen hats, with their shirtsleeves rolled to their thick and glistening forearms, swarm about everywhere, lifting, pulling, shouting, laughing. Steepling above the cargo are the masts of ships that rock, creak and clatter as the sea sways beneath and the wind swaggers above. And the magnificent clippers themselves: all that is daring and adventurous awaits the call to weigh anchor and the unfurling of sails.

Swells of salt, of brine, of fishy sea; it all has the power to repel her. That she loves a man from the West who runs to the sea to find refuge when she a maritime woman flees to the West for hers...

The smell of the sea is the smell of the past; Luke has forced her to face it.

She stops a young dockworker to confirm she is headed in the right direction.

"Aye, pier four, but the *Pacific Treader* sailed half hour ago, M'am."

They didn't tell her that at the office where she first inquired. In fact, she doesn't believe it. He can't have gone. But she rushes now, her heart pounding, a painful lump forming in her throat. She swallows repeatedly, but panic outstrips everything else and she succumbs to tears.

Pier four. A few towers left; empty crates. And where the *Pacific Treader* should be is a cavernous hole that the wind tunnels through.

Jennifer makes her way onto the pier with the sound of deep lapping water and the potent smell of brine all around her.

"Looking for someone, M'am?" a thickset man inquires.

She shakes her head. He tips his cap and moves on.

The pier is deserted.

Finding a lonesome crate, she sits on it and looks out across the harbor.

Too late. *I'm too late.*

Thirty minutes. She thinks of all the delays she suffered getting here; one or two less and things might have been so different.

I deserve to feel heartbroken and disappointed.

Because you were right. I didn't trust you. Or myself. Or us.

And because of that I never gave you hope to think beyond the present. Why would you think that I would help you bear your grief when you knew I didn't trust you? How would that reassure you about the future?

I wasn't brave enough. I was afraid that if I told you about my life you would leave me, but you left anyway, so either way that leaves me miserable and without you and incomplete, whereas once I owned the whole world.

Meg said, 'We know when he's sailing. You have given him time and space to mourn and grieve. If you love him more than anything else in the world, Jennifer Sullivan, you will go to San Francisco and you will prevent him from setting one toe on board a boat. You are the only one who can do it'.

Beneath her the pier shudders and groans as the wind buffets both wharf and water. She gets to her feet and hugs her cloak tightly around her body.

I do love you more than anything else in the world. Love you so much more than keeping secrets.

I came to tell you, my blue-eyed boy, that you belong with me.

But I'm too late.

Jennifer...

There is only one thing to be done.

Jennifer...

Follow you.

"Jennifer..."

I miss the sound of your voice; it comes to me on the wind and the waves, through the tall masts and on the gull's cry.

"Jennifer."

She starts and flinches and tumbles out of her thoughts to feel the wind chilling the tears on her face and chaffing her lips.

She hears footsteps behind her.

"Jennifer, turn around..."

...moving, creating, finding a way.

"Please..."

She glances over her shoulder. Luke hears her sharp intake of breath, but she looks away again.

"I couldn't do it, Jennifer," he forces himself to say, "I couldn't leave you..."

She turns to face him; her eyes, bright and full of tears, stay fixed this time. She wants to know she is hearing the truth and if she can believe what she is seeing.

"I... didn't sail because..."

He attempts to swallow the lumps in his throat.

"... because I couldn't leave you."

He waits, transfixed.

Watches as emotion unfurls inside her like a bird taking flight. She flies at him and he catches her in his arms, snapping them shut with her inside. He buries his face in the hollow between her shoulder and her neck.

And breathes and breathes... fragrance, spirit, presence...

How did he survive without her?

As the pleasure of her body pressed against him penetrates this bittersweet intensity, as touching her gives physical form to what was once an abandoned dream, the tenderest, warmest feeling breaks through. They are together.

Thumbing tears from his cheeks, she says, "Let me look at you. Are you all right? Are you well?"

"Yes, yes, I'm fine... You?"

"I am now. I don't know how I lived, how I drew breath, without you."

"I'm so sorry, Jennifer. I gave you a commitment I had no right to walk out on."

"You didn't sail."

"No, it was wrong. I..."

Softly, she puts her fingertips to his lips. "I have your letter but I don't think you need reminding of how you felt all those months ago. How are you feeling now?"

"Better... at least, I've made decisions, got some perspective."

"That could not have been easy. I'm glad."

"Jennifer, I'm sorry."

She dismisses him with a shake of her head. "Don't."

"Jennifer, I thought I was gonna have to beg you to take me back."

"Oh, Luke. Your letter was so heartfelt, so heart-wrenchingly honest that it made me see something for the first time..."

"What thing?"

"Myself."

He smiles. "You saw how amazing you are?"

"Luke, I saw... I couldn't be what you needed me to be because I had not been honest with you."

He waits. Seems like he's been waiting for this for a lifetime.

"I need to tell you about myself and we need to find out if... if..."

"If it matters."

"It won't be easy."

He swallows hard; more tears appear in her eyes and spill over. He rummages for his handkerchief; dabs her cheeks. And says, "I love you. I didn't try to unlove you all this time. I just tried to live without you and realized it ain't possible. Whatever we face, Jennifer, we have to believe that our love for each other is strong enough to get through it."

"We need to find that out."

"I believe it is."

"It got us this far."

"Pulled us back from the brink."

She tries a smile. "Yes." She hugs his neck, holds him very close. "I've missed you, so much. I missed your stories. And your adventures."

"Me, too," he murmurs. "Yours, I mean..."

"Even details?"

"Every last one of 'em. Maybe not Mrs Pinczewski's tumor."

"I never had a thought I didn't wonder what you would think about it, or make a move..."

"Or take a breath, or read a word, or dream a dream...."

"Yes."

He cradles her head in his hand and looks into her eyes. "Jennifer, you're in my heart. You're kinda locked up in there and you're not coming out."

Her eyes sweep over his face. "I'm locked up?"

"Threw the key away. In the harbor."

Her wide smile gladdens him, warms his blood.

"I have your ring," she says archly.

"My ring…"

"On a gold chain around my neck."

"You like it that much?"

"Well, you gave it to me. Besides, I like what the engraving says. And that reminds me of you."

"*We will not be slaves.*"

"You knew I needed to be free of my secrets. You were trying to tell me. Urging me not to be afraid."

"Never known you to be scared of anything."

"I am scared now… but I don't want to be."

"You can't be scared of me?"

"Being without you."

He trains his eyes on that beautiful mouth and decides it could do with warming. Only it's him that begins to heat up; he'd loaded a lot of clippers to try to forget how kissing her made him feel. But that's in the past, and in her kiss there's no sign of fear he can detect. A gust of wind spatters them with briny spray and cools the heat inside him a little.

He holds her tight and murmurs, "Did I ever tell you about my great grandfather who made my great grandmother sleep with a shotgun under her pillow?"

She shakes her head. "Indians?"

"Not exactly," he grins and traces a line over the bridge of her nose where one girlhood-summer those dainty freckles appeared. "She was very beautiful and very precious to him. And he had a lot to lose. Now I know how he felt."

She whispers, "You'll have to come to St Louis, shy-boy."

"Your brother and his family…"

"Mm…" She lowers her eyes. "Things to be done first…"

Whatever her secrets, she will be brave and he will… love her.

"Later."

Her eyes quickly meet his again.

He smiles. "Let me show you San Francisco first."

"Just the two of us...?"

"Will you be in love with me?"

"Yes," she breathes.

"Then I will be a very happy man."

"Luke, I..."

"What?" he murmurs, smoothing her cheek.

"When I was standing here before, I was planning to follow you..."

"To Hawaii?"

"Mm. Wherever."

"That was a brave decision. An ocean voyage is no picnic."

"Luke," she says in the tone she uses when she wants him to be serious.

"Yes, Jennifer."

"There's no turning back. That's the only direction there is."

So that's how it feels for her. She ain't gonna be the same ever again and she knows it. She is putting herself into his hands. A very brave decision.

"The future?" he says thickly.

"That's you."

"And you."

Love will see them through this.

Love dares, Luke – to hope, and to dream, and endure, you name it; it's a risk worth taking because when you got it on your side, you will prevail...

Come off it, Mart...

No, one day, you'll see. We both will.

He sighs, reaches for her hand, kisses it and places it against his heart.

"Come on, *kettaa pihyen*; there's a whole world to see."

...Edith

Indeed, there is only one thing I will ever regret in my life. That I did not accompany Kelley on that bright autumn morning to call upon Jennifer Sullivan, even though she asked.

"It's a beautiful morning, Auntie. Let's walk. We could see Jennifer. Ask her to lunch with us after this morning's court session. You know how intrigued with her you are. Come on; it'll be fun... Maybe we can even round up Luke."

"Well, Ethan told me that Luke went on an errand out of town, to deliver a package of medicines to one of Dr Sullivan's patients. He may not be back in time."

Kelley frowns. "Oh. He is very good about helping her, I've noticed, I think because of her help with the governor. And she saved his leg."

I smile tentatively. "Possibly. Kelley, have you ever thought that there is more than just gratitude between those two?"

"What do you mean more... oh... What? No! She's a doctor, a city person, and Luke hates cities. They are not at all compatible." Her face is a comedy of expressions. Confusion gets the upper hand for a moment. "Luke with Jennifer...she's pretty, I guess. And she has spirit." Then a sort of defiant rejection seizes her and she is shaking her golden head adamantly. "No, Auntie, I think not. But since I'm headed that way, I will ask Jennifer myself."

"Trust me, darling, I believe they are being very discreet."

She flashes a grin. "Don't worry, Auntie. I'll be casual. I'm sure it will be news to Jennifer."

All I can do is curve my mouth into a sort of acquiescent smile.

And she departs with a spring in her step and a twinkle in her eye, tossing over her shoulder, "If you change your mind, you know where I am."

I will never forget where I was; I will never forgive myself for being there and not with her.

Thankfully, Sara is with me now, here at home in New York. Her journey to the city where her forebears first set down in this country is a significant one. Certainly, we comfort and console one another, but for Sara it is a tribute to our darling one, our beloved. For when Luke left for San Francisco and he asked Sara what she would do in his absence, she told him, "I won't be waiting for you." And added, "I owe her that much." Sara's presence here reminds us both of that wonderful spirit which had the power to change people's lives. Kelley's Cimarron lives in our hearts.

My Kelley was both a Manhattan woman and a frontier woman, a curious mix constantly at odds. But I believe she had finally discovered that freedom for her was to live and work as one, in harmony and with the passion of the other. To the call of her heart, which began with so much promise, she responded sincerely, inimitably, and with endearing purity. And as I tip Keith's gleaming gold watch into the palm of my hand, so many memories come flooding back to me. I can hardly bear it.

"My dearest girl, can you ever forgive me..."

THE END OF VOLUME ONE

THE LIBERTY & PROPERTY LEGENDS
A saga of The West and Gilded Age America

by
TERRI SEDMAK

America 1880's. Lives taken, justice sought. Love won and love lost.
Friendships forged and families fractured.
As terror grows, heroes rise.

EMPIRE FOR LIBERTY
Dangerous Lullaby

VOLUME TWO
WYOMING, 1885... THEIR DARKEST HOUR IS COMING...

In this fast-paced, character-rich second volume and sequel to Heartland, warmed by humor and romance, we witness the best and worst of humanity. We are now deep in the heart of The Liberty & Property Legends and there is no going back.

'This second instalment in The Liberty & Property Legends sees the ghastly consequences of Ed Parsons' land grab, and the accompanying murder, begin to spread. Ambitious reporter Emmaline Roberts arrives in Cheyenne to investigate and is soon relying on the not-so-tender mercies of Sheriff Cliff Ryan to stay alive. With the scope and intrigue of a great soap, this story makes for compulsive reading.'
That's Life! Fast Fiction

'It's easy to get immersed in the vibrant history. As you are swept into the lives of an engaging Cliff and a feisty Emmaline, you start caring for the characters. Another emotional rollercoaster is assured with Empire for Liberty, a second instalment in a six-part series. This Australian author certainly knows how to paint a vivid picture!'
PS News

'This is one of the best fiction stories I have read in a long time, regardless of genre. Empire for Liberty is a very clever second book.'
NSW Writers' Centre

CPSIA information can be obtained at www.ICGtesting.com
Printed in the USA
LVOW06s1951010913

350473LV00001B/301/P